INDIAN PRAIRIE PUBLIC LIBRARY

W9-DCL-603

3 1946 00343 6380

T 42
2015-2
2017-1
L4/18

Donated by

**Darien Woman's Club
2005**

INDIAN PRAIRIE PUBLIC LIBRARY
401 Plainfield Road
Darien, IL 60561

Miss Julia's
SCHOOL OF
BEAUTY

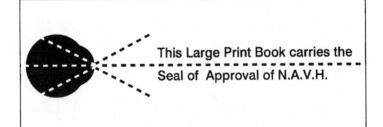

This Large Print Book carries the
Seal of Approval of N.A.V.H.

Miss Julia's
SCHOOL OF
BEAUTY

Ann B. Ross

Thorndike Press • Waterville, Maine

INDIAN PRAIRIE PUBLIC LIBRARY
401 Plainfield Road
Darien, IL 60561

Copyright © Ann B. Ross, 2005

All rights reserved.

This is a work of fiction. Names, characters, places, and incidents either are the product of the author's imagination or are used fictitiously, and any resemblance to actual persons, living or dead, business establishments, events, or locales is entirely coincidental.

Published in 2005 by arrangement with Viking Penguin, a member of Penguin Group (USA) Inc.

Thorndike Press® Large Print Basic.

The tree indicium is a trademark of Thorndike Press.

The text of this Large Print edition is unabridged.
Other aspects of the book may vary from the original edition.

Set in 16 pt. Plantin.

Printed in the United States on permanent paper.

Library of Congress Cataloging-in-Publication Data

Ross, Ann B.
    Miss Julia's school of beauty / by Ann B. Ross.
        p. cm.
    ISBN 0-7862-7619-3 (lg. print : hc : alk. paper)
    1. Springer, Julia (Fictitious character) — Fiction.
2. Beauty contests — Fiction. 3. North Carolina —
Fiction. 4. Married women — Fiction. 5. Large type
books. I. Title.
PS3568.O84198M59 2005b
    813′.54—dc22   2005005054

This is for Deborah Schneider,
with many thanks.

As the Founder/CEO of NAVH, the only national health agency solely devoted to those who, although not totally blind, have an eye disease which could lead to serious visual impairment, I am pleased to recognize Thorndike Press* as one of the leading publishers in the large print field.

Founded in 1954 in San Francisco to prepare large print textbooks for partially seeing children, NAVH became the pioneer and standard setting agency in the preparation of large type.

Today, those publishers who meet our standards carry the prestigious "Seal of Approval" indicating high quality large print. We are delighted that Thorndike Press is one of the publishers whose titles meet these standards. We are also pleased to recognize the significant contribution Thorndike Press is making in this important and growing field.

Lorraine H. Marchi, L.H.D.
Founder/CEO
NAVH

* Thorndike Press encompasses the following imprints: Thorndike, Wheeler, Walker and Large Print Press.

Acknowledgments

My thanks, as always, to Pamela Dorman, Lucia Watson, and Zaidee Rose for mustering the might of Viking Penguin on Miss Julia's behalf.

My thanks, also, to Abby Ramsey for knowing the words to "There Is a Time"; to Cathy Sink (she'll know why), and to Millie Wareham (her mother will know why).

And special thanks to Ruth Sternemann of Wisconsin, the winner of the Name the Baby Contest, for naming Binkie and Coleman's little daughter.

Chapter 1

I am sick and tired of people asking how married life's treating me. Every time I've turned around in the three weeks we've been back from our honeymoon — and don't get me started on that subject, since Dollywood is hardly my idea of a romantic getaway — somebody's wanted to know how Sam and I are doing. You'd think I'd come fresh and new to the conjugal state with no idea in the world of what it means to share a bed. Because that's exactly what's on their minds when they ask. So I'm going to answer it one more time, and that will be my final word: We're doing as well as can be expected, and I'll thank you not to ask again.

Of course, if I'm honest, which I always am, living with a man after enjoying several years of solitary peace takes some getting used to. Not that Sam is anything like Wesley Lloyd Springer, who I never got used to, even though I tried for more than forty years. That marriage ended in Wesley Lloyd's sudden demise, although for all intents and purposes it had ended some years before he did. I just hadn't noticed.

But you better believe I'm going to be on my guard this time.

My foot set the chair rocking as my hands gripped the wide arms. Sam's front porch was one of the few places I felt at ease in his house. I just had not been able to get settled in at his place, although I knew that's what generally follows when you marry — the woman leaves her home and lives with her husband, and is usually happy to do it. But I'd think, at our age, we could've at least discussed the matter. After all, it wasn't as if I were a young thing, eager to leave my parents' home.

But no, on the day we returned home from our communal honeymoon, which was spent with Hazel Marie, Little Lloyd, Lillian, Latisha, and Mr. Pickens, one car went one way and one went the other. Without a by-your-leave, Sam had driven right past my house, went another few blocks, and turned into his driveway, saying, "Well, here we are, Mrs. Murdoch. Welcome home." And that was how I ended up here, and not all that happy about it, either.

So Hazel Marie and Little Lloyd were alone in my house, four blocks over, where I couldn't keep an eye on them. I suspected, however, that Mr. Pickens was a frequent and welcome guest. By them, not necessarily by me. I declare, if I could take a chance on marriage, it seemed to me he could do the same.

The rocking chair began to die down, as I returned to thoughts of what I'd unknowingly put up with where Wesley Lloyd was concerned — how he'd secretly and scantily supported a mistress and a son for almost a decade before his passing brought them out of the woodwork. Of course, Hazel Marie and Little Lloyd had proved a blessing to me in the long run, but hardly in the short one. So, even though I am not averse to receiving blessings, I could do without any more of that particular kind. Which meant that I was determined not to put up with a stunt like that from another husband.

Not that I intended to follow Sam around or check up on him or never let him out of my sight, but I thought I could recognize the symptoms of a distracted husband now. Besides, Sam is retired from the practice of law, so he doesn't have the excuse of working late or of meeting a client or of any other alibi for being out of the house. He'd better be where he's supposed to be, when he's supposed to be. I'm taking no chances of being made a fool of again, and Sam knows it. At least, he ought to, for I've told him often enough.

"Julia?" The screen door squeaked as Sam opened it and stepped out onto the porch. "What're you doing out here by yourself?"

"Watching the world go by."

"Mind if I watch with you?" He smiled as he pulled another rocker up close. "Lots to see this time of day."

I couldn't help but smile. There wasn't a soul on the sidewalk, nor had there been more than two cars that passed in the last hour.

"It'll pick up soon," I said, learning to give back the wry humor that he delighted in. "It's almost rush hour."

"So it is." He glanced at his watch. "There'll be a veritable traffic jam when people start heading home. Glad I made it out here in time."

He reached over and took my hand. "No regrets?"

I rested my head on my unoccupied hand, and said, "No, I guess not. It's just that I can't help wondering how it'll all work out."

"Worry about today, Julia. If today works out, then tomorrow will, too."

"Sufficient unto the day? I guess you're right, but you know what they say: Marry in haste, repent in leisure."

"Good Lord, Julia. If you call what we did marrying in haste, how long do you think we should've strung it out? I started courting you almost from the time old W.L. was buried."

"You did? Well, I'm sorry, Sam. I didn't notice." Then, fearful of having hurt his feelings, I quickly added, "But you have to admit, I had a few other things on my mind." Namely, the discovery of Wesley Lloyd's rascally nature and what it had produced in the form of Hazel Marie and Little Lloyd. Which, of course, Sam knew all about, since he had helped me through most of it.

"No," I went on. "I'm not talking about the length of your courting efforts. I'm talking about our quick jump into marriage without thinking through the consequences. You have to admit that running off to that tawdry all-night wedding chapel in Pigeon Forge and honeymooning at Dollywood — a theme park of all things — constituted a spur-of-the-moment decision. If that's not marrying in haste, I don't know what is."

"Well, I don't want you repenting in

leisure or any other way. What's bothering you, Julia? If I can make it right, I will."

"Some of it's Lillian. She's unhappy. She and James just can't seem to get along. And I can't blame James. He's been looking after you for so long that it's natural he'd resent somebody else coming in. But they're at each other all the time, Sam, and I wonder if I should've asked Lillian to work here. Except, I don't know what I'd do without her."

"Would she be happier with Hazel Marie and Little Lloyd?"

"I don't know. Maybe. She misses that child something awful. Even though she still has Latisha, probably for the duration since that little girl's mother is showing no signs of sending for her." Latisha was Lillian's great-grand, as she called her, and had been in Lillian's care for some months now, ever since her mother decided to head for the bright lights of New York. I smiled, recalling how Latisha, barely six years old, had ridden the log flume at Dollywood two dozen times, then came home telling everybody she was ready for another honeymoon.

Starting the chair rocking again, I couldn't help but think how our rush to marry had been so woefully lacking in any

14

long-range planning. "I thought," I went on, "that with her house finished and Latisha needing supervision, Lillian would welcome more time at home. With just you and me to do for, and James to help, she has a much easier time of it, and for the same salary, too. Instead, she's moping around like she's on her last legs, and giving James the evil eye whenever she can. And," I went on, giving him a glance, "James is doing the same to her."

"If she's that unhappy, why don't you see if she wants to go back to your house? I expect Hazel Marie would love to have her."

"I know she would. Why, Sam, Hazel Marie couldn't cook a decent meal if her life depended on it. I worry about that child getting the proper nutrition. But to let Lillian go? I couldn't do that. I'd be all alone over here."

"Alone? With me here?" Sam frowned, showing real distress. "I'm your family now, Julia. You're not ever alone with me around."

Well, I wouldn't tell him, but I could do with a little more aloneness than he was giving me. Lord, I'd about forgotten how arduous it was to get a sound sleep with another body in the bed. But that was something I wasn't ready to say, particularly

15

since he seemed to take such comfort in having me near. But, I'll tell you the truth, such close contact is hard to put up with every night of the week.

I'd thought that a late-in-life marriage would entail little more than having a friend to talk to and discuss things with, and of course have by my side for social engagements. But, to my consternation, I'd found that Sam had more than companionship on his mind.

But the fact of the matter was that I missed my own home and the people in it. I missed the activity and the give-and-take among us and that little boy's heart-lifting smile. Oh, of course, Little Lloyd turned up at Sam's just about every day, but visiting together is not the same as living together.

But, to answer Sam, I said, "I know I'm not alone. It's just that here we are, two old people, sitting around by ourselves."

"We're not old, Julia." Sam leaned over and lowered his voice. "Don't you know you've put a spring in my step and a sparkle in my eye?"

"And don't you know that I don't like referring to such things in the light of day? I declare, Sam, you beat all I've ever seen."

"Where's your mind, woman? All I'm referring to is being in your company. But," he went on, "if you have certain things on your mind, I'll be glad to accommodate you."

"If you don't behave yourself, I'm going in the house. You can just sit out here by yourself and wave to the cars." I sounded severe, but he knew me well enough to know it was all I could do to keep from laughing. That's what the man did to me and, I guess, that was the reason I'd married him in spite of my misgivings.

Take that night, barely a month ago, when he'd swept away all my inhibitions with his sudden insistence that we drive over the mountain to Tennessee and marry before sunup. At the time, the whole idea was so tantalizing that I hadn't stopped to think of what I was getting myself into. Why, we didn't even tell a soul what we were doing — just took off in the dead of night and eloped. I still couldn't get over how I'd done something so unlike myself. I, who had always preferred things done decently and in order, and as close to Emily Post's recommendations as it was possible to get, had just thrown caution to the winds.

To tell the truth, the whole thing had been like having an out-of-body experience. Not that I go in for all that new age claptrap, but it was as if I had watched somebody else stand beside Sam and promise to love and honor — but not to obey, I assure you — him till death did us part. I didn't get back into my right frame of mind until the next morning when I looked at the two of us in the cold light of day, and realized that I'd become tangled up again in the ties that bind.

When our one-line wedding announcement came out in the local paper several days later, why, you can imagine what a splash it made all over town. As soon as we got home, Mildred Allen called to tell me that the announcement should've included the schools Sam and I had attended and all the clubs we belonged to, as well as the committees and panels we'd sat on. "People read those things, Julia," she'd said. "And they want to know."

Then Emma Sue Ledbetter had dropped by, all red eyed and splotchy. Her feelings were mortally wounded because we hadn't been married in the church with her husband officiating. "What you did was a slap in the face, Julia," she'd sobbed. "And that smidgen of an announcement in the paper made it clear that you had snubbed your own pastor." Well, wasn't that the truth, and furthermore, it was done with deliberate aforethought.

As for the pastor himself, there'd been not one word out of him so far. Which suited me fine. Hazel Marie, now, was another story. She couldn't decide whether she was thrilled to death that Sam and I were married, or too mad to speak to me. "I wanted you to have a *big* wedding," she'd wailed, "with all the trimmings. I can't believe you'd do this without telling me." But Lillian had just smiled and said, " 'Bout time you got off yo' high horse an' married that man, I don't care how you do it."

And there're some people who aren't real sure that a Dollywood wedding will hold up over time. I occasionally wondered about that myself, but I wouldn't go so far as to mention it. Old Mrs. Estes, who's never believed that anybody's walked on the moon, squinched up her eyes at us the first time we walked into church together. And that old fool, Thurlow Jones, wrote a congratulatory note, but spoiled it by saying that he would've done better by me.

But, back to that night and the high spirits that Sam kept me in the whole two hours of driving it took to get to the altar. He talked all the way, telling me about the wedding packages offered by the Wedding Ring Chapel, which, I discovered, he had previously investigated and had on tap anytime he could turn my head enough to get me to agree to such a scheme.

"I want nothing but the best for us," Sam had said. "So let's decide which ceremony we want. There's the deluxe package that includes a bridal gown and a groom's tuxedo, complete with bouquet and boutonniere."

"Too much, Sam," I said, laughing, although if they'd offered a nice dinner suit I might've gone for that. I certainly hadn't been appropriately dressed for a wedding.

"Okay," he said. "How about the package that includes wine goblets and sparkling cider? Oh, you'll like this, Julia. They all include a garter."

"A garter! That is the tackiest thing I've ever heard of. I thought I'd faint when Binkie lifted her wedding dress, exposing her whole leg, and took hers off. No, let's bypass the garter."

"Well, I'm disappointed, but you can keep it as a souvenir. Now, we have to have the candlelight ceremony. That'd be nice, don't you think? And the photograph album with twenty pictures. Don't worry about the cost — it's all included. And the framed marriage certificate — that's important. I want it hanging over our bed so you won't forget the liberties it allows me."

"Oh, Sam, you are too much."

The whole trip was one of the best times of my life. I'd never been happier, mainly because I'd simply closed my eyes to the grief that woman is heir to in the marital state. And, believe me, I'd had plenty of grief in my previous experience of that state. Instead, I'd just enjoyed the moment, something I'd never done before. Or since.

"Now, listen," I'd finally said. "Let's just have a plain ceremony with no extras. I can do without candles, cameras, and bouquets. Just make sure everything is legal, that's all I ask."

"Well, if it's plain you want, we can do the drive-through special. It's the cheapest, too, and I want to know if they ask, 'You want fries with that?' when you drive up to the window."

By the time we walked into the chapel, after filling out the necessary forms and swearing that there were no legal impediments to our merger, I was amazed at what followed. First off, the officiating minister glanced over our license and the various forms, then broke into a wide grin. "Well, bless me, Lord. I see you folks're from Abbot County, North Carolina. Real nice place. I got kin over there. Y'all know any Kincaids? I guess you don't, they all married and remarried now. But I'm still a Kincaid,

Aaron Kincaid, to be exact, and happy to be of service. Now if you folks're ready to be united in wedded bliss, step right up to the altar and we'll get this show on the road."

I almost turned and left, right then.

But that was just the beginning of wonders. In the small room, arranged like any other chapel, except for the naked plaster angels hanging from the ceiling, we were met by a large woman of uncertain age dressed in a flowing white robe. She handed us a card printed with a dozen or so song titles, any one of which she would be happy to render with piano accompaniment, for a cost of twenty-five dollars over and above the price of the basic package.

I rolled my eyes, but Sam was ever the gentleman. He politely handed the card back to her and, with a slight bow, said, "Maybe next time."

Leaving the soloist with her mouth open, we proceeded to the front to meet the smiling officiator. We had been assured that he was ordained and legal in all manner of ways approved by the state of Tennessee. Which should've made me leery, right there, but we were too far along to raise questions by that time.

Before getting to the ceremony, the preacher, who was all decked out in a white suit and white suede shoes, asked if we wanted the candlelight ceremony. He waved his hand at the plethora of candles on white metal stands flanking the pulpit. "We'll light 'em all for a mere twenty-five dollars more," he said. Then expansively added, "The golden glow will be an immeasurable addition to your wedding pictures."

Sam cocked his head at me. "Candles, Julia? Or would you rather use that money for a motel room?"

Now, I know that the ceremonies of life should be approached with dignity and solemnity, but, I declare, it was all I could do to keep my composure. Sam had enough money to buy an entire motel, with plenty left over for whatever else he wanted. I think he thought that if he could keep me amused, I'd be married before I knew it. And that's just about the way it happened.

I have come to the conclusion that the most important ingredient of a good marriage is laughter. And Sam provides plenty of that, yet he never steps over the line to play the fool. So, is there any wonder I married the man?

But I'll tell you the truth. Given all the subsequent second thoughts I'd been having, he'd do well to stay on his toes and keep me entertained.

Chapter 2

The screen door squeaked as Lillian poked her head out. "Miss Julia, Miss Hazel Marie on the phone. She say she got something to tell you, you gonna love. She don't say what, but she say hurry up an' come to the phone."

Sam and I looked at each other, the same thought running through our minds.

"You suppose?" I asked.

Sam raised his eyebrows. "You never know."

Hurrying past Lillian, I dashed through the hall and into Sam's study. "Hazel Marie," I gasped, out of breath by the time I picked up the phone, "has Mr. Pickens proposed?"

"*Him?* Why would you think that?"

"Oh, no reason. I just keep hoping, and when Lillian said you had something to tell me that I'd really love, well, I thought . . ."

"You know how he is, and I don't guess he's ever going to be the marrying kind. No, it's something else, and I really need your help with it. Coleman just called to tell me that the sheriff wants to buy two

24

more dogs for the canine unit and some bulletproof vests for them. And guess what? They want me to put on a beauty pageant!"

Coleman Bates was a deputy sheriff, my erstwhile boarder, husband of Binkie, father of little Grace Elizabeth, and as fine a young man as I'd ever known, except for his habit of calling his baby girl Gracie, when she already had a perfectly lovely name. But his coming up as a proponent of a beauty pageant made me wonder how level his head was situated.

"I don't understand the connection between police dogs and beauty contestants."

"Well, I don't either," she admitted, "but it's all part of their public awareness program — you know, to make the public aware of what the department needs. So they want to raise money by selling tickets to the pageant, and they're hoping that businesses will donate prizes and things to the winners." She stopped for a long minute. "And maybe we could get some sponsors for the contestants, too. Oh, I know, we could give them credit and free advertising in our programs. But, listen, Miss Julia. The sheriff thinks that a lot of sheriffs' departments all across the state will be doing the same thing. I mean, he doesn't want this to be some tacky, local kind of thing. Our winner might compete in a statewide contest, and for big prizes, too. Isn't that exciting? I can't wait to get started."

"You're going to be a contestant?" I asked, marveling at the thought. Hazel Marie was eye-catching, there was no doubt about that, especially with her blonde hair and full-bosomed figure and the way she dressed and carried herself. But, let's face it, you don't normally see a forty-something-year-old woman prancing around publicly in high heels and a bathing suit. Not that I wanted to see any younger woman do it, either.

"No, no." She laughed. "They want me to be the organizer. You know, do all the planning and setting up, telling the contestants what to do and what they can expect and so on."

"Do you know anything about beauty pageants?"

"Well, I've been to a lot of them, and I almost entered one one time, except I couldn't afford all the clothes you need. But we can do this, Miss Julia, and it'll be loads of fun. I've already looked up pageants on the Internet. I mean, Lloyd found them for me, and you wouldn't believe all the different kinds they have — from babies to women over the age of sixty."

"Hazel Marie," I said with a perilous warning in my voice, "you're not suggesting . . . ?"

"No," she said, laughing again. "I wouldn't do that to you, but mainly because I don't think you'd do it. Of course, you'd win, if you did."

I rolled my eyes, even though she couldn't see them go back in my head. "I don't need flattery, Hazel Marie, because there's no way in the world I'd hold myself up to public ridicule by displaying myself in such a fashion."

"Well, here's what I'm thinking. First of all, Coleman said that as a local pageant, we'll have a lot of leeway. It's the first time they've done this, so it can be pretty much anything we want it to be. So that's the first thing we have to decide — what to call it and what age group we want and where we'll get the contestants."

I noticed she kept saying *we*, so I changed the pronoun. "Why don't you have a baby contest, so little Grace Elizabeth Bates can win?"

"I thought about that, but she'd be ineligible since Sheriff Frady put Coleman in charge of it all. And I've thought about young girls, eight or ten years old, and do a Little Miss Sheriff's Department or Little Miss Deputy or something. What do you think about that?"

"You don't want to know."

"You're right." She sighed, then said, "What it comes down to, Miss Julia, is we have to have contestants of an age to generate interest."

Uh-huh, I thought, *nubile* contestants is what she means. "Little doubt of that," I said. "I don't think many people would come out for a Ms. Senior Citizen or a Mrs. Homemaker of the Year contest. Or a Little Miss Doberman Puppy, either."

"Well, listen. We need to put our heads together and make some decisions. The sooner we know what we're going to do, the sooner we can start publicity, and —"

"Why do you keep saying *we*, Hazel Marie? Beauty pageants have never been my cup of tea, and I don't know what I could do to help you." Nor, I thought, would I especially want to.

"Oh, I should've told you. What I want is to have something elegant and tasteful, and you do that better than anybody."

I had to sit down. Elegant and tasteful were the last adjectives I'd ever have tacked onto a beauty contest. But then again, perhaps my influence would have a moderating effect on what could easily become a parade of youthful flesh for the titillation of a certain percentage of the public.

"Details, Hazel Marie. I need some details."

"Well, like, you could show the contestants how to walk and sit in a ladylike manner. You could be at all the rehearsals and correct their posture and so forth. And help them with how they present themselves before the judges, you know, when they have to answer questions about their platforms and ambitions. Just general etiquette, Miss Julia. Besides, I'm not going to do this if you don't help me."

"Don't put that on me, Hazel Marie. I'll have to think about it." And, I thought, talk to Sam about it.

Then I immediately thought better of that. The quickest way to ruin a marriage is to start asking permission for the least little thing you want to do. It sets a pattern, don't you know, and before you know it, somebody else is telling you what to do and when to do it. And, I'll tell you, if I had to get Sam's approval every time I turned around, I'd have to reconsider the wisdom of marrying him in the first place.

"On second thought," I said, "I'll do it."

"Oh, good! Now, we need to start right away."

"Wait a minute, Hazel Marie. I'll help you with ideas and suggestions and so on, but you've got to keep me in the background. I have a husband to tend to now, so I can't be at the beck and call of meetings and rehearsals. Besides, I don't have any experience with putting on shows of this nature. So the first idea I have is for you to find somebody who knows what they're doing."

"Don't worry, I've got it covered. You'll just kinda be around to keep us on the straight and narrow. But I would like to talk it over with you before I get too far along." She stopped, thought a minute, then went on. "I could ask you and Sam to come over for dinner tonight, but, well, you know I'm not very handy in the kitchen."

I walked out onto the porch, and said, "Sam, Hazel Marie, and Little Lloyd, and I guess Mr. Pickens, too, are coming for dinner." It was all I could do to keep from saying, if that's all right with you. But I held the line and didn't. "I need to tell Lillian and James to prepare enough for everybody."

"It's about time they came over," he

30

said. "We've not seen enough of them. But come on back out and sit with me when you're through."

Well, I thought, as I walked back to the kitchen, telling, instead of asking, hadn't been so hard. So I took heart from the ease of making a decision on my own.

I slowed as I got to the dining room, mentally placing all of us around the table. It would be the first time I'd entertained in Sam's house, and I was struck by the fact that I would not be using my table, my china, my silver, or anything else that was still in my house on Polk Street. Here, I'd moved into another woman's place and was about to use her household goods. And I hadn't even counted her place settings or checked her linen closets. Sam's first wife had passed so many years before that I'd hardly given her a thought. I'd known her, of course, but not all that well. Sam had been Wesley Lloyd's attorney, so we all had some social contact. It had been limited, though, since Wesley Lloyd didn't believe in mixing pleasure with business.

The fact of the matter was that Sam hadn't become important to me in a personal way until after we'd both become spouseless. That was why, I guess, I never thought of him with another woman. Until

I found myself preparing to use her Haviland china and Gorham silver on her mahogany table, which was acceptable enough, but not nearly as nice as my own.

I bit my lip, wondering if Hazel Marie would be interested in a swap.

Then I pushed through the door to the kitchen and found Lillian and James silently fuming at each other. James was cleaning the sink, but I caught him sending a glare in Lillian's direction where she was viciously rolling out pastry on the counter on the other side of the room. I decided that the better part of discretion was to ignore the tension and pretend we were all one happy family.

"Lillian, everybody's coming for supper, so we'll need to set three more places. I hope whatever you're preparing will be enough to go around."

"Won't be," James said. "She jus' got that little ole rib roast cookin', an' it not enough to feed hardly nobody."

"That's a ten-pound roast," Lillian shot back at him. "An' like I done tole you, it's a plenty."

"Not with them bones, it won't." And James gave a quick nod of his head as if that settled the matter. "You gonna be lackin', lady."

I held up my hand, as Lillian appealed to me with silent fury. "Wait," I said. "Let's don't argue. Lillian, will it be enough? I mean, with Mr. Pickens at the table?"

"Well," she said, her eyes sliding away, "he make a difference. But I don't want nobody tellin' me what to cook and how to cook it."

At this pointed comment, James turned from the sink and brought his argument to me. "I been cookin' in this kitchen longer'n I can count, Miss Julia, an' Miss Lillian come in here an' try to take over. I know what Mr. Sam like, an' he like chicken. *Fried* chicken."

"Good," I said. "Perfect, in fact. Lillian, you tend to your roast and whatever you plan to have with it. James, you fry up a chicken and make rice and gravy. Then everybody'll be happy, and we'll have plenty for the table. I want you to set the table, Lillian. You know how I like it. James, you can clear the table when it's time and put things in the dishwasher. Let's all work together, since it's our first time of having company."

They both thought through my distribution of tasks, anxious that one not be privileged above the other. It was the most unlikely thing to me — they seemed to feel that the one who had the most to do was the most preferred.

Then James mumbled, "What about dessert? Who get to do that?"

Lillian slapped a round of pastry into a pie pan. "What you think I'm doin' here? Can't you see I'm makin' a choc'late pie hard as I can? See, Miss Julia, he jus' don't think I got a lick of sense."

"Won't be enough," James mumbled again.

Lillian's mouth tightened. "Well, I jus' make two of 'em."

"Mr. Sam, he like lemon."

Lillian's face began to crumple, so I stepped in. "He can eat chocolate tonight, or, James, you can give him a bowl of ice cream. But he's going to have to learn to eat what we give him or do without."

James turned a shocked face to me, but he didn't say a word. A satisfied smile tugged at Lillian's mouth. She was pleased that I was taking control and, from her point of view, putting James in his place. She knew her position was unassailable with me, and it didn't matter who I was married to or whose house we were in.

"Lord, Sam," I said, as I walked out onto the porch. "We're going to have to do something about those two. Now they're fussing about who gets to cook what, and what you'll eat and what you won't."

He laughed. "You know I'll eat anything, Julia. Don't let James get away with that. He decides what I like by what he has a mind to cook."

I took a seat beside him again, sighing as I did so. "Well, if they both insist on cooking, the only thing I see to do is add on another kitchen. With no connecting doors."

Chapter 3

I wanted to grab Little Lloyd and hug him good when he and his mother and Mr. Pickens came in that evening. I knew it would embarrass him, though, so I stood back and looked on with pride as he shook hands with Sam, one of the many social courtesies I had taught him. I waited to see how much of a welcome he wanted from me, and was warmly gratified when his eyes searched me out. We smiled at each other, sharing a special bond from all the experiences we'd had together. I was relieved that my precipitous move to Sam's house seemed not to have disturbed his feelings for me.

As soon as we were seated at the table, Mr. Pickens's black eyes roved back and forth over the abundance of dishes. Then he made a comment about the food, a most impolite thing to do, as everybody but him seemed to know.

"Roast beef *and* fried chicken," he said as he surveyed the table. "Man, Miss Julia, you must've worked your fingers to the bone getting all this ready."

"Not at all, Mr. Pickens," I said, knowing full well that he was aware of my lack of culinary experience. "Lillian and James just knew you were coming."

Hazel Marie laughed as she took the platter of chicken I passed to her. "Oh, J.D.'s amazed at such a full table. He thinks I starve him to death. When I ask what he wants me to make for supper, he always says reservations."

We smiled at the old joke, but I knew it was fairly close to the truth. Sooner or later, and probably sooner if Little Lloyd's health was to be maintained, I'd have to help her find a cook. Which brought to mind the possibility of sending Lillian to her, and I didn't want to think about that.

"Well, listen, everybody," Hazel Marie said, when we'd finished and James began to clear the table. "We need to make some plans. Let me get my notes." She sprang up from the table, brought back a yellow legal pad, and settled herself in a businesslike manner to plan a beauty contest to aid the sheriff's canine deputies. Mr. Pickens watched her with an indulgent expression on his face.

"First thing," she said, "is to decide what age contestants we're going to have."

Mr. Pickens put his elbow on the table and leaned his head against his hand. "Are we talking women or dogs?"

"J.D.," Hazel Marie said, flapping his arm with the back of her hand, "behave. We're talking women, young women, of course, and don't you start with me. I'm thinking maybe seventeen or eighteen, in that range."

"That'll do it for me," Mr. Pickens said. "What about you, Sam?"

"On the grounds that it might incriminate me," Sam said, "I respectfully decline to answer." He winked at me from the head of the table where he sat.

"Oh, that's right," Mr. Pickens said. "With your bride sitting right here, I commend you on your discretion."

Little Lloyd piped up then. "I think that's a good age, Mama. That's about the age of the contestants I've seen on television."

I raised my eyebrows, concerned at what the child was watching, but Mr. Pickens put his arm around the child's chair and said, "That's my boy."

"All right," Hazel Marie said, writing on her pad. "That's decided. Now, what are we going to call it? I mean, what title will the winner get?"

"Why, Miss Top Dog," Mr. Pickens said, as if there were no other answer.

Sam laughed, but Hazel Marie didn't. "Absolutely not. And if you keep that up, I'm not going to talk to you the rest of the evening."

He stretched his other arm across her chair, so that he encompassed both her and the child. I looked again at my unbalanced table, with the three of them on one side and no one on the other. Nothing would do but that both Little Lloyd and Hazel Marie had to be seated next to him. It was a continual marvel to me how they circled around him, and a continual cause of distress that Hazel Marie allowed him familial comforts without one iota of legal commitment from him. It wasn't right, and I didn't like it. Still, little by little, I'd come to accept, if not condone, what I couldn't seem to change. Which is exactly the way sin sneaks up on you.

And, I thought with a sudden jolt of insight, my being so attracted to Sam, but not wanting to fall into sin, might've been the very reason I'd plunged headlong into another marriage.

Mr. Pickens smiled down at Hazel Marie. "I'm just teasing you, sweetheart. Don't get in an uproar."

She frowned at him, but it didn't last long. "Anybody else have a suggestion?"

"Tell us," Sam said, "just what the winner will be expected to do. Will she have any duties after the contest, or is the contest all there is?"

"Well, Coleman said that she might represent Abbot County in a state contest for the Miss North Carolina Sheriff's Department. If their plans get that far, I mean. Because, see, I think we'll be sort of a pilot program. Anyway, our winner will ride on a float in all the local parades throughout the year, and they want her to maybe go around to the schools and tell about attack dogs and arson dogs and the other kinds of dogs that do all sorts of things. They're deputies, too, you know. She'd maybe speak to the Rotary and the Kiwanis, that kind of thing, to let them know what the department needs and what it's doing. Sort of a goodwill ambassador, I think."

I sat at the foot of the table, cringing at the thought of all the *uh*s and the *you know*s and the lame jokes that litter the orations of unaccomplished public speakers. Somebody was going to have their work cut out for them, whipping young contestants into enough shape to be a credit to the sheriff and his canine deputies.

"Then," Sam said, "why not Miss Abbot County Sheriff's Canine Unit? That says it all, right there."

"Well," Hazel Marie said, frowning, "I don't know. I kind of wanted something

40

with a little zip to it, but I can't think what it would be."

"Miss Serve and Protect?" Little Lloyd put in.

"Good one, son," Mr. Pickens said. "I don't think your mother'll like it, though."

"No, I don't. People might not know what she was serving and protecting. Let's think of something else."

Sam said, "Miss Canine Handler?"

Mr. Pickens shared a grin with him, and offered, "Miss Four-Legged Deputy?"

From the look on her face, Hazel Marie was about to get enough of their carrying-on.

"How 'bout Miss Point and Retrieve?" Sam said, as I glared at him.

Then Little Lloyd piped up again. "I know! Miss Sniff and Seek!" He threw his head back and laughed until he almost fell off his chair.

Hazel Marie threw down her pen. "That's enough. Miss Julia and I'll just do it ourselves. You decide, Miss Julia. What should the title be?"

"I think Miss Abbot County Sheriff's Department says it all," I said. "Especially if she's going to be in a state pageant. It may not have the zip you want, but trying for zippiness tends to get us sidetracked. As we've just seen."

41

"I guess you're right," she said, writing down the title. "We can always change it, if we think of something better."

Mr. Pickens mumbled, "I still like Miss Top Dog."

Hazel Marie poked him in the ribs and said, "I'm gonna Top Dog you." Then to the rest of us, she said, "All right, we have the age and the title. The next thing is to figure out how to get the contestants. Should we just advertise and let any girl enter who wants to?"

I asked, "What if no one wants to?"

"Oh, that won't be a problem," Hazel Marie said. "I think the problem'll be having more enter than we want. There's not a woman in the world who wouldn't love to win a beauty contest."

Well, I didn't know about that, but I let it go.

Sam pondered for a minute, then said, "You know, it might be more interesting if each of the contestants already represented something. Like, if a business or something sponsored each girl, or, uh, woman."

Mr. Pickens nodded. "That would work."

But I shook my head, recalling the diverse sponsors we'd gotten for the Poker Run some months before. "Hazel Marie, if you do that, you're going to have the likes of

Thurlow Jones turning heads with the offer of exorbitant amounts of money. You better think of something else."

"How 'bout this," Mr. Pickens said, as Hazel Marie pursed her mouth and glared, expecting more nonsense from him. "Why don't you let the various sections of the sheriff's department choose their own contestants? Then the winner will represent the whole department."

"How would that work?" Hazel Marie asked, laying herself open to more of his teasing. But he surprised me by coming up with a halfway sensible suggestion.

"Well," he said, "say you have the detective squad choose a Miss Detective Squad, and the SWAT team, a Miss SWAT Team. There could be a Miss Dispatcher and a Miss Patrol, and if you want a big bunch, you could have the Misses First, Second, and Third Watches." He thought for a minute, then went on. "I think you'd better leave off a Miss Canine Unit, since there's only one dog and one handler now, and expanding it is the whole purpose of the contest. Right?"

We were all silent, thinking over Mr. Pickens's proposition, waiting, I thought, for the punch line.

When it didn't come, Hazel Marie gazed at him with some wonderment. "Why, J.D., that's a great idea and so fitting."

His black mustache twitched at her praise. Then he spoiled it by moving from the sensible to the ridiculous. "You'll need a Miss School Crossing Guard, too," he said, when everybody knew that crossing guards weren't sworn deputies.

Little Lloyd's face lit up. "And a Miss D.A.R.E. Officer!"

"You both better quit while you're ahead," Hazel Marie said, frowning as Little Lloyd and Mr. Pickens slapped hands. Then turning to us, she went on. "Let's think about how the squads would choose their representatives."

"Wouldn't matter," Mr. Pickens answered her. "They could do it any way they wanted, just so each squad came up with one. It could be somebody's girlfriend, or a sergeant's daughter. Whoever they wanted."

"Not a wife," Hazel Marie said, firmly. "Let's keep this for single women only."

"Oh, yeah," Mr. Pickens agreed. "You don't want that kind of trouble."

"This is perfect," Hazel Marie exclaimed, writing furiously on her pad. "I can't wait to tell Coleman. He'll love it." She looked up from her writing, and went on, "Now we need judges."

Mr. Pickens raised his hand. "I'll be one."

"No, you won't," she said, without looking at him. "Think of somebody else. Sam, what about you?"

Sam smiled and shook his head. "Better not. My lady-wife might not like it."

I straightened up at my end of the table. No, no, I thought, I didn't want to have to ask his permission for every little thing, and I didn't want him asking mine either. There's nothing worse than a weak-kneed, henpecked husband. Unless it's a mealy-mouthed doormat of a wife.

"I have absolutely no opinion on the subject," I said. "If you want to do it, Sam, then do it. You certainly don't need my permission."

"Oh, good," Hazel Marie said, writing down Sam's name. "Everybody knows how fair you are, Sam, so you'll be perfect. Now, who else? We need some women, too."

Mr. Pickens kept a straight face as he said, "What about what's-his-name, Tonya Allen?"

"That's a wonderful idea!" Hazel Marie said, her face lighting up. "I just love her, and she knows so much about fashion and what's in and what's not. I mean, with her New York background, she'll add a cosmopolitan atmosphere to the whole thing."

I was trying my best to keep my distance

from the pageant planning. Having bitten off more than I could chew on any number of occasions before, I figured I'd learned my lesson. Besides, I had all I could handle with a new husband and didn't need any more problems. So, when Tonya Allen's name came up, I had to bite my tongue. Tonya was Mildred Allen's erstwhile son, Tony, who'd had an operation to rearrange certain delicate bodily areas, and was now a gingerly accepted member of the social scene in Abbotsville. After recovering from her son's sudden switch in gender, Mildred had reminded us that Tonya was a legacy and had to be inducted into all our clubs. See, that's the problem with all this modern technology — you never know whether someone belongs in the Sons or the Daughters of the American Revolution.

I couldn't help but ask, "Would Tonya count as a male or female judge?"

"Doesn't matter," Hazel Marie said, since she was so taken with Tonya and admired her taste in clothes and home decor to the extent that I worried about leaving my own house in Hazel Marie's hands. "Tonya'll be the perfect judge. Now who else? We need an odd number."

"Seems pretty odd to me, already," Mr. Pickens said.

Chapter 4

"What kind of prize will the winner get?" I asked, as we rose from the table and made our way into Sam's small front room. I suppose you'd call it the living room, although Sam did most of his living in the large study across the hall. I took my seat in an upholstered chair, although Sam had made it clear with a cocking of his head that he'd wanted us to sit together on the sofa. But I thought it best that Hazel Marie and Mr. Pickens sit there so she could pinch him when he got too rambunctious.

"I don't know," Hazel Marie said. "What do you think?"

"I believe they're mostly scholarship prizes now," Sam said. "But that means you need money to start with. You'll have to find some heavy-hitting sponsors."

Hazel Marie frowned. "You don't think ticket sales will bring in enough?"

Sam shook his head. "No, because you'll have expenses to cover, too. And you'll want to have enough left over to buy the trained dogs that the sheriff wants."

Hazel Marie's face fell, and she put down her pen. "Oh, me, I'd forgotten about that. Buying those dogs will mean big money, and I bet we won't make enough to buy their flea collars."

Sam smiled at her. "I tell you what. I'll help you with the sponsors, and to start it off, I'll make the first contribution."

"Oh, thank you, Sam. Because I really want to present the sheriff with a big check. And have a scholarship prize, too, because that'll just elevate the whole pageant."

That got me started. "I wouldn't worry about handing out scholarships. It does me in to hear contestants say that the only reason they entered is to get money for college. But you'll notice that intelligence and aptitude tests aren't on the agenda. And to tell the truth, I don't know what a shapely pair of legs has to do with getting an education, anyway."

"I can think of a few things," Mr. Pickens said, and got another poke from Hazel Marie's elbow.

"We'll all have to help with getting sponsors," she said, tapping her pen against her mouth. "Because we'll need some more prizes, too. You know, for the first and second runners-up and so on. Like, maybe, an outfit from one of the shops downtown

48

or a makeover from a beauty salon."

"My word, Hazel Marie," I said. "I should hope the winner wouldn't need a makeover. I'd hope she'd be as pretty as she could be, already."

"That was just a suggestion. We can come up with some more ideas as we get into it. And, Sam, we'll make a list of everybody we can think of who'd be willing to donate something for the good of the sheriff's department." Hazel Marie got a faraway look in her eyes as she considered who might be persuaded to part with a little cash.

"One thing, Hazel Marie," I warned. "Don't put Thurlow Jones on your list. He'd ruin everything."

Sam smiled at me as we heard laughter issuing from the back of the house. Little Lloyd had helped James clear the table, then had stayed in the kitchen with him and Lillian. Maybe he was what we needed to bring about a truce between the two sparring cooks.

Excusing myself on the pretext of thanking James and Lillian, I walked back to the kitchen. What I really wanted, though, was to be in the company of that child. When I pushed through the door, I found him sitting on a stool beside the large butcher block in the middle of the room. Lillian sat across from him, laughing at something I'd just missed. James leaned against a counter, a smile lighting up his face.

"Hey, Miss Julia," Little Lloyd said, turning his sweet face to me. "James was just telling us about the time he was mowing the lawn and ran over a yellow jacket nest. He said he never ran so fast in his life."

"Goodness, James," I said. "Did you get stung?"

"No more'n two dozen times," James said, laughing. "They was mad as hornets, comin' after me for all they was worth. I had a mind to run in the house, but they'd of followed me in. So I hit about sixty and turned the hose on myself. They lost some steam after that."

"Did you have to see a doctor?"

"Oh, no'm, I jus' chewed me up some tobacco and put that on 'em. Took the stingin' right out, too. 'Sides, this all happened two summers ago an' I ain't had no lastin' effects from it. 'Course I'm not too quick to go mowin' no lawns, neither."

"I don't blame you. Well, I just stepped in to tell you and Lillian that dinner was just perfect. You both did a fine job, but I guess you already know that from all the empty plates."

"That Mr. Pickens sho' can put it away," James said admiringly.

Lillian frowned and looked away. She didn't want to share Mr. Pickens or any of us with James.

"Lillian," I said, stepping closer to Little Lloyd so I could touch him. "Your pies were wonderful, and I hope you noticed that Sam had two pieces."

That brought a smile to her face, and a triumphant glare aimed at James.

"Anyway," I went on, "I just want to thank you both. Little Lloyd, how're you getting along in school and at home?"

"School's almost out for the summer," he said. "Home's okay, but I miss Miss Lillian's cooking. And I miss you, too, Miss Julia. It's not the same without you there."

I declare, when you teach a child good manners, you never know whether he's practicing them or telling the truth. I chose to assume he was telling the truth, and it made me wonder again at what had possessed me to give up raising this child in favor of taking another husband.

I soon returned to the living room and

took my seat again, as Hazel Marie was jotting down more notes. Mr. Pickens put his arm around her and leaned close to read what she was writing and, to avoid staring at this incidence of close contact, I glanced around the room. I didn't know how Sam felt, but some changes had to be made. Not one thing had been done to the decor since his wife, I mean, his first wife, had passed. And it was past time for some refurbishing. The dining room needed it, too. There was a fine breakfront there that I would keep, but it badly needed something better behind the glass doors than stacks of mismatched china. I could picture a collection of lustrous oyster plates, for instance, or some Boehm birds or the like. As for the room we were in, I busied myself with plans to turn it into a morning room with a pastel color on the walls and a lot of chintz, plus that nice desk that no one was using in one of the guest rooms. In other words, I would make it into a room for myself, where I'd catch up with bills and my correspondence.

I bit my lip as I thought of what I'd like to do, realizing that Sam might not approve, seeing that it was his house and his furnishings. But, I reminded myself, if he wanted me to feel at home in it, then it had to be made into my house, too. I just didn't know how to approach him with the idea.

That was another problem with marrying somebody set in their ways while you were set in yours. It made me tired to think of all the complications.

"Miss Julia?" Hazel Marie gathered her notes, readying herself to leave, while Sam and Mr. Pickens went back to the kitchen for Little Lloyd. "We really need to think about a big party to celebrate your wedding. The etiquette book says that's what you're supposed to do when you have a small wedding. And they don't get any smaller than what you and Sam had."

Hazel Marie still hadn't gotten over our elopement. She said she'd been counting on being a bridesmaid again, and not even sharing our honeymoon at Dollywood had calmed her down.

"I know it's the thing to do," I said, "and I've had it on my mind. Let's get together soon and make some plans."

"Good! There's no reason we can't handle a beauty pageant and a big blowout in the same month."

By the time the three of them took their leave, Hazel Marie had several pages of her yellow legal pad covered with notes, and she was even more excited than when she'd started. Sam and I walked out onto the porch to see them off and stood watching as they went down the walk, arm in arm, to Mr. Pickens's sports car. Little Lloyd hopped into the back seat and waved to us, his face remaining like an afterimage in my mind. My spirits sank lower and lower as the car backed down the drive and roared off into the night.

"I don't know how I'm going to manage this, Sam," I said, feeling his arm slip around my waist. "I miss them so much."

"Give it time, sweetheart," he said. "It's not as if they live miles away. They're practically next door."

"Well, I know that. But I miss being with them, talking and laughing and, well, feeling at home." I didn't want to tell him, but I felt like a visitor in his house, and when you're a visitor, sooner or later you're liable to be told it's time to leave.

"I want you to feel at home here," Sam said, searching my face in the glow of the carriage lamps beside the door. "It might help if you'd move all your things here. Right now, you're practically living out of a suitcase. And, Julia, you know I'll do whatever it takes to make you feel at home."

I could certainly take that as my go-ahead to redecorate his house, but by that time I didn't have the heart for it. So, I could only nod, because I felt like crying. Homesickness, I thought, that's what this lonely feeling is. It was a wonder to me that I could put a name to a feeling I'd never had before. But once you have the affliction, you know what it is.

After a sad and lonely night, even though Sam exerted a mighty effort to distract me, I awoke with a hard resolve to try to make the best of my situation. Saint Paul said that he had learned to be content in whatsoever state he was in, and the least I could do was try to do the same.

Some might think that being Sam's wife would be enough, but, take it from me, that's a recipe for disaster. I'd lived too long with no life other than just being a wife, and had learned a bitter lesson from it. So the only thing I knew to do was start planning a complete redecoration of the house, tell Emma Sue that I would be a circle leader next year, and rejoin the garden club. Somehow I had to fill my life with something of my own.

Later that morning, as I was measuring windows for draperies, Hazel Marie called.

"Miss Julia," she said, "you're not going to believe this, but I just ruined your microwave oven. But don't worry — I've already called for a replacement. I just wanted you to know, in case you came over and saw the mess."

"What happened, Hazel Marie? Did it die on you?"

"No, it was working fine. But, see, I washed a pair of J.D.'s jeans and didn't know there was about fifty dollars in one of the pockets. And, Miss Julia, when I opened the washer after it got through spinning, there were fives and tens and ones all over the place. I thought I'd ruined that money, but it was just kind of pale and limp. And wet, of course."

"I don't understand, Hazel Marie. What does that have to do with the microwave?"

"Well, see, I wanted to get the money dry before J.D. saw it. Not that he'd get mad, but he'd laugh a lot. So I put it in the microwave to dry and, well, it exploded."

"Exploded! Hazel Marie, are you all right? My word, I can't believe that."

"Yes, well, I didn't think you would."

I hung up the phone and marched myself back to Sam's bedroom. I dragged out my suitcase and opened it on the bed, then proceeded to fill it with gowns and underclothes and personal hygiene paraphernalia. Then I took the few dresses I'd brought from home out of the closet and laid them on the bed. All I could think of was how fortunate I was not to have moved in completely.

"Julia?" Sam stood in the doorway, concern spread over his face. "What are you doing?"

"I'm going home. You can stay here, or you can go with me. But either way, I'm going home before Hazel Marie blows up my house with her and that child in it."

Chapter 5

"Wait, Julia," he said, coming over to put his hand on my arm. "Let's talk about this. Aren't you happy here with me?"

"No, sir. I am not. I need to be in my own house with my own things. Since Wesley Lloyd's been gone, I've fixed it the way I like it, and I don't want to be anywhere else."

"Well, Good Lord, woman. What about me?"

"I've already told you. You can come with me if you want to. We'll be more than glad to have you. And," I went on, rounding on him, "I will tear out walls, repaint, and get new furniture in my bedroom, so you won't feel like you're in somebody else's place."

Sam put his arms around me. "Is that what this is about? Honey, you can tear out, repaint, and replace all you want to right here. We can tear down the whole house and build another one, if that's what you want."

"Oh, Sam. It's not that, at least not all of

it. I need to be with Hazel Marie and Little Lloyd, and I want to be with you, too. So the only answer is to live in my house. If you want to, that is."

"And if I don't?"

We stood almost as close as two people can get, looking into each other's eyes. I didn't cringe or blink. "Then I guess I'll be going."

"Well, hell, you put it that way, I'll get my toothbrush." And he had the audacity to start laughing before he started packing.

"You don't mind going with me?" I thought for sure he'd get mad and tell me he'd be glad to see the last of me. That would not've stopped me, but still.

"You think you can get rid of me that easy? No way, sweetheart. You pitch a tent, I'll be crawling right in beside you."

When I told Lillian we were moving back home, she let out a whoop that could've been heard down on Main Street. She helped me get my things together, and told Sam she'd come back later to pack up and move everything he wanted. She was so happy she could hardly stand it. In fact, she lifted my spirits so much that the more we loaded in the car, the better I felt. And Sam, why, he seemed just as lighthearted as the two of us. It was a wonder to me that he could take picking up and moving out of his home of so many years with hardly a second thought. The only one who wasn't happy was James, but Sam assured him that he was still needed and he was to stay on to look after the house.

"I guess I'd better call Hazel Marie," I said to Lillian. We were standing on the lawn, waiting for Sam while he discussed a few things with James. "To warn her, you know, and not just land on her out of the blue."

"Yessum, you better. No tellin' what she be up to."

As I walked into Sam's study to use the telephone, I had a moment alone to reconsider what I'd put in motion. I was doing exactly what I wanted to do, but sometimes that's not enough reason to disrupt everybody else. So far, Sam had been nothing but amenable to anything I suggested, but I had to ask myself if I was expecting too much from him. But then I recalled that within the few days that we'd been man and wife, he had changed his will, making me his primary beneficiary. And he'd done it of his own free will, for I'd known nothing about it until it was signed, sealed, and notarized. If that's not true love, I don't know what is.

I was still studying what to do about my own will. I was reluctant to replace Little Lloyd with Sam as my primary beneficiary, mainly because the child had longer to live than Sam and could make better use of an inheritance. Besides, Sam didn't need it. He had plenty of his own.

The same could be said of me, but I was of a mind with Mildred Allen, who'd once said to her husband, "What's yours is mine, and what's mine is mine." Besides, Sam had said not one word about a mutual will change, so I'd determined to leave well enough alone, at least for the time being.

As I stood there, hesitating before calling Hazel Marie, I also had to consider the disruption to her life by our moving in, lock, stock, and barrel. What if she didn't want all of us descending on her? Of course, it was my house and I could live in it if I wanted to. But she had every right to expect to have it to herself, since I'd given her to understand that I'd be living with Sam.

Well, there was nothing for it but to tell her, and so I did. "Hazel Marie," I said, when she answered, "I know this might be a shock to you, and you might not like it. But I'm moving back in with you and Little Lloyd."

There was dead silence, while I cringed at the prospect of hearing dismay and disappointment in her voice. I knew she'd try to make the best of it, and would never in this world come right out and tell me I wasn't welcome.

Then she said, "Oh, Miss Julia, you've not given it enough time. Please, you and Sam just need to talk to each other. You'll work something out. I know you will."

"They Lord, Hazel Marie. I'm not *leaving* him. I'm bringing him with me. We're both coming home."

"You are? And Lillian, too? Oh, thank goodness. You don't know how bad my cooking is. And I've missed you so much. I hate to admit this, but when J.D.'s not here, I get scared to death at night. I tell you what, Miss Julia," she said, with a sudden lift of excitement. "Why don't I move upstairs into your old room, and you and Sam take mine? My room will give you all the privacy you could ever want, and it has a king-size bed, too."

"Thank you, Hazel Marie," I said, feeling a great relief at her response, "and it'll keep me from having to climb those stairs every day of my life. That will work just fine."

It would, in fact, work better than fine.

After sleeping alone these many years, I couldn't get used to the narrowness of a double bed with two people in it. Why, I could hardly turn over without disturbing Sam, or him me. One of those wide king-size beds would be just the ticket. And if that didn't give me a more peaceful sleep, why, I'd just change it for twin beds. Just because you're married doesn't mean you have to be in close proximity night and day, with never a bit of room to spread out in.

By the time we got to my house, Sam in his car, following Lillian and me in mine, Hazel Marie was in the throes of emptying her closets. Her bed was piled high with clothes, and the floor was a minefield of shoes, boots, and pocketbooks.

"I don't know if your closet will hold all of this," she said, as I walked into her room. "I didn't know I had so much."

"Lord, Hazel Marie, you could start a clothing store if you had a mind to." As I surveyed her possessions, I knew the closet in my room would barely accommodate half of what she had. "There's only one thing to do. Let's get some hanging racks and put them in the guest room where Lillian sleeps when she stays over. Wait, I have a better idea. Why don't we line that room with closets, then have a door cut from my bathroom into it? That way you'll have your own dressing room."

"Oh, like a suite. I love it! And, if we have guests, we can put them in Coleman's old room. Now," she said, pushing back her hair and considering the job in front of her, "I've got to start getting this stuff up the stairs."

Sam and Lillian came in about then, both carrying suitcases and bags. Sam put his down and looked around. "You sure there's room for me?"

"Oh, Sam," Hazel Marie said, "there's always room for you. I'm moving everything upstairs, and pretty soon you're going to have a clean, neat room to move into." She sighed. "As soon as I get organized."

Lillian said, "I hate to bring this up, but we might could use James right about now, 'cause somebody gonna be makin' two million trips up and down them stairs."

"Good thinking, Lillian," Sam said. "I'll call him and tell him to come on over. Julia, you mind if I use your phone?"

I stared at him, then took his arm and led him out into the back hall. "Now, listen, Sam. If you're serious about living here, you're going to have to get used to

64

this being your home. You don't have to ask if you can use the phone or anything else in it."

He ran his fingers down the side of my face. "Okay, but I'm beginning to get an inkling of how you felt in my house."

I smiled at him, congratulating myself for having chosen such an agreeable man to spend the last years of my life with.

"I can't wait for Little Lloyd to get home from school," I said. "He's going to be thrilled to have you here all the time, and you're going to relieve Hazel Marie's worries about him being surrounded by nothing but women. I just hope you can put up with people coming and going, and all the noise and something going on all the time. You might miss your peaceful days after a while."

"I'm looking forward to it. Besides," he went on, "I've already thought this through. Since I've started a new project, I'll just keep on using the study at my house every day. Like an office, you know."

"What project are you talking about?" From the way he'd pestered me about getting married, I'd thought I was the only project he had.

"I'm writing a legal history of Abbot County. Didn't I tell you about it? Anyway, all my research and notes are at my house, so I can spend a few hours every day working over there, then just shut the door and come home."

"You better remember to come home," I said, moderating my words with a warm smile. "And I mean every day at the exact time you're supposed to." I stopped and frowned. "Listen, Sam. You think our being here will put a crimp in what's going on with Hazel Marie and Mr. Pickens? I mean, I'm fairly sure — but I'd never come out and ask — that he's spent a night or two here since we got married. I doubt he'll feel so free to come and go with us here."

"I expect you're right. But that could be good. It might make him realize what he's missing."

"Lord, I hope so. I'm about to think that Hazel Marie's wasting her youth on that man. She's going to end up an old maid, if she's not careful."

James came in about that time, and Lillian, taking command since she was back in her domain, gave him his orders. The two of them began carting clothes up the stairs, with Hazel Marie making burdened trips right behind them.

"Let's just put everything in Coleman's

room," she said, "until we get my bedroom suite fixed up."

At the same time, I began emptying the closet and drawers in my old room to clear it for Hazel Marie's things. Lillian and James made heavily laden trips both up and down the stairs, and it was beginning to look as if we'd never get the house straight again.

When Little Lloyd came in from school, he dropped his book bag and looked around in wonder. "What in the world's going on?"

"Miss Julia's come home!" Hazel Marie said, with enough pure pleasure in her voice to gratify me. "And Sam's with her, and so is Lillian."

"Really?" Little Lloyd said, his eyes wide. "Everybody's going to live here with us every day and all the time?"

"That's right," Sam said. "You think you can stand us?"

"Oh, boy, I sure can. Where's Miss Lillian?"

"Somewhere on the stairs, I expect," Sam said. "And you and I ought to be giving her a hand."

The boy started toward the back hall, but not before giving me one of his special smiles, which confirmed for me that I'd at least made one right decision.

Chapter 6

We were at breakfast a couple of days later when Luther Pruitt showed up at the back door. Sam, who had asked him to come, opened the door for him, and in he came, so lanky and tall that his white hair almost scraped the top of the door. He was wearing bib overalls and heavy work boots, and carrying a tool box, a thermos, and a heavy hammer. Behind him came a shorter man, younger and more muscular, wearing jeans and a white T-shirt. A loaded tool belt was strapped around his hips. He, too, was carrying a thermos, as well as a portable radio.

Sam introduced us, and I thanked Mr. Pruitt for agreeing to construct a dressing room for Hazel Marie.

"Won't be nothin' to it," he told me. "I built a many a closet in my time." His eyes twinkled, as he jerked his thumb over his shoulder. "This here's Willie, my brother's boy. He's not good for much but holdin' a plumb line, but he keeps me comp'ny."

Willie grinned, revealing a gap where once an eyetooth had resided. It gave him a roguish air, and I began to have my doubts if these two were the best carpenters available. Sam had vouched for them, though, and after asking about their families, he turned them over to me. But not before he planted a kiss on my cheek in front of them all and told me he'd be at his house most of the morning. Pretending that such an overt show of affection hadn't mortified me to my bones, I joined Hazel Marie in leading the workmen up the back stairs.

"Here it is," I said, opening the door of the guest room, which had been emptied the day before by Sam and James. "Hazel Marie, show them your plan."

She spread out the hand-drawn plan. "This is not to scale," she said, "because I don't know how deep closets should be. But, see, I just want closets all the way around. Except for the doors and windows, of course. And a door knocked through this wall to the bathroom."

Luther held the paper close to his lined face, then squinted his eyes at the walls. "Hit'll work. And if hit don't, well, good thing we brought the sledgehammer."

"Lemme see," Willie said, reaching for the plan. "Yeah, it will, with a few changes. How 'bout we put you in some shelves and drawers, too. That'll still leave plenty of room for hanging clothes."

"That'll be wonderful," Hazel Marie said.

"And a full-length mirror."

"Oh, yes."

"You might want to have the closet doors decorated, too. Maybe use paneled doors, and have some dentil work on the crown molding. And you might think about a built-in dressing table with some real good lighting over it."

Hazel Marie was nodding, her smile getting wider. "Yes, yes. You know exactly what I want."

During all this, Luther had twitched out his tape measure and was taking measurements. He glanced at me, gave me a wry smile and said, "See, he ain't good for much, but he keeps me in business."

Yes, indeed, I thought, Willie had just about doubled what I'd expected to spend on housing Hazel Marie's clothes.

We'd not gotten halfway down the stairs when we heard a crashing and splintering racket as the carpenters began to knock out a wall. A cloud of dust rolled out into the hall, along with the strains of a country music station from the portable radio.

"My word, Hazel Marie," I said, turning to see the dust drift down onto the hall floor. "We'd better do something about that. Everything in the house will be covered in dust if they keep that up."

"I'll tell them to keep the hall door closed," she said, running back up the stairs. "That'll help with the music, too. Although I don't mind listening to Tim McGraw."

Lillian came to the bottom of the stairs, looking up. "What they doin' up there?"

"Knocking out the wall to put in a door," I told her. "Let's close off everything downstairs."

Another splintering crash resounded through the house, as Hazel Marie hurried down the stairs. "They're both wearing masks," she said. "We might ought to get some, too."

"I'm not wearing a mask in my own house," I said. "Surely they'll be through with that demolition before long."

"I want to see," Little Lloyd said, passing me on the stairs. "I might want to put in a door one of these days."

"Don't be long," I said. "You'll be late for school."

"Listen," Hazel Marie said, as she stood by the kitchen sink, draining the last of her coffee. "I'll drop Lloyd off at school, then I've got a meeting with Coleman and the

71

sheriff to get the beauty pageant under way." She looked at me. "You want to go with me?"

"No, indeed. I don't have any business at the sheriff's department. You get your plans made, then tell me what you want me to do."

"Well," she said, gathering up her notes and her purse. "I'll tell them they have to come up with the contestants. Then we'll figure out what parts of the department should have a representative. I'll push for no more than ten. Fewer would be better, don't you think?"

"Lord, Hazel Marie, I don't know. I'm in uncharted waters when it comes to beauty pageants. From everything you've told me, you can do whatever you want and nobody'll know the difference."

"Well, that's true, and such a relief. We won't have to worry about following too many official guidelines, like we're the Miss America contest or something."

"Thank goodness," I murmured, having no desire to be involved with anything official or guided along lines I had no wish to follow. "I think I'll walk downtown," I went on, just as another splintering noise echoed from upstairs. "Anything to get away from that racket. Lillian, why don't you think of some place to go until they get through up there?"

"Yessum, I'm gonna go to the grocery store an' stay as long as I can. You want me to fix them mens some lunch?"

"Oh, I hardly think so. I expect they've brought their own. You might offer them a snack later in the afternoon, if you want to."

"I'll do it," Hazel Marie said. "One thing I know about working men. They do better work if they like the people they're working for."

"Lord, Hazel Marie, don't tell me that," I said. "If they're getting paid, they should do the best work they're capable of, regardless of who they like and who they don't."

"It don't hurt nobody to be nice," Lillian said. "So I'm gonna take 'em some of these muffins right now. An' see if they want some of my coffee."

I threw up my hands. "Do what you want, but don't start pampering them. They'll charge me by the hour, whether they're working or sitting around eating all day."

We all turned to look as a heavy-footed clattering came down the back stairs. Willie Pruitt bounded into the kitchen, saw us, gave a missing-tooth grin, then tiptoed toward the door. "Sorry," he said, "didn't know y'all was in here." He waved a crumpled piece of paper with penciled figures on it. "Goin' to the building supply to get lumber."

As he passed me on his way to the door, I couldn't help but look to see if his tool belt had pulled his jeans down below the modesty level. Not that I'm interested in such things, don't you know, but there was a child in the house.

I gazed longer than I should have, and was only brought up short by Hazel Marie's giggles. When Willie went out the door, she took her hand from her mouth and said, "That sure looked good, didn't it?"

"I don't know what you're talking about, Hazel Marie," I said. "He's just a fine-looking young man who badly needs some dental work."

"I wasn't looking at his teeth," she said, cutting her eyes at me. "And you weren't, either."

"Law, you two," Lillian chimed in. "Let that man do his work, and don't be eyeballin' all over him. Though," she went on, "them tight pants do make a mighty fine rearview picture."

Little Lloyd pushed through the dining room door with his book bag on his shoulder. "I'm ready, Mama."

"So am I," I said, collecting my pocketbook and preparing for my walk downtown. "And I hope we all have better things on our minds by the end of the day."

I waved as Hazel Marie and Little Lloyd left in the car, and I turned toward Main Street. I couldn't remember the last time I'd walked downtown without a specific purchase in mind. It wasn't like me just to wander off to look in windows or stroll the sidewalk in order to get out of the house.

I couldn't help but smile to myself as I waited to cross a street. What had I told Sam? Why, just that I'd missed the hustle and bustle of a busy household, with people coming and going and giving and taking. Now, all of a sudden, it was too much for me, what with disorder everywhere and two new people hammering and sawing and creating an uproar for who knew how long. And Sam underfoot most of the day and the entire night, with Mr. Pickens yet to be heard from. But he'd show up sooner or later, as he always did, and add his carryings-on to the general mixture.

I was a woman who liked things neat and in their place, a quiet and serene household, and it looked as if that was a thing of the past. And only because I'd married Sam and had to make room for him and Hazel Marie's clothes.

"Well, Lord," I said, under my breath. "I hope he proves worth the sacrifice of my peace and quiet."

A young person in baggy pants and sweatshirt with shaggy hair and unknown gender gave me wide berth as I passed by. So maybe my words hadn't been as far under my breath as I'd thought. I straightened myself and marched on, undeterred by being thought an old woman talking to herself. And why wasn't he in school, anyway?

I got to the corner of Main Street and turned right on the sidewalk. It was a beautiful morning with late-spring flowers blooming in the beds built up along the block. If I hadn't been so self-consciously at loose ends, I could've enjoyed a leisurely hour, like the old men sprawled on green benches watching the early shoppers were doing. As it was, I moved along with the people who were hurrying to offices and shops, readying themselves for the day.

I hardly knew what to do with myself,

but I acted as if I had a purpose for being there. The new park, I thought. That's what I need to see. The garden club had taken on a small area of the courthouse lawn to improve with a gazebo and enhance with plantings, and I had contributed to the project. It was well within my province to see what my donation had accomplished. That's my purpose, I decided, and the reason I'm walking Main Street.

With a goal clearly in mind, I was no longer concerned about what anyone might think, which made me mad as soon as I realized it. It was nobody's business what I was doing or where I was doing it, and I didn't have to make up an answer for people who wouldn't ask in the first place. Still, I felt a whole lot better, now that I knew where I was going.

Striding along, enjoying the aroma emanating from Baston's Bakery and anticipating a rest in the gazebo, I could have missed her. And, oh, would that I had.

Chapter 7

LuAnne Conover came flying out of a shop in her usual hurry, digging deep in her pocketbook and hardly looking where she was going. She glanced to the side, saw me, and pulled up short.

"Julia! I didn't expect to see you. What're you doing downtown?"

"Errands, LuAnne. Just first thing and another. Besides, it's a nice morning for a walk. What brings you to town?"

"Well," she said, leaning in close and darting her eyes around, "don't tell anybody, but I just had my hair done in this new shop." She pointed at the door she'd just exited. "You like it?" Meaning her hair, which she patted with her hand.

"It looks very nice. But you know Velma's going to hear about it, sooner or later. Especially if you don't go back to her."

"I'll tell you the truth, Julia. I am tired of Velma's same-old, same-old. She never wants to do anything new, even when I go through magazines and show her the styles

I want to try. She always says my hair won't work that way. Well, you never know until you try, do you? But she won't even do that. I think she doesn't know how, that's what I think."

"That may be so," I said, thinking to myself that I appreciated not being made a guinea pig for every new style that came along. I like to know what I'm getting when I put my head in somebody else's hands. "Well, I must be on my way, and I know you have things to do, too. Good to see you, LuAnne."

"Wait, Julia, don't go yet. I wanted to tell you what I just saw, speaking of magazines. See, I was under the dryer, and you know I don't buy these things, but that was all they had to read. So, I was just leafing through this *Country Weekly*, and guess what happened to Sonny Sutton!"

"Who?"

"Oh, you know." She flapped her hand at me. "He's the Singing Sensation from San Antone. That's in Texas, but he's everywhere now. Of course, I don't listen to country-western stations, but you can't help but read or see something about him in everything you pick up. In fact," she went on, getting a studious look on her face, "Leonard was watching the news not too long ago, and even Dan Rather mentioned him."

Since we were standing in the middle of the sidewalk, causing people to walk around us, I sidled closer to the building. LuAnne sidled right along with me.

"So," she continued, "when I saw his picture in *Country Weekly*, well, I had to read it. And he is really good-looking. I mean, in a rugged, outdoorsy kind of way, if you like that kind of thing. Black hat, he always wears that, with little silver things on the band, and a denim shirt with the sleeves rolled up, and this real big buckle on his belt. I think an old girlfriend gave him that, and he always wears it. In remembrance, you know. And real tight jeans." She stopped and giggled. "That may be why he sings so high."

"LuAnne!"

"Oh, I'm just teasing. Anyway, I've got to go. Good to see you, Julia."

"Wait a minute. Is that what you wanted to tell me? That you saw his picture in a magazine?"

"Oh, for goodness sakes, that's just like me to start something and not finish it. No, what I wanted to tell you is he and his new girlfriend got married a couple of weeks ago. They flew down to Pigeon

Forge and had a quickie wedding in one of those chapels they have over there. You know, so they could have a private ceremony, away from their fans and all the reporters in Nashville. That's where he lives now. Anyway, all I could think of was that you could've had a double wedding, if you and Sam had run into him."

I didn't say a word, hoping she'd not pursue the subject. I'd kept my silence about the details of my and Sam's wedding, not wanting to advertise the unlikely setting. All anybody knew was that we'd left town and eloped, which had been enough to be the lead topic of any number of dinner party conversations. On the other hand, we'd made no secret of our Dollywood honeymoon, since it had turned into a family outing.

I started to move off down the sidewalk, and she edged along with me, taking up where she'd left off. "*Any*way, the big story was not the wedding, but the breakup. Seems the preacher who did the ceremony wasn't ordained or something. I didn't understand it, but here the new couple has been living together and all, and I know these big celebrities do that all the time, but Sonny Sutton's a Christian man, and he didn't hesitate a minute — not wanting to besmirch his reputation and create any more of a scandal than he already had, you know. So he up and moved out on his wife, or whatever she was by that time, and went to a hotel until they get their legal status rectified. I feel so sorry for them. Just think of it — they went to all the trouble of getting married, only to find out they're not married. Can you believe that?"

Well, no, I couldn't. My head had begun to spin, and my knees were trembling so bad I had to lean against the wall of the Artisan jewelry store. I was having a hard time swallowing, and had to put my hand to my throat to get my breath. Surely, I thought, as my mind swirled, Sam and I had not had the same preacher as Sonny Sutton and his bride, or ex-bride. There'd been wedding chapels on practically every corner in Pigeon Forge. How likely was it that we'd gone to the same one?

LuAnne, unmindful of my reaction, chattered on. "On the other hand, it is funny when you think about it. I mean, with all the places they could've gone to, how on earth did they end up there? Serves them right for sneaking off from their fans."

She stopped and peered closely at me. "Are you all right, Julia? You look like you're having a spell or something. You want me to drive you home? I can run get the car."

"No, don't do that," I managed to get out in a reasonable facsimile of my normal voice. I took a deep breath and pulled myself together. "I'm all right, really. Thank you for your concern — it was just a little dizziness. It's passed now, and walking in the fresh air will do me good."

"Well, okay, if you're sure." She suddenly swung aside and headed into Baston's Bakery. "I've got to get some dinner rolls. You take care, Julia."

I stood there after the door closed behind her, trembling all over as the impact of her words hit me again. Fearful of fainting dead away right there on Main Street, which would make the "Emergency Calls" column in the newspaper, I carefully proceeded toward the Sure-Save drugstore. Feeling that I was moving in slow motion, I pushed through the door and headed toward the magazine display.

I scanned the garish covers, looking for the one LuAnne had spoken of. My head spun again, as I realized that Sonny Sutton's picture, complete with black hat and big belt buckle, was on more than half a dozen. Which one would give me the details I needed? Trying to get my bearings and steady my limbs, I read the glaring headlines: SONNY SINGS A SAD SONG! SONNY MARRIED — NOT! SONNY'S NOT MARRIED, HE'S MAD!

Looking around to see if my interest in fan magazines was being observed, I quickly snatched up one that featured a wedding chapel in a yellow box below Sonny's picture. I gathered all my considerable reserves and marched up to the cash register, determined to stare down anyone who questioned my choice of reading material.

I dug out a five-dollar bill from my pocketbook and put it on the counter in front of a bored-looking cashier. "I'm buying this for my friend, Hazel Marie Puckett, who enjoys keeping up with country music stars."

The cashier was a young woman with a spikey hairdo, a gold stud in her lip, and a wad of gum in her mouth. I mustered up the courage to look her square in the face, daring her to make a comment about my purchase.

I needn't have worried. She didn't even look up, just made change, put the magazine in a paper bag, and pushed it toward me. "Come back 'n' see us," she said, and went back to work on her chewing gum.

I clutched the bagged magazine to my

chest and headed out, my head held as high as I could get it. Hurrying on down the sidewalk, I nodded to people I knew and to some I didn't. I put purpose in my stride, not wanting to be sidetracked by anyone with nothing to do but make inane conversation about the weather. Even though I made myself appear resolute and purposeful, I was a quivering mess of shock and confusion inside, fearful of what I was going to read if I ever got to the privacy of the gazebo.

"How do, Miz Springer, or should I say Miz Murdoch?" The voice stopped me in my tracks. What kind of greeting was that? Was my marital status being questioned already?

I turned to see Mr. Harris, generally called Red for obvious reasons, although his hair was now more white than anything else. He raised his hat to me, then settled it back on his head. He wore a rumpled suit and a tie that had seen better days. Red Harris had a law practice of sorts, but as long as he'd been at it, he'd never made much more than a bare living from it. Most people attributed that fact to drink, though I'd never personally seen him take one.

"It's Mrs. Murdoch, of course," I said, watching closely for any hint of a smirk or of a knowing glint in his eyes. "And I'm doing fine, as I hope you are."

"I got no complaints," he said, as we stood in the middle of the sidewalk as if both of us had all the time in the world. "How's married life treatin' you?"

"Quite well," I returned, fearing that he was leading up to the subject clutched to my bosom. Realizing how thin the paper bag was and fearing he could read through it, I quickly tucked the package under my arm. "If it wasn't, I wouldn't be in it. Now I bid you good morning. I've just picked up something for Hazel Marie, and I must get it to her."

I took myself off as fast as I could, leaving him with his hat raised again. Lord, that was a close call. What else did he have to do, but read whatever was printed and comment on it?

Crossing another street, I gained the courthouse grounds and headed for the gazebo. Thank goodness, it was empty. After carefully scouting my surroundings, I collapsed on the bench and slid the magazine out of its bag.

I quickly read the lead article, but was hardly the wiser when I finished. It seemed that the attorney general of Tennessee was looking into the qualifications of people who ran what he called "fly-by-night marriage mills," one of which Sonny Sutton and his erstwhile bride had patronized. He and Maylynn Simmons had undergone a wedding ceremony suspiciously similar to the one Sam and I'd had, in which we'd said our vows before a white-suited preacher. The article went on to quote the attorney general, who said, "There may be couples, like Sonny and Maylynn, who went through a marriage ceremony in good faith, but who may not be legitimately married."

Lord, the blood drained from my face, and I felt as if I was about to faint dead away.

It was Sam's fault. That's all there was to it. As soon as he caught me at a weak moment, when I agreed to marry him, he'd been bound and determined to give me no chance to change my mind. He struck while the iron was hot, so to speak. So, nothing would do, but we had to hurry across the state line and be married before the sun came up. If that didn't qualify as a quickie wedding just like Sonny Sutton's, I didn't know what did. And here, I had lived with Sam and conjugated with him, and walked around in public with him, and I might not be his wife at all. We could be breaking the law, right and left.

He would have to answer for this.

Chapter 8

My mouth tight with anxiety, I closed the magazine and slid it into the paper bag. Then I stood up carefully, making sure I was steady on my feet, as I readied myself to do battle with Sam.

Then a frightening apparition, that had seemingly sprung out of the azaleas, set me back on my heels, startling me so that I gasped in alarm. Just as quickly, though, I recognized the visitor, and had to sit down abruptly. Of all the people in the world I didn't want to see, it was Pastor Larry Ledbetter. Yet, there he was, smiling in pleasant surprise at seeing me. He walked right into the gazebo and took a seat, as if he didn't have a sermon or a Bible study lesson to prepare anytime soon.

"What a surprise, Pastor," I said, shoving the magazine sack under my pocketbook. I clasped my hands together, so he wouldn't see the state they were in. "I declare, I didn't expect to run into you here."

"Nor I you, Miss Julia." He stretched his legs out, as if he planned to stay a while.

"But I'll take this opportunity to ask your opinion on the serenity garden we're planning for the courtyard between the sanctuary and the Sunday school building. I've been told that this new garden here is well designed, so I thought some of their ideas might work for us." He twisted his head around, checking out the decorative ceiling above us. "I like this gazebo, don't you? Something like it would be a nice addition to our garden."

"Yes, it would, and I'm glad to see you taking an interest." I couldn't help but make a little jab, since he spent most of his time holed up in his office. "Gardening is quite a healthful occupation."

I gathered my things, preparatory to leaving, hoping I'd get away before he brought up the fact that Sam and I had left him out of our marriage arrangements. A decision that, after learning of the perilous state of affairs we were now in, I heartily regretted having made.

The pastor shifted himself on the bench, glanced my way, and I knew I was in for it. "You know, Miss Julia, I've been meaning to come by and extend my warmest wishes to you and Sam on your nuptials. You must accept my apologies for being so lax. I wanted to let you get settled in first, but I guess the Lord had other plans, since he's brought us together this morning."

Surely, the Lord wasn't so unthinking as to arrange this meeting just when I was in no shape to deal with the pastor's hurt feelings. But I had to put the best face on it, and try to make amends.

"Well, Pastor, I want to explain why we —"

"No, no," he said, holding up his hand. "No explanations are necessary." He plastered on a too-hearty smile as evidence that he didn't mind two of his most faithful church members hightailing it somewhere else to get married. "I understand how these things happen."

I was glad he did, because I didn't, especially after reading what had happened to a certain celebrity of country music fame. That thought jolted me again, for the last thing I wanted was for the pastor to learn what I now knew, and what I was so anxious to put before Sam.

"My goodness, look at the time!" I jumped up and started out of the gazebo. "Do come by to see us, Pastor, anytime. And give my regards to Emma Sue."

He got to his feet and mentioned something about blessing our marriage, however precipitous it had been. I pretended I didn't hear him and took off for Sam's house without looking back.

I was out of breath by the time I climbed the porch steps, not only from the pace I'd set in getting there, but also from the head of steam I'd built up on the way.

"Sam!" I called as I opened the screen door and let myself into the hall. "Where are you?"

"In here, Julia," he called from his study. "Come on in."

He was rising from his desk chair as I entered the room, as courteous as ever. His desk was strewn with notes and ledgers and law books and old photographs, but I hardly gave them a glance. Sam was going to have to put aside ancient history and turn his hands to current events, and I didn't mean maybe.

"I'm glad to see you," he said, reaching for me. "I do better work when my lady-wife is around."

I turned away from him and took a seat in a leather chair across the room. "I may not be your wife, Sam, and if I'm not, I'm certainly no lady, taking into account what we've been up to."

He got the kind of quizzical look on his face, moderated by the beginnings of a smile, which often appeared when I made some pronouncement he hadn't thought was coming. "I believe you are my wife, or else my dreams have been mighty realistic. What's got you so upset, Julia?"

"Have you seen this?" I asked, my mouth so tight I could hardly get the words out. I held up the magazine with its gaudy cover.

He leaned against the desk, smiling. "No, I don't believe I have."

"Well, just read it." I turned a few pages and pointed to the offending article. "Look at this."

He took it, read it, and his smile widened. "This doesn't concern us, Julia. You've gotten yourself all worked up over nothing."

I jumped to my feet. "Don't patronize me, Sam Murdoch! I may be worked up, but it's not about nothing. Don't you see? We may not be legally married and . . ." I glanced at the door to see if James was around, and lowered my voice to a hiss. "We've engaged in *marital acts.*"

"We sure have," he heartily agreed. "And I, for one, enjoyed them and intend to keep on enjoying them."

I rolled my eyes back into my head. He was not taking this with the seriousness it deserved. "Forget about what we've enjoyed," I said. "What we've done was certainly done in good faith, but that doesn't matter a hill of beans when it comes to the legal system. And you should know that better than I do. What are we going to do, Sam?" I threw out my hands, and almost dropped my pocketbook. "You know what the Bible says about what we've been doing, don't you?"

"No, I don't believe I do," he said, and the twinkle in his eyes infuriated me even more. "Give me chapter and verse."

"I can't, exactly, but it concerns *fornication!*" Then I clamped my hand over my mouth for saying such a thing out loud.

"Lord, Julia, you're about to get me stirred up with that kind of talk." Then, seeing that teasing was getting him nowhere, he changed his tune. "Look, I don't think this affects us. I admit it sounds like the same chapel we went to, but there're dozens of them over there. And each one has four or five ministers to cover twenty-four hours, seven days a week. They couldn't all be questionable. It's just gotten blown out of proportion because of this singer."

"Are you sure?" I asked, reaching for the magazine. "Let me read it again."

I did, but it gave me little comfort. "Look, Sam. It mentions the candle stands and the drive-up window. Everything!" I slung the magazine aside and threw back my head. "My Lord, we could've gone our merry way for years, thinking we were man and wife, and all we'd be is man and woman, living in sin."

"Julia, Julia," Sam said, putting his arms around me. "Calm down, now. Do you think I'd let this go by without looking into it? I had to tease you a little, but I have every intention of making sure that everything is legal and aboveboard. I want you to put it out of your mind, while I make some calls. Then I'm going to reassure you that we are married so tightly that only the Grim Reaper can separate us. And maybe not even then."

"Oh, Sam," I said, leaning my head against his chest, "I hope you can. I couldn't live with myself, much less with you, if we're not legal. This all serves me right for not wanting to be married by Pastor Ledbetter. I may not like him, but he'd never set us on a course that had any question about it."

"Don't start having regrets, sweetheart. I liked the way we did it. It was fun and exciting, something you've had too little of, and that's what I wanted to give you. Now, let's just go on the way we are, and in a few days, after I've checked with some officials in Tennessee, we'll look back on this and laugh."

"I truly hope so, but, right now, it's not anywhere near laughable. How long do you think it'll take till we know for sure?"

"Not long. I'll get our marriage certificate out of the lockbox at the bank, and get the minister's name from it. Then I'll start making some calls."

"Good. I feel better already, knowing you're working on it. Now, Sam," I said, stepping back from him, "until we know for certain, we have to live accordingly."

"Oh?" he said, frowning. "I'm not sure what you mean."

"I mean that I can't live as your wife until I'm sure I *am* your wife. And you shouldn't want me to."

"I don't know, Julia," he said, shaking his head. "That's an awful lot to ask. Wait, wait, now, don't get mad. I can't help but tease you. I'll do whatever you want — you know that — but I don't have any doubt that we're firmly and legally married, and I'd hate to miss out on any of the benefits, even if it's only for a day or two."

"All the more reason for you to expedite this investigation with every means at your disposal. And as soon as you confirm that we're married, I'll welcome you back."

95

His eyebrows shot straight up. "You're really kicking me out? Julia, good grief, woman. Don't tell me I have to move everything back to this house, live here by myself, and start courting you all over again."

"Well," I said, studying the problem, "that would be noticeable, wouldn't it? I mean, we'd have so many questions to answer, and no telling what the pastor would say if we let it be known that we've been significant others, not a married couple. He might not even marry us, if we needed to do it again. No, let's keep on the way we are with you living in my house, just not sleeping in my bed. We'll do something with Hazel Marie's clothes and put you upstairs in Coleman's old room."

"Julia, I'm going to give you my best legal advice: You are overreacting."

"No, I'm not. I'm just making sure that you don't fiddle around with this. If you want back in my bed, then you better get a move on and get this resolved."

"I'm going to the bank right now." He laughed as he guided me out of the room with a hand on my back. "Who would've thought that I'd get my woman, then lose her before a month is up?"

Chapter 9

"Don't move me out yet, Julia," Sam said, as he pulled to the curb at my house to let me out. "Hold off till I get the phone number of the chapel. I'll call them and —"

"Why, Sam, don't do that. They're not about to admit to being unqualified. They wouldn't have the job of marrying people if they told on themselves."

Sam picked up my hand and kissed it. "That's not the only call I'll make. But I want to start with whoever owns the chapel, and with the minister who married us. Then I'll call some folks in the register of deeds office in the county seat. But for now, let's not disrupt everybody in the house by moving me upstairs. You'd have to tell them why, you know."

Pondering the humiliation of explaining our separation to Lillian and Hazel Marie, to say nothing of Mr. Pickens, I slowly took back my hand. "I guess we couldn't keep it from them, could we? They'd be seeing us go our separate ways every night." I opened the car door and started to slide out. "Well, one good thing — we won't be in the tabloids like Sonny Sutton. But, Sam," I said, turning back, "take a lesson from him. He did the right and gentlemanly thing by moving out without a lot of moaning and groaning about it. And it seems to me that you'd want to protect my good name and my honor at least to that extent."

"Oh, I do, Julia. It's just that I don't think we have to do anything drastic right away."

I got out of the car, then leaned back in. "Then it would behoove you to get it settled today. Besides, I'm tired of moving clothes up and down the stairs."

As soon as I walked into the living room, I almost turned around and walked back out. The most nerve-wrenching, screeching racket filled the house as a power saw screamed its way across a piece of wood. Even with doors closed everywhere, you could hardly hear yourself think, and we were going to have to put up with it for days on end. I was about ready to move back to Sam's house, where there was peace and quiet. But, with a wry twist of my mouth, I realized I was stuck where I was. There wouldn't be the option of moving in with Sam until I knew how closely related we were.

In one of the infrequent moments of silence, I pushed through the door into the kitchen. Hazel Marie was at the table, working on her notes, while Lillian stood at the counter, making sandwiches for lunch.

Before I could say a word, another scream of the saw split the air. They looked up at me, as we waited for it to die down.

"Lord, I don't think I can stand that," I said, pulling out a chair. "Are all the doors closed?"

"Ever'one in the house," Lillian said. "An' still you can't get away from that racket. Them mens say they gonna try to get through with their sawin' today, or maybe tomorrow, then all we have to listen to is nailin' an' hammerin'."

"You'd think they'd do their sawing outside, where it wouldn't be so loud," I said.

Hazel Marie turned a page of her notes. "They told me that if they did that, they'd have to troop through the kitchen a dozen times, taking things upstairs. I didn't think any of us would want that."

"Yes, well, I guess you're right." In an attempt to carry on as normally as possible, in spite of my frazzled state of mind, I tried to settle my nerves and pretend I wasn't about to jump out of my skin. So, gingerly taking a seat across from Hazel Marie, I asked, "How did your meeting with Coleman and Sheriff Frady go?"

We all stopped and covered our ears as another shriek of the saw attacked us. When silence reigned again, Hazel Marie said, "They love our idea of having each unit in the department pick its own contestant, and the sheriff is going to tell them to get right on it. But there may not be more than six or seven contestants the way it works out, which suits me fine. Sheriff Frady said it'd be better to let each squad decide how they want to pick their representative. And, Miss Julia," Hazel Marie went on, looking up at me, "we're going to have to stop calling Coleman Deputy Bates. He's a sergeant now, in charge of the first watch. Isn't that great?"

"Well, it certainly is. And high time, too." I plucked a napkin from the holder on the table and began shredding it. "Where're you going to hold the pageant, Hazel Marie?"

"Oh, I'm glad you asked, because it's all arranged. We're going to rent the high school auditorium. School will be out pretty soon, so it's the perfect place. But, look, I need you to help me decide on the various looks the girls will be judged on."

"Looks?"

"Yes, you know, bathing suit, evening gown, casual wear, and so forth. Each one will be a kind of mini-competition."

"Well," I said, arranging the napkin shreds into a little pile, "I vote against bathing suits."

Lillian grinned. "I knowed you would."

"We have to have a bathing suit competition," Hazel Marie said. "That and evening dress are the basics. But, see, they don't call it the bathing suit competition anymore. It's called Physical Fitness, and the contestants aren't judged just on how they look, but on what kind of shape they're in." She stopped and smiled at what she'd just said. "I guess there's not much difference, is there?"

"Not a bit, as far as I can see."

"Anyway, we'll call it Physical Fitness, which makes it sound more like a sports competition, rather than a comparison of figure sizes." She stopped and looked at what I was doing. "Are you all right, Miss Julia?"

"I'm fine," I said, quickly gathering up what was left of the napkin and wadding it in my hand. "Why do you ask?"

"Just wondering," she said, tapping her pen against the pad in front of her. "You seem a little distracted."

"Not at all. You have my full attention." I stuffed the napkin remnants into my pocketbook. "Tell me about the other categories."

"Well, the evening dress category will be Beauty and Poise, and casual wear will be Expression of Personality. That can be anything from jeans to shorts to sundresses — whatever they want. But, what I want to know is, do we want to add any other competition?"

"What about talent? Aren't you going to have that, or will the judging just be on how these girls look in their various outfits?"

"Oh, yes. Of course, we'll have talent. And that means we'll need music, an orchestra or something, because I'm sure some of the contestants will sing."

"Have mercy," I said, leaning my head on my hands. Then, in an attempt to be helpful, I went on. "Where're you going to get an orchestra?"

"That won't be a problem. I know a local bluegrass band that would love to play. And we'll need music for when the contestants parade around, too."

"Bluegrass, Hazel Marie? What if one of

the girls wants to sing opera or something? Heaven forbid, but it's possible."

"Then she'll have to bring her own music. On a record or a CD. The auditorium has a wonderful sound system, so that'll work out. I better check it, though." She leaned over her pad and made a note. "As soon as we know who the girls are, we'll get them to tell us their talent. Then we'll know what kind of backup they'll need."

"This is getting awfully complicated," I said, but my words were drowned out by another wood-eating scream from above. It was just as well, for Hazel Marie was not to be deterred by any cautionary words from me. "I'm going outside," I said, getting up from my chair. "Lillian, if you need me, I'll be in the far corner of the yard, as far away as I can get."

"I'll bring these sam'wiches," she said. "An' we'll have our lunch out there."

Hazel Marie jumped up. "I'll go with you. Let me take some things, Lillian."

I left them to it, and walked out to the arbor, where there were chairs and a table in the shade of a wisteria vine. I needed a minute to myself, for I had more on my mind than a beauty contest. Namely, my status as a married or a single woman. I had fully expected either Hazel Marie or Lillian to draw my attention to the celebrity news of the day, but it looked as if they'd not yet gotten the word.

I sat down in one of the white wooden yard chairs and leaned my head back. Where was Sam? And why hadn't he let me know something? A couple of telephone calls shouldn't have taken this long.

I had almost confided my concerns to Lillian and Hazel Marie, but when Hazel Marie started in on her plans for the pageant, I'd decided not to. No need to upset them if Sam found out that our marriage was legitimate, after all. So, I was trying to keep my worries to myself. But, let me tell you, it was hard to appear interested in half-naked women parading around with their navels in view, when my mind was torn up over the possibility that Sam and I had been doing a different kind of parading.

The screen door slammed behind Hazel Marie and Lillian, as they came bearing trays of sandwiches and lemonade. They sat the trays on the table, and drew up chairs.

"Come on over here an' eat," Lillian said. "Them mens is about to stop for they lunch, too, so we get a little peace an' quiet."

"Where's Sam?" Hazel Marie asked as she poured tea into the glasses. "I thought he'd be home for lunch."

"He'll be along shortly," I said, hoping that was true. "He had to go downtown on business for a little while, and he may've gotten held up. He's going to have to learn to fit into our schedule, though."

"You better stop bein' so hard on that man," Lillian said. "You gonna run him off, you not careful."

I took a bite of an egg salad sandwich so I wouldn't have to answer. Lillian didn't know how close she'd come to what I might have to do.

"You couldn't run him off with a stick," Hazel Marie said, laughing. "He's so happy he finally got you to marry him, he'll put up with anything. I can't wait for J.D. to wrap up his case in Atlanta, and find out that we're all living together."

It pleased me that Hazel Marie was taking the conversation in another direction, so I said, "We could find room for him if he'd get over his aversion to marriage."

Hazel Marie started to say something, but Sam's car pulled into the driveway. I immediately got up and started across the lawn to meet him.

As I walked away, I heard Hazel Marie

say, "Isn't that sweet? They just adore each other, and can hardly stay apart."

"I never thought I'd live to see the day," Lillian said.

Let them think what they want, I thought — all I want to know is what he's found out. And if it was good news, there'd be no reason for them to know that any question had ever been raised.

Chapter 10

"Sam?" I asked, my whole question in the one word. I walked up to him as he got out of the car and reached out to him.

"Julia," he said, as he put his arms around me and pushed my head against his chest. "I hate to tell you this."

"Then don't," I said, straightening up and stepping back from him. "Oh, Sam, I don't want to hear it. It's bad news, isn't it?"

"I'm afraid it is. But, Julia, there's no reason to be upset. The situation's not irreparable, just questionable."

"Questionable? Still? I thought a person was either married or not married, not something in between. Didn't you call people in charge of such things? Couldn't anybody say one way or another? I don't understand."

"Well, it's like this. I called the Wedding Ring Chapel, but the minister, if that's what he was, who did our ceremony has flown the coop."

"What! Why, Sam, it's hardly been a

month since we had the ceremony. And you're telling me he waited to do ours, then disappeared?"

Sam rubbed his face, trying not to smile. "I don't really believe he was waiting just for us before he took off."

"Well, what was his reason? Didn't he give notice, a forwarding address, anything? Can't we track him down and find out his qualifications? What's his name, anyway? You had me in such a whirlwind that night, I didn't know what was going on or who was doing what."

"His name's Aaron Kincaid, current address unknown." Sam blew out his breath. I think he'd been holding it, waiting for my reaction.

"Unknown! Get the police on him. Hire Mr. Pickens to track him down." I stopped and reconsidered that suggestion. "No, don't do that. The fewer people who know about this, the better. But we have to find him. He's a perpetrator of illegal marriages."

"Julia," Sam said, putting his hand on my shoulder. "Listen, now. The man told us he had family around here, remember?" I shook my head. I hardly remembered anything of that night. "And," Sam went on, "I've called every Kincaid in the book, and nobody knows him. So it looks like we're not going to find him. The chapel folks think he left Tennessee, but they're not even sure of that. Apparently, he'd only been employed for a few months, and he came with good recommendations. I finally got them to admit that they hadn't checked his ordination, because they were hard up for somebody to take the night shift. If he hadn't come along, they would've had to give up their twenty-four-hour service."

"Well, they Lord," I said. "And, just think, they would've lost a few fifty-dollar weddings."

"Ninety-nine dollars, Julia."

"Don't quibble. I want to know if he was ordained — that's what's important. Didn't the chapel inquire as to his standing in a denomination, or did they just hire him off the street?"

Sam leaned against the fender of the car, his arms crossed in front of him. "They didn't much want to talk about that. But I spoke with someone in the register of deeds office who was very helpful. They knew him, or rather, knew of him, because he's listed as the presiding minister of some twenty-six marriages, of which ours is one. As is Sonny Sutton's, so I guess we're in good company, if you want to look at it that way."

"I don't. But you didn't leave it there, did you?"

"No, I asked what denomination he'd listed." Sam stopped, looked off into space and rubbed his chin. "Thinking to check with a conference headquarters, you know."

"And? Don't keep me in suspense. Tell me."

"Well, it took them a while to find the record, but it looks as if he provided proof of ordination from something called the East Tennessee Fire and Water Baptized Holiness Church, Sanctified."

"Never heard of it."

"Neither had they."

"Well, what does that mean?" I demanded. "Sam, I declare, you are driving me to distraction. Just tell me the bottom line. Are we married or are we living in sin?"

"I'll tell you what's a fact, Julia," Sam said, as he put his arm around me and drew me close. "I don't know. I've called every official in Tennessee I can think of, trying to find out if that Fire and Water whatever church is legitimate, and so far nobody even knows what it is. I've got Binkie working on it, too —"

"You told Binkie! Sam, I didn't want

anybody to know the mess we're in." I could've cried at the idea that he'd lay out our troubles to somebody else without consulting me.

"Now, Julia. Binkie's got the contacts and the means to follow this up. And, she's an attorney — your attorney and mine. She's not going to tell anybody anything."

"Oh, me," I moaned, bowing my head. Then, looking back at him, I said, "So what do we do now? How long will it take until we know? I'm confused, Sam. Are we looking for that Kincaid man or are we looking for his church?"

"What I've got Binkie doing is looking for the church headquarters, their conference or synod or whatever organizational setup they have. When we find that, they'll have a list of who they've ordained, and if Kincaid's on it, we're home free."

"And what do we do in the meantime?"

"Keep right on as we are. We married in good faith, and as far as I'm concerned, you're my wife now and forever."

"Yes, well," I said, stepping back. "And if we keep on as we are for the next seven years, there won't be any question about it at all. That may be your idea of a proper marriage, but it's certainly not mine."

"Then here's what we'll do. Let's go

down to the courthouse, take out another marriage license, go over to the church, and get Ledbetter to marry us again. Nothing to it, Julia."

"Nothing to it! How can you say that? You want us to announce to the world that we *thought* we were married and *lived* like we were married, and all the while we weren't? And" — I suddenly had another thought — "what if it turns out that we're legally married after all? We'd have gone through another marriage and the attendant gossip for nothing. No, I say we do nothing until we know for sure where we stand."

"I'll do whatever you want." Sam turned to me and lifted my face so that we were looking at each other. "But, Julia, if you send me packing while we wait, everybody'll think that our marriage didn't work out. Are you ready for that?"

"Oh, Lord," I moaned. "I thought I'd about outgrown worrying what other people think. But I guess I haven't. No, we've got to keep up a good front. Then if we have to get married again, we'll sneak out to another town. But in *this* state, Sam, where we know the attorney general is looking out for us." Sam started to laugh, but I soon fixed that. "That is, if I decide I want to get married again. And in the meantime, to keep the gossip down, you can stay here, but you have to move up to Coleman's old room."

"Huh," he said, "so you're going to banish me. That means, you know, that you're going to have to tell everybody in the house what's going on. You ready for that? If you don't want anybody to know, we're going to have to stay together."

"You mean, sleep in the same room, in the same bed, so they'll think we're still . . . ? No, Sam, I don't trust you."

"Smart woman," Sam murmured, brushing the hair from my face.

"Don't start in with your teasing."

"I'm not teasing."

"Well, whatever it is, I'm not in the mood for it." I looked across the yard where Lillian and Hazel Marie were eating egg salad sandwiches and laughing together. I was about to shock them out of their good mood with our startling revelation, but there was nothing for it, so I took a deep breath and Sam's hand. "Let's get it over with."

We walked across the lawn toward them, with me dreading every step. Lillian jumped up and poured a glass of tea for Sam, as Hazel Marie handed him a plate.

"We 'bout to give you up," Lillian said to Sam. "Set down an' eat, now, 'fore you cave in. You, too, Miss Julia. Some folks think love be enough, till they stommicks start growlin' on 'em."

"Thank you, Lillian," I said, as she handed me a plate with my half-eaten sandwich on it. "But I don't think either of us have much of an appetite. We have something to tell you. Go ahead, Sam."

Sam shot me a quick glance. "You want me to tell them?"

"I do." Then, recalling the last time I'd said those words, I cringed.

"Well," he said, "it seems there's some question as to the validity of our marriage."

"What's that mean?" Lillian asked, as Hazel Marie frowned, trying to understand.

"It means," I said, "that we may not be married at all." And between us, Sam and I laid out the whole pitiful situation for them.

"Oh, my goodness," Hazel Marie said, patting her chest. Then she frowned, thinking hard. "I guess we better not have a reception, don't you?"

"Don't none of it make no difference," Lillian pronounced, quick to come to our defense. "You done been livin' together, so you as married as you can get. That's what I think."

"It's not that simple, Lillian," I said. "We have to be sure that the marriage certificate is a legal document. It may not be worth the paper it's printed on. We can't just pretend to be married, so what we're going to do is separate for the time being. But not really separate. We'll be living together, but not *together*. Just until we find out one way or another. Sam will keep on living here, but upstairs in Coleman's room. That way, nobody but us will know the problem, yet we won't be breaking the law by cohabiting."

"By what?" Lillian asked.

"Sleeping together," Hazel Marie told her. Then to Sam, she said, "How do you feel about this?"

"Not too good, if you want to know the truth," he said. "But if that's what Julia wants, that's what we'll do. Frankly, I think we're as legal as we can be, but I'm willing to wait to be sure." He smiled and reached for my hand. "It'll be hard, though."

"Law, goodness," Lillian said, as the implications sunk in. "I never heard the like. Here, you married one day, an' the next day, you not. What yo' preacher gonna say?"

"That's just the thing, Lillian," I said, putting aside my sandwich. "We want to keep this under wraps. If we have to get married again, well, we'll face that when we have to. Right now, as far as the town is concerned, we're married, period. Though, Lord knows, it'll be hard to put a good face on it."

"I know what you can do," Hazel Marie said, sitting up with the dawning of a new idea. "You've been thinking of going on a real honeymoon, anyway. So why don't the two of you go off on a cruise or something while this is getting straightened out? And," she said, her face brightening with a new thought, "if you find out you're not married, you can have the ship's captain do it. That would be so romantic."

"Hazel Marie, I am not going to have another slipshod wedding. No, we'll stay right here, and do the best we can. Besides, we need to keep after this and get it resolved. I can't go off and have a good time without knowing who or what I am."

"Julia," Sam said, tightening his hold on my hand, "we've said our vows to each other, and that's not changed one bit. And, believe me, I'm going to move mountains and a few officials, and whatever else it takes, to put your mind at rest."

"Oh, that's so sweet," Hazel Marie said, but I just nodded. I'd believe it when I saw it.

"And just think," Hazel Marie went on. "You're going to have the beauty pageant to take your mind off of it. While Sam makes sure you're legal, you'll be so busy you won't have time to worry. The pageant couldn't've come at a better time, don't you think?"

I refrained from saying what I thought, because Hazel Marie always meant well. But if anybody thought a few young women strutting around half dressed would distract me from worrying about my legal status, they'd have to think again.

Chapter 11

"You're really moving me out?" Sam asked, as I emptied drawers of his shirts and socks, readying them for removal from our bridal chamber. Sam was sitting across the room in a chair, watching me with some disbelief. Although by this time, he should've known that when I say I'm going to do something, I do it.

"I certainly am," I replied, opening a closet door. "And I know you wouldn't have it any other way. You'd lose every bit of respect you have for me, if I treated this matter lightly."

"I'd respect you, Julia. You know I would."

"Uh-huh. I've heard that before."

"From who? Who else has been courting you?"

"Nobody, and you know it. I heard it on those soap operas Lillian and Hazel Marie watch. As soon as one of those men, who're too handsome for their own good, tells an innocent young woman he'll respect her, you'd better watch out. It's as bad as

118

some crook saying, 'Trust me.' Lillian warns them about it, too, although those actors go right on and get themselves in trouble."

Sam rubbed his fingers across his mouth. "I didn't know you watched soap operas."

"There's more than watching soap operas you don't know about me, and, obviously, you don't know how I feel about sleeping with a man who may not be my husband. If you did, you wouldn't be giving me a hard time about moving you upstairs."

"Well, my land, woman, you can't expect me to be happy about it. But what I'm holding on to is sneaking down here at night and crawling in with you."

I whirled around. "Don't you dare, Sam Murdoch. We're going to do this right, or we're not going to do it all."

"Looks like we're not going to do it at all."

"I'm talking about being married, not . . . what you're talking about."

I kept myself busy so I wouldn't have to think about the awful mess we were in. I declare, to have to pretend to be married, after having acted like I was married, when all the time I probably wasn't married, was more than I could contemplate with any equanimity at all. Every time I was struck anew with what I'd gotten into, I couldn't help but wonder if somebody was trying to tell me something.

As I followed Sam up the stairs and down the hall to Coleman's old room, both of us carrying armloads of clothing, Willie stuck his head out of Hazel Marie's closet-to-be.

"Y'all movin'?"

"Not at all," I answered, as if it were any of his business. "Just switching rooms."

"Need some help?"

"No, sir, we don't. I don't want to take you away from your work." I tried to be pleasant, but I was seething at his eagerness to lay down his hammer and piddle with something else.

Sam and I distributed his clothes in his new room, which didn't take long as he hadn't quite moved everything from his house.

"Julia," Sam said, closing the door to the hall, "I'll tell you what's a fact. This wasn't the way I'd envisioned being married to you. Although" — and he stopped, almost overcome with laughter — "I always figured life with you would be one surprise after another. But being exiled to the far corner of the house is more than I expected."

"You may treat this as a laughable matter," I said, folding my arms across my chest, "but I assure you, it is not."

"I know that," he said, and sobered his face. "But what I want to know is how long do I have to put up with this?"

"Why, Sam, I told you. Until we know absolutely and positively that we are married."

"And what if we don't ever find out for sure? What if there's no such thing as a Fire and Water Baptized Holiness Church, Sanctified or not, registered as a legitimate church? I'll tell you what's a fact, I'm ready to remedy the problem right now. What we ought to do is either get a preacher to re-marry us or go down to the magistrate's office and do it there. And I mean, today, right now. Then you'll have peace of mind and I'll have my rightful place beside you again."

"Is that all you can think about?" I threw up my hands in exasperation. "There's more to this than just bodily contact. There's the matter of living within the law, and of our Christian witness. Do you really want to flaunt our neither-nor situation in front of young people who're likely to follow in our footsteps?"

"Well, no, but it's more like us following in their footsteps. As you know, a good many of them seem to cohabitate without benefit of licenses and ceremonies."

"Yes, and they'll suffer for it, too. But that's neither here nor there." I brushed what other people did aside, and paced the room. "It's bad enough that Little Lloyd sees the way his mother carries on with Mr. Pickens whenever he takes it into his head to show up. Do we want to be another example of promiscuous behavior? No, we do not. At least, I don't."

"Far be it from me, too, Julia," Sam said, but the glint in his eyes belied the meaning of his words. "But, speaking of Little Lloyd, how do you intend to explain our new sleeping arrangements to him?"

"There's no need to explain anything," I said. "I'm hoping he won't notice."

As Sam's eyebrows shot up, but before he could answer, we heard a commotion emanating from the kitchen. The screen door slammed, Lillian dropped a pan, Hazel Marie shrieked, and Mr. Pickens announced his arrival with his usual upheaval of the household. As I opened the door to the hall, I could hear him telling Lillian he was starving to death and telling Hazel Marie he'd never seen her looking so pretty. He knew how to make a warm welcome for himself.

"Julia," Sam said, as I walked out into the hall, "are we going to hope that Pickens won't notice, either?"

I rounded on him, my hands on my hips. "I don't believe everybody is as interested in where other people sleep as you seem to be."

"Well, Good Lord, Julia. I'm only interested in where *I* sleep. I don't care about anybody else, and I'm here to tell you that I am not happy about this."

I stopped at the head of the back stairs, turned to him, waited for a flurry of hammering to stop, and said, "I'm not happy about it, either. I was just about to get used to being your wife and having a little domestic comfort, and" — I stopped and leaned my head against his chest — "I'm going to miss you, Sam."

He ran his hand over my hair, messing it up as usually happened when he did that, and said, "We'll get this straightened out real soon, don't you worry. Then I'm going to jump in your bed and make up for lost time." He lifted my head and frowned at me. "But what I want to know is, what do you mean by a *little* domestic comfort?"

"Oh, you," I said, pulling away from

him, but smiling in spite of myself. "Let's go down and greet Mr. Pickens."

Mr. Pickens was in rare form, warm and expansive, and noticeably pleased to be home. Such as it was, for he was not a permanent member of the household. He lived in a suburb of Asheville, maintaining a small ranch-type house that suited his unmarried state. J.D. Pickens was a private investigator, a designation he preferred over private detective, and which I was careful to call him. I'd made his acquaintance not long after Hazel Marie and Little Lloyd took up residence in my house, when she disappeared on me. I had engaged him to find her, which he subsequently did, although not without considerable help from yours truly. From the first time he laid eyes on Hazel Marie, he was smitten, although that hadn't kept him from laying eyes on any number of other women, as well.

I will have to say, however, that in spite of his roving eyes and his aversion to marriage, his heart seemed to belong to Hazel Marie. So, why he couldn't bring himself to make that attachment permanent, I couldn't understand. Oh, he had plenty of excuses, the major one being Little Lloyd's inheritance of half of my late husband's estate. He said he didn't want anybody thinking he'd married for the access he might have to those assets. Which was ludicrous to begin with, for Mr. Pickens had the least interest in wealth as anybody I knew. Just look at that souped-up and heavily dented vehicle he drove, for one thing.

Another excuse he gave for avoiding marriage was because he'd been married before, not once or twice, but three times, and none of them had taken. And I had to admit, that made him an exceptionally poor candidate for another stab at it. Hazel Marie, of course, was more than willing to take a chance, but then, the woman had never been married at all and, in spite of the fact that she was the mother of a son, she was fairly close to spinsterhood.

I got myself together as best I could as Sam and I descended the stairs into the kitchen. One thing about Mr. Pickens I could depend on, he was a tease beyond compare. I dreaded the moment when he found out our sleeping arrangements and the reason for them. I'd never hear the end of it.

He and Sam shook hands, and the first thing out of Mr. Pickens's mouth was: "So,

Sam, how's married life treating you?"

"Just dandy, up till now," Sam said, laying himself open to a follow-up question that would open a can of worms.

Mr. Pickens's eyebrows went up at that, but, thank goodness, he didn't pursue the matter. Instead, he turned to me and said, "Well, now. I'd say married life agrees with you, Miss Julia. I've never seen you looking so, well, blushing and blooming."

Did I say that Mr. Pickens was a tease? I knew good and well that I was neither blushing nor blooming, particularly with the burden of possible fornication hanging over my head. But leave it to Mr. Pickens to make sly remarks that would bring a rosy color to any woman's face.

Hazel Marie spoke up right about then and brought it all out into the open. "J.D.," she said, "there've been some changes while you've been gone. Sam and Miss Julia may not be married at all, so it's best if you don't ask how they're doing."

I closed my eyes so nobody would see my utter dismay, for Hazel Marie could no more keep a secret than she could fly. Of course, I knew Mr. Pickens would find out sooner or later about our separation, but I would've preferred later rather than sooner. And would've much preferred telling him in private, rather than having it reannounced in the presence of all of us, except Little Lloyd who was expected home from school any minute.

Mr. Pickens turned a disbelieving, but somewhat amused, face to us. "Say what?"

"And, you haven't heard it all," Hazel Marie went on, holding on to Mr. Pickens's arm and gazing at him with adoring eyes. "I've moved up to Miss Julia's room so she and Sam can have mine because it's so much more private, except now, Sam has to sleep in Coleman's old room until they track down the Fire and Water Baptized Church, and all that hammering you hear is coming from Luther and Willie Pruitt, who're putting in closets for me."

"Run that by me again," Mr. Pickens said to Hazel Marie, but he was looking quizzically at Sam.

Sam said, "I believe we are married, but Julia wants to make sure. It's a temporary setback, that's all."

"Well, dang," Mr. Pickens said, scratching his head. "You mean to tell me that Miss Julia, *our* Miss Julia, who is so hell-bent to have everything proper and correct, has been engaged in some premarital — or is it nonmarital? — activity? Now

127
INDIAN PRAIRIE PUBLIC LIBRARY
401 Plainfield Road
Darien, IL 60561

I've heard everything."

Lillian started laughing, Sam had been on the verge of it all along, and Hazel Marie joined in. I broke a smile to appear congenial, but it nearly broke my spirit to have the tables turned on me like that.

"You may continue to believe that I want things done as they should be, Mr. Pickens," I said, turning from them and walking over to the counter where the coffeepot was. "And that is the reason for this interlude of celibacy, which I highly recommend to you. It builds character, doesn't it, Sam?" I reached for cups and saucers and placed them on the counter. "Now, who wants coffee?" I asked to indicate that the subject was closed as far as I was concerned, although I'd noticed that Sam had not answered, much less agreed with, the question addressed to him.

Of course, the subject was not closed as far as Mr. Pickens was concerned, and as we sat around the kitchen table, he insisted on knowing all the ins and outs of our current situation. I let Sam tell him how we'd come to such a pass, as I pretended to have little interest in the sad tale. Still, I had to endure the retelling, while not only Mr. Pickens but Lillian and Hazel Marie, as well, displayed an uncomely avidity in hearing it again.

"Hazel Marie," I said, ignoring Mr. Pickens's merriment, and in an attempt to distract him, "tell us how the beauty pageant is going. How far along are you?"

"Well, I'll tell you, I had a real hard time deciding if I should ask Tonya Allen to be a judge or ask her to be your assistant. She'd be so good at either one, but I finally decided that she should be a judge, because I remembered somebody else. This is somebody who's had a lot of experience with beauty pageants, and will be a lot of help to you. You know her, Miss Julia. Etta Mae Wiggins is going to be your right-hand man." She laughed. "Woman, I mean."

I could've slid under the table. *Etta Mae Wiggins?* That little twit of a home health care supposedly professional, who'd been all over Sam when he'd been laid up with a broken leg? And now, here she was, coming back into our lives just when Sam could well be footloose and fancy-free again.

At that point, I was firmly convinced. Somebody *was* trying to tell me something.

Chapter 12

The next day dragged on until I thought it would never end. I kept trying to come to terms with the sudden uncertainty in my life, as well as with the prospect of having Etta Mae Wiggins underfoot for the duration of the pageant. I tried to appear interested that afternoon, as Hazel Marie ruminated over her plans for the pageant.

"I'm having everybody come over tonight," she said, tapping her pen against the pad on her lap. "Etta Mae said we could meet at her place, but you know she lives in a single-wide trailer, so there wouldn't be enough room. It was nice of her to offer, though."

"I suppose so," I said, reflecting that it was easy enough to appear generous when you know your offer won't be accepted. "But, I tell you, Hazel Marie, a trailer park would not be suitable even if she had a double-wide. We own that place, you know, and I wouldn't want to be assailed with a list of demands from the tenants."

"I'd forgotten about that. Well, don't

worry, we'll be meeting here, if it's all right with you."

I nodded, resigned to not only putting up with Miss Wiggins's presence, but also, since she'd be a guest in my home, gritting my teeth and being polite to her.

"Now, here's the plan," Hazel Marie went on. "We can't use the auditorium until school is out, so we'll have to meet here for the next week or so. I know you have a lot on your mind right now, but I would like you to at least meet the contestants. And, really, all we'll need to do is see what we have to work with." She sighed. "From what Coleman's told me, none of the girls have had much experience with pageants."

"That might be a good thing, Hazel Marie," I said. "They won't know whether we're doing it right or not."

"I guess," she said, distractedly. "But now, I have to figure out how to get a runway built and installed, on top of everything else. And how to uninstall it when we're through."

"Why don't you ask Mr. Pruitt?"

"I'd love to. I just didn't know if you'd want them to stop what they're doing to work on another job."

"The Lord's sake, Hazel Marie, there's

no need for them to stop. I meant that they could build a runway after hours or on the weekends. I don't see where that could possibly be a problem. A lot of people work extra jobs."

"Are you feeling all right, Miss Julia?" Hazel Marie turned a concerned face to me. "You sound a little edgy today."

"I'm *feeling* a little edgy," I said. "And who wouldn't, what with my current situation, and having that Wiggins woman to deal with on top of that. To say nothing of all the hammering and nailing going on upstairs, and worrying about a bunch of giggling young women who don't know how to conduct themselves in a genteel manner, and I've already said I didn't see how I could be involved with a pageant." I stopped, hoping I hadn't gone too far. "I'm sorry, Hazel Marie. I think I'm having an emotional crisis, and I don't even believe in such a thing. But I get a raging headache whenever I think of all I have to put up with."

She gave my face a good going-over with a minute-long stare. "What do you have against Etta Mae?" she asked, ignoring most of what I'd said and going right to the heart of my problem.

I sniffed. "I really don't know the woman."

"She's very nice, and awfully hard-working. And she'd do anything for you."

"That may be, Hazel Marie. I'm just surprised that you'd want her around Mr. Pickens, knowing how he is about attractive women."

She laughed. "I'm not worried about that. Oh, I know how J.D. can be, but he doesn't mean anything by it. Especially since I know Etta Mae would never go after somebody who's already taken. And, believe me, J.D. is taken. Besides," she went on, "Etta Mae wouldn't even look at a friend's man."

Well, wasn't that the problem? Etta Mae Wiggins was no friend of mine and, if she learned the truth of my marriage or lack of same, she might well assume Sam was untaken and go after him again. I recalled all too well how she'd hung on him and pampered him and did personal things for him when he was laid up. And how he'd loved every minute of her totally unnecessary ministrations. The thought of it set my teeth on edge.

"Well, you just make sure she minds her manners around me," I said. "I'm in no mind to put up with her gushing over . . . well, whoever."

Hazel Marie frowned; then her eyes

widened and her face lit up. "Sam?" She laughed. "You think Etta Mae'll go after *Sam?*"

I drew myself up. "Well, it's not so far-fetched. Not that I'm worried, you understand. It's just that I've seen that woman in action, and Sam is a very attractive man."

"But, Miss Julia, for all Etta Mae knows, Sam is a married man. Nobody but us knows any different, and I sure won't tell her. And I can promise you that she respects the marriage vows." Hazel Marie stopped and bit her lower lip. "Of course, not all married men respect theirs, and she's had a little trouble along those lines — you know, them going after her."

I swung around, my hand pressed to my forehead. "Don't tell me that, Hazel Marie. I've got enough to worry about without adding anything extra."

"Shoo," Hazel Marie said, waving her hand. "You don't have enough to worry about if you think Sam's going to take up with another woman."

"Well," I said, darkly, "any man can be vulnerable. Especially to an all-out attack by the likes of her."

"Well, yourself," she came back at me, but with a smile. "All you have to do is keep Sam so occupied that he doesn't have the energy to think of anybody else. And you can't do that in separate bedrooms."

"Hazel Marie!"

"I'm just telling you the truth, and you know it. Now listen, the girls will be here before long, and they're going to be so excited. Just think, Miss Julia, one of them's going to be Miss Abbot County Sheriff's Department. It's the chance of a lifetime."

"Then Lord help them if that's the high point of their lives. No, I'm sorry, Hazel Marie," I said, as her face fell. "I didn't mean it quite like that. It is a wonderful opportunity for all of them, and I know they'll appreciate what you're doing. So, tell me," I went on, trying to set aside my own troubles, "do we know any of them?"

She consulted the list she'd gotten from Coleman, then handed it to me. "I know some of the family names, but not the girls themselves. See if you do."

I scanned the list and, like Hazel Marie, recognized some surnames. "I know a Peavey, and you do, too. Let's hope it's not the same family. And here's a LaVane. Is her father the young man who works at the radio station?"

"Oh, I hope so. We'd get a lot of advertising if he is. I don't think he's so young, though."

"Everybody's young to me, Hazel Marie," I said, feeling every year of my age.

"Well, when we get into this, it's going to young you up, as Lillian would say. Now, Miss Julia, since we're talking about this, I might as well tell you, even though I know you're not going to like it. But I've had to ask Thurlow Jones to be a judge."

"Oh, no, Hazel Marie. Don't tell me that. The man's as crazy as a loon, and he'll ruin everything. Why in the world did you ask him?"

"I knew you wouldn't like it, but I was put on the spot. Sheriff Frady told me that Thurlow wants to do it, and he asked me to ask him. I didn't have a good reason not to."

"I could've given you a dozen." All I could think of was how that grizzled old man had thought he was the answer to all my prayers, and how he'd put me in an unseemly position — namely, astraddle a Harley Davidson motorcycle — by giving me a challenge I couldn't turn down. He'd lured me into participating in a Poker Run, of all things, to raise some much needed money for Lillian and her neighbors. I still hadn't recovered from it, and Hazel Marie should've known that. "What I'd like to know is, how did Thurlow know about the pageant. We've not done any advertising yet."

"Oh, I expect the sheriff told him. They're big buddies, you know. Anyway, now we have Sam, Tonya Allen, and Thurlow Jones as the judges. That's enough, don't you think?"

"More than," I said, my heart sinking at the thought of putting up with both Thurlow Jones and Etta Mae Wiggins. Then I had another thought. "Hazel Marie, do you think Miss Wiggins could get interested in Thurlow?"

Hazel Marie nearly fell out of her chair, laughing. "Etta Mae and Thurlow? You've got to be kidding! *No*body would be interested in him."

"Well, it would solve a lot of problems," I said, because I still didn't trust the Wiggins woman around Sam, and I didn't trust Thurlow Jones around me.

By the time the contestants were due to arrive that evening, I was ready to see the last of Mr. Pickens and his playfulness. He had dropped by in time for supper, as was his wont, and he'd kept everybody but me entertained with one humorous story after another, none of which I was in the mood for. Afterward, Hazel Marie suggested that he and Sam make themselves scarce and find something to do somewhere else. The contestants, she said, might be self-conscious if they had an audience this early in the game.

So Sam told Mr. Pickens that they could go to his house, and Mr. Pickens told Sam that he had a video they could watch if he'd been feeling a little deprived lately. It had taken me a minute to get his meaning, then to understand that Mr. Pickens was ragging on me, as usual.

He laughed and put his arm around me. "Just teasing, Miss Julia. You know I wouldn't do that."

"I wouldn't put anything past you, Mr. Pickens. So you'd better mind yourself around me." I smiled and slipped out from under his arm. But if he thought I didn't mean what I said, he was dead wrong.

Little Lloyd wanted to go with them, but his mother said he'd be too late getting to bed on a school night.

"That's all right," Mr. Pickens told him, with a pat on the shoulder. "We need you to stick around and take notes. Pictures, too, if you can sneak downstairs."

"Mr. Pickens," I said, "stop putting ideas in that child's head. He never knows when you're teasing."

"I'm not teasing," he said, but he grinned at Little Lloyd.

So with Little Lloyd safely upstairs with his door closed and homework on his desk, Hazel Marie ran to greet our first arrival after the doorbell rang. It was Etta Mae Wiggins, and you would've thought they were the best of friends, as they squealed greetings and hugged each other. I knew they were not. They had both gone to the same county schools, but Miss Wiggins was some few years younger than Hazel Marie, so they couldn't have been too close. Both had checkered pasts, though, which I suppose accounted for some of their feelings of companionship.

"Etta Mae! I'm so glad to see you," Hazel Marie cried before the woman got in the door good.

"Hazel Marie!" she cried in return. Then she stood back and gazed at her. "You look gorgeous! I love that silk shirt. And your gold necklace! Girl, you look like a million dollars."

Which, I thought, was reasonably apt, since, by way of Little Lloyd's inheritance, Hazel Marie had the use of a million and then some dollars.

"This? It's old as the hills," Hazel Marie said, looking down at herself. "Come on in, Etta Mae. We sure need your help. Oh, I love your hair. What've you done to it?"

"Cut, dyed, and permed it," Miss Wiggins said, shaking her curly head. "I was sick and tired of my real color, which was hardly any color at all, so I got me a new 'do. If I'd gone red, I'd be Orphan Annie. You like it?"

"It looks great on you. Come on in and have a seat. You and Miss Julia know each other, don't you?"

The sparkle in Miss Wiggins's eyes died away as she turned to me. I quickly offered my hand, mindful of my duties as a hostess.

"We've met," I said. "How are you, Miss Wiggins?"

"I'm fine, ma'am," she said, with considerably less enthusiasm than when she'd greeted Hazel Marie. "Thank you for asking, but you can call me Etta Mae if you want to."

I didn't, particularly.

Hazel Marie guided Miss Wiggins to a seat beside her on the sofa, while I took one of the Victorian chairs by the fireplace. As she studied the copies of the pageant agenda that Hazel Marie handed to her, I had the opportunity to study her.

Miss Wiggins was a small woman, a bit

shorter than Hazel Marie, but much more rounded. Whereas Hazel Marie verged on the skinny side, except for her up-top area, Miss Wiggins had a more balanced figure, one that would draw stares, backward glances, and leers from those so inclined.

She had a bouncy personality, as I'd perceived at our first meeting when she was supposedly caring for Sam. *Perky* is a better word, though I am not impressed by perkiness in the best of times. I noticed her glancing occasionally in my direction while listening to Hazel Marie's description of the pageant and the decisions that had to be made.

"Well, I hope I can help," she said, as Hazel Marie finished. "You know I'll do whatever I can. I'm really excited about it, 'specially since you asked me. I just admire you so much, Hazel Marie. It's a real honor to work with you."

That was a little much for me, but I held my tongue because I do believe the woman was being honest, though just a little over-the-top with her flattery. Of course, she could do worse than idolize Hazel Marie, who, I don't mind saying, had bloomed in my nurturing care.

It was remarkable to me, though, as I sat and studied this little upstart whom I didn't trust for a minute, how she could turn the charm on and off. When she spoke to Hazel Marie, she was animated, her eyes sparkling, her hands gesturing, and her voice lilting with excitement. But when she cut her eyes at me, as if she were checking on my response, all her liveliness petered out. Her eyes darkened, the hint of a frown showed up between her brows, and a worried look passed across her face.

"Miss Julia?" Hazel Marie said.

I shook myself out of my concentration on Miss Wiggins's facial expressions. "Yes?"

"Is there anything I've forgotten? Anything you've thought of that might help."

"Ah, well, yes," I said, trying to turn my mind to the work at hand. "Miss Wiggins, uh, Etta Mae, that is. I've already told Hazel Marie that I don't know a thing about this pageant business. I am perfectly willing to lend a hand occasionally, but that's all I can do. I have too much on my plate for any more. So, for Hazel Marie's sake, I hope you know how beauty pageants are supposed to be run."

"Yes, ma'am, I think I do. I've been to a lot of them, and a friend of mine was a contestant in the Miss Apple Festival contest several years ago. She didn't win, though."

Well, Lord, that was hardly a glowing resume of Miss Wiggins's beauty pageant experience.

"Then I guess the two of you will have to stumble through as best you can."

Miss Wiggins seemed to shrink into the sofa, as she glanced at me from under her thick eyelashes. She murmured, "I'll do my best."

"Oh, you'll do fine," Hazel Marie said. "I know you will. I wouldn't have asked you if I thought you couldn't."

Miss Wiggins's face brightened at Hazel Marie's vote of confidence. As I watched the transformation on her face, it struck me that I was the one who was making her so unsure of herself. In fact, I do believe she was intimidated by being in my presence. I didn't know whether to be flattered or offended.

Still, it never hurt to have people recognize my position in this town and deal with me accordingly. But, I will admit to feeling a softening of my heart toward Miss Wiggins. She was being properly respectful, and if she continued to remember her manners and kept her eyes off Sam, we'd get along just fine.

Chapter 13

"I hear them," Hazel Marie said, as a couple of car doors slammed outside. "Sit still, Miss Julia. I'll let them in."

As she walked toward the door, she added, "Get ready, everybody. We're gonna have us a beauty pageant."

Well, of course I couldn't sit still with guests at the door, so Hazel Marie and I greeted the young women as they straggled in by ones and twos. Now, I know that first impressions often have to be reconsidered, but first impressions were all I had to go on at the time. And, believe me, I sincerely hoped to be able to reconsider them, since the contestants in aggregate did not engender a great deal of confidence in their ability to show well, either up close or onstage.

Most of them were quite attractive, or they would've been with different hair styles, less makeup, and more suitable clothing. But I kept my thoughts to myself as Hazel Marie quieted their chatter by taking charge of the meeting. She started off in a soft voice and with a noticeable trembling of the pages in her hand. But she persevered, giving them an overview of the way the pageant would be organized, what would be expected of the contestants, and the categories in which they would be vying. Then she handed out the schedules that listed the various competitions and the types of dress each one required.

"Any questions?" Hazel Marie asked, and waited a few seconds while the girls looked over the pages. "Well, I'm sure you'll have lots to ask as we get further along. Now, I'm going to introduce everybody by their names and titles so we'll all know who is who." She turned to me. "But first, this is Mrs. Julia Springer. Oh!" Hazel Marie's hand flew to her mouth, as she blushed and giggled at her slip. "I mean, Mrs. Murdoch. I'm sorry, Miss Julia, but you being a new bride and all, well, I'm not used to your new name."

Six pairs of young eyes openly stared at me, as if they couldn't comprehend that someone could be a bride at my age. I composed my face as best I could and settled myself stiffly in my chair in order to withstand their frowning scrutiny with some measure of serenity. But I was embarrassed at the attention, considering the questionable circumstances of my marriage. Even if few were aware of it, Hazel Marie might have been correct in reverting to my former name.

"Anyway," Hazel Marie went on, trying to regain their attention. "This is Etta Mae Wiggins. She and I will be your official guides, instructors, and chaperones. So, tell your folks that you're in good hands."

I wondered about that, as Miss Wiggins gave a little wave to the girls and Hazel Marie continued with her introductory remarks.

"Etta Mae'll be showing you how to do the runway walk, how to turn and how to sit. Both of us will help you with your responses to the questions and the interviews with the judges. And we'll spend a lot of time on your choice of outfits for the different events, your makeup, and how you wear your hair. We have a lot of work to do, so I hope everybody's ready to buckle down."

By this time, I was becoming more and more impressed with Hazel Marie. She'd started off with a nervous quaver in her voice, but she'd gradually attained strength of purpose and confidence in herself. I expect it was because even she could not fail to notice how raw and uninformed these young women seemed to be. Anything Hazel Marie could offer had fertile soil to take root in.

"Now, let's see who everybody is," Hazel Marie said, consulting her notes. "Miss First Watch, that's Melanie Easley, right? Stand up, Miss First Watch."

The young woman who jumped up, grinning and flinging out her arms so we could get a full view, looked like a carhop, if they still have those jobs. She had on shorts that were so short I had to avert my eyes when she leaned over to take a mock bow to everybody's applause. Her tank top barely covered her middle and was so tight in the bodice that nothing was left to the imagination. A slenderizing diet wouldn't be amiss, either, for the kindest thing I could say for Miss Easley was that she had retained a soft layer of baby fat.

I took pad and pen, and wrote down her name and title so I could remind Hazel Marie and Miss Wiggins what that child needed to be told.

"Thanks. You can sit down now." Hazel Marie looked around. "Now we have Miss Third Watch, Ashley Knowles."

Miss Knowles rose slightly from her chair, then quickly sat back down, letting her long hair, black and stringy, veil her face from view. Shy, I supposed, feeling some pity for the girl who looked less like a beauty queen than anybody I'd ever seen.

Then, to my consternation, I detected a flash of gold embedded on the side of her nose. Lord, my own nose began to twitch so bad, I had to fumble a Kleenex out of my pocket. She wore jeans that were so long they dragged along the ground, gathering up dust and dirt and whatever else she walked through. Taking in all that, along with her poor posture, I knew she'd need a lot of work if she was going to withstand the kind of scrutiny she'd let herself in for.

I jotted down a note to that effect, noticing as I did that Miss Knowles sat some little distance from the others.

"All right," Hazel Marie said. "Now, Miss Second Watch, Tasha McKenzie." Hazel Marie glanced at the heavily made-up young woman. "You wouldn't be Preacher Skeeter McKenzie's daughter, would you?"

"I sure would," she answered, pleased to be recognized. "Everybody knows my daddy, don't they?"

Lord, I was taken aback at hearing that bit of information. Preacher Skeeter, as he insisted on being called, had a splinter church somewhere out in the country and, from what I'd heard, pretty much made up his own doctrine. He preached it every

Sunday morning on the local radio station, which a lot of people listened to for its entertainment value. But what I wanted to know was why in the world a fundamentalist preacher, who disapproved of everything from television to assertive women, would allow his daughter to compete in a body-baring beauty contest. Yet, there she was in skintight pants, slung so low I wanted to jerk them back up. Underneath her bouffant hairdo, she was smiling and simpering with what seemed to me an unwarranted confidence in her own allure.

I made a note that she might need bringing down a peg or two.

"Hazel Marie," I whispered, while Miss McKenzie did a twirl in the middle of the room, "does that girl's father know what she's in for?"

"I guess he does," she whispered back. "I sent all the girls a general outline of the events."

Strange, I thought to myself, as Miss McKenzie confounded me even more by announcing that she'd been to modeling school in Greenville.

"I'll be glad to help any of y'all," she said, taking a stand beside Hazel Marie, as if she'd just promoted herself to coleader of the band.

But Hazel Marie was not to be intimidated. "Have a seat, Tasha. If we need help, I'll let you know. But right now, we have to move on."

Well, I thought, this beauty pageant business would seem to have heretofore unnoticed benefits. My retiring and usually submissive Hazel Marie was showing a little backbone, and I was quite proud of her.

Just as she opened her mouth to introduce another contestant, a persistent ringing sound made everyone look around to see where it was coming from. An attractive black girl dug into her drawstring bag and fished out a cell phone. She laughed as if in apology, but did nothing to end the call. Turning her head to answer it, she ignored Hazel Marie's glare and my frown of annoyance. We all waited while she finished a conversation that consisted of little more than several *really*s? and a few *you know*s. There were some eye rollings and exaggerated sighs among the other girls at the interruption.

When the girl finally clicked off the phone with a pleased smile and an insincere "Sorry," Miss Wiggins spoke right up. "The very first rule: No cell phones during rehearsals. If you have one, turn it off now."

Every head, except Miss Knowles's, leaned down to purse or backpack on the floor, as they followed her instructions.

"Good," Hazel Marie said, scanning her notes again. "Let's see, the next one I have is Miss SWAT Team. That's Heather Peavey, right?"

Miss Peavey jumped up with a cheery smile. "That's me, and I'm going to do this if it kills me! Because if I don't, my dad's gonna kill me, anyway."

All the girls laughed as if they knew her, and indeed they did. Miss Heather Peavey, I learned, was an athlete of some local renown, having excelled on a school volleyball team. And, as I noted the resemblance, I realized that she was the daughter of Lieutenant Peavey of the sheriff's department, he of the most unlikely tenor voice who sang at Binkie and Coleman's wedding, and of the most inquisitive nature into some of the expeditions I'd have preferred nobody knowing about.

Yet I was quite taken with Miss Peavey, even though she unfortunately took after her father in build and stature. She was a healthy-looking girl with a sturdy, boyish physique and an engaging smile. She, too, had on shorts, but they were of a length of

151

your average modern dress. She wore what looked like a man's shirt, tucked in with the sleeves rolled up. Of them all, she had the most cheerful countenance.

"Thanks, Heather," Hazel Marie said. "Well, it looks like I got out of sequence here, but let's have Miss Vice Squad, Bethany LaVane."

There was some tittering at Miss LaVane's title, but she didn't seem to mind. As she stood, she exhibited some of Miss Peavey's outgoing qualities, but she put me off right away, for she seemed to have no concept of how she sounded when she opened her mouth.

Lord, that country twang! Miss LaVane was going to need a lot of help, not only with her elocution and clothing, but with that dyed-to-within-an-inch-of-its-life hair that badly needed a pair of scissors and a brush taken to it. Add three-inch-high heels on her clogs, and you have a picture of modern pulchritude.

"I'm so excited I can't hardly stand it," she announced as she teetered on her wooden platform soles. "An' I'm just proud to represent the vice squad, I don't care what y'all say."

Her long earrings tinkled when she moved her head and — to my shocked eyes

— a gold ring in her navel winked at me between her cropped shirt and hip-slung pants. What was the world coming to? It was beyond me to figure out why a nose and a navel needed decorative accessories.

"And our last contestant is YoShandra Washington, Miss Detective Squad."

"You can call me Shandra," Miss Washington said, as she stood before us with a large smile on her face.

This young woman was just like the rest in her clothing, if not her complexion, and I'm speaking of the fact that all of them, with the exception of Miss Peavey, seemed to have on clothes about two sizes too small. Everything was too short, too tight, or too skimpy, and if that was the current style, I didn't care for it. Miss Washington, for instance, wore orange pants and a yellow T-shirt, both stretched so tight that I wondered how she got them on, much less how she'd get them off. But polyester does have a lot of give to it, molding itself to every convex and concave feature of the figure. Which is why I don't wear it.

"Well, that's all of us," Hazel Marie said. "I'd hoped to have two or three others, but for some reason, not all the sections of the sheriff's department came up with a representative."

Miss Peavey's hand shot up. "I know why. Most of the guys are married, and you said wives aren't eligible." She laughed. "They were afraid to vote for anybody else."

Hazel Marie raised her hand to calm down the laughter. "Okay, let's move on. Now, girls, I want you to know that this is serious business. It's real, and not something to be taken lightly. I expect each and every one of you to be at every meeting and every rehearsal. I understand that none of you have done this before —"

"But I've had training," Tasha McKenzie interrupted. "I know what we're supposed to do, and how to act and all."

"I think we have it covered for the time being, Tasha," Hazel Marie said, but I heard a note of uncertainty in her voice. It was plain that Miss McKenzie would take over if Hazel Marie gave her the chance. I hoped Miss Wiggins would prove her worth, and keep her in line.

For myself, I was glad the pageant was Hazel Marie's project, and not mine.

Chapter 14

Hazel Marie brushed a lock of hair out of her face. "I'll turn things over to Etta Mae now. She knows how it's done, so everybody pay attention." Then she added, "You're all going to be wonderful contestants, and I know you'll be a credit to the deputies you represent. Etta Mae, it's all yours." And Hazel Marie took a seat.

Miss Wiggins stood, and I, wanting to sneak out to the kitchen, started to, as well. But as she announced her intentions, I sank back down, deciding to stay for the show.

"What we're going to do first," Miss Wiggins announced, "is get some idea of how you present yourselves. That way, we'll know how much practice you'll need. Now, if you'll help me move these chairs out of the way, we'll make a runway from here through that door into the dining room. When you get to the table, turn around and walk back."

Well, I thought, she could've at least had the courtesy to ask my permission before she started rearranging my house, but the five young women who sat in a clump eagerly started in. They jumped up and, with a lot of laughing and talking, made a makeshift runway the length of the living room and half the dining room. Miss Knowles stood up and moved her chair, but kept herself apart from the others. Or they kept themselves apart from her.

"Hazel Marie," Miss Wiggins said, "if you'll stand at this end, I'll stand by the table. That way, we can see each girl walk and turn. Everybody line up now, and I want you to walk and smile like you're going to do for the judges."

Heather Peavey laughed nervously and said, "I'm used to having referees watch me, but this is a little out of my league."

"Oh, you'll do fine," Melanie Easley said, tossing her hair. "There's nothing to it. I was on the homecoming court, and all you do is smile and look good. And try not to trip."

"All right, girls," Miss Wiggins said. "Listen up, now. You're going to learn the right way to walk when you're presenting yourself to the judges and the audience. It's been tested and approved by all the major pageants, because it shows your figure and poise better than any other way. So let's get started."

Ashley Knowles edged to the back of the line.

"I'll go first," Tasha McKenzie said. "Then you'll all know what to do."

"Go ahead, then," Miss Wiggins said, none too graciously.

And she did, bouncing along with the most unusual gait I'd ever seen. She walked as if she had springs on her feet, bouncing up and down in a stilted and unnatural way, with her hips swiveling enough to throw them out of joint. When she got to the table, she stopped, swung herself from one side to the other with her legs spraddled out, then made a swift turn with her head high in the air and an aloof expression on her face.

During this unlikely display, I noticed the other girls putting their heads together. One of them murmured, "Have we got to do *that?*" With worried frowns, they watched as Miss McKenzie bounced back to stand in front of Hazel Marie, did another turn, and flashed a confident smile, thoroughly pleased with her performance.

"See?" she said. "It's easy once you get the hang of it. All you have to do is work it."

"Well, I don't know," Hazel Marie said

with a worried frown. "What do you think, Etta Mae?"

"That may be the way models do it," Miss Wiggins said, "but for a pageant, it's all wrong. You'll look ridiculous swinging yourself around like you're wearing Calvin Klein."

My eyes widened at Miss Wiggins's tone, but Tasha tossed her hair. She set her mouth in a thin line of displeasure, and muttered, "I know what I'm doing, even if nobody else does."

"Okay, now," Miss Wiggins said, taking charge again. "I'm going to show you how it should be done. Watch."

She squared her shoulders and, to my consternation, jutted out her bosom. Then she turned her head and shoulders toward the girls, put a wide smile on her face, and began to walk with a scissoring movement of her jeans-clad legs, her arms swinging from side to side. The remarkable thing about it was that from the waist up, except for her arms, not a single muscle moved. Even though she was striding swiftly across the room, the profile of her bosom stayed locked in the most advantageous position for viewing from the judges' table.

"Now," she said, as she stopped. "You end with one foot in front of the other so you can keep your balance and pivot smoothly. There's no need to take an extra step on the turn." She demonstrated a stumble-free about-face. "Then you walk back, always keeping your face and shoulders turned toward the audience. Who wants to try it first?"

Well, I was impressed. Miss Wiggins had managed to exhibit a tightly controlled pace and an error-free turn without missing a step or losing her bright smile. I do admit, though, that the performance seemed on the stiff side to me, and quite unnatural. I mean, who walked around the mall like that? But I could see the reasoning behind it, which was to show a woman's assets in their best light.

"That looked good," Heather Peavey said with a troubled frown. "I just don't know if I can do it."

"Sure you can," Etta Mae told her. "Come on, somebody. Let's see you try."

"I will." Melanie Easley jumped up and stood by Etta Mae. "Get me started."

As Etta Mae pushed on her back to make her straighten her shoulders, I noticed with some satisfaction that Miss Easley had eschewed shorts for a pair of cropped pants. Or as they were once known, pedal pushers.

The next several minutes were taken up with tryouts of the pageant walk, accompanied by too many squeals and too much laughter for my strung-out nerves. Hazel Marie tried to remind them of the seriousness of getting it right so they could move on to other things, but still some couldn't get the hang of a smooth walk and turn.

Miss Peavey, for one, always started with correct posture, but by the time she got to the turn, she was slouching with her knees athletically bent.

Miss Vice Squad, Bethany LaVane, started that thigh-swishing gait in good form. But then she walked right out of her clogs and sprawled on the floor. Etta Mae was immediately at her side, helping her up and assuring her that she wasn't hurt.

"This is a good example for all of us," Etta Mae said, turning to the group. "You'll need to practice in high heels every day. If you're not used to them, you might can get away with mid-highs."

Tasha McKenzie couldn't let that pass. "Three-and-a-half-inch heels make your legs look better. That's what I'm planning to wear."

"Yeah, and you're likely to bust it on the runway," Etta Mae said, which wasn't the most elegant way of expressing it, but she got the point across. "We want a uniform look to all of you. You can express your individuality by the color and design of your outfits. Now, Tasha, let's see you try it again."

Having taken in everything, Miss McKenzie proved an apt pupil, but she didn't like it. If Miss Wiggins took her eyes off her for one minute, Tasha broke into her former stilted gait.

"Tasha," Etta Mae said at one point, "it's got to be smooth and even, with your bottom tucked in. Don't bounce and swivel your hips like that. Just do like I showed you."

Miss McKenzie tossed her head, even though her sprayed-stiff hair didn't budge. "I think you're wrong. This walk you want us to do is outdated, and if it was up to me, I'd do it the correct way. The professional way."

Miss Wiggins stalked right up to her. "It's not up to you."

That quieted everybody down, as they looked from one to the other. As for me, I was pleased to witness the firmness Miss Wiggins exhibited in putting Miss McKenzie in her place. She probably got it from dealing with cranky old people.

With a glowering frown, Tasha mumbled,

"I didn't say I wouldn't, did I?"

With that display of temperament, I decided it was time I left them to it. I edged toward the kitchen, but Hazel Marie, probably wanting a diversion, stopped me before I got to the door.

"Miss Julia, before you go, do you have anything you'd like to say?"

Not a thing, I thought, but for her sake, I managed to come up with a few encouraging words. "Well, I think it's important that each and every one of you present yourselves as well-bred young ladies. When you are in the public eye, you should make sure that you sit modestly, walk gracefully, speak softly, dress tastefully, and not chew gum. Above all," I said, as six blank faces looked at me, a few knees gradually came together, and Miss LaVane swallowed hard, "remember that, regardless of how attractive the outside is, it's one's inner beauty that counts. Now, I expect you're ready for a break, so I'll see what we have in the kitchen."

With that, I pushed through the swinging door into the kitchen, but not before noticing a little eye-rolling from one or two of the contestants. What I'd told them was undoubtedly nothing they'd not heard before. But if they'd taken heed to begin with, I wouldn't have had to repeat it.

I'd barely gotten the refrigerator door open to get out the lemonade pitcher, when Little Lloyd crept down the back stairs.

"I thought you were in bed."

"No'm, homework made me hungry." He grinned at me. "And I wanted to see the beauty queens."

"Then you can help me take those cookies to them." I pointed to the covered plate Lillian had left on the counter. "Grab a handful of napkins, and I'll put some glasses on a tray. We'll set them on the dining room table and they can help themselves."

When he and I walked into the dining room, laden with refreshments, the Misses LaVane, Peavey, and Easley immediately stopped practicing and swarmed around us. I thought it was Lillian's cookies that had drawn them, and they didn't hesitate to partake of them, but it was Little Lloyd they were most interested in.

"Oh, you're so cute," Miss Easley said, sidling up to him in a friendly manner. "Where do you go to school?"

"You gonna be our talent coach?" Miss Peavey asked. "I bet you'd make a good one."

"Look at that hair," Miss LaVane marveled. "It's so fine and soft." And to prove it, she was bold enough to run her hand across his head.

Little Lloyd blushed and stammered and ducked his head, overcome by the attention. He wasn't accustomed to being made over and flirted with and cooed at. But he liked it, I could tell. Though Lord knows why they were doing it, for the boy was no poster child. I could still see too much of his daddy in him.

"They need to get on with their practice," I said, guiding Little Lloyd back into the kitchen and letting the door close behind us. "Here, I've saved some cookies for us."

He sat down, but his eyes were on the door. "They sure are pretty. No wonder they're beauty queens."

"Pretty is as pretty does," I said, worried that their teasing had turned his head. He was much too young to be noticing girls.

A burst of laughter from the front room made us swivel our heads toward it. Little Lloyd got up, saying he wanted to see what they were doing. He crept up to the door and cracked it so he could peer out without being seen.

A heavy thump was the next thing we

heard, and the child turned to me, his eyes big and his mouth open. "One of 'em fell!" Then he hunched over to peer out again. "She's all right. They're all laughing." He continued to watch, while I sat at the table wondering if he should be watching such sights from a concealed place. He turned to me again. "I can't wait to see them on the stage. You know, in their evening gowns and bathing suits."

"You've seen enough already," I said, rising from my chair. "It's time you were in bed."

Chapter 15

After getting the child off to bed and hearing the bustle of leavetaking, I wandered back into the living room. The young women were gathering their things while Miss Wiggins kept up a barrage of last-minute instructions and directions.

I'm not sure how much they heard, for they were talking excitedly among themselves. All except Ashley Knowles, who kept her distance, and Tasha McKenzie, who flounced toward the door without a good-bye, thank you, ma'am, or kiss my foot.

"Hazel Marie," I whispered, drawing her aside, "I take back all my hesitancies where Miss Wiggins is concerned. You are fortunate to have her. Just keep her away from me."

"Girls!" Miss Wiggins called over their chatter. "Next time, I'll expect everybody to have their walk down pat, so be sure to practice. We'll be taking up fashion tips and beauty products, especially your stage makeup. Okay, everybody, that's enough for tonight. Hazel Marie, you have anything else?"

"Just that I think we've had a good rehearsal. You all know what to be working on, and I want you to begin thinking about your various outfits. Oh, and what you're going to do in the talent category." Hazel Marie giggled. "Can't forget that, can we? Anyway, we'll discuss that next time. And, one other thing," she went on, "we're starting the advertising tomorrow, which means the pageant will be on us before we know it. So be sure and talk it up. We want a full auditorium with all your families and friends."

It was with more than a little relief that I wished them all a good night and closed the door behind the last of them, except one.

"Oh, Etta Mae," Hazel Marie said, turning to her, "I can't tell you how glad I am that you're helping me. I was about at my wit's end, but you really know how to handle them."

"Yes," I said, handing Miss Wiggins her jacket, "they need a firm hand, and you certainly have that." Then, thinking I'd sounded less than gracious, even though I'd meant it as an expression of praise, I added, "My compliments, Miss Wiggins, especially for coming to Hazel Marie's rescue."

"Thanks, but you can call me Etta Mae," she murmured in case I'd forgotten. "If you want to."

After repositioning the chairs in the living room, Hazel Marie and I collapsed, side by side, on the sofa. Hazel Marie looked as done in as I felt.

"I hope we haven't bitten off more than we can chew," she said. "I don't know what I expected, but it certainly wasn't this. And I didn't know we'd have to put up with a know-it-all like that McKenzie girl."

"She's a handful, all right. But the Knowles girl, Hazel Marie. What's her problem? I don't think she said a word all evening. And did you see that thing stuck in her nose? I won't even mention Miss LaVane's navel."

"Body piercing's all the rage now," Hazel Marie said. "But that's not what worries me. They can take out the studs and the rings, but if any of them have tattoos, they're stuck with them."

"Stuck? Needles? Don't even talk about that." I squirmed in my seat.

"We could've used a little more help," Hazel Marie said, giving me a sidelong glance. "I wish you'd been more outspoken."

"Well, Lord, Hazel Marie. I've rarely been told that. Besides, you know I don't have the time nor the aptitude for this sort of thing." I stopped and plucked at my dress skirt. "I have a lot on my mind right now. It's awfully hard to put a beauty pageant in the forefront of my thinking when I don't even know who or what I am."

"I know." Hazel Marie patted my hand. "And I appreciate what you're doing. Has Sam found out anything?"

"No, and you'd think he'd be anxious to get this matter resolved, what with being put out to pasture, as he calls it. I'm beginning to think that our room separation suits him just fine."

"Oh, I don't think that's true. I think he's suffering. Why, the poor man is in the same situation you are, and you're not happy with it, are you?"

"Well, no, Hazel Marie. Of course I'm not. Being neither one thing nor the other is hard on the nerves, especially when I have to pretend to be happily married in front of other people. Then, I come home and have to get into a single state of mind again."

We sat in silence for a few minutes; then I mustered the courage to say what had been bothering me more and more lately. "Hazel Marie, I'm afraid the Lord is trying to tell me something."

"What?" She looked at me with those big, innocent — though I knew they were not — eyes.

"Maybe I should've never married Sam in the first place."

"It'll work out," she said, as if my words had not penetrated her own cloud of worries. "But I'm not sure this beauty pageant will." We sat in silence for a while longer, too overwhelmed with what we'd each let ourselves in for to get up and go to bed. Then she said, "At least I've got Etta Mae now, and you'll always have Sam."

I wasn't too sure about that, but I knew enough to know that Hazel Marie didn't have her mind on my problems. We finally rose and went our separate ways to bed, she to my former room and I to my lonely one. Glancing at the clock as I readied myself for retiring, I wondered when Sam would get in. Although he would not be joining me, I was uneasy when he wasn't where he was supposed to be, which was right upstairs, far from Mr. Pickens's baleful influence. It didn't look good for him to be out all hours of the night, and him a newly wedded man. As far as most everybody knew, that is.

I sighed and crawled under the covers, leaving the bedside light on while I read my daily devotions. I couldn't keep my mind on them, though, for my thoughts went spiraling far from the recommended reading.

So I closed the book and settled back against the pillows, determined to examine all the random thoughts that had troubled me throughout the day.

Ever since this mess we were in started, I'd been recalling my loudly proclaimed reasons for urging Binkie and Coleman to marry. Then there were the many times I'd harped on the unsanctified manner in which Hazel Marie carried on with Mr. Pickens. I'd left no stone unturned in making myself the staunch advocate of legal and church-sanctioned marriages. And now, just look where I was.

I hated to admit it, but if it'd been someone else in my situation, I would've found it amusing, even laughable. Which it certainly would be to any number of people, if the word ever got out. There are always people who take pleasure in seeing the mighty fall. Or, more aptly, seeing those who take the high moral ground, as I was so well known for doing, slide into the common ditch.

And common was just the way I felt. The idea of finally jumping into another marriage, only to find myself in what only amounted to a *relationship* — and we all know what that means — went against the grain of everything I'd stood for all my life.

Then it hit me. I rose up in bed, stunned by the realization that I was no better than Wesley Lloyd, both of us having gotten ourselves into immoral associations.

Well, Lord, I sighed, taking myself in hand. There was absolutely no comparison. Wesley Lloyd had been legitimately married when he took up with Hazel Marie, but I'd been free as a bird when I went to Sam's bed. Wesley Lloyd had been an adulterer, while I was merely a fornicator. And there was still a chance that I wasn't even that. Besides, there was a world of difference between the two, wasn't there?

I plumped up my pillow and leaned back, trying to get comfortable. Then, being the fair-minded woman I am, I confirmed to myself that there certainly was a difference. In adultery, there was always a third, sometimes a fourth, person who is betrayed and hurt. In fornication . . . Well, who did it hurt, really, when all was said and done?

It hadn't hurt me, and Sam's only problem was wanting more of it. Still, it was a sin according to Paul and Pastor Ledbetter, although the Ten Commandments were notably silent on the matter.

I turned off the light, deciding that, since I was not theologically trained, my interpretation of the difference was as good as the next person's.

"Julia?" Sam tapped lightly on my closed door, just as I was about to drift off. "May I come in for a minute?"

I switched on the bedside lamp and looked at the clock. It was close to midnight, and he was just getting in after viewing some questionable video provided by Mr. Pickens.

"What for?" I answered, pulling up the covers.

I heard a muted laugh; then he said, "Why, for whatever you'll let me."

"Go to bed, Sam. It's late, and I'm in no mood to wrangle with you tonight."

"I don't have wrangling on my mind. I just want to say good night."

"Well, come on in before you wake the whole house." I moved the pillows and sat up in bed, smoothing my gown and the covers in order to be presentable.

Sam pushed open the door and walked over to the bed. He sat beside me and took my hand. "How was the rehearsal?"

"Dismal, Sam, that's the only way to describe it. You wouldn't believe what they have to work with."

"I expect Hazel Marie'll whip them into shape."

"I don't know if she will or not. Sam," I said, putting my other hand on top of his while avoiding his eyes, "Etta Mae Wiggins is helping her. I wasn't too happy about having her around, but after tonight . . . Anyway, I just want to ask you — well, this is hard to say because you know I'm not a suspicious woman."

"Just jump right in, Julia. What's bothering you?"

"You are. And our situation. And Etta Mae Wiggins. Put all those together, and there's plenty to bother me."

His eyebrows went up and his mouth went down. "You're worried about me and . . . ? I think I feel complimented." At my frown, he went on, "But maybe not."

"You shouldn't, because, in spite of what Hazel Marie says, that woman will go after anything in pants."

"What does Hazel Marie say?" He reached up and smoothed my hair.

I turned my head. "She says, and I guess I have to trust her on this, that Miss Wiggins has a high moral character and would never look at a married man."

"So what's the problem? I'm a married man."

"*That's* the problem. We don't know if you are or not."

"You may not know it, but I do. I'm as married as a man can get. You don't need to worry about me, Julia."

"Well, but what if she finds out that we're temporarily separated? There's nothing to stop her then."

He leaned down and put his face next to mine. "Don't you trust me, Julia?"

"About as far as I can throw you," I said, unable to resist teasing him, since he was getting awfully close and my chaste resolve was ebbing away.

He laughed against my neck. "Just tell me one thing. Why would I want anybody else when I have you?"

I slid away from him. "Now you're being ridiculous. If some young, sexified thing threw herself at you, you wouldn't give one thought to me. I'm not blind, Sam, and I can see the difference."

"I can, too. And I've made my choice." He sat up and looked directly at me. "You don't need to worry about me, Julia, whether we're married or not. And you know that I believe we are, and it wouldn't hurt either of us to live like we are or just go on and ask Ledbetter to remarry us."

"I can't face him, Sam. You know how he gets. Let's wait and see if it works out." Then, clasping his hand tightly, I asked, "You haven't heard from anybody? No word at all?"

He lifted my hand and kissed it. "Not yet. But there're lots of people working on it, since we're not the only ones in this boat. But, Julia, if we find out that the first one didn't take, you will marry me again, won't you?"

"I'll have to think about it." I said it lightly, drawing a smile from him. Deep inside, though, I couldn't help but wonder if the continuing silence from Tennessee was another ominous sign that I'd taken a wrong turn somewhere.

But with his comforting presence beside me, I felt my resolve begin to slip another notch. I took my hand away from him before I fell off the high principled stand I'd taken. "It's time for you to be in bed. Upstairs."

Chapter 16

The telephone rang as I sat at the breakfast table with Sam and Little Lloyd the next morning. Lillian started toward the kitchen phone, but turned back when she heard Hazel Marie call down the stairs that she was getting it.

"Not long before school'll be out," Sam said to Little Lloyd. "What're you going to do with all that time?"

"First thing I'm going to do is help Mama, if she'll let me." The boy smiled, a dreamy, half-asleep expression on his face. "That Miss Easley sure is pretty."

Yes, indeed, I thought. He'd stayed up too late, showing entirely too much interest in those young women.

Lillian came to the table with the coffeepot and began to refill our cups. I thanked her with a smile, but she wouldn't meet my eyes. Her face looked closed off and tight, filled with troubled thoughts.

I watched her, wondering what the matter was, but Sam distracted me. He reached for the hand in my lap, enclosing it in his warm one, a welcome habit of his, especially since our cessation of otherwise physical contact. But, I declare, it was difficult to butter a biscuit with one hand.

He turned to Little Lloyd. "I'm feeling a great need to catch a few fish. If you're not too busy with beauty pageants, I could use a little help."

Little Lloyd smiled wider. He nodded his head up and down. "That'd be good. Except I don't know how."

"We'll take care of that. The ladies of the house have their hands full, so we men have to find something to keep us busy." Then with a final squeeze of my hand, he stood up. "If you've finished, I'll drive you to school. Julia, I'll be at my house, making some phone calls, if you need me. Maybe I'll have some news for you later today."

He leaned down and kissed me, part of his homecoming and leave-taking routine that I was still trying to accustom myself to. "I'll see you at lunch," he said. "Lloyd, give me a minute. I need some papers from upstairs."

When Sam left the room, I checked Little Lloyd's plate to assure myself that he'd had an adequate breakfast.

"Have a good day, sweetheart," I said, as he checked his book bag. For some reason, terms of endearment to those I cared for seemed to come more easily to my tongue these days. They came naturally and easily from Sam, but I was always surprised when one slid out of my mouth.

"Miss Julia?" Little Lloyd zipped up his book bag, then cut his eyes toward me. "Can I ask you something?"

"May I," I corrected him. Then, "Of course you may. What is it?"

"I thought married people lived together, but you and Mr. Sam don't."

"Why, we certainly do," I said, distressed that the child had noticed our peculiar living arrangements. Of course, given his background with a father who made only weekly visits and a mother who had an on-again, off-again relationship with Mr. Pickens, the child didn't know what a normal family was. You'd think one more unusual pair wouldn't disturb him. But here he was, bringing it up before I'd formulated a good explanation. "Sam lives right here in our house."

"I kinda meant in the same room together," he mumbled, as he made some unnecessary adjustments to his book bag.

Lillian glared at me across the kitchen counter, her look plainly saying, "Le's see how you get outta this."

179

"Well," I started, fumbling for a reply, "sometimes adjustments have to be made. And this is only temporary while" — truck doors slammed outside and the heavy footsteps of the Pruitts stomped onto the side stoop — "while we have work done on the house."

"Oh. Okay." Little Lloyd turned to greet Luther and Willie Pruitt, his concern about where people laid their heads seemingly put aside, at least for a while. But his question brought me up short. Something had to be done, and the sooner Sam got it done, the better.

In the ensuing confusion of getting the Pruitts through the kitchen and Sam and Little Lloyd on their way, Hazel Marie burst through the swinging door.

"Miss Julia, we have a problem. Morning, Lillian. How are you?" Hazel Marie took a seat at the table and propped her elbows on each side of her plate.

"That was Etta Mae on the phone," she said. "She said one of the girls just called her, wanting to know what kind of bathing suits they should wear. What do you think?"

"Well, my goodness, a bathing suit is a bathing suit. How many different kinds could there be?"

"Dozens. There're maillots, for instance, which we've eliminated since they don't flatter the figure. But the basic question is one-piece or two."

"One," I said.

"Wel-l-l, the problem with them is they're kind of hard to find. The in look is two-piece, and the major pageants allow them now. So, Etta Mae and I think we should, too."

"You mean, bikinis?" I asked, ready to do battle.

"No, no. Not bikinis, and certainly not thongs —"

"I should say not! That's not even a bathing suit. All it is is nasty."

"Well, we're thinking two-piece suits with adequate coverage, but even those will be cut fairly high on the legs. High-rise cut, I think it's called. But listen, Miss Julia." Hazel Marie reached across and laid a reassuring hand on my arm. "That's about the only kind the stores carry now. We have to keep up with the times, you know."

The times were hardly worth keeping up with, in my opinion. But since I wanted to hold the line somewhere, I said, "All right, but no navels."

Hazel Marie laughed. "You might as well

prepare yourself. Navels are in, too. Or rather, out, so you'll see plenty of them.

"Anyway," she went on, "Etta Mae's going to come by on her way to work and drop off some catalogs. I have so many things to do today that I'd like to leave them with you. If you have time, would you look through them and mark what you like?"

"What kind of catalogs, Hazel Marie? Lord knows, they're stacked up all over the house now. We certainly don't need any more."

"Oh, these are different. They're catalogs that show various kinds of trophies and things. We'll need some for the winners of the different contests, and something outstanding for the grand winner. And a tiara, too."

She looked off in space for a minute, thinking. "Since there're only six contestants, maybe we ought to give each one a trophy of some kind. A small one, you know."

"Why, Hazel Marie, that would take away from the overall winner. And what are you going to do? Rig the judging so that each girl wins in some category?"

"Oh, I wouldn't do that. I'm just thinking a small trophy engraved with, like,

Miss Vice Squad or Miss First Watch. It would be like a keepsake or a memento of their big night."

"Well, I'm glad it's not my decision to make," I said, laying my napkin beside the plate. "But it seems to me that the funds you raise ought to go to the purpose they're raised for."

"They will. Every penny of it." Hazel Marie smiled and ducked her head. "I'm sorta backing the pageant a little."

That didn't surprise me at all. When Hazel Marie threw herself into something, she went all the way.

I was sitting in one of the easy chairs by the window of my room, formerly Hazel Marie's room, leafing through the catalogs that Miss Wiggins had dropped off. I'd never seen such offerings before. There were pictures of everything from trophies to medals to ribbons to sashes to crowns. And they came in every material and for every purpose known to man. You could order athletic trophies, homemaker trophies, Worker of the Week trophies, Salesman of the Year trophies, medals for The Greatest Mom, and sashes for the Miss, Mrs., or Ms. Whatever-in-the world-you-wanted.

I took a pencil and marked a few of the less ornate trophies for Hazel Marie's consideration, then looked up to see Lillian standing in the doorway.

"Miss Julia?" she said, waiting hesitantly on the threshold. "You busy?"

"Not very. What is it?"

"I got to tell you somethin'."

"Well, come on in and tell it." I put aside the catalog, and removed the stack of them from the chair that should've been Sam's, but currently wasn't.

Lillian came in, but she didn't sit. She stood in front of me, wringing her hands, an anguished expression on her face.

"What in the world is wrong with you?" I asked. "Sit down and tell me."

She sidled toward the empty chair and sat gingerly on the edge of it. "I don't know if I ought to, an' I don't know if I oughtn't to, either."

"For goodness sakes, don't be like LuAnne Conover. She's the world's worst to bring up something only to back out of telling the whole of it. Whatever it is, we can deal with it."

"I don't know if we can or we can't." Lillian looked down at her hands in her lap. " 'Cause it not s'posed to be tole. Miz Conover, she be mad at me if I tell it, an'

184

you be mad at me if I don't."

"Well," I said, sitting up straight, "if LuAnne has anything to do with it, you'd better tell me. I love her to death, Lillian — you know I do — but sometimes she doesn't have a lick of sense. What is it?"

"She make me promise not to tell, an' now I jus' worriet sick about it. I mean" — she stopped and twisted her hands again — "seein' how things not 'zactly how they oughta be 'tween you and Mr. Sam."

I popped up out of the chair and stood over her. "What's she saying about Sam and me? Has she found out what I'm trying to keep secret?"

"No'm, she don't know a thing, but she plannin' another secret, an' I don't 'spect you gonna like it."

Then she took a deep breath and plunged in. "She tell me I got to keep this secret on pain of death. That what she say, on pain of death. But I know you have my hide if she spring it on you, an' you find out I know about it an' don't tell it."

"Lillian," I said, as calmly as I could, "I appreciate your wanting to keep a secret that you've promised to keep. But if it has anything to do with me and Sam, you have a higher obligation to let me in on it."

"Yessum, I guess so. Well," she said with

a great sigh, "Miz Conover, she say look like you an' Mr. Sam not gonna do the proper thing, what she say you oughtta do after runnin' off an' marryin' 'thout tellin' nobody. So she gonna do it for you."

I narrowed my eyes. "What's she going to do?"

"She gonna th'ow a big weddin' party for you an' Mr. Sam at that country club an' ast everybody in town. An' she say it gonna be the biggest do she ever done, an' she say you better not find out about it, 'cause she want it to be a surprise."

I collapsed into the chair, my limbs spraddled out and my eyes rolling back in my head. "Oh, Lord," I moaned. "Of all the things I don't want, it's a mockery of a wedding celebration." This was just one more thing I had to deal with, and all because of one rash decision. "Lillian, what am I going to do?"

Chapter 17

Grasping the arms of the chair, I pulled my-self to my feet, so rattled I could hardly bear it. Lillian, relieved at last of her burdensome secret, leaned back in her chair and watched as I began to pace the floor.

"A surprise party!" I cried. "How in the world did LuAnne come up with that idea? She *never* entertains on such a scale. It's just two tables of bridge or dinner parties for six, and that's it. Oh, Lord," I said, flinging out my arms and pivoting like I was on a runway. "Why did she have to pick me to change her entertaining habits on?"

"She real excited about it. She say she found a way to pay you back for all you done for her."

"I'm going to do something for her, all right. I'm going to wring her neck. Lillian," I said, swinging around to face her, "we've got to put a stop to it. Can you imagine celebrating a wedding that may not've been a wedding?"

"No'm. That why I thought I better tell

you, so you not be shamed with all them people 'gratulatin' you, with you an' Mr. Sam bein' separated an' all."

"I'm glad you told me, Lillian, and don't you feel bad about it, either. I never liked surprises in the first place, and this one beats all. How did she think she could pull it off?"

"Well, that's why she tole me. Miz Conover, she say she an' Mr. Conover gonna invite you an' Mr. Sam to that country club for dinner, an' I'm s'posed to get you to dress up so you look real smart. An' all the guests gonna be there to surprise you. She plannin' dancin' an' toasts an' all like that. Like I say, she real excited about it, but she kinda mad, too."

"Mad? Why?"

" 'Cause you not doin' it yo'self. She say when people run off an' get married by theyselves, they always th'ow a big party to 'nounce it to they friends. She don't know why you bein' so lax 'bout doin' it."

"You didn't tell her, did you?"

"Oh, no'm, I don't tell her nothin'. I jus' say, 'Yessum, I do this' an' 'Yessum, I do that.' An' Miss Julia, she gonna invite me, too."

"Well, I should hope so. You're a part of any celebrating that's going to be done.

But this one is not going to be done. Why, Lillian, think of the embarrassment if we have to get married again! And I mean, *after* the reception. It doesn't bear thinking about." I began pacing again, my mind filled with images of people laughing their heads off at us. I stopped then, and whirled around. "Does Hazel Marie know about this?"

"No'm, she don't know nothin'. Miz Conover, she say she don't trust nobody but me, an' the more that knows a secret, the less likely it stay a secret."

"She should know. She's never kept a secret in her life."

"What you gonna do, now you in this mess?"

"I'll tell you what I'm *not* going to do. I'm not going to be an unmarried guest of honor at a reception to honor my wedding. Let me think, Lillian. We've got to stop this in its tracks. When is this thing supposed to be?"

"Next Sat'dy night. She say she not gonna invite you too early, 'cause you might figure it out. But everybody else gonna get they invites."

"Well, she'll just have to uninvite them. Help me think, Lillian. We've got to do something."

"You an' Mr. Sam could go outta town."

"That's good. Yes, we could go out of town. Oh. No, we couldn't, not with all that construction going on, and the Pruitts needing an eye on them all the time. And Hazel Marie wanting me to help the contestants with their verbal presentations, though I'm going to put that off on Miss Wiggins. Think of something else, Lillian."

"You could get sick, maybe."

"That's a possibility, because I almost already am. My stomach is churning at the very thought."

"Maybe Mr. Sam get sick. If he have to take to his bed, Miz Conover can't celebrate no weddin' with jus' half of you."

"That's it, Lillian!" I cried, my face lighting up. "We can put it all on Sam. That way, I can help Hazel Marie and keep an eye on the carpenters, but be unable to accept LuAnne's invitation because of Sam. Oh, what a relief!"

"How you gonna get Mr. Sam to take sick on us? I think he be glad to celebrate yo' weddin', since he pretty sure y'all already married."

"You're right. I'll have to fix it so he'll be the one who can't go."

Lillian stood up, put her hands on her hips, and glared at me. "Don't tell me you gonna make Mr. Sam sick. That's no way to do, Miss Julia, an' nothin' gonna come outta my kitchen what make him th'ow up."

"No, no, Lillian. What do you think I am? I wouldn't do that to him. No, what I'm going to do is this." And I told her how I would make it impossible for LuAnne to hold a wedding reception for what looked to've been a nonwedding. "All I have to do is get him out of town."

And for that purpose, I took myself off to Sam's house, with Lillian calling after me to wait, since he'd be home for lunch any minute. But so would Hazel Marie, and the Pruitts would be marching through the kitchen, and there was no way that lunchtime would be conducive to handling a delicate negotiation like I had in mind.

Interrupting what I hoped was Sam's pursuit of a certain renegade preacher, I rapped on the screen door, then let myself into the front hall.

"Sam?"

"Come in, Julia," he said, standing to greet me. "Come on over here and give me a kiss."

"Kissing is not on my mind. But since

it's on yours, I've come up with something that'll make it and everything else possible in the very near future."

"I'm all for it, whatever it is." Sam took my arm and led me to the leather sofa. We sat down together, he turned toward me, and I sitting precisely two feet away. I didn't want to risk inflaming him, since he stayed so close to the combustion point anyway.

"Well, Sam," I began, "I'm not happy with the way things are."

"I'm not, either." He ran his hand up and down my arm.

"I know you're not, and I appreciate your gentlemanly conduct in the face of it."

"I'm a gentleman only because you won't let me be anything else." His other arm slipped around my shoulders.

"Well," I said, looking down as the warm smell of him wafted over me. "Well, what I want to say is that I know you've got Binkie looking into it, and I know you've made a lot of phone calls, but I think we need to speed things up considerably."

"I certainly agree. And I may have something up my sleeve that'll do just that." By this time his head was next to mine, and I was only half listening.

But I managed to get said what I'd come there to say. "I think you should go to Tennessee and stay there until you get it settled."

He straightened up. "Exactly what I've been thinking."

"Now, I know Binkie's doing the best she can, but there's nothing like pursuing it in person. Just go on over there and look every official in the eye. Then you can track down that preacher and find out what we need to know. I think you ought to stay until there's absolutely no question, one way or another. Then we can do what needs to be done — or if nothing needs to be done, why, then, we can resume what we started out doing."

"I'm all for that, and the sooner I go, the sooner I'll be back. I'm thinking of leaving right away."

"Well, my goodness," I said, taken aback by his eagerness. "You don't have to be in that big of a hurry. I mean, I want you to get it done, but shouldn't you pave the way with some phone calls, and talk to Binkie again? I think you could leave any time next week, and plan to stay over the weekend at least. That would give you plenty of time."

Sam looked at me, a smile playing

around his mouth. "What are you not telling me?"

See how well he knows me? I declare, I can't put anything over on him.

I heaved a big sigh and told him. "It's LuAnne. She's planning a big reception for us at the country club next Saturday night, and they're going to toast us and wish us a happy married life. And, Sam," I said, putting my hand on his chest, "I just can't bear to let that happen, in case we have to get married again. Everybody'll think it's the funniest thing they've ever heard. The only way to stop what's supposed to be a surprise — only Lillian told me about it, thank goodness — is for one of us to be sick or gone, and it can't be me, because Hazel Marie's busy with those beauty contestants and the house is torn up with closet construction. So it has to be you, and we can't have you getting sick, and, besides, Lillian'll be watching every bite you take. So the thing to do is have you gone, and LuAnne'll have to call the whole thing off."

"Julia," Sam said, shaking his head and looking at me with those smiling blue eyes. "I'd ask you to marry me, if we weren't already married. Which I'm convinced we are. Wait, now, I know you're not sure.

But, honey, I just admire the way your mind works."

"It happens to be working overtime, right now. And don't change the subject. You have to be gone, so LuAnne can't have a party for us. And we can't let on that we know anything about it."

"She'll just reschedule for another time," Sam said, trying not to laugh. "Will I have to be gone then, too?"

"Not if you do what you're supposed to do. And when you get back, we'll know we're either already married or we'd better get that way fast. Then we can attend her party with a clear conscience. And keep in mind that there's a place for you downstairs."

"I'm halfway to Tennessee already, and I'll stay gone long enough to miss the party, if that's what you want. As it happens, I've got a little something in the works that might move faster if I'm there to push it along. In some of those phone calls you've taken me to task for, I've managed to get through to one of Sonny Sutton's people and —"

"Sonny Sutton! You actually talked to him?" I didn't know one country-western singer from another, but a star is a star.

"No, not yet. But he may want to talk to me. Seems he's not happy with his lawyer,

195

and he thinks I might be more helpful. Since we're in the same boat, so to speak."

"That's all well and good, Sam, but we don't want the kind of publicity he's been getting. You stay out of camera range, if you get anywhere near him. Besides, I don't see what he can do that you can't do better yourself."

"Well, it may not amount to anything. But with all the people he has out looking for that preacher, he has a better chance of finding him than I do." Then he stopped to think something over. "Lloyd's out of school in a couple of days, isn't he? Think he'd like to go with me?"

"I'm sure he would. And with his mother so busy, it'd be a real treat for him." Then I stopped, wondering if the idea was all that wonderful. "But, Sam, you'll have to be careful and not let him know what you're up to. I don't want to confuse the child about married life any more than he already is. Would you believe he asked me why we're not sleeping in the same room?"

Sam smiled. "What'd you tell him?"

"I didn't tell him anything. We were interrupted by the Pruitts coming in to work. So, see, the sooner this matter's resolved, the fewer questions we'll have to answer."

Chapter 18

It took all the inner strength I could muster to walk into church Sunday morning, knowing what I now knew. The four of us took our places in our regular pew. Hazel Marie and Little Lloyd slid in first, and I followed with Sam behind me. He was unaccustomed to sitting on our side of the center aisle, but he was proving pleasingly adaptable to the changes I was bringing to his life.

In those few weeks between our return from the wedding and before I learned of its doubtful legitimacy, I had taken great satisfaction in proceeding down the aisle on Sam's arm — man and wife, for all to see. So, on this Sunday, there was nothing to do but keep up the pretense in order to keep down the scandal. But I could pretend with the best of them, so I held my head high and smiled graciously at the two or three widow ladies who would've given their eyeteeth to be in my place.

Oh, but if they only knew.

I settled back in the pew, content to be close to Sam without having to worry

197

about any untoward activity from him. As amorous as he was proving to be, even he wouldn't go beyond the bounds of decency in the sanctuary.

As I glanced through the bulletin to see Pastor Ledbetter's sermon topic, Hazel Marie reached across Little Lloyd to get my attention.

"LuAnne's waving at you," she whispered.

I looked across the aisle where LuAnne and Leonard Conover were sitting close to the front. She was indeed waving, her fingers wiggling over her shoulder and a gleeful expression on her face. She was mouthing something I couldn't make out, and if I hadn't known what she had up her sleeve, I'd have figured right then and there that she was about to rope me into something. I smiled at her, then studiously avoided her eyes, putting my mind firmly on the business at hand, which was the worship service. LuAnne was customarily sedate and composed in church. She took the service seriously, and I'd never known her to offer a word of criticism toward the pastor or his sermons. Something I couldn't say for myself, but then, I take pride in my ability to think. And Pastor Ledbetter knew it well. He knew I'd take him to task if he strayed into politics, like the time he dared tell us that he'd had word from the Lord on who we were to vote for. And the time he preached on certain domestic matters, when he told us that the Lord didn't want women in the workforce. What did the pastor think washing and ironing and cooking and cleaning and the myriad other housewifery duties constituted, if not work?

But would LuAnne openly disagree with him? No, she would not. Mainly because whatever he said went in one ear and out the other, never lingering long enough to give her any distress.

I glanced again at the bulletin and nearly passed out. The sermon text was from the Gospel of John, and the sermon topic was "A Wedding Celebration." The pastor prided himself on giving sermons that were relevant to current events without straying from the teachings of Scripture. And, indeed, he had an uncanny and often far-stretched ability to make Scripture fit whatever he had on his mind — which, this morning, seemed to be awfully close to what was on LuAnne's mind, and on mine.

I poked Sam and pointed to the printed topic, but he just nodded and smiled.

I struggled to my feet as the congregation rose when the choir started down the aisle, singing the processional. We joined our hesitant voices with their loud and tuneful ones. I normally enjoyed holding a hymnal with Sam while his warm baritone drowned out my quavering soprano, but that morning I could hardly mouth the words.

Trying to put the best face possible on what I was in for, I draped my arm across Little Lloyd's shoulders. For the moment at least, I had the two most important men in my life on either side. It crossed my mind that if Mr. Pickens would only soften his hard heart enough to darken the door of the church and take his place beside Hazel Marie, I'd have all my chickens under my wing. And while that unlikely occurrence ran through my mind, I dared to fantasize that Pastor Ledbetter would accept a call to another church. When you're dreaming of an ideal world, you might as well include everything.

After the usual presermon activities, Pastor Ledbetter assumed his position behind the podium. He made a remarkably authoritarian figure in his black robe with velvet inserts. A large man, anyway, with a voice amplified by a lapel microphone, he was a commanding presence in the pulpit.

To open his sermon, he read several

verses concerning a certain wedding that took place in a town called Cana. I pulled a Bible from the rack on the back of the pew in front of us, and followed along as he read. We Presbyterians believe in making sure that we're getting a correct reading. Baptists do the same, only worse.

Then, with all the power vested in him, the pastor began his verse-by-verse explication.

"It is worth our notice," he said, "that the Lord's earthly ministry began at a wedding. It was at this wedding — we don't know whose wedding it was, and we don't know in whose house it was performed — all we know is that it was in Cana — but it was there that he performed his first miracle — turning water into wine. Now, notice that it was a happy occasion, a joyful occasion, one that had brought guests from far and wide to join in the celebration. Jesus was there, and his mother and his disciples, and apparently many, many more. There were so many that the host ran out of wine before the festivities were over. And that was a shameful occurrence in that day and age — it indicated a lack of foresight and a lack of planning, and it was a lapse in hospitality, so much so that it would bring shame to the host. So the

Lord's mother appealed to him to save the day. And the Lord looked around and saw six stone water pots, each holding two or three firkins apiece, and he said, 'Fill the water pots with water.' And lo and behold, when the host tasted it, he said it was good — that is, the best — wine."

Firkin, I thought. *What is that?* Glancing in the margin of the text, I found the answer: *firkin, about nine gallons.* I blocked out the pastor's drone, and made a few calculations. Each water jug held about three firkins, which translated into about twenty-seven gallons. So, six water jugs, holding twenty-seven gallons each, meant that the guests had one hundred and sixty-two gallons of wine, on top of what they'd already put away. No wonder they had a celebration.

The pastor paused, as he always did when he got to a subject he found hard to explain. "Of course," he went on, "it was *new* wine, unfermented, so this was not a drunken celebration. But it *was* a celebration, and we should ask ourselves why the Lord would choose what some might see as a private and personal event at which to begin his public ministry. These few verses, recorded only by John, reveal to us the Lord's stamp of approval on the marriage ceremony itself, and on the public celebration thereof. A marriage is not supposed to be undertaken in the dark, hidden away from family and friends and neighbors. It is to be performed in the light of day — that is, with the approval and goodwill of the community, as illustrated by this joyful celebration in Cana."

I sat stiff as a board next to Sam, listening intently as the pastor raked us over the coals for eloping over the mountains. Then he began cutting closer to the bone.

"So God blesses and honors the public union of a man and a woman. We have the proof right here." He held up his Bible. "In these verses, God shows us that we are not to cohabitate, willy-nilly, with first one, then the other, with nobody knowing who belongs to whom. We are to pledge ourselves publicly to one partner until death do us part, and we are to make that pledge openly and publicly so that the whole world knows who we are and what we are doing. That's why we celebrate weddings — they are public acclamations of private commitments."

He went on and on in this vein, but his message came down to one thing: Neither he nor God liked fornicators and adulterers, who worked their wiles under the cover of darkness, and if we knew what was good for us, we'd get married in plain view and stay that way.

Well, of course, that's what I was trying to do. But over and over, one thing ran through my mind: What did he know, and when, how, and from whom did he learn it?

Sam took my hand and slid a little closer, trying to soothe my agitated nerves and keep me calm. He knew what I was feeling, and how the pastor could get to me, especially when he couched directly aimed criticism in sermonic terms.

"What God is telling us," the pastor rolled on, "is that he honors with his very presence the union of man and woman when that union is sanctified according to his precepts and acknowledged by friends and neighbors. But those who would disdain what he has given for our joy and benefit, when they discount and ignore and ridicule his precepts, and claim they no longer apply in this day and age . . ." He paused for an extended moment of silence. "Those, he will surely judge."

He didn't have to tell me that. I already knew it. Why else had I banished Sam from my bed? I certainly did not want to have to defend myself before the Judgment Seat.

He'd reached a good stopping point, and I waited for him to give the signal to the organist for the closing hymn. Instead, he leaned away from the pulpit, swept his gaze across the congregation, and let us know that he had something further on his mind.

"Let us now," he said in a lighter tone, "officially welcome into the bosom of our church family Mr. and Mrs. Sam Murdoch." Then, to make known that he still had something against us, he said, "We've not had the pleasure of publicly acknowledging your recent union, so let us rectify that now. Sam, Miss Julia, will you stand so we all can share your joy. My friends, let us celebrate the blessed, sanctified, and honorable marriage of two of our most beloved members."

There was nothing to do but to stand in front of them all, while they smiled and clapped for what he had already said was all but an unblessed, unsanctified, and dishonorable union. I was trembling by the time we sat down, and kept on trembling while the pastor moved on through the rest of the service.

"Sam," I whispered as the collection plates were passed, "that was a repeat sermon. I thought it sounded familiar, and what he did was go through his files and come up with something he'd already preached on. And, if I'm not mistaken, he aimed it at me the first time around, too."

Sam leaned close and whispered, "He doesn't know a thing, Julia. As long as he's been here, he's bound to recycle a few sermons, and this one just happened to hit us. Don't let it bother you."

Easier said than done, as so many things are. But all I could do was carry on in my usual manner. But there was one thing I was even more determined to do, and that was to get Sam on the road so he could hold a few Tennessee feet to the fire. I wanted some answers, and I wanted them sooner than I was getting them.

As soon as the service was over, I hustled us out before Sam could get caught up in greeting people and shaking hands and asking after their families. He was a friendly and outgoing soul, but I didn't want to hang around to receive congratulations on our marriage, regardless of what Pastor Ledbetter had said about needing the approbation of the community. And I especially didn't want to risk getting a dinner invitation from LuAnne on the church steps. I wanted Sam well out of town, so I could tell her in good conscience that we had to regretfully decline. If I told her he was only *planning* to be gone, she'd insist he delay his trip, then get all upset and mad when I told her — as I would have to — that he couldn't. I was in no mood to deal with any of it.

Chapter 19

When we got to the house, Hazel Marie and I headed for the kitchen to heat up the lunch dishes that Lillian had left.

"I want everybody to listen to this," I said as Sam and Little Lloyd followed us in. "If LuAnne Conover calls this afternoon or in the morning, I am not available. Tell her anything you want, but do not call me to the phone."

"Yes, ma'am," Sam said, and saluted.

"Oh, you." I couldn't help but smile. "Wash your hands, Little Lloyd. It'll be on the table in a minute. Sam, what time are you leaving tomorrow?"

"I'll pick up Lloyd as soon as school lets out. About eleven o'clock, Hazel Marie?"

She nodded. "Yes, all he has to do is get his report card and clear out his locker. And, Lloyd," she went on, turning to him, "don't lose that report card. I want to see it as soon as you get back."

"No'm, I won't." He ran his hands under the faucet at the kitchen sink. I handed him a bar of soap, and told him to try again.

I didn't know why Hazel Marie was so eager to check his report. There were never any surprises on it. Straight A's, because he was smart as a whip. I attributed his good showing mainly to my influence and the educational atmosphere I'd created for him in my home. I'd even bought a set of encyclopedias, for I'm a strong believer in education, although I often felt that the school system could spend taxpayer money more efficiently.

"If there's time, Julia," Sam said, "I'm going up and get out of this Sunday-go-to-meeting suit. Lloyd and I have lots of work to do this afternoon."

"Don't be long," I said. "We're almost ready to eat."

After he left, a knock on the back door interrupted our lunch preparations, and Hazel Marie answered it. "Why, James, what brings you here?"

In he walked, his hands full of covered dishes. He put them on the counter, and said, "This here's fresh creamed corn right outta my garden. I jus' pulled them ears this mornin'. And I got you a pot of green beans cooked with a chunk of fatback, like Mr. Sam like. An' 'cause I was in the kitchen anyway, I made him this peach pie. He like that, too, if you put a little ice cream on it."

"My goodness, James," I said, surveying his handiwork. "This looks wonderful. But what're you doing in the kitchen on Sunday? It's your day of rest."

"Well, I seen Mr. Sam lookin' kinda peaked here lately, an' look like he fallin' off a little. He need some good cookin', an' I knowed Miss Lillian, she don't work on a Sunday."

"That's very thoughtful of you. Thank you, James. I'm sure we'll enjoy it." I knew the offerings were going to send Lillian into orbit when she learned of them. "Sam'll be down in a minute, and I know he'll be so appreciative. But sit down, James, and have lunch with us."

"No'm," he said, heading toward the door. "I got to be movin' on. Tell Mr. Sam I brung him something he like."

When he'd left, I looked at Hazel Marie. "We'd better eat it all today. I don't want any of it left over for Lillian to see."

Little Lloyd cocked his head at me as I put a plate of deviled eggs on the table, picking up on a subject I thought had been closed. "Why don't you want to talk to Mrs. Conover? Are you mad at her?"

"Oh, goodness no," I said, with a little laugh, catching Sam's eye as he came to the table in time to hear the child's question.

But of course I was, or if not exactly mad, somewhat put out because of her propensity for creating turmoil in my life. "We just have to get you and Sam packed and ready for your trip. I want to spend the time with the two of you without any interruptions, and LuAnne loves to talk on the phone. Interminably so."

Hazel Marie said, "I'm afraid we're going to have one interruption, Miss Julia. I set this up with Etta Mae before I knew Sam and Lloyd would be going off. She's coming over this afternoon so we can see where we are with the contestants. Maybe I should call and postpone it."

"No, don't do that. I'll help them pack, and your meeting will be the perfect excuse for me not answering if LuAnne calls. Everybody can say that we're having a meeting here, and it won't be a story."

Sam grinned and winked at Little Lloyd. "We think you'd better sit in on that meeting, just to be on the safe side."

Well, Lord, yes. I certainly did not want to put the boy in the position of having to outright lie. "I'll put in an off-and-on appearance, if that's all right with you, Hazel Marie."

"Sure. We could use your input," she said.

As Sam and Little Lloyd discussed what

they'd need to pack, a sudden lost feeling swept over me at the thought of them being gone, even though it was in a good cause. Little Lloyd had been beside himself ever since Sam had broached the subject of an extended trip. The only hesitation he'd expressed concerned the beauty pageant. "Will we be back in time to go? I want to see who the winner is." And Sam had reassured him by saying that, since he was a judge, there couldn't be a winner until he showed up.

I looked at the child across the table, then back to Sam beside me, wondering which one I'd miss the most. "Eat your beans, sweetheart."

"Yes, ma'am," Sam said, and winked at Little Lloyd, who got so tickled he had to cover his mouth.

Having helped Sam pack his shirts, but leaving his undergarments for him to manage, I sat with Hazel Marie in the living room, awaiting the arrival of Miss Wiggins.

"I've got Lloyd all packed," Hazel Marie said, "except for that last load of clothes in the dryer. Nothing would do, but he has to take that T-shirt Coleman gave him, and of course it needed washing. He's upstairs, packing books and games for his Game

Boy and no telling what else. Sam's awfully good to take him, but the car is going to be loaded down." She laughed at the thought. Then she frowned. "I hope they won't stay too long."

"I do, too. Not only because I'll miss them, but because I hope their return will put an end to the dilemma we're in. And you know Sam'll look after Little Lloyd. You don't need to have any worries about that."

"Oh, I don't. It's just that this will be his first long trip away from home." She got up and went to the window. "Here's Etta Mae now."

Just as Hazel Marie opened the door for Miss Wiggins, Sam came downstairs, making a most ill-timed entrance. I watched him as Miss Wiggins bounced in, all peppy and perky in tight blue jeans, boots with high heels and a sleeveless turtleneck sweater. Sam's face lit up with a welcoming smile.

"Why, Etta Mae," he said, extending his hand. "How good to see you. You're looking fine and fit."

I stiffened in my chair. He had no business noticing how she looked. I knew that Sam was a friendly man, always making whomever he met feel that they were the very ones he'd been hoping to see. He could talk to anybody and make them feel welcome and at ease. But I'll tell you, there's something to be said for a taciturn man in certain situations. Like this one.

"Mr. Sam," she cried, ignoring his hand and giving him a quick kiss on the cheek, and giving me a flash of heartburn. "You are lookin' so fine. How's that leg? It giving you any trouble?"

"Not a bit. And it was your good nursing care that put me back on my feet. How's the world treating you these days?"

"Just great," she said, stepping back. "And I know it's treating you even better. I heard about your good news, so congratulations." She cut her eyes at me. "I hope you'll both be very happy."

She didn't hope any such thing. I expect she hoped we'd be miserable, and Sam would be single again. Hazel Marie was wrong about that woman, for here she was smiling and laughing and throwing herself around in front of Sam, obviously trying to show him what he'd missed.

The sooner Sam got on the road and away from temptation, the better. And the sooner he settled our marital status, the sooner I'd feel safe from the likes of Etta Mae Wiggins.

"Thank you," I said, with a quick nod of acknowledgement. Then, "Hazel Marie, let's get to work."

Sam left us then, saying that he and Lloyd were going to the Gulf station to check the oil and gas up the car. It suited me fine for him to be out of the house.

Hazel Marie and Miss Wiggins started right in discussing the contestants and their talents and attributes, so I allowed my mind to wander. They didn't need me, and as I had nothing to offer, I took the time to think over Pastor Ledbetter's sermon, as well as a few other matters.

As much as he could get my dander up in the best of times, I had to admit that his sermon had hit me where it hurt. I didn't ordinarily put all that much stock in whatever the preacher said, especially when he began wandering far afield in order to make a point, but he'd been right this time. The ceremonies of life, such as births, marriages, funerals, and debuts, should be observed with the appropriate social rituals. And the fact that Sam and I had not toed the line, socially speaking, brought me up short, making me question the decision I'd made to marry him in the first place.

Too much had gone wrong, and was still going wrong.

215

I rubbed my face, trying to get with the beauty pageant program, as Miss Wiggins giggled at something Hazel Marie had said. But my ruminations had made me realize that I'd better begin taking note of the signs springing up everywhere, warning me that all was not well.

Chapter 20

Well, Lord, I had the most sorrowful feeling when Sam backed the car out of the driveway on his way to pick up Little Lloyd on his last day of school. The two of them would then head out for Tennessee, and who knew when they'd return. I had taken Sam aside before he left, or rather, he'd taken me aside for a private good-bye. "Hurry back, Sam," I said. "But don't leave one stone unturned. There's got to be a record somewhere. That would prove something, wouldn't it?" And Sam had hugged me close and said, "There's a record, Julia. I told you that. The problem is with the man's qualifications."

"Then find him and shake the truth out of him."

I stood with Hazel Marie and Lillian in the yard, watching until the car was out of sight.

"I don't think I can stand Lloyd being gone so long," Hazel Marie said, as tears welled up in her eyes. She blinked several times, and gave a little laugh. "I know he's old enough to be away from his mother.

But I don't think *I'm* old enough to bear it."

"He be all right, Miss Hazel Marie," Lillian said, putting an arm around her. "Come on in the house now, an' put yo' mind on that beauty contest. That baby be back 'fore you know it."

"I should've gotten him from school," Hazel Marie said, wiping her eyes. "I could've kissed him and told him good-bye again."

"You done all that 'fore he went to school. I 'spect he have enough kissin' an' huggin' to last him till he get back."

I followed them in, fighting a few tears of my own. Here I was, barely married, or maybe not at all, and I was having to endure a worse separation than the one I'd suffered by denying Sam my bed. And that child was gone, too. I declare, it's a lonesome feeling when the ones you care about go blithely off, leaving you with an empty house and a hole in your heart.

Well, of course the house wasn't empty. Hazel Marie and Lillian were there, and so were the Pruitts, whose presence no one could miss, what with all the racket they made. And soon a half dozen contestants would be over, plus Miss Wiggins. And, if I knew her, LuAnne wouldn't be far behind.

She'd called three times the previous afternoon while Miss Wiggins was there and once that morning, asking to speak to me. Both Lillian and Hazel Marie had answered the telephone, and each time they'd faithfully put her off, saying that I was unavailable or busy or out. Sam was another matter, because he was so tenderhearted that he might've felt sorry for spoiling her plans, and begun backpedaling about making the trip. He didn't ordinarily answer the phone anyway, but I'd specifically cautioned him against it as long as LuAnne was gunning for me.

Not wanting to put Hazel Marie and Lillian in the position of telling an out-and-out story, I'd jumped up every time the phone rang. Hurrying out of the room, I'd mumbled that I needed to be excused. I made so many trips that Miss Wiggins asked Hazel Marie if I needed to see a doctor.

So, we'd barely gotten back in the house after seeing our men off, when LuAnne showed up on my front porch, just as I'd expected. When I opened the door, she barreled in, steaming.

"Don't you ever return your calls?"

"I was just getting ready to," I said, as I motioned her to the sofa.

She plopped down and crossed her arms.

"I've been trying for *two days* to get you. And you're always gone or too busy or too something to pick up the phone. I declare, Julia, you're the hardest person in the world to do something for."

"Well, I'm sorry, LuAnne. It's just been a madhouse around here, what with beauty contestants in and out, and Hazel Marie handing me a dozen different things to do, and Mr. Pruitt needing praise for every nail he hammers in, and Miss Wiggins demonstrating the proper way to walk, and Little Lloyd's school getting out for the summer, and, well, a million other things. But I was just about to call you, now that I have a little quiet time to enjoy a chat."

"Yes, well, please do fit me in your busy schedule." LuAnne was not going to be appeased so easily.

"So, tell me, what did you want to talk about?" Then I jumped up, not yet ready to hear what was on her mind. "Would you like some iced tea? I'll ask Lillian to bring it in."

"No, I wouldn't like iced tea or anything else. I want you to sit down and give me one minute of your time."

I eased back onto the sofa. "All right."

She inhaled deeply, her mouth still set in a tight line. "Leonard and I want to invite you and Sam to have dinner with us at the club this Saturday night."

"How very nice, LuAnne. I'm sure we'd love it —"

She began to rise. "We'll pick you up about seven."

"— except we can't."

She fell back against the pillow. "What? But you have to. I mean, I already have our reservations and everything."

"I am so sorry, LuAnne, but Sam and Little Lloyd just left for a week or so in Tennessee. That was another reason I couldn't take your calls. Busy getting them ready to go."

"Tennessee! *Why?*"

"Well, you know that Sam's working on a legal history of Abbot County. Apparently there're some judges and attorneys he wants to interview who've retired there." I thought that was a reasonable and perfectly logical explanation, although not entirely true.

LuAnne's eyes began to smoulder as she squinched them at me. "Who ever heard of *any*body retiring to Tennessee? I have a feeling I'm missing something here."

She hefted herself to her feet and loomed over me. "And you know what I think it is? I think you're so stuck up that you don't want to be seen with me and Leonard, or any of your friends. You're so proud of yourself for finally catching Sam that you think you're too good for us."

"LuAnne!" I scrambled off the sofa and did a little looming of my own. "I'll have you know I am not stuck up! And as far as *catching* Sam, why, *he's* the one who did the chasing. And the catching. And it took him a number of years to do it, too!"

"All right, then answer me this. Why haven't you had a reception for your friends to celebrate your wedding? Even Pastor Ledbetter's noticed that failing, and you know it's the decent thing to do, after running off who knows where to get married. And, furthermore, where're the wedding announcements? They should've been in the mail as soon as you got back from that tacky honeymoon at Dollywood. And no thanks to you for that announcement in the newspaper. I happen to know that the community news editor had to call you to confirm it." She paused to get a breath, then lit into me again. "You've not done one thing, Julia, and it's either because you're too stiff-necked to care about the proprieties, which is totally *un*like you, or you're ashamed of yourself or of Sam or of something."

I drew myself up. "I am not ashamed of anything, and certainly not of Sam."

"Well, that's the way you're acting. You've completely cut yourself off from your friends, and the only time you and Sam are ever seen together is in church. And you're out of there before the last amen is sung. I'll tell you, there's something real fishy about your behavior, and if I didn't know you better, I'd think you were trying to hide something really bad."

"Why, LuAnne," I gasped, trying to laugh as I clutched the back of my Victorian chair. "What a thing to say! Have you ever, *ever* known me to go beyond the bounds of decency and proper conduct?"

LuAnne narrowed her eyes and studied me with an intensity that I could barely tolerate. I dropped my eyes. "Come to think of it," she said, "I have."

My mind was going a hundred miles an hour, trying to think of a rebuttal. "Well," I stammered, "not in matters of morality, you haven't."

"There's always a first time. And you're certainly acting like something's wrong. In fact, you haven't been married a solid month and here Sam has taken off to do *interviews?* Don't make me laugh, Julia. Newlyweds don't separate like that."

She stopped, her eyes got wider, and her mouth dropped open. "Is that it?" she whispered. "Have y'all separated already?"

"No!"

"It's all right, Julia," she said, immediately sympathetic. "You can confide in me. I won't tell anybody. Being married is a hard row to hoe, and I ought to know if anybody does."

Lord, yes, being married to Leonard Conover would be a burden to anybody. But I said, with a barely suppressed sigh of exasperation, "LuAnne, let me say this so you won't misunderstand. Sam didn't leave because of a disagreement or any other reason, except for some work he has to do. And it's perfectly all right with me for him to be away for a few days. We don't have to be constantly underfoot to have a good marriage. In fact, I think a little breathing room now and then is not at all a bad thing." I had to hold myself together while I said it, for LuAnne was right. A new husband leaving his bride so soon after getting her didn't exactly indicate a state of conjugal bliss. But I'd about had my fill of being separated in ways she knew not of, and hoped with all my heart that Sam would return with proof of our right to be one flesh again.

"That may be," she said. "But you haven't been married long enough to need any breathing room. So, call him and tell him to get back here by Saturday. I want to do something special for you, Julia. And I want the whole town to know that Leonard and I are happy that you and Sam are finally married. Everybody goes to the club on Saturday night, and they'll see you there. It's a good way to announce your new status as a couple. Even though you ought to make a formal announcement, and you know it. So get Sam back here."

I knew she was struggling to keep her plans for a formal reception secret, as she tried to talk me into accepting a dinner invitation. I sympathized with her, for I'd been in similar situations, of saying one thing while hiding another, too many times before.

"I can't, LuAnne," I said, searching as hard as I could to find a reasonable excuse. "I'm not even sure where he'll be. He's got Little Lloyd with him, and they may stop off to see the sights."

"The sights! What's more important, the sights or my party!? I mean, my dinner invitation? I tell you, Julia, this is more than I can take, even from you, who's never been known to honor anybody's wishes but your own!"

"I resent that, LuAnne. You know I do for others all the time. How could you say such a thing?"

"Easy! I just said it, and I'm leaving." She stomped to the door and flung it open. "Now I've got to go home and make ten dozen phone calls, canceling all my plans. Because, and I might as well tell you since it's all off, but everybody who is anybody has been invited. And now they have to be *un*invited. And all because of you, Julia Springer!"

As she glared at me, waiting for a response, I stood riveted to the floor. Julia Springer, she'd called me.

But she wasn't through. "You know what I think, Julia? I think you're doing exactly what you've criticized other people for doing. For all I know, you're *just living* together, because you want Sam, but you don't want him to get his hands on Wesley Lloyd's estate. You just want to have your cake and eat it, too. That's what *I* think!"

The windows rattled when she slammed the door.

I couldn't move, just stood there listening to her stomp off the porch. Before I could get my breath good, though, she retraced her steps and flung the door open again. She walked right up to me.

"Tell me one thing, Julia, and I'll leave you alone. Just *where* did you and Sam get married?"

"We, uh, well, we eloped."

"I *know* that, but where did you elope *to?*"

I tried, but I couldn't get a word out of my mouth. And she bored in like a prosecutor. "You had your honeymoon at Dollywood, didn't you? You didn't make a secret of that, because Hazel Marie and Lillian and everybody went, too. So, is that where you got married? Is it? And did you get married where Sonny Sutton did? Because if you did, I don't see either you or Sam moving into a hotel room, which is what Sonny had the moral fiber to do. And I guess that goes to show, doesn't it?"

She turned on her heel and flew out the door again, slamming it so hard I hoped the hinges would hold. I was so stunned at her lucky guess that I stood trembling in the wake of her passage.

LuAnne didn't know, I reminded myself. She was only reaching for anything to get back at me for spoiling her party plans. Even though I'd never been a Methodist, I took her stab in the dark as one more sign that I'd started on a backslide somewhere.

Chapter 21

Another loud crash from upstairs shook me out of my shocked state, as the Pruitts, uncle and nephew, wreaked closet-building havoc. I had half a mind to go up there and give them their walking papers, but once a crew of carpenters starts a job in your house you're pretty much stuck with them until they're through. And the job always takes longer and is more complicated than they let on before they start.

I gathered myself and sighed in resignation, acknowledging with a sinking heart that I had to put up with them for the duration, as well as with the possibility that LuAnne would share her suspicions on the state of my marriage with everybody she met. All I could hope for was that people would laugh her off. With my reputation, surely no one would believe her, since LuAnne was known for exaggerating everything she passed on. Most people didn't give her stories the time of day.

Of course that didn't prevent them from being passed on to somebody else.

"Lillian," I said, heading for the one person I always turned to in time of trouble. I pushed through the swinging door into the kitchen, just so tired of putting up a good front, only to have it so easily penetrated by LuAnne's wild speculations. "Lillian, I think it's all falling apart."

"Yessum, it sound like it. Them mens be comin' through the ceiling, next thing you know."

"That's not it." I fell into a chair at the kitchen table and covered my face with my hands.

Lillian immediately walked over and stared down at me. "What's the matter with you?"

"I'm sick, Lillian. Just sick. I try my best to do the right thing, and whichever way I turn, it turns out to be wrong."

"What you talkin' 'bout? You need a dose of something? Or you jus' missin' Mr. Sam an' Little Lloyd?"

I nodded my head, then shook it. "No, I mean, yes. Of course I am. But that's not the main thing. It's LuAnne Conover." I uncovered my face and looked up at her. "She *guessed*, Lillian! She guessed we're not married, just like Sonny Sutton's not, and she knows Sam is living here!"

"Oh, Jesus!" Lillian's hands went up in the air; then she leaned over the table. "I don't know no Sonny Sutton. Who you talkin' about?"

"He's a country singer or something. And he didn't get married the same way we didn't, and it's in all the papers and magazines. And LuAnne put two and two together."

"Well, I 'spect you didn't 'firm it up for her."

"Didn't what? Oh, no, I didn't confirm it. I was too shocked to say anything. And she didn't give me a chance. She flung it at me, said, from the way I'm acting, she thinks we're not married. Then she left. Slammed the door, too."

"She don't know nothin', Miss Julia. She jus' tryin' to get yo' goat for upsettin' her party plans, jus' th'owin' out anything she think of."

"I know, but she was so mad. There's no telling what she'll do, who she'll tell it to, and you know what gossip is like. She may say, 'I *think*,' but the next person'll tell it like it's the gospel truth."

"Maybe when Mr. Sam call, you tell him to come on back home. That put a stop to it."

"I *can't*, Lillian," I wailed. "Not until he

finds out for sure. If he comes straight back, why, we'll still be up in the air, and we'll have to go to that reception and have everybody congratulate us on something that may not even *be*."

"Yessum, you pretty much up against it, any which way you do. But Miz Conover, she won't go talkin' 'bout something she jus' *think*. When she get through callin' all them guests, sayin' they won't be no party, she be over her mad, an' she be over here 'pologizin' to you."

Hazel Marie came breezing through the swinging door, heading for the refrigerator. "Hey, everybody. Who's apologizing to who, and for what?" She stuck her head in the refrigerator and looked around. "Lillian, can I help fix lunch? I'm about to starve."

"You might as well come over here and listen to this," I told her. "Lunch is going to be delayed."

She straightened up and closed the refrigerator door. As she slid into a chair at the table, she gave me a searching look. "You look like you've lost your best friend."

So I went through it all again, and she was properly concerned about the threat that LuAnne posed to my carefully constructed marital arrangement and to my peace of mind.

"And, Hazel Marie," I said, "she is so taken with that singing sensation, that it didn't take her any time to jump from his predicament to ours."

Hazel Marie bit her lip, then put her hand on my arm. "You've just got to be above it all, if she does talk about it. Besides, not even LuAnne would spread such a thing with no proof whatsoever."

"But you know," I said, "when she calls people to cancel the party, she's going to say how upset she is, and go into a lot of detail about how I've spoiled everything. She'll never admit that it's her fault for not making sure the guests of honor could be there. She's brought it all on herself, but a lot of good that does me."

"Everybody loves LuAnne," Hazel Marie said, "but everybody knows how she is, too. They're not going to pay any attention to what she says."

"Well, but," I said, "it's a fact that I haven't formally announced our marriage, and I haven't had a reception, and Sam and I've kept pretty much to ourselves. And now that Sam's gone off, that doesn't look good, either. She even jumped to the conclusion that we'd separated, of all things. When people think of everything I've done, or *not* done, it'll just add fuel to the fire."

"Law," Lillian said, "it do look bad, don't it?"

"You need to eat something," Hazel Marie said, recommending Lillian's cure for every ailment. "Let's have lunch, and you'll feel better. And Etta Mae and the contestants're coming over to talk about the talent category. I'm going to keep you so busy, you won't have time to think about anything else."

Hazel Marie was wrong. I had plenty of time to think about LuAnne's tendency to tell everything she knew and a lot of what she didn't. Yet the contestants did provide some distraction, for I was amazed at the confidence they displayed about their individual talents. Not a one exhibited any trepidation about being in the spotlight before an audience of hundreds, to say nothing of three judges.

"Let's go around the room," Hazel Marie said, as the girls took their places in my living room. "I want each of you to say what your talent is, and be specific. Don't just say you're going to sing. I need to know what you'll be singing and what kind of backup you'll need. Melanie, you go first."

Miss First Watch, Little Lloyd's early favorite, leaned forward eagerly. "Well, I've taken dance for twelve years, so I'm going to do an original interpretation of Johnny Cash's 'Ring of Fire.' I'll be using scarves and silver rings and things like that." She sat back and smiled confidently. "Oh, and I'll have my own CD, so all I'll need is a way to play it."

"Uh, okay," Hazel Marie said, but she didn't seem too impressed with Miss Easley's talent. "That's good. Shandra, what's your talent?"

YoShandra Washington said, "Baton twirling. I was the head majorette with the school band, and I've kept in practice. I've not decided on my music, but I'll bring my own CD, too. Maybe 'When the Saints Go Marching In,' or something like that."

Etta Mae Wiggins spoke up like she knew what was involved with baton twirling. "If she's going to use fire, Hazel Marie, we need to check with the fire marshal. We'll be in an auditorium, not on a football field."

"Oh, I'm going to use fire," Miss Washington said. "And there won't be a problem. I've done it before."

"Are you sure?" Hazel Marie was frowning even more.

"Sure, I'm sure. It might be dangerous for some people, but I know how to handle it."

Miss Easley spoke up again. "I may use fire, too, on my rings. All I need is a little more practice, and there won't be any danger."

You see what I mean by self-confidence? These girls had more than their share of it. If it'd been up to me, I'd have struck off baton twirling and ring dancing to begin with. I'd never looked on either as a talent. An ability, maybe, but not an inborn talent. But nobody was asking me, so I kept quiet.

"Ashley?" Hazel Marie looked over at the one whose stringy hair covered her face. "What's your talent, hon?"

"The guitar, I guess," she said, then ducked her head, letting her hair fall around her face. The girl was so shy, it was painful to watch her. "I guess I'll need a microphone."

"Oh, we'll have a microphone," Hazel Marie said, "so don't worry about that. Will you sing, too?"

She shook her head. "I don't think so."

"Okay, great." Hazel Marie made a note,

then looked up. "Bethany, what about you?"

"I'm going to play the piano, so I'll need one on the stage, and of course a microphone next to it. My music teacher is helping me decide what piece to play, but it'll be something by Yanni. You know, a classical piece."

"Good, we're getting a good range of talent here." Hazel Marie turned to Miss Peavey. "Heather?"

Lieutenant Peavey's daughter sat with her elbows on her knees and her chin in her hands. "I guess I'll be singing. But I'd sure like my dad to do a duet with me. We're real good together."

Hazel Marie looked at Etta Mae. "We can't do that, can we?"

Miss Wiggins shook her head. "Sorry, but this has to be individual talent. Can you do a solo?"

Miss Peavey shrugged. "Sure. I'll probably do a Faith Hill number, or a Shania Twain. Something a little bit on the country side." Then she laughed. "Anyway, if we let my dad sing, he'd win the whole contest."

Well, hardly, but he'd certainly win the talent competition. Lieutenant Peavey had a beautifully clear tenor voice, and had proved it at Binkie and Coleman's wedding. If his daughter had anything close to his talent, she'd do all right.

Hazel Marie consulted her notes. "Tasha, what's your talent?"

"Well," she said with cool assurance, "I've had a hard time deciding. I could do a dance or a gymnastics routine or model some of my own fashion designs, but I'm going to do something that'll show two of my talents at the same time. I write poetry and I'm a good public speaker. So I'm going to do a recitation of a poem I've written. You see," she went on, "this is an opportunity for me to witness for Jesus, and that's what my poem is about. It's called 'The Wreck on Interstate 85,' and it's about what can happen on prom night. I'll do it with a lot of emotion and graceful hand gestures, and the music I'll have in the background will make it heartrending."

Both Hazel Marie and Etta Mae were frowning by this time, but it was Etta Mae who said, "You sure you want to do that for a beauty pageant?"

Miss McKenzie drew herself up. "Why, I certainly am. We're supposed to witness wherever and whenever we can. But I guess if you haven't been saved, you wouldn't understand that."

That comment didn't go over so well with the other girls, and certainly not with Miss Wiggins.

"We're trying to help you here, Tasha," Miss Wiggins said as calmly as she could manage, but I noticed two bright spots of color in her cheeks. "For your own sake, I'd suggest you show another of your many talents. The judges may not like something that deliberately plays on the emotions."

Tasha McKenzie looked off at the ceiling and smiled. "We know we'll be persecuted for our beliefs."

I wanted to get up and shake the girl till her teeth rattled. But Miss Wiggins just glared at her; then she shrugged as a smile played around her mouth. "So be it then, if that's what you want."

Chapter 22

I went to my bed early that night, feeling as if I'd been run over by a steamroller. LuAnne had weighed on my mind all afternoon, and even the chatter and laughter of the contestants had not distracted me for long. All I could think about was what LuAnne might be spreading around town, to say nothing of wondering where Sam and Little Lloyd were and what they were doing. It had not been a pleasant day, and the night wasn't shaping up to be any better.

I'd missed Sam when he was upstairs in Coleman's room, but that didn't compare to the emptiness I felt with him away and gone who knew where.

When the phone rang, I snatched at it, my heart speeding up a notch. "Sam?"

"Hey, sweetheart. How're things going?"

"Awful. You won't believe what's happened now. LuAnne all but guessed, and she suspects the worst. She accused us of just living together, Sam, simply because it's not convenient for us to attend a reception in our honor."

"Now, Julia," he said, in that placating tone that infuriated me. "She can guess and suspect all she wants, but that doesn't change anything."

"Well, I tell you what's a fact. I *want* something changed. I'm tired of living like this, not knowing if I'm Julia Murdoch or Julia Springer, which, by the way, she called me. So what have you found out, and when will you be home, and where are you now?"

"We're in Pigeon Forge at the Ramada Inn. I'll go to the Wedding Ring Chapel in the morning and see those folks. Then I thought we'd spend a little time at Dollywood —"

"Dollywood! Sam, we don't have time for playing around. You have business to attend to, and you ought to stay at it."

"Julia, I have Lloyd with me, remember?" He stopped, and I realized that the child was hearing every word Sam said.

"Well, yes," I said, toning myself down. "I guess he wouldn't understand if you got that close to a theme park and didn't visit it. But, Sam, please don't fiddle around too long. We need to get this matter settled. Because, I'll tell you another thing, the longer it drags on, keeping me in a state of constant anxiety, the less I'm thinking that being married is worth all the trouble."

"Don't say that, sweetheart. You'll break my heart."

"Then get a move on." I just had absolutely no sympathy for people who say they want something, yet won't move heaven and earth to get it.

Sam's soft laughter came over the line, and he said, "I have a plan, Julia. After Lloyd goes on a few rides, we'll head on to Nashville. I've finally made contact with Sonny Sutton's manager, and —"

"Sam, you don't have time to be chasing after singing stars. What are you doing?"

"Hold on, Julia. Sonny wants to talk to as many of us who had dealings with Kincaid as he can. Strength in numbers, I guess. Anyway, he has more resources than we have, at least here in Tennessee. I have an appointment with him, so I'll see what he's found out, and what he plans to do. From the way his manager talked, Sonny's mad as thunder and ready to take some kind of action."

"You mean, like a class-action lawsuit?"

"Well," Sam laughed, "if we could find somebody to sue, maybe so. But if I can't settle this business with Sonny's help, right there in the state capital, I'm coming home. Start thinking about where and how you want to get married again."

My spirits sank, for this was the first time that Sam had expressed any doubt about the legitimacy of our original wedding. Lord, we'd have to redo it in secret, for there was no way in the world I was going to make public the fact that carnal knowledge had already been had.

"I just want you home, and all this over. Two more days, and maybe . . . oh, but you can't come home then. You have to stay away through Saturday, or LuAnne will have my head."

He laughed again. "We'll find something to do until you let us come home. Now, you want to speak to Lloyd?"

Of course I did, and had a nice conversation with the boy. He was excited about visiting Dollywood again, so soon after sharing in our honeymoon there.

When Sam took the phone back, I asked, "Is Little Lloyd getting enough sleep? Is he eating right?"

"We're going to get a good night's sleep, and don't worry about his meals. We had corn dogs for lunch and hamburgers for supper."

"That is no way to feed a child, or yourself. Your systems will be all torn up if you

242

keep eating that way. Find a cafeteria or something that serves vegetables. I want you both in good health when you get home."

"I'll take care of him, Julia. But I want you to stop worrying about us, and stop worrying about LuAnne, too. It's not worth getting all upset over something she might say, and probably won't. You and I know that we're married in God's sight, and that's all that matters."

"No, that's not all that matters. We may well be right in God's sight, although I have my doubts about that, but the people in this town don't have his vision."

"I know, and that's why I'm over here, miles away from you before we've celebrated our one-month anniversary. Now, Lloyd," he said, turning away from the phone, "I want you to cover your ears. I've got some sweet things to say that might embarrass you." Then he turned back to the phone and went right ahead and said them, disregarding the fact that any child will perk up as soon as he's told not to listen. But in spite of the fact that Sam had an audience on his end, I enjoyed hearing what he had to say ever so much.

We'd barely cleared the breakfast dishes,

during which we suffered through the noisy arrival of the Pruitts the second day Sam was away, when Etta Mae Wiggins showed up. I wondered when the woman worked, since she seemed to be at my house every time I turned around. But apparently, her home visits to shut-ins and the elderly could be arranged to suit her personal schedule.

Hazel Marie spread her papers and folders out on the kitchen table. "Everybody sit down," she said. "There're some things we need to figure out."

"Hazel Marie," I said, "don't you think it'd be better to work at the dining room table? You'll probably be in Lillian's way in here."

Before Hazel Marie could answer, Lillian chimed in. "You not in my way. 'Sides, I like to hear what all y'all got goin' on. That YoShandra Washington, she in my church, an' all us gonna be there to see what she win."

"Oh, she's a beautiful girl," Miss Wiggins said. "All she needs is a good showing in the talent category, and she'll be a contender."

As Hazel Marie nodded in agreement, Lillian frowned and said, "Well, I don't know 'bout no contender, but she sho' know how to strut herself in front of that marchin' band. I jus' worry how she do without no band behind her."

"She'll be fine, Lillian," Hazel Marie said, shuffling through a pile of papers. "I need to get organized. I can't find a thing."

"Let me have them," I said, reaching for a stack. "And you go on with your meeting." She had the papers in such a mess that I wasn't sure I'd ever get them straight. But it gave me something to do.

"Oh, good," Hazel Marie said, pushing more sheets to me. "Well, here's the thing, Etta Mae. I'm worried about the girls' talents. We have an original dance, which could be awful. And a baton-twirling act that could set the place on fire, if the dance doesn't. No offense, Lillian, but we don't know how good Shandra Washington is with burning batons. Then there's Ashley Knowles, with all that hair and green nail polish, who says she's going to play the guitar. What if she comes out with some sort of heavy metal something that nobody'll like?"

Miss Wiggins frowned. "From the way she looks, it's more likely to be something edgy like grunge rock. We'd better head her off, Hazel Marie, 'cause, believe me, those judges won't go for grunge."

"What?" I asked, suddenly picking up on the conversation. "I know she looks unkempt, but I wouldn't go so far as to call her grungy."

Hazel Marie and Miss Wiggins stared at me, then looked at each other. Hazel Marie sputtered, giving Miss Wiggins an opening to laugh out loud. The two of them sat there, laughing their heads off.

"Oh, Miss Julia," Hazel Marie finally managed to say, "grunge is a kind of music. You know, the kind that Smashing Pumpkins plays."

"Well," I said with some asperity, "I wouldn't want anything to do with such as that. So I hope you put a stop to it before I have to listen to it." I went back to my job of stacking pages in order, trying to ignore their amusement at my expense. "You might not believe it, but I've heard about that so-called music, where bands throw things and break things and set off fireworks and I don't know what all. So, if that girl wants to get up there on stage and throw food and smash pumpkins, I say you ought to put your foot down right now. There're children all over the world who go to bed hungry every night."

Both Hazel Marie and Miss Wiggins laughed so hard they had to put their heads on the table. I didn't let it bother me. I know what's acceptable and what's not, even if nobody else does.

Miss Wiggins finally straightened up and wiped her eyes. Then she tried to make amends for her behavior. "You're right, and we'll make sure it doesn't come to that. Actually, I don't think Ashley'll do anything too in-your-face. She's so self-conscious, she can't even look you in the eye. Besides, she'd need a band to really get into it."

"Well, I for one," I said, "could do without any of that hip-hop music, whoever plays it."

Hazel Marie grinned, then consulted her notes again. "What about Bethany? A classical piece on the piano? I don't know classical from a hole in the ground, so I won't know whether she's doing it right or not."

"Oh, you'll know," Miss Wiggins assured her. "But the one that worries me is Tasha McKenzie. An original poem? With emotion and graceful hand gestures? Talk about awful. That could take the cake."

"That one worries me, too," I said, somewhat surprised to find myself in agreement with my rival. "The one you probably don't have to worry about, though, is the Peavey girl. If she can sing anywhere near as well as her father, she'll win the talent category. Don't you think, Hazel Marie?"

"Yes, I do," Hazel Marie said. "But here's the thing. We need to have a talent run-through. I mean, let's get the girls to meet us at the auditorium, and tell them they have to do their talent just as they plan to do it on the big night. That way we can see what and how they're going to perform, and if their choices are appropriate."

Miss Wiggins nodded, but her mind was on something else. "I tell you what, Hazel Marie, I'm worried about the Knowles girl. She is just pitiful looking, if she'd ever get that hair out of her face long enough to see her. She's going to need one heavy-duty makeover."

"I know," Hazel Marie said, hesitant, as always, to speak ill of anyone. "And I've been thinking about her. It'll take a lot of work to bring her out, and I think she knows it. That's why she's so retiring and all. She knows she doesn't stack up with the other girls. I just wonder why she agreed to enter in the first place."

"I can tell you that," Miss Wiggins said. "One of her uncles or cousins or something is a deputy, and he works the third watch. I heard he twisted a lot of arms till they made her their representative. She lives with her grandmother right across from me, and there're several uncles who really look out for her. And I'll tell you something else. I, for one, wouldn't want to cross any of them."

"She seems like a nice girl," Hazel Marie said. "But she's so shy, I don't know how she'll do in front of an audience."

"Well, that's her problem, not ours." Miss Wiggins twisted her mouth, then went on, "But if she can't do it, I hope she'll drop out before we get too far along."

"Oh, I hope she won't," Hazel Marie said. "We'll keep encouraging her, and maybe she'll surprise us. But back to the rehearsal. What we have to do is be honest, regardless of whose feelings get hurt. If we think a girl needs to pick out another song to play or sing, we have to say so. I just want this to be a real pageant, with beautiful girls and outstanding talents, and not some amateur night with karaoke."

"I don't know what karaoke is, Hazel Marie," I said, "but there's no way you're going to get around amateur night. Amateurs are what you have."

Miss Wiggins grinned at my comment, which I didn't appreciate. She said, "Well, you know me, Hazel Marie. I'll say what I think, and I, for one, am about ready to take Tasha McKenzie *down*. That girl is downright spooky. And the rest of them? They better start appreciating what we're telling them, since all we want is for them to do their best."

"I'm sure that's true," I said. "But what ought to concern you is that their best may not be very good."

"Well, then," Hazel Marie said with a sigh, "maybe the other categories will take up the slack. Talent only counts twenty percent, anyway."

"Why, Hazel Marie, it'd be awful if the winner only came up to eighty percent. Seems to me, anybody who wins should make in the nineties, at least."

A heavy clomping on the back stairs interrupted our discussion, as Willie Pruitt clamored into the kitchen.

"Whoa," he said, grinning his gap-toothed smile as he pulled up short. "Sorry 'bout that. Didn't know y'all was down here."

"Good morning, Willie," I said. "You're getting close to finishing up there, aren't you?"

I might as well have been talking to the wall. Willie's eyes lit on Etta Mae Wiggins, and there they stayed. He just stood there, breathing in and out, his carpentry errand apparently flown from his mind.

Of course, Miss Wiggins noticed it, for she lifted her chest, tightly encased in a pink T-shirt, to give him a better view of her attributes. Then she went so far as to swing around in her chair so he could see her trim ankles — one even had a bracelet on it, which he certainly noticed. Cocking her curly head and giving him a sultry look, she smiled right back at him. It may have been an unconscious reaction to an appreciative pair of eyes, but that just shows what kind of person she was.

"Ma'am," Willie said, nodding to me as he edged around the kitchen counter toward the back door, "I don't think I ever seen so many good-lookin' women in one place before. Y'all about made my heart stop."

Well, he may have said "y'all," which is always plural as any Southerner knows, but he was thinking in the singular. Miss Wiggins, to be exact, and she knew it. She gave him back, stare for stare and smile for smile, confirming my belief that she'd go after anything in pants. Not that Willie Pruitt was just anything. He was, in fact, a healthy, well-made specimen with an easy way about him, notwithstanding that missing canine tooth and the fact that he was covered in sawdust, splotched with paint, and about ten years younger than she was.

"Miss Wiggins," I said, seeing my chance to further the attraction. "This is Mr. Willie Pruitt, who is as fine a carpenter as I've ever come across. He has steady work and makes a good living. I'm sure you'll enjoy getting to know him. He's here every day."

There, I thought, as Willie grinned wider, stumbled over his own feet on his way to the door, and mumbled, "Glad to meet you." If that didn't get her sights set on somebody besides Sam, I didn't know what would.

Chapter 23

After discussing the rehearsal longer than I wanted to hear about it, Hazel Marie told us about the advertising campaign she'd started.

"I'll pick up the tickets from the printer today," she said, "and drop some off at the sheriff's department and at several places downtown. Ads in the newspaper and on the radio are already running. Plus, I've got fliers and posters stuck in shop windows all over town. The girls need to pitch in and get the word out, too, so we'll have a big crowd."

"Let me take some posters," Etta Mae said. "I'm all over the county, and I can put them in stores out there. And sell some tickets, too. Some of my shut-ins and senior citizens will buy them."

"How're they going to get to a beauty pageant?" I demanded. I could picture Miss Wiggins wrangling a few dollars from elderly dodderers who didn't know the time of day, much less one contestant from another.

"Oh," Miss Wiggins said, airily, "I'll

borrow a van and take as many as can get in it."

"Well," I said, somewhat taken aback, "that would be commendable." Then I sat back and kept my mouth closed. If Miss Wiggins was willing to pick up a van full of senile and disabled people, and get them to their seats, I didn't need to criticize her.

"Now," Hazel Marie said, looking straight at me, "I've scheduled the girls to come over first thing in the morning, one at a time, so we can prepare them for their interviews with the judges and for the questions the master of ceremonies will ask. Etta Mae has to go see a patient, and I have to check on the printer's, so would you write out a few practice questions?"

"Hazel Marie," I said, about overcome with exasperation. "You know I don't know what you want. What kind of questions, anyway? Somebody has to help me."

"I'll help," Miss Wiggins said eagerly, which was just the kind I could do without.

"I will, too," Hazel Marie said. "But I'd like you to make up some general questions that they might be asked. That way, we can see how they respond, and what kind of presence they have when they're put on the spot."

"Well, give me a hint of what you want."

"Oh," Miss Wiggins said, "you can ask about their ambitions and their platforms. You might include some questions on current events, too, though when I was that age I didn't listen to the news. Don't much now, either."

"Well," I said with a sigh, "I'll try, but don't expect much."

I spent the rest of the day writing out questions for the contestants, having no idea in the world what I was doing. And not much interested in the task, either. My mind was whirling with thoughts of LuAnne out there somewhere, telling tales right and left. Who knew where and what the gossip was at this very minute while I was trying to occupy myself with thoughtful questions for young women who didn't have a thought in their heads?

Hazel Marie answered the door the next day when Miss Wiggins rang the doorbell again, and there she was with Miss First Watch, Melanie Easley. We got ourselves settled in the living room, and Hazel Marie turned the proceedings over to me.

I took a deep breath, determined to take the pageant as seriously as I could manage. "First off, Miss Easley, I hope when you meet with the judges, you'll be dressed for the occasion. I don't want to be critical, but shorts and a halter top just will not do. You should wear a suit or a dress with a jacket. Think of it as a job interview, and remember how important first impressions are."

Her eyes wide and serious, Miss Easley nodded.

"Let's move on, then," I said, reasonably satisfied with her response. "We're going to pretend that Hazel Marie, Etta Mae, and I are the judges, and you've just come in for your interview. You must have good posture, so sit up straight and don't cross your legs. You should speak to the judges in a well-modulated voice — something like, 'How do you do? I'm Melanie Easley, Miss First Watch' — then take your seat in front of them." I turned to Miss Wiggins. "I don't think it's necessary for her to shake hands, do you?"

"No, it might be awkward," Miss Wiggins said, twisting her mouth in thought. "They may be sitting behind a table."

"Then let's get started." I took my seat between Hazel Marie and Miss Wiggins, so that the three of us were facing Miss First Watch. That made her the focus of our attention, which was the idea.

"Miss Easley," I said in a severe tone, "do you think it appropriate to involve yourself in something as trivial as a beauty pageant when there are homeless and hungry people on the streets?"

Hazel Marie cut her eyes at me, and Miss Wiggins turned to stare with her mouth agape. Miss Easley's eyes were going back and forth, trying to come up with an answer. Or maybe to understand the question.

"Uh, well," Hazel Marie said, "maybe we could change that to something like, 'What suggestions do you have for helping homeless people?'"

The rewording didn't seem to be of much help to Miss Easley. "Build more houses?"

"Let's try this," I said, somewhat taken aback by the reaction to my question, as well as by the answer to it. "If you win the title, what would you do to assist the sheriff's department in its public awareness program?"

"That's a good one," Miss Wiggins said, her approbation pleasing me in spite of my natural aversion to her.

Miss Easley's face lit up. This was a question she could answer. "Well, I'd do everything I could to make the public aware of the sheriff's department."

"Like what?" Miss Wiggins said. "You need to be specific."

"Well, uh, talk about it, and, uh, have my picture taken for the newspaper. You know, wearing my crown and all. Oh, and I could wear a sheriff's department ball cap everywhere I go. Gosh, I can't think of anything else. Right offhand."

I closed my eyes so nobody could see them rolling back in my head. I sighed and gave her an easy question. "Miss Easley, what are your plans for the future?"

"You mean, after the pageant?"

I nodded, and she started in with what I soon realized was an answer she was ready for. "Well, I want to dedicate my life to helping people, but I don't know just how I'll do it yet. I'm thinking of going to chiropractic school, or maybe be a veterinarian. I kinda feel like animals need help, too."

"Let me ask one," Miss Wiggins piped up. "Melanie, if you suddenly came into a million dollars, what would you do with it?"

I sank back in my chair, more than willing to give up the questioner's place. Maybe someone else could get some decent answers.

Miss Easley straightened up, her eyes alight. "A million dollars! Let's see, the first thing I'd do is give a chunk of it to my church. For, you know, foreign missions or a new Sunday school building or something. I couldn't enjoy it if I kept it all for myself. Then I'd build my parents a new house and buy them a new car. And put aside some for my little brother's college education. Oh, and I'd set up a scholarship somewhere for needy people, and give to the United Fund and maybe pay somebody's hospital bill, especially a little kid who's real sick or needs a special operation or something. I'd just do all kinds of good works and, you know, like that."

I didn't believe a word. For one thing, the girl didn't know the short distance a million dollars would go these days, which was not anywhere near far enough for her to be a public benefactor on such a grandiose scale.

It went on like that all morning, each contestant showing up at her appointed time and giving the answers she thought we wanted to hear, when she could come up with an answer at all. During the debacle, we learned to limit our questions to those concerning ambitions and public service. And even those were often stumbled over, but current events on the national or world stage drew nothing but blank looks. In spite of that, Miss Washington declared her intent to run for the presidency some day, which hadn't stopped some others, so maybe she would. And Miss Peavey wanted to be a volleyball coach and eventually run for sheriff of Abbot County. She may have thought that would win her points in the contest, but I could've told her that Sheriff Frady did not appreciate competition of any kind.

Miss Knowles either didn't have any ambitions, or she couldn't bring herself to disclose them. All during her painful interview, I kept thinking it might be best if she did drop out.

Bethany LaVane declared her intent to go to medical school if she could get her grades up. "But if I can't," she said, "I'm thinking about learning to do facials and massages and so on. You know, things that make people feel and look better, which is kinda like being in the health care field."

Tasha McKenzie had so many ambitions she made me tired just listening to her. "I plan to use my potential in the modeling world and be an example for young women all over America. Because, see, I'm a Christian, and you don't see many of them on the cover of *Vogue*. But I like fashion, too. You know, designing and marketing. Of course, I could combine designing and modeling, and be the first designer-model. I just want to make an impact on the world." She stopped and drew a breath, for which I was thankful. But then she went on. "But the bottom line is that I want to do what the Lord wants me to do. He hasn't spoken to me yet, but my daddy says he will. All I have to do is wait and be ready for the mission field or whatever he calls me to do. And of course, I want to get married and have children. That's the highest ambition of all, but I think with all my talents I can do that along with whatever profession I take up."

Both Miss Wiggins and Hazel Marie started to wind things up, but Miss McKenzie hadn't finished. "I can write, too, as you'll see when you hear my poem. And I'm real good in science and things like that, so I might be a doctor and find a cure for cancer or something."

Hazel Marie and Miss Wiggins sat in stunned silence at the breadth of the girl's ambitions. I finally managed to mumble, "Very impressive, I'm sure," and showed her to the door.

When the last one left, the three of us

just sat for some little while.

"Let's cut out the judges' interviews," Miss Wiggins said, "and just have a few simple questions from the master of ceremonies."

Hazel Marie nodded. "Good idea."

That was a relief to me, for I didn't see a way in the world we could prepare the present contingent of contestants for a formal interview. The whole thought of them appearing cold before a trio of judges was enough to make me cringe. And who knew what kind of crazy questions Thurlow Jones would be just devilish enough to throw at them? He could have every one of the girls crying and spoiling their makeup and unwilling to go forward with the pageant. And what would Hazel Marie do then?

Miss Wiggins stood up, saying she had to be on her way. Just as we stood with her, there came an awful clanging and banging and a rushing sound of mighty waters. We all looked upward but, of course, couldn't see a thing because of the ceiling.

"Goshamighty!" Mr. Pruitt hollered. "Turn it off, Willie, turn it off!"

Lillian came flying out of the kitchen, her eyes big with fright. "They's water comin' outta the ceilin'!"

We hurried toward the stairs, just as we

heard Willie go clattering down the back stairs. "Where's the main?" he yelled.

I veered off and met him at the dining room door. "What is it, Willie? What happened?"

"Busted a pipe. A big 'un, too." He waved a wrench in the air, then turned and sprinted to the back door. "Gotta turn it off at the main."

I took one look inside the kitchen and shut the door. Water was dripping down the walls and flooding through the overhead light fixture.

"Here, Miss Julia!" Hazel Marie thrust an armful of towels at me. "It's coming down the stairs!"

I hurried toward the stairs and started sopping up the water that was flowing like a fountain. Lillian's shoes were soaked through, so she kicked them off as she stuffed towels on a stair step. Miss Wiggins was doing her part, running back and forth from the linen closet bringing towels and sheets and blankets.

"Don't let it get on the Orientals," she said, surprising me that she knew what an Oriental was.

We could hear Mr. Pruitt stomping around upstairs, yelling his head off. "Dadblame the cussed, dadblamed luck! Hurry up, Willie!

Shut it off! I'm drownin' up here!"

In the midst of our scurrying around, mopping and sponging and damming up the water, wouldn't you know but the telephone rang. Miss Wiggins ran toward the linen closet again, yelling, "Want me to get it?"

Hazel Marie, who was helping me hold back the flood, yelled back. "Take a message!"

It seemed forever before the waters subsided and Miss Wiggins turned up with an armload of towels that were no longer needed. Willie stomped back inside and slunk up the back stairs, his run to the rescue accomplished.

All of us were soaked to the skin, and in our exhaustion, we could only collapse on the floor to get our breaths. I couldn't bring myself to think of the damage the house had incurred. It was enough that we'd held back the flood.

Mr. Pruitt made a careful appearance on the landing. "Miz Murdoch? Sure am sorry 'bout that. These ole houses, well, I never knowed a water pipe to be where that one was. We busted through the wall, an' I be blessed if we didn't bust through a pipe, too. But we're insured, so don't you worry none."

What could I say? "These things happen, Mr. Pruitt, or so it seems. But you can fix everything, can't you?"

"Yes ma'am, we'll get to it." He turned to go, then thought of something else. "Oh, I don't guess you'll have water for a while. Got to get a plumber out here, an' you know how they are."

Lillian looked at me. "How'm I gonna cook supper 'thout no water?"

I put my head on my knees, done in by another thing that had gone wrong. I was about to get tired of it, wondering what I had done to bring down such trials and tribulations on my head.

But that wasn't the end of it, for Miss Wiggins said, "I hate to leave y'all with this mess, but I gotta take a prescription to a patient. Oh, Miss Julia," she called as she headed out the door, "that was Mr. Sam on the phone. He said he'd call back later."

Well, if that didn't beat all. I wasn't sure I'd ever be able to get up off the floor. While water inundated my house, Miss Wiggins was having a private conversation with Sam. And let me tell you, she had stayed on the phone longer than that little message would've taken.

Somewhere it says that God tries those whom he loves, but by this time that was little comfort. I'd had about all the trials I could stand.

Chapter 24

With no water in the house, except what was still seeping from the kitchen ceiling, we decided to go to Sam's house for dinner. I'd called James to let him know we were coming, and you would've thought I'd given him a present.

"Y'all jus' come right on over here," he said. "I'll put something on what be the best dinner you ever had. You tell Miss Lillian she don't have to lift a hand. *I'm* cookin' tonight!"

And he did give us an outstanding meal, though no better than Lillian could've done. I didn't tell him that, though, just complimented him and thanked him for saving us from eating at Hazel Marie's favorite hamburger place.

Lillian, herself, was less than gracious, sullenly letting James fill some Tupperware containers to take home for Latisha's supper. "We ought to be mopping up that water," she told me. "It gonna rot out the flo'boards."

She was not happy with the way matters

stood, and James's antics didn't help. I walked into Sam's kitchen and caught him jiving around her, chanting, "Po' Miss Lillian ain't got no kitchen. Can't do no cookin', 'thout no kitchen."

Lillian was so mad she didn't see me, and I'm not sure it would've mattered if she had. She picked up a long wooden spoon and waved it at him. "How you like tryin' to cook with yo' head rollin' down Main Street? You sorry thing you, git off from me an' stay off."

I cleared my throat, and they backed away, both looking a little shamefaced. James, though, was full of himself and couldn't stop smiling. I wished Lillian good night, assured her that we'd soon have the water back on, and sent her off, only slightly mollified.

"Lord, Hazel Marie," I said, as we entered our damp house a little while later. "I don't think I can take another catastrophe. If it's not a broken water line, it's James and Lillian at each other. I hope I can stand up under it all."

"I just hope our beds're dry, that's all I hope."

Even though Lillian had mopped the stairs and the kitchen before we'd gone to dinner, water had continued to seep down and collect in the corners. Hazel Marie and I delayed our bedtime to swab up the puddles and wipe down the walls.

"Careful on the stairs, Hazel Marie," I said, as she went up to bed. "They may be slick."

By the time I'd locked up and gotten to my room, I was almost too tired to prepare for bed. I glanced at the clock, noting that it was not as late as it felt, but wondered why Sam had not called back as he'd told Miss Wiggins he would.

I slid off my shoes and started rolling down my hose, almost tripping myself, getting to the phone when it rang.

Expecting Sam and ready to unburden this latest disaster onto him, I eagerly answered it. Instead of Sam's warm voice, though, I heard a deeper, more rhythmic one.

"Good evening, madam. Aaron Kincaid calling for Mr. Sam Murdoch, if you please."

"He isn't in at the moment. May I . . . *Who* did you say? Are you that preacher from Pigeon Forge?" I gripped the receiver, fearing that if I didn't hold it tight I'd lose him.

"Indeed, madam, I am a minister of the Gospel of our Lord, Jesus Christ, and my ministry has carried me to many places, including that of which you speak."

"Well, for goodness sakes, Mr. Kincaid. We've been looking for you." I sat down abruptly on the bed. "And not only us, but any number of other people."

"Yes, I've been made aware of that. It doesn't suit the Lord's purposes, though, for my whereabouts to become known at this time. Suffice it to say that I am no longer in Tennessee. I had the misfortune to perform a blessed ceremony for a certain Nashville star —"

"Sonny Sutton?"

"The very one. I was honored to do it for him and his beautiful bride, especially since he'd slipped off from that bunch of managers and agents and lawyers that follow him around everywhere he goes. Of course, they've gotten in their licks since then, looking into my background and checking my references and in every way delving into matters that belong only to the Lord and me."

I tried to break in and get an answer to my urgent question, but when a preacher gets on a roll, it's hard to slip a word in edgewise. He kept right on, but losing more and more of his dignified locution as he went. "But the Lord has showed me the reason for all that digging and delving they started in to do. That bunch of hangers-on of his didn't want Sonny marrying that girl. I don't know why, but they'da done anything to break 'em up, an' it just so happened that they used my Holy Ghost ministry to get 'em broke up, an' I've had to stay low ever since."

"Mr. Kincaid!" I was able to break in at last, talking quickly to get in what I needed to say. "Answer me one question. Are you or are you not qualified by the state to perform marriages?"

"Madam, I am qualified by the power vested in me by the grace of God and the baptism of the Holy Ghost, as well as by the authority of the East Tennessee Fire and Water Baptized Holiness Church, Sanctified, which unfortunately no longer exists."

"That doesn't answer my question." But I was afraid it did. "Please, Mr. Kincaid, just tell me. Does Tennessee, or *any* state, recognize the marriages you performed?"

There was silence on the line; then he said, "I have a higher authority than any state you could come up with. The Lord recognizes me, and that's all I need. I don't need the government telling me what I can and can't do."

Well, there it was. Sam and I were as unwed as we'd been before taking that road trip. "Mr. Kincaid," I managed to get out, "do you realize the position you've put us in? And not only us, but more than two dozen other couples? You may be able to flout the government, but we can't. My husband — I mean, my whoever-he-is — is an attorney, for goodness sakes, and this will ruin his reputation and his Christian testimony. To say nothing of my own. And, Mr. Kincaid, I can't imagine what my friends and neighbors would say, if the word got out that we haven't been legally married. I can't believe you could be so . . . so callous as to set up to marry people and not really do it." I was so mad by this time that I had to exert a mighty effort to get myself under control. "You've put us in a situation that is just ruinous, both spiritually and legally speaking."

I stopped to catch my breath, and waited for a response. It was a long time coming, and I began to wonder if I'd get one.

Then he said, "I can see you put a lot of stock in not getting crossways of the government. Me? As long as they don't bother me, I don't bother them. Now, Miz Murdoch, 'cause that's who you are in my view, I been reading the Abbotsville newspaper, 'cause I got kin here. I mean, there. I might've mentioned that to you folks on your weddin' night. Anyway, I got something real important to talk to Mr. Murdoch about."

"Well, he certainly wants to talk to you, too. In fact, he's in Nashville looking for you right this minute. Where are you, Mr. Kincaid? How can he get in touch with you?"

He waited so long to speak again that I was afraid he'd broken the connection. Then he said, "I been thinking. Seems like we both want something from the other, so there's no reason we can't help each other out."

"What could you possibly want from us?"

"Well, I heard from my folks that Mr. Murdoch's gonna judge a beauty contest, and it's real important to me that my niece come away with the crown. So, I tell you what, you get Mr. Murdoch to swing his vote her way, and even if Sonny or the law catches up with me, I won't let on that you and Mr. Murdoch stood before my altar. Seein' that you don't want it known."

"For goodness sakes, Mr. Kincaid, I can't do a thing about that contest. I'm not a judge. And Sam, well, Sam is absolutely incorruptible. There's no way he'd throw a contest."

"All I'm asking is for you to do your best to sway him. Use your influence on him. 'Cause, see, I'm about tired of layin' low, especially since everybody wants to interview me. I been keeping up with it, and one of them grocery store papers is offerin' five thousand dollars if I'll come forth and tell all about my weddings. They want to know who all I married, so they can track 'em down and see how they feel about doin' it over again."

"Oh, no, you don't want to do that. You'd be arrested or fined or something."

"The law won't do nothing but tell me not to do it no more. Sonny might come down a little harder, but whatever way it turns out, I got a list of all my weddings, and I guess it'll make good reading in the newspapers. Be headlines on CNN and Fox News, too."

I made a quick decision. "Who is your niece?"

"Ashley. Ashley Knowles."

Oh, my word, the worst contestant of them all, and he wanted her to win? And if I did manage to put a tiara on her head, who would believe it?

But he was running on, making his case. "She ain't never had a thing. Never been nowhere, never had a chance. All I'm asking is that she win this one thing, 'cause she's a good girl and all us Knowleses and Kincaids, we stick up for one another. Miz Murdoch, it ain't like me to hold something over somebody's head, but since you don't want nobody to know about me and my ceremonies, why, let's just say I'll scratch your back, if you scratch mine. And you can go on and get married all over again, if that be your intent, and I'll mark out the Murdoch name on my list."

It was pure and simple blackmail, that's all it was. But, then again, no money was involved, so I wasn't sure if it was so pure and simple, after all.

"Hold on, Mr. Kincaid. I'm thinking." And think I did. I knew that we could hurriedly get remarried on the sly as soon as Sam got back. That would make us legal, but it wouldn't free us from the ridicule if Mr. Kincaid made his full list public. And the public was interested, for which Sonny Sutton could be thanked. His marital mess was what had made the news, and ours and twenty-something others just made the story more interesting. But one thing I was certain of, there was no way in the world Sam would act dishonestly. And even if I could persuade him to, there were still Thurlow and Tonya to contend with.

Getting to the judges wasn't my biggest problem, though. My biggest problem would be Ashley, herself, who could barely open her mouth in my living room, much less in a crowded auditorium.

"Mr. Kincaid? I can't promise anything. But if you'll stay quiet and out of the spotlight until our problem is rectified, I'll do my level best to make Ashley a winner."

"And may the Lord bless you for this good deed you're doing."

When I got off the phone, I could only sit on the bed and stare into space. What had I gotten myself into? How in the world could Ashley be transformed into a beauty queen? The child was not beauty queen material, and so painfully shy it hurt to look at her. Maybe I should throw it all in Sam's lap and tell him to either make her the winner or he could kiss me good-bye. I could move to Florida and get away from the public mockery.

But then there was Etta Mae Wiggins, waiting in the wings for just such a happenstance.

The more I thought about this latest disaster, the more I was convinced that every sign was pointing to one conclusion — the Lord was not happy with me. And all I'd done was marry Sam, or try to, anyway.

Chapter 25

Still in my bathrobe, I straggled into the kitchen the next morning, thinking that I might turn around and go back to bed. I had not slept well, what with one plan after another for transforming Ashley Knowles thought up and discarded. I would've liked to've enlisted Tonya Allen's help, or Hazel Marie's or even Miss Wiggins's, since any one of them could perform cosmetic miracles. But I didn't dare risk it. If she got special help from one of the pageant officials, she'd be disqualified before I turned around. I didn't know what I could do on my own, being unschooled in makeups and makeovers, but I was determined to make do as best I could.

Hazel Marie, dressed in a bright blue silk dress and matching cardigan, was busy helping Lillian, but getting in her way more often than not.

Hazel Marie turned from the counter, a sugar spoon held in midair. "Are you sick?"

Lillian closed the oven door and said,

"What's the matter with you?"

I slid into a chair and brushed back my hair. "Nothing, and I don't know why everybody's so worried about my health. I'm perfectly all right."

"No, you're not." Hazel Marie came over to the table and searched my face. "You never come to breakfast in your nightclothes. You're always up and dressed before anybody else. So I know something's wrong."

"Well, I'm not sick. I just didn't sleep well, and I'm thinking of going back to bed."

"You need something on yo' stommick," Lillian said. She put a plate of eggs and bacon in front of me. "An' here's some orange juice, so you can lay off drinkin' so much of that coffee, like you us'lly do."

Hazel Marie settled herself at the table. "I guess you don't feel like going to Helen's, then."

"Why would I want to go to Helen's?"

"She's having the book club, remember?"

"Oh, Lord, I'd forgotten. And I don't even know what we were supposed to read. I declare, Hazel Marie, I'm not sure I can make it. I didn't hear from Sam last night, but he was going on to Nashville to meet with some country music star. Though what good that will do, I don't know."

"I know," she said. "Lloyd called this morning and told me. He's real excited about meeting Sonny Sutton. Which is strange, because I didn't think he liked country music."

"I thought I heard your phone ring. Did you ask him about his bowels?"

"His *bowels!*" Hazel Marie doubled over, laughing, and Lillian was just as bad.

"Hazel Marie," I said, sternly, "Sam's letting him eat all kinds of trashy food, and that could get him in a terrible bind." As far as I was concerned, irregular movements were no laughing matter.

Hazel Marie finally got hold of herself, although with no little effort. "He's all right, Miss Julia. I'm sure he's just as regular as clockwork. But I'll ask next time he calls."

"I wish you would. I have enough to worry about without adding the state of Little Lloyd's system to the mix. I want that preacher found and muzzled before he tells what he knows."

Hazel Marie frowned. "I thought you wanted him to tell what he knows."

Realizing that I'd misspoken, I quickly said, "I meant that if he had anything good to say, he wouldn't be running around all over creation."

Hazel Marie reached over for my hand. "They'll find him. Preachers aren't that good at running off and hiding. They have a calling to get up in front of a congregation and preach. He's probably holding a revival somewhere."

"Don't say that, Hazel Marie. That means he could be up in the hills where we'd never find him." Actually, I now hoped he wouldn't be found, but I didn't tell her that. I ate a bite or two of eggs and refilled my coffee cup. Then with a sigh, I said, "I better go get ready. Helen hates to start late."

"Oh, you're going? Good, but you don't have to hurry. We have plenty of time."

Lillian frowned. "People what wander 'round in they nightgown ought to get back in bed. You be sick an' not know it."

"I'm not sick, Lillian. I'm just worried and anxious, wanting this mess to be over and done with. If I don't show up at Helen's, they'll all figure LuAnne's suspicions are true, because you know she can't keep anything to herself, and they'll be waiting to see how I handle it." I got up from the table, mentally girding myself to keep my composure. "If I stay home, they'll think I have something to hide," I said, on my way out of the kitchen. "Besides, I don't intend to give them the satisfaction of talking behind my back."

As Hazel Marie drove us to Helen's house, I sat stiff and apprehensive in the passenger seat. I didn't want to go, but I knew I had to appear serene and unfrazzled, despite the fact that LuAnne was probably talking her head off, and I had to turn an ugly duckling into a talented swan, and my house was still soggy, and Sam was gone, and God was mad at me.

"LuAnne'll be there, won't she?" I turned to look at Hazel Marie.

"She always is. But there won't be many. Helen said we're just going to discuss a summer reading list. You know, before everybody gets busy with vacations and all."

"Well, you stay close, Hazel Marie, because there's no telling what tales LuAnne's been spreading." I sighed, dreading the ordeal ahead. "I'll tell you what's the truth, I am sick and tired of having to face down gossip every day of my life. You'd think people would find somebody else to talk about."

"Oh, they do," Hazel Marie said,

glancing at me with a sympathetic smile. "But you have had more than most to put up with."

"That's the Lord's truth," I murmured, holding on to the door handle as she took a curve. "And none of it is my fault. It looks like, when it comes to husbands, I am a snake-bit woman."

LuAnne was there, all right, glaring at me as soon as we walked in the door. I nodded a greeting, but she switched herself around and started talking to Mildred Allen as if I were a perfect stranger and not someone she'd often confided in about Leonard's most intimate failings. The details of which, I assure you, I would rather not have known.

I took a deep breath and pretended I hadn't noticed the snub. Tonya Allen noticed it, though, for I saw her eyebrows go up. Emma Sue Ledbetter was too busy helping Helen put out cheese and fruit trays and trying to talk her into leading a circle next year to pay any attention to what other people were doing. And Helen — well, Helen, bless her heart, was too gentle a soul to pick up on any unkind thoughts roiling through the air. Even in her own living room.

Kathleen Williams was there in her Pink

Lady uniform, which meant that she was either going to or coming from her volunteer work at the hospital. I declare, that woman volunteered for every do-good organization in town, and thank goodness for her and others like her, because I had all I could handle just managing my own life. Miriam Hargrove, the wife of Dr. Hargrove, who I hated to see at church since he'd seen too much of me in his office, was telling all who would listen that she'd found the perfect summer book — something about an elderly widow woman who overcame all obstacles with a straight back and a sharp tongue.

After getting coffee or tea and placing a few nibbles around the edges of our dessert plates, we took our seats in the living room. I made sure to sit beside Hazel Marie, giving LuAnne a wide berth. LuAnne hadn't given me a moment's notice, making out like she had urgent business to talk over with everybody else in the room. And by acting like I wasn't there, she was making it obvious that I was, and that she wanted everybody to know that she had something against me.

I had never been known to press myself on anyone, much less someone who wouldn't give me the time of day. So, if

LuAnne could snub me, I could snub her back, and I could do it better than she could any day of the week.

I drank my coffee and ignored her, turning my attention to Helen, who called the meeting to order. Our book club had been meeting off and on for any number of years, with members coming and going, but with a core group continuing to hold it together. Helen was the force behind it, for she enjoyed reading more than anybody I knew. Except for Sam, but he didn't need a club to keep him at it.

I didn't want to think of Sam for fear that I'd get so blue I'd give myself away. So I put my mind to the business at hand.

"Does anybody have any suggestions?" Helen asked.

Mildred raised her hand. "I do. I suggest we read something light and entertaining, for a change. That last book we read about did me in, it was so dark and gloomy. I want to be uplifted."

"It would've uplifted you if you'd read it," Kathleen said. "I know you, Mildred, and I'll bet you didn't get past the second chapter."

"Well, what if I didn't?" Mildred said without a lick of shame. I hadn't finished it, myself, but I didn't care to admit it. "I don't see the use of having a book club if all the books are too deep to understand."

"But that's the whole point!" Kathleen took everything to heart, and was always trying to improve herself, and us, too. "The whole purpose of the club is to read things that we wouldn't read on our own, so we can *learn* something."

Mildred came right back at her. "Well, what're we going to learn if we can't even read the thing?"

"Ladies," Helen cautioned, but it didn't do much good.

"Speak for yourself," Kathleen murmured, but Mildred heard her, and murmured right back, "Some *new* members think they can come in and change everything."

Helen was beginning to look a little frazzled by this time, for her eyes were going from one to the other of us. "Anybody else have a suggestion?"

"I do," Miriam said, then went into a long spiel about this series of books she was so enamored of. "If they don't take your mind off your troubles, nothing will. I kept my husband awake the other night, laughing out loud. I mean, this woman gets into the most gosh-awful predicaments you can imagine."

That was enough to put me off the books right there. I had enough predicaments of my own. I didn't need to go looking for somebody else's.

"All right," Helen said, "we'll consider that. Anybody else?"

"I sorta agree with Mildred," Emma Sue ventured. "I mean, about reading something uplifting, but maybe not anything too light. I think we ought to do some devotional books, something that will help us in our daily life. Just because it's summer doesn't mean we should put the Lord in second place."

There were a few under-the-breath groans, because Emma Sue was always suggesting something devotional. We'd read a few of her suggestions, and I'm here to tell you I'd not learned one thing I hadn't already known.

"What about you, Tonya?" Helen said, turning to our newest member, who had a certain authority, being a former resident of New York. Tonya had a particular viewpoint, as well, seeing as how she had grown up as Tony, had undergone and survived a gender-changing operation, and was now flourishing as the most lively, but levelheaded, woman among us. Which was a marvel to me, since Tony had been the giddiest young man you'd ever want to meet. But I expect that a surgical experience of the likes of what he'd gone through would be enough to make you stop and think before opening your mouth again.

"Well," Tonya said, thoughtfully, "we're going to have a list of books, aren't we — not just one or two? Maybe we could put one of each kind on the list and let people read what they want to."

"That won't work," Kathleen said. She was generally quick to state her opinion, which wasn't always appreciated. "How're we going to discuss something we haven't all read?"

"We won't need to discuss them," Tonya said. "At our first fall meeting, we can have brief reports from whoever's read a particular book, with recommendations to the rest of us. Then we can read them or not."

"That makes a lot of sense to me," I said, although I'd earlier determined to keep my mouth shut and not draw attention to myself.

LuAnne drew herself up, and snapped, "It doesn't to me. We're a *book* club, and that means everybody reads the same thing so we can discuss the same thing."

Hazel Marie leaned forward. "But it doesn't mean that we can't make a few changes, if that works for everybody." My heart went out to her for defending me, because I knew it took great effort for Hazel Marie to speak up in public, much less to disagree with anybody. "I mean, if everybody wants to do it that way."

LuAnne sniffed, then cut loose. "I think it's a mistake. We ought to keep the club like it's always been, and not go changing it to suit people who don't have a sense of the *traditional* and the *correct* and the most *proper* way of doing things."

Well, that outburst got our attention, for it was obvious that LuAnne was talking about more than which paperbacks to take to the beach that summer. Tonya cut her eyes at LuAnne, and Hazel Marie stiffened beside me, while Mildred looked ready to jump down LuAnne's throat. They were all offended, but none more than I, because I knew what LuAnne was referring to, and it certainly wasn't books.

"Well, you don't have to get *personal*," Mildred said, huffing a little as she assumed that LuAnne was attacking her reading preferences. "Just because I want to read some light romances and Emma Sue wants to read something theological doesn't mean that we're not perfectly proper and traditional. Besides, we read that book you recommended last year, and that was the trashiest thing I've ever seen."

"Ladies," Helen said, her eyes darting around for help.

"How do you know?" LuAnne shot back. "You didn't read it. And a few others didn't, either." Then she turned straight on and glared at me. And about that time, the rest of the room began to get the message. "And *some* people don't ever follow the rules and do what they're supposed to do."

Everybody got real quiet, as eyes turned to watch for my reaction. I could feel Hazel Marie building up a head of steam on my behalf, and knew I had to divert her as quickly as I could. Hazel Marie had been known to do a little hair pulling in her time, and since I'd had to twist a few arms to get her in the club in the first place, I rose from my chair.

"Helen, thank you so much for having us." I put my coffee cup and plate on a side table and gathered my purse under my arm. "But it's getting late and I'm expecting Sam to call. He wants me to join him and Little Lloyd on their educational trip through Tennessee, and I may just do that. He is a dear man, and can't bear to be away from me. Hazel Marie, are you ready?"

And she and I marched out of there with our heads held high, having avoided a public showdown with my oldest friend. I felt quite proud of myself for the way I'd handled the crisis.

On our way home, Hazel Marie stopped for a red light. Frowning, she looked over at me. "I didn't know you were going to Tennessee."

"I didn't either. It just seemed the thing to say at the time." I sighed, overcome again, now that the adrenaline had eased off, by the state of affairs in my life. Well, just the state of my life, now that I was averse to thinking of *affairs* in any context at all.

Chapter 26

Hazel Marie turned onto Polk Street, as we headed toward home. She suddenly pursed her mouth and took a white-knuckled grip on the steering wheel. "I could just wring LuAnne's neck! She had no call to jump on you like that, and I don't know why you didn't let her have it."

"I didn't want to create a scene."

"Well, she certainly created one. And you let her get by with it, which is what I don't understand. Everybody was staring at her like she was crazy or something."

"That was sort of the idea," I said, although, truthfully, my failure to respond to LuAnne in kind came more from wanting to get away from her before she made her meaning clear. "You see, Hazel Marie, a soft answer turneth away wrath. Solomon said that, I think, and it's good advice. Especially," I went on, "when all you want is to shut somebody up."

Hazel Marie nodded, but she didn't seem convinced. "Maybe so, but to see her turn a perfectly nice discussion about books into a personal attack on you just made me mad as fire."

"I know it did. That's why I thought I'd better get you out of there."

We looked at each other then, and began laughing. Hazel Marie's grip eased up on the steering wheel, as she visibly relaxed in her seat. "I guess we didn't decide anything, did we?"

"About what?"

"What to read this summer."

"Lord, Hazel Marie, I can't get myself exercised over what to read or not read. I'll decide when the time comes. Besides, Helen'll let us know. But for now, I've got all I can manage just trying to get through each day without losing my mind." I heaved a long sigh. "Considering all I have to contend with."

"Oh, I know," she said, quick to agree with my mood. "I was just thinking about when it's all over, and you and Sam settle down to a normal married life."

"I'll tell you what's a fact. I don't know what a normal married life is. I haven't had one yet." Then I bit my lip, fearing I'd made her feel bad. But she hadn't been the only woman in my first husband's life, so maybe she wouldn't take it to heart. "And I'll tell you another fact," I went on, trying to dig myself out of the hole. "I'm not convinced that married life is normal for anybody."

"Oh, don't say that," Hazel Marie cried with some consternation. She turned into our driveway and pulled to a stop in front of the garage. "I've been trying too hard to get into it. I'd hate to think it's not natural."

"Not normal, Hazel Marie, is what I said. I expect it's natural enough, since so many of us get into it one way or another." I opened the car door and began to unfold myself enough to get out. "Let's go in, and — oh! Wait a minute." I swung my feet back into the car.

"What is it?"

"I just had a thought. Do you think it's possible that LuAnne hasn't told anybody her suspicions about Sam and me? I was so sure she couldn't keep it to herself, that it just occurred to me how everybody seemed just the same. Not one person looked at me crosswise. At least, not until she made it obvious how mad she was."

"Well, you know," Hazel Marie said, frowning in concentration, "you may be right. Nobody said a word to me, and I didn't see anybody smirking behind your back."

"It's hard to believe," I said, my heart lightening at the thought of my friend's unexpected ability to keep something juicy to herself. "But maybe I've done LuAnne a disservice. I declare, Hazel Marie, that makes me feel one hundred percent better, and renews my faith in the value of friendship."

"Good. Now, let's get inside. I've got a dozen things to do on the pageant."

We'd barely gotten through the door when Lillian said, "Miss Julia, Miz Ledbetter call an' she jus' this minute hang up. She say she comin' to take you to lunch."

"Take *me* to lunch? When has she ever done that?"

"She say she tho'win' a tuna fish salat together, an' y'all can talk while you eat."

"Oh, me," I moaned, holding my hand to my head. "When Emma Sue throws something together, that's exactly what she does. Why is she doing this? The last thing I want to do is eat her tuna salad." I turned to Hazel Marie. "We just saw her at Helen's, and she didn't say a word about lunch."

"Well, she sayin' something now," Lillian said. "An' why she doin' it is 'cause she got to counsel with you, so you go on over there an' see what she want."

I grabbed the back of a chair to steady myself. "*Counsel* with me! Oh, Lord, Hazel

Marie. What if LuAnne was so mad that she told Emma Sue her suspicions after we left? You know it would only take a few hints for Emma Sue to think I needed some counseling. What am I going to do?"

Hazel Marie came over and put an arm around me. "You don't know what she wants, Miss Julia. It could be something else entirely. But if LuAnne has talked, then you do what you always tell me to do. You hold your head up and keep your own counsel. You don't need any from anybody else."

"Well, but," I said, "what if she asks me straight out if Sam and I are married? What if she tells me we're living in sin? And you know she'll tell the pastor, and then he'll preach a sermon on the moral depravity of the age, complete with examples and case histories, and by that time everybody'll know who he's talking about. Call Emma Sue, please, Lillian, and tell her I'm sick."

"Too late," Lillian said, leaning across the sink to peer out the window. "She jus' pull in, come to pick you up, so you go on an' get it over with."

"Lillian's right," Hazel Marie said, but with a frown of concern on her face. "You'll just worry yourself really sick, if you put it off. Because you know Emma Sue won't give up. She'll be after you and after you, so go on and don't admit to anything."

I straightened up, took a deep breath, and got my backbone up. "All right, if I have to. But what I want to know is, where is Sam when I need him? Gone, that's where, and here I am having to deal with this mess by myself. Maybe I really don't have a husband if this is the way it's going to be."

And I went back out the door to meet Emma Sue, leaving Hazel Marie and Lillian staring after me in shock.

By the time I was seated at the table in Emma Sue's breakfast nook, I had myself girded for battle. Nothing was worse than being counseled, which just meant somebody wanted to tell you what you're doing wrong. And I wasn't going to have it. Wasn't going to listen to it, wasn't going to cry and confess and promise to do better. I was already doing the best I could, and that would have to suffice.

Emma Sue was behind the counter, throwing her tuna salad together, talking and talking about any and everything to cover her nervousness. She wasn't finding it so easy to confront a sinner with her sin, with the sinner sitting right there waiting for lunch.

"Here we go," she said, setting plates onto our place mats. She slid into her chair and shook out a napkin. "Now, Julia, I want you to know that my heart is truly burdened for you, and anything you tell me will go no further. Well, of course, I'll lay it before the Lord, but I mean I won't tell anybody else."

"This looks lovely, Emma Sue," I said, poking my fork into the tuna salad that rested on a lettuce leaf.

"Oh, my goodness," she said, jumping up and going around the counter to the kitchen. "I forgot the tomatoes. It's too early for good ones, but I just got these yesterday and they look pretty good."

"Most of the out-of-season ones are as hard as a rock inside," I said, putting down the fork to wait for my hostess. "If they can put a man on the moon, I don't see why they can't grow decent tomatoes."

"I don't, either," Emma Sue agreed, slapping down a plate of sliced tomatoes and resuming her seat. "But have some, anyway. And eat, Julia, you don't have to wait for me."

I took a bite of the salad. Not bad, but not Lillian's. Too much mayonnaise, for one thing. And it was Miracle Whip, and not Hellmann's, for another. "Delicious, Emma Sue."

"There's plenty more, so eat all you want. Now, Julia, I have to get this off my chest, because if there's anything I can do to help, I want to do it."

"I appreciate that," I said, hoping I was being noncommittal, while inside I was seething at the thought of LuAnne spreading her unconfirmed suspicions. "But everything that can be done is already being done, so it's best to just leave it as it is."

"But Julia, you can't do that! It behooves us all to be up and doing all the time, putting on the whole armor of God, of course, beforehand. And it's not like you to just let things slide. You've got to get it straightened out."

"There's nothing I'd like better, but some things can't be hurried along." I ate some more tuna salad. "Emma Sue, do you think we could have a few crackers or a piece of bread with this?"

"Oh, my goodness, I forgot." Up she jumped again to bring a basket of crackers to the table. "I am so upset over this, I don't half know what I'm doing."

"It's all right. I appreciate your concern,

but believe me, you don't need to be upset. As soon as Sam gets back, it'll all be worked out. *If*," I continued with some asperity, "he ever gets back. And I really wish you wouldn't say anything about this to anybody."

Emma Sue's eyes got big, and she leaned across the table. "You're going to bring *Sam* into it?"

"Why, yes. Who else would I bring?"

"You mean —" Emma Sue's voice got lower and more intense. "You mean, that *Sam's* involved?"

"Well, Emma Sue, of course he is."

"Oh," she said, slumping back into her chair. "Then it's worse than I thought. I thought you'd just had a little misunderstanding, and a few words to the wise would put things right. And some prayer, of course."

"Believe me, it's not just a little misunderstanding. It's more like a major upheaval of my life." What was the woman thinking? It seemed to me that the unsettled state of my marriage was a crisis of the first magnitude.

"Well, of course you've known each other for a long time," Emma Sue said, "and it's not easy to deal with a falling-out."

I frowned at her. "A falling-out? I

wouldn't go that far, although we certainly aren't as close as we have been." I thought of Sam sleeping upstairs, while I tossed and turned alone downstairs. "But that seemed the best way to proceed under the circumstances."

"Well, see, that's just it," Emma Sue said, as if I'd just expressed some insight into the problem. "You need to be closer. Much closer."

I smiled. "That's what he says."

"Who?"

"Why, Sam. He would agree with you completely."

Emma Sue suddenly found her silverware of immense interest, moving around the spoon and lining up the knife with the edge of the place mat. "Julia," she said with a sudden catch in her voice. Her face reddened, and her hand began to tremble. "I thought you were just at cross-purposes over some little something, and I could help you get back together. But — but if Sam's involved — oh my goodness, Julia — you have to talk to Larry and do it without delay. I had no idea it was this bad."

My head snapped up and I glared at her. Larry Ledbetter was the last person I'd take my marital problems to, because I knew what he'd say. As a dyed-in-the-wool fundamental Presbyterian preacher, he would insist on an immediate remarriage with families and witnesses present, along with public proclamations. And he'd do everything he could, including applying to the presbytery, to make it retroactive to cover the probable lapse from grace when we thought we'd been married, and acted accordingly.

"It is pretty bad, Emma Sue, but at this point, not bad enough to disturb the pastor with something that we can work out ourselves." I cut into a slice of tomato and pushed it around my plate, wondering how I could change the subject. "By the way, did the club decide on a summer reading list?"

"I don't give a flip about a summer reading list!" Emma Sue threw her napkin across her plate. "How can you sit there and worry about reading, when you've just shocked me to the core! *You,* of all people! I don't know how you can be so calm. Why, it's just . . . it's, well, I can't even think about it, much less talk about it." And the tears began gushing out of her eyes. "Oh, Julia," she sobbed, covering her face with her hands. "I didn't know you had this burden. I'll pray for you, that's all I can do. It just breaks my heart."

I knew this would happen. I just knew it. And now I had to deal with it. "Emma Sue, listen, we went into it with the best of intentions. We had no idea what we were getting into, and my conscience is as clear as a bell on that point. And when Sam gets back, everything will be straightened out and we'll take up where we left off."

Emma Sue sprang from her chair with such force that the chair fell backward. Her face was streaked with tears and blotched with outrage. "How *could* you? How could you even *want* to take up where you left off? The idea! I can't even conceive of Sam and LuAnne together, much less *involved!* It's sickening and disgusting and — and I don't know what all. And at their age!"

I sprang from my chair, too. "What are you talking about?"

"You know what I'm talking about. Open marriages may be the thing in big cities, but I never in my life thought that you would condone such outright sin."

I collapsed into my chair, and raised my head to heaven. "Emma Sue, you need help."

Chapter 27

It took me forever to convince Emma Sue that Sam was not involved with LuAnne in any carnal way, either with or without my knowledge and approval. It was all I could do to get it across because neither of us could bring ourselves to speak in plain words. Emma Sue had already suffered all the shocks she could stand. And while we talked about something neither of us could come out and say, it was taking me a mighty effort to shut out the picture she'd brought to mind of Sam and LuAnne. Well, I refused to think about it. But Emma Sue had, and not only thought about it, but had leapt on it.

In my effort to set her straight, I came just short of admitting what was really burdening my soul. Namely, that Sam and I had biblically known each other in a dubious state of matrimony, and that LuAnne didn't have a thing to do with it, except get mad at me for turning down an invitation.

"Oh, Julia," Emma Sue said, crying now in relief. "I'm so glad that you're not involved in such carnal activities."

"Not even remotely," I said, with some regret.

"But, you see, I was just so concerned at the way you and LuAnne avoided each other at the book club, and those sharp words going back and forth, well, all I could see were two longtime friends on the outs. But then when you mentioned Sam, I guess I just jumped to conclusions."

"I guess you did."

"But see, I thought if I could get you to apologize to her, you'd both get over whatever caused the spat in the first place."

That stung. "I'm not the one who needs to apologize," I snapped. "LuAnne is who you should be talking to, because it would do her a world of good to have some counseling. Talk about jumping to conclusions! She is the world's worst, and I don't know why you think I'm to blame for her behavior this morning. She's the one who flew off the handle and got mad and tried to get even by starting rumors and airing her anger in public." I took a deep breath and steamed for a while. "In fact, I think I handled myself with commendable restraint at the book club and, if you but noticed, here in your kitchen when you accused me of condoning morally indefensible behavior.

If anybody's owed an apology, it's me."

"Oh, Julia, I do apologize. I really do. I don't know why I thought . . . Well, it just came into my mind, unwanted and unbidden."

"What books have you been reading?"

"None, Julia! I promise I haven't. Nor magazines, either." She stopped short and a look of wonder passed across her face. "I know where I got the idea! It was those magazine covers in the checkout line at the grocery store. They had all these titles of articles on how to please your mate and what to do when he suggests things you don't want to do and how you can rejuvenate your marriage and whet his appetite."

"Whet his appetite! Lord help us, Emma Sue. I'd think that'd be the last thing a woman would want." I couldn't help but think of Sam and his zealous activities.

"Well," she said, somewhat abashed as color flooded her face, "you haven't been married as long as I have. This time, anyway."

"You can say that again," I said, and thought, *hardly at all.*

Emma Sue reached out with her hand and put it on mine. "I am truly sorry, Julia. Please forgive me, and tell me what I can do to help mend your friendship with LuAnne."

I moved my hand and pushed back my plate with most of the now-soggy tuna salad staring back at me. "Don't do anything, Emma Sue. This is something that has to run its course. I appreciate your concern, but if you give her a hint of what you hit me in the face with a while ago, she will never get over it. Misunderstandings are LuAnne's stock in trade, and you don't want it spread all over town that you've allowed yourself to be tantalized by magazine covers at the supermarket."

She reared back in shock at the thought. "Oh, goodness no! Would she do that?"

"LuAnne will tell everything she knows, thinks, or suspects. So, a word to the wise, Emma Sue. Don't believe anything she says. And you know I think the world of her."

There, I thought. Maybe I'd made an end run around LuAnne's doubts about my marriage.

"Now, Emma Sue," I went on, thinking this was as good a time as any since I had now taken the high road. "I'd like to ask your opinion about something."

"Oh, yes, Julia, I wish you would." She stopped and thought for a minute. "You know, I don't think you've ever asked my opinion about anything before. So I'm truly honored. What is it?"

"I want to know what you think about signs."

She frowned. "What kind of signs? Are you coming down with something?"

"For goodness sake, Emma Sue. Signs from the *Lord!* That's what I'm talking about."

"Oh, that kind. Well, you know I believe in them. There's the rainbow, for instance, and Gideon's fleece, although we're not supposed to test the Lord. All we're supposed to do is recognize his leading. Why, I couldn't get through the day without watching for signs to guide me in my every endeavor."

"Well, but what are they? What form do they take, and how can you tell if they're from the Lord or just something that happens? I mean, what if you were cooking supper and it burned? Would that be a sign that the Lord didn't want you to eat it, or would it just mean that you talked too long on the telephone?"

"Well, let me see. First off, in that case, the Lord would probably be telling me to keep my mind on what I'm doing and stay off the phone when I'm cooking. Though that's hard to do when it keeps ringing like it does here. But I don't think he'd necessarily be telling me not to eat it. If it's not too burned, anyway. He'd just be showing me the consequences of taking my hand off the plow. So to speak." She paused and thought some more. "I'm not sure that qualifies as a sign. You do have to be in a constant state of prayer, Julia, so you'll be open to recognizing and interpreting a sign. Not just anybody can do it."

"I think I'm one of those."

"Probably so," she agreed with great solemnity. "I've long been concerned about your spiritual condition, Julia, but you can easily rectify that. As I said, you need to be in a constant state of prayer. Then you'll begin to see signs everywhere you look and know that the Lord is guiding you."

It didn't sit well with me to hear her voice concerns about my spiritual condition, but I sucked in my breath and persevered in my quest to determine what qualified as a sign and what didn't.

"Well, I don't know how to do that, Emma Sue," I said. "It seems to me that you wouldn't get anything done if you were stuck somewhere praying all the time. I know I wouldn't. And I admit that there are hours and hours of the day when I don't think of the Lord at all. Too busy holding onto the plow of everyday life, I guess."

"Well, see, that's your problem. And I don't mean that you have to have your head bowed and your eyes closed all the time. You just have to have a prayerful attitude."

"I think I have that. Maybe not all the time, but every now and then. But, Emma Sue, can't the Lord give a sign to somebody who's just doing the best she can, even if she's a little on the lax side about praying?"

"Oh, absolutely. And it ought to shake you up something awful to have the Lord reach down out of the blue and show you what he wants you to do. You know, when you're not expecting it and haven't been praying for it."

"Then maybe mine qualifies, because I've really been shaken up."

"I wish you'd tell me what it is, Julia. I could be ever so much more help if I knew just what is concerning you. All that cooking and burning you brought up wasn't much of an example."

"I know, but I can't tell you exactly, Emma Sue. If it is a sign, then it's between the Lord and myself. But let's try this. Say you took a certain step, and took it in good faith and with a clear conscience, and it wasn't a step that no one else had ever taken before, by any means. And you took it after long consideration and a good deal of prayer, and when it came down to it, you did it without any hesitation or doubts as to its benefits and advantages."

I was stretching things here, because I'd married Sam in an almighty rush, ignoring all my doubts and hesitations. But now those doubts and hesitations had come back tenfold, because it looked as if the Lord was trying to get my attention. Why else would one catastrophe after another be befalling me? And why else was I suddenly being given the option again of staying single? And if that option constituted a sign from the Lord, I certainly wanted to know it.

But I wasn't about to give Emma Sue all the particulars.

She frowned, willing me to go on by the intensity of her gaze. "And . . . ?"

"And, what if after you took the step, you discovered that it wasn't a step at all, but a *mis*step. Would that misstep be a sign that you ought to take the step again and take it right, or would it mean that you shouldn't have taken the step in the first place?"

If Emma Sue had frowned any deeper, her face might've never straightened out. She worked her mouth back and forth, rubbing her hand across her chin and never took her eyes off me. "Julia, have you joined that new health club in town?"

"What?"

"Because, if you have, I can assure you that the Lord wants us to take care of our bodies, and exercise is one way to do it. Just because you hurt something by stepping wrong doesn't mean he wants you to quit." Her face cleared, as she gave her interpretation of my sign. "Don't worry about a thing. You just keep right on taking those steps. They're good for you. Just be careful about missteps — you can really damage something that way."

I sat there, stunned at her literalness; then I gathered myself and stood up. "I better be getting back, Emma Sue. I hope you don't mind running me home, or I could call Hazel Marie to come for me."

"No, no, don't do that. I'll take you. I would suggest that you walk for the exercise," she said, smiling to show that she didn't mean it, "but I guess with a sore foot — or is it your ankle? — you ought to stay off of it for a while."

"You're right, Emma Sue." And I purposefully limped off to her car, thanking her for lunch and the counseling session, all the time praying that she wouldn't begin thinking of my last example and come up with another interpretation closer to the truth.

Chapter 28

"Lillian," I said, walking into the kitchen after thanking Emma Sue for the ride, and plopping down my pocketbook. "You couldn't get a straight answer out of Emma Sue Ledbetter if you tied her to a tree. And I just wanted to know one thing. Is the Lord telling me something or not?"

Lillian closed the refrigerator door and turned, frowning at me. "Who you been listenin' to?"

"That's the problem. Either I'm not listening hard enough, or nobody's saying anything. See, Lillian, I think this marital mess I'm in may be the Lord's doing. I think he's giving me one more chance to get it right."

Lillian stood looking at me some little while, thinking over what I'd said. Then she lit into me. "You think gettin' rid of Mr. Sam be what the Lord want you to do? Miss Julia, I'm here to tell you, the Lord, he like marri't folks. What you think he mean when he say, 'Go, and sin no more'? He mean, don't be havin' no relations till

311

you get that knot tied good an' tight. An' that's what you been doin'. I mean, not doin'. Not havin' no relations, I mean."

"Oh, Lillian, I can't talk about such things." I turned away, embarrassed at discussing intimate details of the bedroom in the family kitchen. "And that's not the problem. The problem is whether I should've married Sam at all."

"You think the Lord be up there, frownin' on you an' Mr. Sam, sending troubles on yo' head all the time? No'm, he be laughin', 'cause he been tryin' to get you two together, an' now he done it, but you can't let it rest. You got to keep on worryin' it and worryin' it. I tell you what I think, Miss Julia." She put her hands on her hips and gave me her last word. "I think you been watchin' too much *Montel* an' *Oprah* an' *Judge Judy*. You jus' lookin' for trouble."

I'd just opened my mouth to refute her, when Hazel Marie burst through the swinging door. "Miss Julia! You won't believe what's happened. It's just awful. We've got to do something."

My heart caught in my throat as I thought of Sam and Little Lloyd in some dire circumstance. I couldn't even speak, standing there holding on to the counter, waiting to hear the dreadful news.

Hazel Marie stormed over to me, her face screwed up in agitation. "Ashley Knowles has dropped out!"

"What?"

"She's dropped out of the pageant. Etta Mae just called and told me. Six contestants was the bare minimum, and I wanted eight, but couldn't get them. Now we're down to five. I am just sick about this."

I eased my grip on the counter as relief flooded through me. "Lord, Hazel Marie, I thought something had happened to Little Lloyd and Sam. Don't scare me like that."

That brought her up short. "Oh, I'm sorry. I'm just so upset, I'm not thinking straight. Etta Mae thinks Ashley doesn't have what it takes, and we ought to just let her go. But I just can't."

"You've put a lot of effort into the pageant, Hazel Marie, and you have a right to be upset. But, I'll tell you what. Why don't I see if I can do something with Ashley. Maybe she just needs a little encouragement, and since I'm not a pageant official, why, it would be all right for me to help her, wouldn't it?"

Hazel Marie's face lit up. "Oh, would you? You've saved my life, Miss Julia. Thank you, thank you."

She'd saved mine, too, for now I had a perfectly good reason to go all out to whip Miss Knowles into shape, and maybe learn something of her uncle's whereabouts. But first, I had to keep her in the contest.

About that time, there was an almighty crash upstairs, and we heard Willie Pruitt laugh and say, "Whoops."

I looked up, expecting water, or maybe the ceiling, to start falling. "What are they doing now?"

"Still puttin' in them closets," Lillian said, shaking her head.

"Yes," I said, "and they need to get through with it. I think they've found a home up there."

"You ought to go up and see," Hazel Marie said. "I don't think you've been up there once, and they're doing such a good job."

"Maybe later, Hazel Marie. But right now, let's talk about Miss Knowles. Why is she dropping out? Did Etta Mae say? And, by the way, Willie Pruitt was certainly taken with Etta Mae. Did you notice? We need to get her back over here, so we can nurture that relationship."

"Oh." Hazel Marie laughed. "I don't think she's all that interested."

"You never can tell," I said darkly, convinced of Miss Wiggins's interest in any stray male who crossed her path. "But, back to Miss Knowles. What's her problem?"

"Etta Mae said she would only say that she didn't fit in. That she thought she wasn't beauty contestant material. And I hate to say this, but she really isn't."

"Well, who is? I mean, all the girls are attractive, certainly, but not a one of them would set the world on fire."

"Just wait, Miss Julia. When Etta Mae and I get through with them, they're going to knock your eyes out. By the time we get the right makeup on them and their hair fixed and get them in their outfits, they'll all be beautiful. You won't recognize them, they'll be so glamorous."

"If that's so, can't you do the same for Miss Knowles? She may need more work than the others, but that would just make the change more startling. Wouldn't it?"

"Sure it would, but not if she won't let us work on her. And, really, it wouldn't be fair to do any more for her than the others. Oh, Miss Julia." Hazel Marie collapsed in a chair by the table. "We've worked so hard, and I'll be so disappointed if she doesn't participate. We need her, even though there's no way she could win."

"Now, Hazel Marie, let me talk to the girl. She was willing enough at first, so something must've happened to make her change her mind. I'll find out what it is and fix it."

"Oh, I hope you can," she said, jumping up from the chair. "I'll leave it all to you, because right now, I don't know if I'm coming or going. I miss Lloyd so much, and J.D. is making himself awfully scarce here lately, so no telling what he's up to. And then this pageant, which is about to drive me crazy. Etta Mae and I are meeting the girls at the high school auditorium in — oh, my goodness — ten minutes. I'm going to be late, and we're having their first stage rehearsal. I can't take on one other thing, so Ashley's all yours." Hazel Marie grabbed her pocketbook and headed out the door.

"Wait. Wait a minute, Hazel Marie. I don't even know where she lives, and besides, I don't . . ."

Hazel Marie stuck her head back in the door. "She lives in the Hillandale Trailer Park. You know, where Etta Mae lives. Not sure exactly where, but the park's not that big. You can find it — just ask somebody." And off she went, leaving me with a job I didn't want, but badly needed.

I turned to Lillian. "Well, you heard her. Let's go."

"Go where?"

"To talk Miss Knowles into parading around on a stage."

"Uh-uh, I don't know nothin' 'bout that."

"Neither do I." I sighed and picked up my pocketbook again. "But if it has to be done, we might as well get on with it."

"Who *we?*"

"Why, you and me, of course. I'm not going by myself. I hardly know the girl."

"I don't know her any better'n you, an' if I jus' volunteer, it done slip my mind."

"Oh, don't be so literal. I've had enough of that with Emma Sue. I need somebody with me, and Little Lloyd's not here. So you're elected. Besides, it'll do you good to get out for a while."

She kept on grumbling, murmuring about something in the oven getting ruined, but she washed and dried her hands and followed me out to the car.

I drove out to the old highway and turned toward Delmont, one of the several small towns in the county that was trying to compete with Abbotsville. With little success, I might add, even though it'd gotten itself incorporated, hired a town manager, and added another traffic light.

On the other side of Delmont, I turned left onto a narrow paved road named for my late husband. All unbeknownst to me until he passed on and his deals saw the light of day, Wesley Lloyd had bought up a good bit of fairly useless acreage out there. He had badgered the department of transportation to pave the road that ran past the trailer park in hopes, I assumed, of it being worth something someday. So far, he'd been wrong.

The Hillandale Trailer Park was on the right. I turned in, feeling the back wheels slide a little as they adjusted to the park's main road, which could've used another load or two of gravel.

"You better slow down," Lillian said.

"I'm slowing. Lord, would you look at the dust we're stirring up." I bit my lip, as we passed single-wides and double-wides blistering in the sun. "If it didn't belong to me, I'd say the owner ought to spruce this place up a little." I'm sorry to say that I'd taken little interest in the park, having put it in the care of an on-site manager. Most of the residents were long-term tenants, meaning to me that they were pleased enough with the way things were. So it seemed to me that I was providing a needed service by making the place, such as it was, available.

Actually, the park wasn't all that bad, if you could overlook the yards strewn with toys and barbeque grills, the wash flapping on lines strung between trailers, and the occasional rusted-out car up on blocks. To be fair, though, there were some trailers that looked well kept, with neat yards and potted plants, and I imagined that Miss Wiggins's was one of them.

"You know where you goin'?" Lillian asked.

"No, but Hazel Marie said to ask somebody. There's a woman we can . . . My Lord, would you look at that."

I would've driven on, but the only person out in the heat was a deeply tanned woman baking half naked in the sun. She was sprawled out in a child's wading pool, her head, arms, and legs hanging over the rims, while her lower part lay in a few inches of water.

I let down my window and called, "Ma'am? Excuse me, but could you tell us where the Knowles family lives?"

She raised her head and squinted at us. "Who?"

"We're looking for a Miss Ashley Knowles. You know where she lives?"

The woman sat up, the straps of her bathing suit top dangling dangerously, exposing more than I cared to see. She splashed water on her shoulders, then patted some on her face.

"She lives down there on the end," she said, pointing. "Last one on this side."

"Thank you," I said, rolled up the window, and continued on. "I declare, Lillian, some people don't have a lick of shame. Did you see how far down that top came? And it was all tanned, too. Think about that, would you."

"No'm, I don't p'ticklar care to."

"Neither do I." I pulled to the side in front of the last trailer, taking note of the listing awning over the door and a few dusty bushes that lined the foundation. It looked as if somebody had tried to improve the looks of the tiny yard, but had given up before it took effect.

"I don't see no car 'round here," Lillian said. "You reckon anybody home?"

"I guess we'll have to go see," I said with a martyred sigh. I opened my door and began to get out. "The things I do for Hazel Marie. Come on, Lillian. Let's go."

She climbed out, mumbling something about the things she did for me, just to remind me of some of the escapades I'd gotten her into before. I stood for a minute, listening to the hum and rattle of leaking air-conditioning units, waiting as she came around the car. I looked carefully around my property, wondering what it would be like to live there. It could've used some trees to shade those tin contraptions from the sun. It could've used a paved street and maybe a common area with a barbeque pit, picnic tables and a swing set. But then I shuddered, thinking of the lawsuit I'd face if somebody got hurt.

"If it's all the same to you, Lillian, I'd rather not mention that I'm the owner. At least until I make some improvements around here." Then I marched up to the trailer door and rapped on the metal frame.

Chapter 29

A tall, gaunt woman in a flowered housedress and bedroom slippers opened the door. Her gray-streaked hair was pulled back in a bun, but several strands had escaped to hang down around her lined face. She wiped her hands on her apron and pursed her mouth.

"Whatever it is," she said, stepping back, "I don't want none."

"Wait," I said. "We're not selling anything. We're just —"

"Not interested," she said firmly and started closing the door. "You people're all the time bangin' on my door. An' I don't care if you did send two women this time, I still don't want to take *The Watchtower*, nor hear about how just a hunderd and seventy-seven thousand're gonna be saved. You done reached that and more, and here you are after me when you know good and well I'm not in that number."

"Oh," I said, taken aback to be taken for a distributor of religious tracts. "I'm a Presbyterian. We believe in predestination, so you won't find us knocking on doors. But, I'm looking for Miss Ashley Knowles. Does she live here?"

The woman stopped, leaned out, and looked me over, giving Lillian a quick glance in the process. "She done anything?"

"Not as far as I know. Look, I'm —"

The woman's face lit up. "I know who you are! You're Julia Springer. I seen your pi'ture in the paper last year, ridin' on that Harley. I wanted to do that so bad, you just don't know. Come on in, Miz Springer. Ashley's not here right now, but she oughtta be back any minute."

I decided not to get into my name change, since I wasn't sure of it myself. She opened the door wide, smiling and glowing, seemingly pleased to have such distinguished guests, while I grasped the door frame to steady myself on the wobbling cement-block steps.

"Have a seat," the woman said, grinning broadly and waving us in. "Anywhere, it don't matter. Don't mind the mess. I'm kinda slow today."

Seeing that it was my first time within the confines of a trailer, I looked around the combination living-dining-kitchen area with interest. The cramped room would've sent me up the wall if I'd had to live in it, but it was hardly a mess. It was neat, without the clutter that usually accumulates in a small living space. But, then again, it hardly came up to the standards of one of Hazel Marie's home beautification magazines. A florid sofa, to the right as we entered, listed badly, hardly helped by a chunk of wood that had replaced a leg. A leatherette La-Z-Boy recliner was aimed toward a small television set on the counter that separated the kitchen from the living area. Two stools at the counter made up the dining room.

I ventured to sit on the sofa, trusting that the substitute leg would hold, while Lillian perched on a straight chair by the door. She was never comfortable in a stranger's house, but then, I rarely was, either.

"Thank you," I said, settling my pocketbook on my lap. "This is Lillian, who helped me find the right address. And you are . . . ?"

"Eunice Knowles," she said, taking what appeared to be her usual seat in the recliner. "I'm Ashley's grandma. She's lived with me ever since her mama's been gone."

"I'm sorry to hear that. It's always sad when a child has to face death so young."

"Why," she said, letting out a cackle, "that sorry woman's not dead. She just picked up and run off years ago, leavin'

Ashley with Elmo. And that boy don't know a diaper from a dishrag. Even if I did raise him. But he done all right, till the army sent him to I-raq, and, honey, talk about prayin', I been doin' some. So they won't nobody to take care of Ashley, 'cept me, and, you know, you do what you have to do."

"That's exactly what I say," I agreed. "I know Ashley must be a comfort to you, and a help, too."

"She's not bad," Eunice Knowles said, frowning as if she had to consider it. "She don't give me no trouble, 'cept for all that guitar playin' she does. Lord, she's pickin' on one thing or another day and night. If it's got strings, she plays it. 'Course, Elmo can, too, so she come by it natural. I told her she had to give it up and get herself a job. I mean, she made it through high school, which is a feather in her cap I can't claim, and it's time for her to find a full-time job and start pullin' her weight."

When the woman took a breath, I was able to get in a comment. "I take it she's not planning on college, then."

"Lord, no, honey. 'Less she goes through it like I did, in the front door and out the back." She laughed, then suddenly leaned forward, peering closely at me. "What'd you want with her, anyhow? You got a job for her? That's where she is now, in Delmont, lookin' for work, and she'd hate to miss out on a good offer. She's been workin' after school and on weekends at the McDonald's over there, and I told her she'd have a good chance of movin' up if she stayed on. I mean, she could be managing that place in a few years if she'd stick it out, and be set for life. But no, she don't want nothing that makes her wear a uniform and a paper cap. You got something that don't call for a paper cap?"

"Oh, no. No, I don't have anything for her. I wish I did, but no, we're here to see why she's dropped out of the sheriff's department beauty pageant. We all want her to stay in the contest, and I'm, well, I guess you could say I'm here as an emissary from the pageant officials to ask her to reconsider. Do you know why she's dropped out?"

"Why, honey, I didn't even know she'd dropped in! You know what these teenagers're like nowadays. They don't tell you nothin'. What kind of contest did you say?"

"Well, they call it a beauty contest, but I'd say it's more of a talent contest." I didn't mind stretching the truth a little, since I was trying to gain Mrs. Knowles's approval and her help. "I understand that

Ashley plays the guitar quite well, and none of the other contestants can do that, so she might have a very good chance." The thought of the girl's stringy hair, green fingernails, and bashful demeanor made me add, "With a little help, of course. Which all the girls need. And you needn't worry about the tone of the contest. It will be strictly on the up and up, being sponsored by the sheriff's department, and I assure you she will be well chaperoned by Hazel Marie Puckett and Etta Mae Wiggins."

"I know that Etta Mae," Mrs. Knowles said. "She lives right across the road from here. Nice young woman, but you don't want to cross her." She cackled again. "She'll let you have it with both barrels, you stand in her way. I admire that, yes, I do, and I wish Ashley had some of her gumption."

"Yes, well," I said, not wanting to get into an assessment of Miss Wiggins's character. "She really wants Ashley to stay in, and I hope she will, too."

Mrs. Knowles slapped her knee and said, "I don't know what's got into that girl! You'd think she'd jump at a chance to show off a little, the way she plays that music. 'Course, the poor thing don't have much in the way of looks, but I tell her if she'd put that lanky hair up in a bun like me, she might be surprised at what she finds underneath. You can't tell 'em nothin', though."

"I'll help with that, Mrs. Knowles," I said, and got a frowning look from Lillian. "We so want Ashley to be part of it, and I hope you'll encourage her to come back. If you don't mind her being in it, of course."

"Well, I don't mind a bit." Mrs. Knowles looked off in the distance, which wasn't all that far in a trailer, and tapped her worn fingers on the arm of the recliner. "You know, it might be just the thing to get her mind off wishing for a record contract. Have you ever heard of such a thing? Just pie in the sky, that's all it is, and she might see what she's up against. It might learn her a lesson, and get her feet back on the ground. I tell you, Miz Springer," she said, shaking her head in wonder, "that girl's got her head in the clouds. You know what she wants to do? Go to Nashville, that's what. And play backup for Reba or Wynonna. Now, have you ever?" She shook her head and clicked her tongue. "I tell her, 'Ashley, if you got to dream, dream something you might could get.' That's why I been pushin' McDonald's. She's got a real chance at managerin' in eight or nine years, but playin' backup? Uh-uh, no way to get a manager job doin' that."

"Uh, yes, I expect you're right. But then, I don't know anything about Nashville."

"You nor me, honey!"

"Yes, well, we must be going. Mrs. Knowles," I said, getting to my feet, "I hope we can count on you to get Ashley back in the pageant. It'll be an opportunity for her to perform before an audience, and you might tell her that it'll look good on her resume if she does get to Nashville. I know you don't want to encourage that, but it might work the other way around, too." I started toward the door, but turned back to try one last time. "Do you know why she doesn't want to do it? I mean, specifically?"

"No, ma'am, I don't. Like I said, I didn't know one thing about any of it. But if I had to guess, I'd guess she took one look at the other girls in that pageant thing, and figured she didn't measure up. In the looks department, I mean. She don't much take care of herself. I tell her she ought to, but she's kinda backward that way, like she don't even want to try. I tell her to go to the Eckerd drugstore and get her some of that Oil of Olay and I'll pay for it if she don't get too much. I even tried to get her to call the Avon lady — there's one right down the road, and I use her myself. But she won't do that, either. Says everybody'd laugh at her if she tried to be something she's not. That never stopped nobody else, so I don't know why it bothers her. Shamed of herself, seems like. What I think is this. I think some of them girls at the high school over there been mean to her, 'cause she don't ever want to be around them. I tell her she's got to be a little forward. Not too far, mind you, but a little. But she's a differunt kettle of fish, and that's the truth."

"There's nothing wrong with being different," I said, feeling for the first time a slight kinship with Ashley Knowles, since I'd never been known to run with the pack, either. Although Ashley's black-rimmed eyes and green nail polish put her far beyond me or the pack. Odd, though, I thought, that this grandmother hadn't mentioned those dramatic cosmetic additions. Maybe the girl put them on between home and school. Some do that, you know, leave home one way and show up at school or work another.

"Here's what we should do, Mrs. Knowles," I said. "You be in charge of getting her back in the pageant, and I'll see to it that she has a makeover that'll put her head and shoulders above anybody who's been mean to her. Lillian, here, is a near-professional when it comes to doing makeovers. Why, between the two of us, we could open a beauty school, if we had a mind to." Lillian shot me a look that would've ordinarily stopped me cold, but there was nothing I liked better than a challenge, and Ashley Knowles was a challenge if there ever was one. Besides, I had to do something to keep her uncle quiet.

"Well, my goodness sakes alive, she can't pass up a chance like that," Mrs. Knowles said, her dark eyes glinting with determination. "Not even the Avon lady is that good." Then she gave a firm nod of her head. "She'll be there. When I put my foot down, she hops to, and I aim to put it down."

"Well, we want her to want to," I cautioned, picturing a sullen Ashley shuffling down the runway. "Thank you for seeing us, Mrs. Knowles. Tell Ashley to be at my house first thing in the morning. We're going to fix that girl up, and give her some confidence in herself. And maybe help her find a job, too. I'm not without influence in the local job market." Although I wasn't sure that my influence went as far as McDonald's.

"Lord, don't I know it. Ashley won't squirm outta this. I won't let her. She'll be there, don't you worry."

331

"Then we'll be looking for her. Oh, Mrs. Knowles," I said, as if I'd just thought of it, "do you by chance know a preacher by the name of Kincaid?"

"Aaron? I guess I do, since he's my boy by my first husband. How come you to know him?"

"By way of a, uh, church service I once attended. He mentioned being kin to a Knowles family around here."

"He's a fine preacher, if I do say so, an' he just thinks the world of Ashley. He called a coupla nights ago to see how she's doin'." Mrs. Knowles squinched up her eyes in sudden concern. "Aaron ain't give you no trouble, has he?"

"No. Indeed not. I've just heard him the one time, and wondered at the connection." I hoped she'd let the matter drop.

She cackled again. "Well, that boy's nigh fifty years old now, and he's seen his share of troubles. But he don't let it bother him, he just follows the Lord an' takes care of his kin."

"Yes, that's what I understand. Lillian, we must be going. Thank you again, Mrs. Knowles."

"Why, honey," she said, springing up from her chair as I opened the door, "I didn't even offer you a Coke or nothin'. I don't know where my manners went. Stay on a while, Ashley'll be on home sometime today."

"No, we have to get back. Thank you anyway. I just wanted to make sure that she'd stay in the pageant. I'm just so pleased to have your help with keeping her in. I'm sure she'll make a good showing."

I opened the door and felt for the top cement step with my foot. Lillian took my arm to help me reach the ground. She worried constantly about falling. Me, not her, but I shook her off when I gained my footing.

"Thank you again," I called back, as I headed for the car, pretending that I couldn't hear Eunice Knowles's voice rattling on behind us about how we should come back anytime, how she'd forgotten to serve the Sara Lee pound cake she had in the freezer, how I was always welcome, and how Ashley'd be sorry she missed us.

"My word," I said, as I closed the car door and reached for the seat belt. "That was an unusual experience."

"Uh-huh," Lillian said, cringing as I narrowly missed a tree turning the car around. After a while, she added, "She sho' know how to talk, don't she."

Chapter 30

"Lillian, you have to help me," I said, elbows propped on the table, my head bowed between my hands. Eunice Knowles had called early that morning, saying that Ashley had agreed to stay in the pageant. "It took me some doin'," Mrs. Knowles had said, "but she finally said okay when I told her she couldn't do no better than to have a fine woman like you help her with her ambitions. She'll be there in a little while."

So now I had to back up my words to turn Ashley Knowles into a beauty queen, and that's why I was appealing to Lillian.

But Lillian went right on stacking breakfast dishes in the dishwasher, showing not one bit of sympathy, while the grating whine of the Pruitts' electric drill added to my distress.

Casting my eyes toward the ceiling and praying for relief from the constant din of closet building, I said, "I can't think with that racket going on. Not that thinking is going to help with this." Spread out on the table in front of me were a curling iron, a large mirror on a stand, hairpins, a comb, a brush, and a basket filled to overflowing with one beauty product after another, most of which I'd never seen nor heard of. "Hazel Marie said we should start Ashley on a beauty regimen, but I don't know what that is. Ashley's on her way over here right this minute, and, Lillian, we have to give her a makeover, and I can't even give myself one."

Lillian grunted. "Wadn't me what said she could."

I raised my head. "Well, but, I told you what that preacher said. The only way to keep my name off *60 Minutes* when they do a fake-marriage segment is to get that girl back in the pageant, and fixed up enough to win. And, I'll tell you the truth, I think that's an impossible job even if I knew what I was doing."

I'd tried to finagle some help from one of the two experts who were running the pageant. But Miss Wiggins had a crisis on her hands that morning. She'd found one of her home-care patients in need of an emergency trip to the hospital, and Miss Wiggins had to be in attendance. Frankly, I thought that was just an excuse. There're plenty of real nurses in a hospital. Then Hazel Marie announced that she had a meeting with Sheriff Frady and the downtown merchants to finalize the plans for the department's public awareness program, of which the pageant was a big part, and she had to be there to make a presentation. She'd been so nervous about speaking before such a prominent group that she couldn't give the proper attention to my concerns. All she'd been able to do was throw together the beauty aids that were now strewn across the table before me. "I can't help you, Miss Julia," she'd said, her hands shaking in her anxiety to look over her notes one more time. "Just do like you've seen me do, and remember, anything you do will be an improvement."

Well, I wasn't so sure about that, especially since Lillian had said that she only knew about cosmetic preparations for tawny complexions. Now here I was, the poorest hand in any two counties you want to name when it came to shading, highlighting, and blending colors, plucking eyebrows, lining eyes or lips, and bouffant coiffuring.

When I'd moaned to Hazel Marie about what to do with Ashley's long, stringy hair, she'd said, "Well, one good thing, Miss Julia. You won't need to use an extension."

Not knowing what an extension was, I

hadn't planned on using one.

On top of finding myself in charge of Ashley's cosmetic enhancement session, Sam had not called the night before, nor had Little Lloyd called that morning. Not hearing from them had put Hazel Marie in an even worse state, and while she prepared herself for her public speaking ordeal, she kept glancing from the silent telephone to me and back again. I'd tried to reassure her by suggesting that their appointment with Sonny Sutton had been delayed, or gone overtime, or some other such reason. But I was anxious to hear from them, myself.

When the doorbell rang, I told Lillian I'd get it. "It's probably Ashley," I said. "Time for us to face the music."

I walked through the dining room, into the living room and opened the front door. I almost didn't recognize the girl. Gone were the black-lined eyes, the atrocious nail polish, and, thank the Lord, the nose button. Her hair looked freshly washed, most of it fluffed out around her shoulders, and with the sun behind her, a few strands stood out in static attention like a halo around her head. I'd like to say that she looked better, but when you're plain, you're plain, and I ought to know.

"Come in, Ashley," I said, noting with approval her denim skirt and cotton blouse, with no flesh showing in between. "We're so glad you're staying in the pageant. It wouldn't be the same without you."

She gave me a brief smile, then ducked her head so that her hair fell around her face. "I'm still not sure about it," she murmured.

Ah, I thought, I might not be a good hand at cosmetics, but encouragement is one thing I can do. "But *we* are. And so are the officers on the third watch. Remember, they chose you."

She shrugged, as if to say she couldn't understand why. Frankly, I couldn't either, but they had, and she was what I had to work with, thanks to Preacher Kincaid. But I didn't want her to know about his meddling.

I led her into the kitchen, introduced her to Lillian, and sat her down in front of the mirror. I stood there for a moment, wondering what to do next and realizing that I'd reached the extent of my expertise. Facing that fact, I didn't know whether to admit I was as ignorant as a stump or keep quiet and try to stumble my way through.

"How about some coffee, Ashley? Or would you like a Coke?" I bustled around the kitchen, sidestepping Lillian, busying myself with anything but that basket of unknown potions.

"A Coke, please, if you don't mind," she mumbled.

Turning to the refrigerator, I said, "I'll get it, Lillian. You sit down and get Ashley started."

She gave me a look that would've frozen me if I'd paid any attention to it. But she sat down and began taking out one item after another, frowning as she read the labels on each one.

I put a glass in front of Ashley and took my seat across from Lillian, who was still studying labels with assiduous care.

"Well, now," I said with forced gaiety, "where shall we start?"

Lillian stared at me, and even Ashley dared to raise her eyes for a brief frightened look. Then I raised my hands and admitted defeat. "Ashley, we don't know what in the world we're doing. I'd hoped that Hazel Marie would do this, but she's in a meeting with the sheriff. Miss Wiggins was the second team, but she's hung up at the hospital for I don't know how long. And that leaves Lillian and me, and neither of us knows one blush from another, and that's the truth."

Ashley looked up from behind her hair, her face brightening, as she said, "I don't either, so I guess I'll be going."

"I tell you what," Lillian said, and I could've hugged her for it. "Le's us all see what we can do. If nobody know the right an' wrong of it, then nobody know the difference."

And that's what we did, although it took the longest time to get Ashley to break down and enjoy herself. When she finally realized that we were truly at a greater loss than she was, she became more comfortable with our experiments on her face. We all played around with moisturizers, toners, cleansers, foundations, eye liners, and lipsticks, and after a while, Ashley was primping and giggling and trying first one thing and another. When we'd used a little of every bottle and jar in the basket, Lillian began to wield the curling iron. She soon had Ashley looking like Shirley Temple in her heyday.

When we'd done all we could, I had to admit that we'd given Ashley a makeover, but into what, I couldn't say. "Ashley, honey," I said, "we may've gone overboard a little." I peered at the colors on her face and the ringlets on her head. "But," I went on with an authority I didn't possess, "show people always go heavy on the makeup. Thank goodness, it's not permanent. I promise we'll get better at it. Still, I hope you're not too disappointed with the results."

"I guess not," she said, turning this way and that in front of the mirror. "It sure is different, though."

Lillian stood back, cocking her head to the side as she gave her assessment. "She look pretty good to me. Miss Julia, you an' me ought to open us up a beauty school, like you say. Miss Ashley done learned us how to do it."

"Lord, Lillian, if we did, I'd have to be the first student. Well, Ashley, at least it's been a pleasant way to pass the morning."

"Actually," she said, still hesitant to look straight at me, "I didn't know we were going to do this. I thought you wanted to hear my talent."

"You did?" My goodness, we had gotten our wires crossed, hadn't we? I didn't know any more about music, guitar playing in particular, than I did about cosmetics. "Well," I said, glancing at Lillian, "I guess we could try, but I don't have a guitar in the house."

"Mine's in the car," she said, rising from the chair. "I'll run get it." She hurried toward the door, then looked around with a shy smile. "I hope nobody sees me."

As soon as Ashley was out the door, Lillian's eyes rolled back in her head. "What you know 'bout guitar playin'?"

"Not a thing. But, according to her grandmother, all she needs is some confidence and reassurance. And we can give her that."

"I don't know if we can or not," she mumbled. "It might be like us puttin' on all that paint 'thout knowin' what we doin'."

"Well, try," I said.

Ashley came back in, giving me a start when I saw the garish colors on her face from a distance. She was lugging a large guitar case, which she put on the floor beside her chair. Taking infinite care, she opened the latches. Then she carefully drew out the instrument and settled it in position across her lap, while I waited to hear the result of all the practice her grandmother had complained about.

Instead, she began to tune the thing, one string at a time, as her newly curled hair draped beside her face. *Plink-plink, plunk-plunk,* on top of sounds of hammering from above, made me want to jump out of my skin. I just can't stand all that screechy tuning that the local symphony orchestra does, either. *Get your instruments in tune beforehand,* I want to scream. *You knew you were going to play them.*

Ashley finally got to the point of strumming one chord, and I thought we'd hear something musical for a change. But no, it didn't suit her, so she went back to the monotonous tuning. At last, she strummed a chord twice in a row, glanced at me, and turned sideways in her chair. After another strum or two, she cut her eyes at Lillian, and would've turned backward if she'd been on a stool.

She stopped, her face entirely hidden from us. "It's no use. I can't do it."

"Can't do what?" I said, jerking upright at that jolting announcement. "Don't tell me you can't play it." I'd about given up hope of her winning even an honorable mention in the looks category, even with the advantage Lillian and I had given her. So if the girl couldn't play the instrument of her own choice, there was no way she could shine in the talent category to make up for it. She didn't have a chance of making any kind of showing, and I was going to be the one to suffer for it when her uncle started talking.

"Yes, ma'am, I can," she whispered, still

unable to face us. "It's just, well, I can't do it with people watching me."

"Well, Lord, honey. Lillian and I aren't *people*. I mean, we're not an audience. If you can't in front of us, how're you going to manage at the pageant?"

Her shoulders drooped and she laid her head against the back of the chair. "That's why I didn't want to be in it," she whispered, her face red with embarrassment. "I just get scared and my fingers stiffen up when I see people watching me."

I listened to this pitiful tale with my mouth open. Then I looked at Lillian, who was shaking her head in dismay. The silence lengthened as I realized that no amount of encouragement or training in charm and poise was going to overcome the problem of somebody so frightened of the spotlight. Especially if being the center of attention required nimble fingers.

"I'm sorry," Ashley mumbled. "I better go on home."

"No, ma'am. You're not going home yet." I had suddenly hit on a tactic that might just work. "Up, Ashley, get up and bring that guitar with you."

I took her by the arm, led her into the pantry, and slid a chair in with her. Then I turned on the light and walked out, closing the door behind me. "Now you can't see us watching you. So you play that thing, and I don't mean maybe."

This time it was Lillian's mouth that was hanging open, but I was determined to keep Miss Third Watch holed up in the pantry until her talent, if she had any, got her out.

After a few minutes of dead quiet, a few clear, though slightly muffled, I must admit, notes emanated from behind the pantry door. Gradually, the notes became chords that stayed close enough together to become what I'd call music. The fact of the matter was, I didn't have much of an ear for any kind of music, but what I was hearing made chills run down my back. Then Ashley's voice rose sweet and true in a mountain ballad that conjured up lonesome ridges and lost loves and tragic deaths. The poignant words touched me deeply, evoking my own muddled situation with Sam. Except I'd yet to see the man I'd hang myself for.

The only thing wrong with the serenade was the volume, which was a mite low. I reached for the knob on the pantry door, intending to ease it open so we could hear better. Lillian placed her hand on my arm and shook her head. "Better not," she whispered. "You might ruin it, an' that be a shame."

As Ashley's voice moved effortlessly into another ballad, Hazel Marie and Etta Mae Wiggins appeared at the back screen door. I moved quickly to them, my finger to my lips. "Sh-h-h, listen. Come on in and listen."

The two women tiptoed in, frowning as they wondered what was going on. Then they both stood stock-still, listening to a plaintive song that made tears well up in Hazel Marie's eyes. I heard a shuffle on the back stairs, and looked up to see both Pruitts standing there. Uncle and nephew were entranced, brought from their work by the music floating up from the pantry. Her song this time was one I recognized, since I'd heard it on *The Andy Griffith Show.* But this time, the words spoke directly to my heart, wrenching it as she sang of days and seasons quickly passing, and of love staying warm in spite of the winter winds.

All I could think of was how much I wanted Sam's warm love, for as far as we were concerned, the winter winds were already at our backs. Tears gushed into my eyes as I thought of the loss of our youth and how we were frittering away the little time we had left.

When Ashley stopped playing and singing, nobody said a word. We couldn't — at least I couldn't — being so moved by what I'd heard.

Then in a small voice, she called, "Can I come out now?"

"Lord, yes," I said. "Come on out here, child, and let us tell you how wonderful you are."

Hazel Marie's hand flew to her mouth, her eyes wide in shock, when Ashley hesitantly walked out. I couldn't tell if her surprise came from seeing who had been so melodious, or from her first sight of Ashley's made-over face, or both. She recovered admirably, though, looking at me as if I'd concocted a miracle. Etta Mae began to clap, and Mr. Pruitt and Willie joined in. Ashley cringed at the sudden ovation, and I had to grab her arm to keep her from retreating to the pantry again.

"That was the prettiest music I've ever heard," I exclaimed. "Ashley, you sing like an angel. Now," I went on, noting the pained expression on her face, "Mr. Pruitt, you and Willie need to get back to work. We have business to tend to, and you can hear more when you buy tickets to the pageant."

Ashley just stood there, her guitar hanging by her side, as she shook her head. "I can't," she whispered. "I just can't."

"Why can't you?" Miss Wiggins demanded in her straight-to-the-point way. "There's no reason in the world you can't do the same thing in front of a few hundred people. They'll love you, and probably'll want you to keep on and on. Now, come on. Don't be silly."

I could've shaken the woman. After all my tender nurturing to get Ashley to warm up her voice and her fingers, Miss Wiggins had just turned the girl into a shaken and white-faced semblance of her performing self.

"She has stage fright," I snapped. "Which is nothing to be sneezed at. It's a real affliction, and I ought to know because I suffer from it myself."

"Me, too," Hazel Marie murmured, thinking perhaps of the public speaking trial she'd just undergone. "Ashley, you're just great, and we really need you to perform. You'll make the pageant worth the ticket price all by yourself. Tell us what we can do to help."

"I don't know," she said, still hiding her face. "I just freeze up when I see people watching me."

I thought for a minute, then said, "I don't guess we could put a pantry on the stage, could we?"

"No," Miss Wiggins said, "but we can put her behind a scrim. Then adjust the lights so that all the audience will see is her outline, and fix it so she won't be able to see out at all. It'll be like she's all by herself."

Well, it seemed that Miss Wiggins was good for something, for Ashley's head came up and she looked from one to the other of us, with a tiny glint of hope in her eyes.

Chapter 31

"What's a scrim?" I asked Hazel Marie when Miss Wiggins and Ashley had gone.

She frowned. "It's like a cloth screen, Etta Mae said. Something that hangs between the actors and the audience to make the actors look kinda hazy, I think."

"It seems to me that if you go to a play, you go to see what's on the stage."

"Well, I know, but it's supposed to give a blurry effect. Kinda like airbrushing a photograph, I guess. I don't know, Miss Julia. I just hope it works."

"I do too, and that's what worries me. Ashley's going to need more than a blurry effect. If she walks out on that stage and sees all those people looking at her, even through a screen darkly, we're going to have one frozen girl on our hands."

"We'll just have to use a thick scrim so that won't happen. I think it could be real dramatic if we backlight her so that she's outlined for the audience. And maybe put a light somewhere that shines right in her eyes, so she can't see out. She could sit or stand in profile, so that she's not even looking out at the audience, maybe with a backdrop of mountains behind her. Wouldn't that be pretty?"

"My goodness, Hazel Marie, you sound like you know what you're talking about. So professional. I didn't know you knew anything about stagecraft."

"I don't, really." She smiled, pleased that I'd acknowledged her newfound expertise. "But we have some good volunteers who're helping us get set up."

"One thing you should keep in mind, though," I said. "If you have Ashley looking away from the audience, there'd better not be anybody watching her from the sidelines. You know, backstage personnel and the like."

"That's the wings you're talking about. And, you're right, we'll have to be careful to keep everybody away when she's performing. Oh, she is so good, Miss Julia. She's just going to *make* the pageant."

That evening after supper, I accompanied Hazel Marie to the high school auditorium to act as a constructively critical observer of the pageant rehearsal. I hated to leave the house, expecting any minute to hear from Sam and Little Lloyd by phone or, even better, to see them pull into the driveway. Hazel Marie was torn, too, and I could tell that worry over their where-abouts was getting to her. But the show must go on, she said, although our show wasn't exactly Broadway material, and for my money it could never open and nobody'd know the difference. To ease our concerns, she put messages on both our answering machines, telling where we were and when we'd be home.

"That way," she said, "they won't be worried about us, and they'll call back."

I hoped she was right, and as I settled myself in a seat some distance from the stage, I tried to put my mind on the matter at hand. Not an easy job, for the confused state of affairs on and off the stage made me so antsy I could hardly sit still. They all needed a firm hand taken to them, from the bluegrass band that couldn't get tuned up to the giddy contestants who were too excited to listen to directions. Add to that Willie Pruitt, who was stomping around on the makeshift runway to be sure it wouldn't collapse under the tread of pumps with three-inch heels; Miss Wiggins, who was shouting orders to any and everybody; Hazel Marie, who was flap-ping her arms in an organizational frenzy;

and a half dozen off-duty deputies serving as volunteers but doing nothing except getting in the way and leering at the contestants, most of whom were in their usual attire of shorts and tops, both cropped beyond decency.

I was pleased to see Ashley Knowles among them, relieved that she hadn't had second thoughts about participating, and that she'd washed her face. I noticed, though, that she still held herself apart from the others. And not a one of those girls tried to include her. *Just wait*, I thought to myself, *she's going to show you all a thing or two*. And I was going to take my share of credit for it, too.

Having heard Ashley's talent, I was feeling much better about the bargain with Preacher Kincaid. If I could only do something about her looks, she had a chance to win fair and square — influence or no influence.

"Okay, everybody," Miss Wiggins bellowed from the stage, as Hazel Marie herded the girls behind the curtains. "The music's about to start, and I'm going to introduce you one at a time. Come out to center stage, pause and pose, then walk down the runway to the end. Stop there and let everybody get a good look, then pivot and return to center stage. Pivot again and face the audience, then walk to your spot at the back of the stage. There're marks where you're supposed to stand, so just stay there until all the contestants have had their turn; then you'll go back down the runway in a line. Be careful when you pass each other — this thing's not very wide." She frowned at Willie Pruitt, who took the criticism in stride as he grinned up at her.

The volunteers took seats up close to the runway, the better to see the parade of beauties, and Miss Wiggins took her place at the microphone on one side of the stage. She looked up at the sound booth over my head, then leaned into the microphone, shouting, "Lights!" There was an electronic squeal, and one of the deputies hurried over to adjust the volume. The lights in the auditorium went out and spotlights lit up the stage.

Miss Wiggins shuffled a few papers, then started out in dramatic tones, "And our first contestant . . . Wait a minute. Where's the music? Ricky, y'all're supposed to be playing."

The orchestra, if you can call it that, cut loose then, with a bouncy tune featuring fiddles, guitars, banjos, and, for all I could tell, a washboard or two.

"Okay," Miss Wiggins said, with a quick look backstage. "We're gonna do it this time. Y'all ready?" Putting her mouth right next to the microphone, she started again. "And our first contestant is Miss SWAT Team, Hea-a-a-the-e-r Pea-vey!"

That was a little much for me, but the off-duty deputies welcomed Miss Peavey's appearance with clapping and whistles. She glided to the center of the stage, her posture correct and her color high. She did everything right, although with obvious self-consciousness, until she got to the end of the runway. She stood for a moment; then, when she pivoted, her hands flew out to the side and her knees bent as if she were waiting for a ball to be passed. When the runway creaked and listed slightly, I realized she was trying to keep her balance.

"Hey!" she yelled. "This thing's falling."

Willie Pruitt ducked down to shore up the runway, telling her, "No, it's not. Keep walking. I'll have it fixed in a minute."

One of the deputies called out, "I'll catch you, Heather!" He'd've thought better of it if her father had been there.

The rehearsal came to a screeching halt while Willie hammered on another brace. Miss Wiggins stood tapping her foot, but he just went about his business with a smile on his face, delighted, it seemed, with any kind of attention from her. "You said to make it temporary," he reminded her.

"But I didn't say half-assed," she snapped back. I cringed at the example she was setting for those impressionable young women. Miss Wiggins, to my mind, could've used some schooling in the social graces even more than the girls, who were at least trying to appear well-bred. But some people don't know and don't care to know.

As the contestants congregated onstage to see what the holdup was, some of the deputies checked out Willie's work, shaking the runway to assure themselves of its stability. Hazel Marie herded the girls backstage again, and Miss Wiggins consulted with the band leader. She seemed to be unhappy with their selection of runway walk music.

I tried to shut my mind to the chaos around me, sinking into wondering where Sam and Little Lloyd were and what they were doing right that minute. Visions of highway accidents or some other unfortunate occurrence raced through my mind, even as I told myself how unlikely such things were. But I am a worrier, and much more apt to expect misfortune than to assume that all is well all the time.

I nearly jumped out of my seat when a head leaned close to the back of my neck. "Well, well," a decidedly unwelcome voice whispered much too close, "what have we here?"

I jerked around, visibly annoyed and not trying to conceal it. "Thurlow Jones! What're you doing here? This is a rehearsal and it's not open to the public."

"I'm not the public. I'm a judge, and I'm just checking out the merchandise." He sat back, smugly pleased that he had startled the life out of me.

Typically, his face was stubbled, not from an effort to follow the current style, but from flat laziness. He'd been lax about shaving all his life. Even though he wore a suit and tie, the one was rumpled and the other stained and frayed. I wondered why he bothered. An old man's musty odor drifted toward me, and I scooted to the edge of my seat, ready to abandon ship if he lingered.

He was a scrawny, short-in-stature but large-in-belligerence man, and the town's premier eccentric, which is saying something, because Abbotsville has a gracious plenty of peculiar people. He lived in a large, run-down house that could've been a show place if he'd taken the trouble to repair it and mow the grass. He had all the money in the world, but nobody could remember how he'd come by it. His family had always been wealthy, but since he'd never married and had no children that anybody knew of, there was talk that he aimed to make the money run out at the same time he did. To that end, he lived a pauper's life, because he was just crazy enough to like it, and gave enormous amounts to the oddest causes anybody could imagine.

"Merchandise!" I hissed. "I'll have you know that is no way to speak of these young women. They have graciously agreed to do this for the good of the community, which is more than I can say for you, Mr. Jones, and I will not have you disparage them in such a manner."

"Well, pardon the hell outta me," he said, sliding down in his chair, with a grin on his face and a glint in his eye.

Thurlow loved to get a rise out of people with his shocking pronouncements, and he'd just gotten one out of me. I knew that the best way to deal with him was to ignore whatever came out of his mouth, but how could I when he irritated me beyond endurance?

"Mr. Jones . . ." I began in a calmer tone, attempting to appeal to his social conscience, as well as to get in a plug for Ashley. "There is one particular contestant that I hope you will look kindly upon. Now, I know that it would be unethical for me to try to sway your vote, but Ashley Knowles is extremely talented and she'd make a wonderful representative of the sheriff's department."

"You mean she'd look good with the canine unit? Or, you mean you couldn't tell her apart from the dogs?"

"No, that's not what I mean, and you know it. I mean that Ashley ought to win the crown, and I would be most appreciative if you gave her every consideration. And, Mr. Jones . . ."

"Just a minute, Julia Whatever-Your-Name-Is. We know each other better'n that. Call me Thurlow. And I'll look at your girl, but I already got my eye on that little chubby one."

Melanie Easley. That's who he was referring to in such uncomplimentary terms, the very one Little Lloyd was so taken with.

"Thurlow, please. It would mean ever so much to me if you would give Ashley every . . ."

"You trying to bribe me?" Thurlow's glasses glinted in the light from the stage. "If you are, I'll need a better offer than just a little appreciation."

He cocked his head to one side, as the music swelled to the swaying walk of YoShandra Washington on the runway. "Hear that? It's 'Pretty Woman,' just the song for you."

"I am a married woman now, and my name is Julia Murdoch. Mrs. Sam Murdoch, and don't you forget it." The last person in the world who needed to know my unsettled marital state was this cocky snip of a man who would've been courting me in a minute if I gave him one bit of encouragement. And if he expected me to offer more for his consideration of Ashley, well, I'd rather take my chances with Preacher Kincaid.

"Is that a fact?"

I half stood, clutching my pocketbook, prepared to do battle or to take myself out of there — one of the two. "It most certainly is a fact, and you'd better hope Sam doesn't learn that you've been pestering me."

With a snort of dismissal, he pulled himself up close to the back of my seat. "How's he gonna know? He's left you, hasn't he? Up and gone, and who knows when or if he'll be back. You know what I think?" He swiveled his head first to the left, then the right, as if he wanted to whisper a secret. "I think you're on the market again, and just so you know, I'm still available."

I stood to my full height, which was some inches above his, and said, "As far as I'm concerned, you'll *stay* available." Then I sidestepped my way to the aisle, aiming to leave until I remembered that I'd come with Hazel Marie and couldn't go until she did.

Even so, I wanted away from Thurlow Jones, who was striking much too close to home. Lord, I needed Sam by my side before LuAnne's speculations started to take hold, and Thurlow raised the woeful specter of me as an abandoned woman.

Chapter 32

But what if I were? Abandoned, I mean. What if it was Sam who was having second thoughts? What if, now that he was free, even if he didn't know it yet, he took a long, hard look at being married to me and didn't like what he saw? I probably wasn't that easy to get along with, always wanting to have my way and thinking I knew what was best for everybody and letting them know it.

Lillian had told me a hundred times or more that I was going to lose Sam if I didn't treat him better. "Mr. Sam, he gonna find him somebody else, you don't get off yo' high horse an' start 'preciatin' what you got." Her words rang in my head, and I knew truer ones had never been spoken. I *hadn't* appreciated him as he deserved. I'd let him do all the courting, rarely responding, and that had carried right over into our marriage, such as it was. And I'd been only too quick to banish him to another room, never letting him know how much I'd missed having him by my side through the night. For all I'd revealed of my own anguish, he had every reason to think I was relieved to have him gone from both bed and board.

So what if he'd had a change of heart when he got off on his own? Out of sight, out of mind, you know. And, even though he had Little Lloyd with him to remind him of me, he might've begun thinking of greener pastures and quieter waters. Neither of which he was likely to get from me.

I stopped, almost stumbling, midway down the aisle, and grasped the back of a chair, weakened as a paralyzing thought hit me. What if our questionable marriage was indeed a sign from above — but to Sam, not to me? I slid into the first chair in the row, hardly able to get my breath. Here, I'd been thinking that the Lord was speaking to me, when all along the signs could've been aimed at Sam. Maybe the Lord had other rows for him to hoe.

Thankful that the auditorium was dark, I leaned my elbow on the chair arm and hid my face as the consequences of my sudden insight hit me full force. And, as I wrestled with that, the beat of "Pretty Woman" reverberating through the room and Miss Wiggins's amplified voice announcing the contestants played havoc with what was already going on in my head.

Lord, I thought. *If that's the case, if all the signs are not aimed at me, but at Sam, where does that leave me?* Out in the cold, that's where.

No. No, it couldn't be so. I shook myself, lifted my head and watched as Tasha McKenzie sashayed down the runway. But I didn't really see her, for I was busy telling myself that surely I would not be hung out to dry.

Sam had made a promise to stay with me until death did us part, but look at the dubious circumstances he'd made it in. For all I knew, those circumstances rendered his promise null and void.

I felt a tap on my shoulder, and mortally shaken by the range of my thoughts, I switched around, pocketbook held high, ready to smack Thurlow Jones out of his seat and across the aisle.

"Whoa!" Mr. Pickens said, grinning his pirate's grin and holding his hands up to ward off a blow. "Don't hit me. I give up."

"Oh, Mr. Pickens," I said, the air suddenly taken out of my sails. "I didn't know it was you." I leaned my head against the back of the chair, just undone at how on edge I was.

"Hey," he said, leaning close so that his aromatic aftershave cologne nearly overpowered me. "Are you all right?"

"I don't know." I sat upright and tried to pull myself together. "As all right as I can be, I guess. I'm sorry, Mr. Pickens, I thought you were Thurlow Jones. He's been pestering the life out of me."

He looked around, scanning the auditorium. "Is he here?"

"I hope to goodness he's gone. He wasn't supposed to be here in the first place." I was trying to put up a good front for Mr. Pickens, letting him think that Thurlow was the cause of my unsteady nerves.

"How long you think this'll last?" he asked, his black eyes watching every move that Hazel Marie made as she showed the contestants their marks on the stage. "Hazel Marie doesn't know I'm back, and I'm gonna surprise her with a great big kiss." He transferred his twinkling gaze to me, expecting to be taken to task for such graphic language. "And speaking of kissing — yours, not mine — where's Sam? He around?"

"Oh-h-h," I wailed, as softly as I could, so as not to attract the attention of outsiders to my dire straits. "He's gone, and, Mr. Pickens, I think he's left me and may not ever come back, and I guess it's Aaron

Kincaid's fault, who falsely presented himself as qualified to join a man and woman in holy matrimony, which you already know about. But what you don't know is that it may be my fault, as well, because I haven't been much of a wife, and that may be why I've been judged and found wanting, and doomed to a lonely old age for the rest of my life."

"What are you talking about?" Mr. Pickens frowned, giving me his full attention, now that sudden tears were revealing my inner turmoil. "Hey. Hey, now, it can't be that bad."

"You just don't know, Mr. Pickens," I said, fumbling for a Kleenex in my pocketbook.

"Well, tell me about it."

"I can't. Not here, with all this commotion going on." I waved my hand toward the runway, where the contestants were passing each other in the most disorderly fashion imaginable. Giggles and laughter almost drowned out the music, as one young woman after another teetered on the turn, almost falling off.

"Then come on." Mr. Pickens stood up, took my arm, and hoisted me out of my seat. Before I knew it, we were headed out of the auditorium and into the dusky evening outside. "You want to sit out here," he said, indicating the cement steps, "or go to my car?"

"Your car, Mr. Pickens. You're not fully aware of the delicate nature of my concerns."

He nodded and led me out to the sidewalk and toward his car, gratifying me with the concerned look on his face, although his mouth did twitch occasionally.

"Now let's hear it," he said, when we were settled in his low-slung sports car, which caused great inconvenience to anyone trying to get in or out.

I straightened my dress, smoothing it over my knees, and began to unburden myself. "I guess I'm worried about Sam. You've been gone, so you may not know that he and Little Lloyd took off several days ago to track down that preacher who supposedly married us but apparently didn't. See, Mr. Pickens," I said, then had to swallow hard before proceeding. "I wanted him to go, urged it, in fact, and banished him to Deputy Bates's old room until he agreed to go. I wanted him to find out for sure, you see, so I'd know where we stood. And that's part of the problem. I've been so concerned about *myself*, and *my* reputation, with little or no concern about his needs. Or what he might want." I dabbed at my eyes, just overcome with my own shortcomings. "And I wanted him gone because LuAnne Conover had planned a wedding reception for us that I wasn't supposed to know about, but Lillian told me anyway, and you know I couldn't have that under the circumstances. I mean, a wedding reception when there hasn't been a real wedding? That wouldn't do at all, but I couldn't admit that to her, so the only thing to do was to have Sam out of town, which was a good excuse to give her. And now, now, I haven't heard from him since night before last, so it's been two whole days of silence, with not even a call from Little Lloyd. And for all I know," I moaned, as my voice broke, "Sam's decided that he's better off without me."

Dead silence from Mr. Pickens. I glanced over at him, seeing his dark profile against the open window. The fingers of one hand tapped softly on the steering wheel.

"And that's not the worst of it," I went on. "All this upset may be a sign from the Lord that Sam and I shouldn't have even tried to get married. I mean, why else would this be happening to us, if the Lord's hand wasn't in it? And I haven't even told you the half of it. Of the signs, I mean."

"Well," he said, finally breaking his silence. He handed me his handkerchief, which I accepted gratefully since my damp and wadded-up Kleenex had lost its usefulness. "I can't help you with the Lord's business, seeing that we're not in close communication. I just go along the best way I know how until I hit a brick wall; then I do something else."

"That's exactly what I'm afraid of! I'm afraid that the Lord is telling Sam that I'm the wrong woman for him. And it just breaks my heart, because I *know* I've not been all that pleasant to him. Nor very warm," I mumbled, looking out the window on my side. "Nor, well, responsive to his overtures, which I know a husband has every right to expect. But, if he'd just given me a little more time to, to adjust, I believe I would've sooner or later. But now he's gone and I'm afraid he's not coming back."

I covered my face with Mr. Pickens's sweet-smelling handkerchief and gave in to my grief.

He rearranged himself in his seat, so that he was leaning against the door, facing me. He took a couple of deep breaths, and turned his head so he was looking through the windshield. Then he ran his hand over his mouth a few times. He coughed and breathed deeply again.

My head shot up. "Are you laughing?"

"No! Lord, no, Miss Julia. You know me better than that."

"That's the trouble," I said, gritting my teeth at the thought of his playful nature. "I do know you."

"Listen, now," he said, and I could hear the change of tone in his voice. "A couple of things. Number one, if Sam was planning to leave you, he wouldn't've taken Lloyd with him. So put that out of your head. Number two, three, and four, where was he when he last called you, where was he headed next, and does he have a cell phone with him?"

"He doesn't have a cell phone, I don't think. At least, I've never seen one. And he was in Sevierville when he last called, and on his way to Nashville to see Sonny Sutton's manager. He's the Singing Sensation from San Antone, you know. Sonny, I mean, not the manager." I blew my nose and wiped my eyes again. "Sam thinks that Sonny's people have a better chance of finding the preacher than he does by himself. But I don't even know if he got there or not. And, Mr. Pickens, thank you for reminding me about Little Lloyd. I'm not thinking straight, or I'd have realized that he wouldn't keep that child from his mother. That means . . . Oh, Lord, that means that something has happened to them."

"Hold on, now. Don't go off the deep end on me. First thing in the morning, I'll start tracking them down. And if I have to, I'll go after them."

"Oh, thank you, Mr. Pickens. I feel better already, because if Sam Murdoch wants off the hook, I want him to tell me to my face."

Mr. Pickens's white teeth flashed in the dark car. "Yeah, hold his feet to the fire." Then he tapped the steering wheel again. "How's Hazel Marie taking it?"

"Well, she's concerned, of course. But not as much as I am, because she trusts Sam to look after the boy." I did a little tapping of my own on the arm of the door. "Which with this silent treatment I'm getting, is more than I can say."

He reached over and patted my arm. "Put your mind at rest. I'm on the case."

"Mr. Pickens," I said, my voice sounding hollow, "I declare, I shouldn't say this to you, but you beat all I've ever seen. You're the world's worst when it comes to what is considered proper behavior." I sniffed, then went on. "In fact, you are the flight-iest and most unsettling man I know, yet every time I get in trouble, you're the one I turn to."

"Yeah, and I get you out of it, too. Don't I?"

"So far," I said, nodding in agreement. "Let's see how you do this time."

Chapter 33

I drove Hazel Marie's car home from the auditorium so she could ride with Mr. Pickens. Following them, I noted that their seat belts kept them separate, after they'd spent an inordinate amount of time close together before buckling up. I didn't begrudge them, although seeing those two heads as one had made my pitiful heart ache.

When the rehearsal was over, and Hazel Marie met us out front, she expressed her joy first at seeing Mr. Pickens waiting for her. Then she launched into a discourse on Ashley Knowles's deficiencies.

"That girl is so self-conscious, you wouldn't believe. She had that hair swinging down in her face, and she looked like she was just cringing all the way down the runway. I don't know what we're going to do with her."

Mr. Pickens smiled down at her, then smoothed her hair with his hand. "I can tell you what you're going to do with me."

It crossed my mind as I drove home that I'd let Hazel Marie down by making not one comment on the rehearsal. Somebody, even Miss Wiggins, would eventually ask for any constructive criticism I might have, since it was in that capacity that I'd attended. And what was I going to say? That between fighting off Thurlow Jones and pouring my heart out to Mr. Pickens, I hadn't had a minute to study a pageant rehearsal?

As I say, it crossed my mind, but that's all it did. It wouldn't be hard to make up something to tell Hazel Marie. In her excitement at seeing Mr. Pickens, she'd chattered away about all that had gone wrong. I would just repeat that to her, if she even remembered to ask what I thought.

Mr. Pickens parked his car at the curb, while I pulled into the driveway. We met in the front yard and went into the house together, both Hazel Marie and I hurrying to check our answering machines. My heart jumped in my breast when I saw the blinking light.

I carefully punched the PLAY button, fearful of erasing whatever was on the tape. Sam's voice soothed my shattered nerves. "Julia? Sorry we've been out of touch, but you won't believe what we've been doing. We met with Sonny's manager early yesterday, and first thing I knew, Sonny himself came in. We compared notes on what we've done to find Kincaid. And, I tell you, Sonny's pretty steamed about the situation. He's got every county in the state looking for that man. I mean, when Sonny Sutton speaks, people listen. Real nice fellow, though." There was a brief silence on the line; then Sam's voice started again. "Anyway, until we hear something, there's not much else we can do, so Sonny took us out on his houseboat yesterday, then to the Grand Ole Opry last night. Lloyd's had a big time and he can't wait to tell you about it. But we're on the way home now. It'll be late when we get there, so we'll go to my house for the rest of the night. But I want to see you in the morning." He paused again, and I thought that was the end of the message. Then he said, "We need to sit down and talk."

The machine clicked off, and I almost did, too. *Sit down and talk?* About what? His change of heart? I sat on the bed, my breath coming in gasps, while I thought over what I'd not heard in his message. Not one teasing word. Not one sweet one. Nothing warm and embracing in the tone of his voice. And what had he been doing while I was home, worried sick? Out running around with a singing sensation and taking no thought of the morrow.

Hazel Marie came down the stairs, calling, "Miss Julia? Did you hear from them? I didn't."

I blew out my breath and got to my feet. No need to throw cold water on her happiness, I thought, as I went to meet her.

"Yes, they're on their way home."

"Oh, I can't wait," she said, then turned toward the living room where Mr. Pickens waited. "J.D., did you hear that? They're on their way. Surely they'll be here soon."

"No, wait, Hazel Marie," I cautioned. "Sam said they'd be quite late, so they're going to his house. Didn't want to disturb us, I guess."

"Oh, I wouldn't care, would you?" But she didn't wait for an answer. She hurried over to Mr. Pickens, standing much too close to him. "Now that I don't have to worry about Lloyd, we could go out for a while."

Mr. Pickens put his arm around her. "Then that's what we'll do." He looked across the room at me, his black eyebrows raised. "Things're looking up, right?"

Well, no, they weren't, but I nodded, told them to have a good time, and locked the door behind them. I knew where they were going — to his house — and what they were going to do, but I didn't dwell on it.

Lord, for all the times I'd been dismayed by what went on between Hazel Marie and Mr. Pickens, I was now overcome with envy. They had something special, even though it wasn't blessed by either church or state. Come to think of it, neither was what Sam and I had. If we still had anything.

Mr. Pickens would go off on his business now and again, but he always came back. And he never changed. As true as any husband could be, even though he wasn't one.

And Sam! The one man I'd thought I could trust, the one I'd been willing, though somewhat reluctantly, to commit myself to, and here he was, wanting to sit down and talk. I knew what he wanted to talk about. I wasn't dense, and I wasn't starry eyed. He'd gone to Tennessee, found out somehow that we weren't legally married, and wanted his freedom back.

And why? Why, because he'd seen Etta Mae Wiggins again in her tight blue jeans, and realized what he'd bypassed for me, who wouldn't be caught dead in a pair of Levi's. Or Liz Claiborne, either.

I checked the back door, turned off the lights, and headed for my room, becoming madder by the minute. I slung my pocketbook off the bed and turned down the covers, building up a head of steam with each movement. I'd torn up my house to accommodate Sam Murdoch. Moved downstairs so we could have privacy. Privacy for what? I ask you. Moved Hazel Marie upstairs, which took two million trips up and down the stairs. Hired Mr. Pruitt and Willie to tear up jack, building closets we no longer needed, and did everything I knew how to do to make him feel at home.

Well, except sleep with him. But that wasn't my fault. It hadn't been my idea to go to a fantasy chapel and have what turned out to be a fantasy wedding. And it hadn't been my idea to spend our fantasy honeymoon at Dollywood, either.

I stopped midway of removing my clothes as I prepared for bed. He wants to talk with me? Well, he'd better be ready to get an earful, too. I wasn't about to show up, full of joy and welcome, only to have him tell me he'd had second thoughts. I'd had a few, myself, if he but knew it. And he was going to know it. I'd beat him to it, that's what I'd do. If he thought he'd take my hand and tell me, with pity in his eyes, that I'd be better off without him, that our make-believe wedding had been a blessing in disguise, that it was all turning out for the best, then he had another think coming.

I lay in bed with the lights off, imagining just how it would go. He'd expect me to be stunned, and he'd feel sorry for me. He'd do all he could to let me down easy. He'd even have a handkerchief ready, in case I started bawling. Oh, I could picture the whole sorry episode, him trying to be kind, since that was his way, and all the while he'd be rejecting me out of hand.

I squirmed around in the bed, turning first one way, then the other, unable to get fixed regardless of what I did. The big rejection scene played over and over in my mind, as I rehearsed what he would say and what I would say in return. Of course, he was a lawyer and could outtalk me any day of the week. So what I would have to do was get my say-so in first. No woman wants to hear that she's unwanted, and I didn't intend to hear it from Sam. If he thought he could break my heart and expose me to the ridicule of the town, I was going to head him off at the pass. I aimed to do a little breaking and exposing, myself. And we'd just see how he liked it.

I didn't think I'd sleep a wink, and I didn't for the longest. But I must have, for I awakened to sunlight shining through the curtains where I'd failed to draw them, and to voices and laughter in the kitchen. Dressing quickly, I hurried in to find Hazel Marie smothering Little Lloyd with hugs and kisses, telling him how she'd missed him and how glad she was to see him. Lillian beamed as she stood by the stove, watching the child as her pancakes almost burned.

Little Lloyd looked fine and healthy, in spite of his questionable diet in the past few days. He was tanned from his time on the rides at Dollywood or on a houseboat somewhere, and full of himself, telling his mother all they'd done, with Sonny this and Sonny that. I reached over and patted his shoulder, wanting to feel him again and reassure myself that he was safe.

He pushed up his glasses, reminding me that we needed to get them adjusted, and turned to me. "Miss Julia, you should've been with us. We did everything, rode the rides and saw a show at Dollywood, and went to the clerk of court's office and looked through records. Real interesting, because you can find out all kinds of things. Then we went to Nashville, and did you know they have a Greek temple there? And a university? Real nice town. I liked it. And Sonny took us on his houseboat and we stayed on the river all day and fished and everything. And he took us to the Grand Ole Opry and I got to meet Lonesome Will — he's their new comedy act — and then we went to some more offices and asked a lot of questions. Sonny and Mr. Sam were looking for somebody — I don't know who — but I think I'm going to be a lawyer when I grow up. I liked looking in those dusty old books."

"Sit down, now," Lillian said, bringing a plate to the table. "You need to eat yo' breakfast. I'll fix Mr. Sam's when he get here."

"Oh, he's not coming," Little Lloyd said, sitting down at his place. My heart dropped like a rock.

Lillian frowned, and Hazel Marie said, "Why not?"

"James wanted to cook for him, so he's eating over there." Little Lloyd busied himself with pouring syrup over his pancakes, unaware of the looks that were aimed my way by Hazel Marie and Lillian. "He said he'll be over later."

Lillian gave me a hard look. "I guess you better get yo'self on over there. No tellin' what that James give him, prob'bly not fit to eat no how."

"No," I said, somewhat stiffly, as I tried to hide my dismay at my husband's reluctance to be welcomed home. "I prefer your cooking, Lillian." Might as well make somebody feel good.

Hazel Marie kept glancing at me as we took our places at the table. She was frowning, hesitant to pursue the subject of my missing husband, but wanting to know what was going on. Finally, she murmured, "Is everything all right, Miss Julia?"

"Certainly," I almost snapped, on edge from trying to hide the hurt I was feeling. "I declare, Little Lloyd, your hair is almost as yellow as your mother's. I hope you didn't get too much sun while you were gone."

In spite of my aching heart, I couldn't help but smile when I looked at him. He still had some resemblance to Wesley Lloyd — wispy hair, thin face, and slight build, but I was beginning to see some of Hazel Marie in him, too, thank the Lord. Mostly in his disposition, for he was as sunny and cheerful as his mother, which changed his features remarkably. Wesley Lloyd had always had a frown on his face, with beady eyes that roved about, looking for something to criticize and disapprove of. He always found it, too.

Little Lloyd smiled. "No'm, I didn't get too much sun. We spent a lot of time in the car, and Mr. Sam's gonna teach me to drive real soon. Then we can take turns when we go on another trip."

"Oh, don't be planning another trip!" Hazel Marie cried. "You just got home. I can't let you go off again for a long time."

"Worry less about another trip, Hazel Marie," I said, "than about Sam letting him drive. You have a few years, Little Lloyd, before you get behind a wheel."

"I know," he said happily, not at all put off by the thought. "But Mr. Sam said he'd take me out in the country and let me practice. I'll need a cushion, though, to be high enough. He said we'd take J.D., too."

"Mr. Pickens," I corrected him.

He nodded. "Yessum. Mr. Pickens."

Well, Lord, I thought as I nibbled at a pancake, Sam is certainly making a lot of plans for the future. Too bad they didn't include me, but then, my plans for the future were unlikely to include him.

And if, as Little Lloyd had said, Sam's immediate plans included coming over *later,* then my plans just might include not being at home to receive him.

"Hazel Marie," I said. "Don't you have something for me to do today?"

Chapter 34

Well, yes, she did. Hazel Marie jumped up to get her notes and her calendar. Then she sat back down and picked up her fork. Between trying to eat and figure out what she had lined up for the day, she didn't do either one very well.

"I've got to do something about Melanie and Shandra, because the fire marshal said absolutely no fire in the auditorium." She looked up at me, her eyes big. "They're so upset — Melanie, especially. She had a crying fit, then changed her talent to a lyrical dance, whatever that is. I just hope she'll be ready, because the pageant's almost upon us." She glanced down, consulting her calendar. "The girls need to rehearse onstage again, so they're going to meet with Etta Mae and me today at the auditorium. Lloyd, you can go with me if you want to, and maybe help up in the sound booth." She made a note to herself in the margin of her notebook. "Then, let's see — oh, not all the band members can get off work today, so we'll just have a run-through and meet again tonight for, well, not exactly a dress rehearsal, since they don't all have their costumes ready. But at least they can do their routines to music. Oh, I need to check the CD's that some of them are bringing. Make sure they'll work on the sound system there. And, let me see — what else?" She took another bite of pancake, while I waited for my assignment.

"What about Ashley?" I asked. "Do you think she'll rehearse? I mean, you don't have the scrim up yet, do you?"

"Oh, it's there. They have a couple of them up in the whatever you call it. The ceiling, I guess. We'll try it tonight when it's dark and can get the lights where they need to be. She might freeze up this morning, even with just the girls watching her. They'll laugh at her or snub her even worse than some of them're already doing. Since you've sorta taken her under your wing, why don't you rehearse her in one of the classrooms? Use a closet if you have to. She needs some help with her walk, too."

"I can do that. I do better one-on-one, anyway. I'll take my car, though, so I can come home when we're through."

"Oh, wait," Hazel Marie said. "I know you want to see Sam." She gave me a teasing smile. "I keep forgetting you're still in the honeymoon phase."

"My honeymoon's come and gone, Hazel Marie," I said. "I think I can manage a tutorial rehearsal this morning without having to see him."

Hazel Marie and Lillian exchanged worried glances again, but I refused to be more forthcoming. I was in no mood to bare my soul to anybody but Sam, and, believe me, my soul was the only thing I intended to bare.

Confusion, noise, and laughter reigned again in the auditorium when we got there. All the contestants except Ashley were beside themselves with excitement, for there were not many more days before the big one. Miss Wiggins was making her presence felt, trying to run everything as usual. The woman made my mouth tighten so much that I could barely speak to her.

I took Ashley aside and led her to an empty classroom. I noted again the lack of makeup, the lank hair, and the absence of the gold stud in her nose. One could only hope that the hole would close of its own accord.

"Now, Ashley," I said, once the door was shut and we were alone. "I want you to run through your piece with just me here. I don't know one note from another, so you don't need to worry about what I think. You could sing and play off-key all the way through, and I wouldn't know the difference."

"I'll try," she mumbled, letting that hair hide her face.

"Well, to make it easier, you sit so that you're looking out the window at the ball field, and I'll go over here." I took myself across the room and slid into a student desk.

I'm pleased to report that Ashley did even better under those circumstances than she had in my pantry, because she sang a song I recognized. I extended my congratulations on a particularly beautiful rendition of "Scarborough Fair," and got a shy smile in return. Then without any encouragement and right in my presence, she launched into "Greensleeves," stunning me with the clear beauty of her voice.

"I don't think you need any more practice," I told her. "It sounded fine to me, although I admit I don't have a musical ear. You do need to decide, though, which one you're going to render as your talent." Then, thinking that she needed to be warned, I asked, "You know about the light they're going to aim at your face, don't you?"

"Yes, ma'am. I hope it works."

"And I hope it doesn't blind you. So don't look right at it. It'll keep you from seeing the audience or anything else. All you have to do is think about the words you're singing. Pretend you're sitting on the side of a mountain somewhere, with no one within a mile of you. I want you to close your mind to everything else, and open it up to what you do best. Which is sing and play that guitar."

She took a long breath and said, "I'll try. I just get so nervous in front of people."

"I understand, but you've done just fine in front of me. Think of it this way: How many of the other contestants can play the guitar?"

"Not any, I don't think."

"That's right, and how many will there be in the audience who can play it?"

"I don't know. Maybe a lot."

"And maybe not. And those who can will recognize your talent, because, honey, you are *good*." I stopped then, wondering if an admittedly unmusical listener's critique held any water at all. But she smiled at the praise, apparently not considering the source.

Then her smile faded. "I think Heather sings better than I do."

"I wouldn't know. I've not heard her, and besides, you won't be singing the same thing. I tell you, Ashley, when you lift your voice in song it sends cold chills down my back. Heather's going to have to go some to get to me like you do.

"So you keep that in mind," I went on. "You are the best in this town at what you do. And how do you ever expect to get to Nashville, if you let a bunch of untalented people stop you?"

She hid her face. "My grandmother tell you about that?"

"Yes, she did. And if that's what you want to do, then this is a good place to start." Not that I would want to go to Nashville, but I believe in encouraging young people to pursue their dreams. "So you're going to have to get over this stage fright of yours, and remind yourself over and over that you're doing something that few others can do. And nobody in this town, much less in this pageant.

"All right, now," I continued. "Put that instrument down, and let's practice your runway walk and your pivot."

She grimaced, but she put the guitar in its case and stood with her shoulders hunched over, as if preparing herself for an ordeal. Which, for her, it probably was.

I pushed back a row of desks to make room for her to walk. "Let's see what you do. Walk down to the wall, turn, and come back."

She did, but it was a pitiful performance.

"Look now, this is one place where we can't hide you behind a scrim or put you in a pantry. You're going to have to do better than that. Pull your shoulders back and hold your head up high. And walk from your hips down, like Miss Wiggins showed you."

"Yes, but I'm not pretty like the other girls. And all those people will be looking at me."

"They certainly will be, and you're going to give them something to look at." I tapped my mouth with a finger, trying to think of anything that would help. "Ashley, do you know why so many beautiful women use makeup?"

"Because they want to?"

"No. It's because they think they need help. Makeup is a cover. It hides faults, smooths out imperfections, brings out eye color, and puts a glow on the face. And none of it is natural, but that doesn't matter. What matters is that it makes any woman look better, if it's done right."

I paused, trying to decide whether to lay

it on the line and risk losing her altogether. I took a deep breath and plunged in.

"There're some people who're just naturally better-looking than others. I should know, because I'm not one of them. When you can't rely on beauty, you have to call on your strengths, which, in your case, is your talent. You mustn't be disheartened by that makeup job Lillian and I did on you, and forget what she said about us opening a beauty school. We'd go broke in a week. Hazel Marie's going to give all you girls some beauty tips and show you how to use product. Whatever that is. When she gets through, you'll walk out there with confidence, because the real you will be behind a layer of cosmetics. And you can pour out the real you in your music when they can't see you."

She'd frowned all the way through my discourse, and hadn't stopped by the time I'd finished. So I kept trying. "I think, if Hazel Marie pulls your hair up and back, and puts some color on your face, you're going to be so pleased that you'll want everybody to see you."

"I don't know . . ."

"Well, I do. Just think of the entire pageant as a rehearsal for the Grand Ole Opry." Or, I thought but certainly did not say, for a job behind a cash register. "Let's go back out and see what the others're doing. And, remember, shoulders back, head high."

That lasted about about five minutes, as long, in fact, as it took us to walk into the auditorium, where her shoulders began sagging again. Hazel Marie was getting the contestants lined up for one more practice on the runway, and she motioned for Ashley to join them.

"I'll be sitting about halfway back," I told her. "And I want you to look at me when you come out. I'm going to remind you of what we just talked about, so keep your eyes on me and imitate what I do. Okay?"

She nodded, and headed for the stage. I stood and watched, vaguely wondering where Miss Wiggins was, while Hazel Marie went over the instructions again.

When Ashley reached the stage, I saw three of the girls put their heads together and begin whispering. They cut their eyes at Ashley, then whispered again.

Tasha McKenzie tossed her head and said loudly enough for me to hear, "I don't think it's fair for some people to get special attention. If you can't do it on your own, you shouldn't do it at all."

Bethany LaVane glared at Ashley, agreeing with Tasha, but not having the nerve to come out and say so.

Melanie Easley said, "Oh, leave her alone. She's just that much less competition."

I don't think Hazel Marie heard them, but she knew they weren't paying attention to her. "Girls, girls, get backstage, now, and let's run through it one more time. Where's Etta Mae?"

I looked around, but didn't see her, so I went up the aisle to find a good seat from which to direct Ashley when her turn came. As I started to enter a row of seats, I caught a glimpse of Sam out in the foyer, deep in conversation with someone. My heart gave an extra thump, and I started toward him. I did so want to see him, and in my sudden joy at just a glimpse of him, I was about to forget all the plans I'd made the night before.

So I hesitated, torn between the urge to tell him off before he told me off and the urge to run out there and hug his neck. While I vacillated, not knowing my own heart, I saw him smile at someone, then throw his head back and laugh. He was certainly enjoying himself, and not at all in a hurry to find me.

I moved across the aisle to get a better

look, and wished I hadn't. Etta Mae Wiggins! There she was laughing up at him as they shared — *shared* — some pleasurable communication.

I slid into a seat, overcome with anger and humiliation. He couldn't even wait until he'd put me aside to go after her. He was already making plans with someone who was no more than a common flirt. Oh, the shame of it. The words of Ashley's song popped into my head, *Alas, my love, you do me wrong,* and it was all I could do to hold myself together. I felt my face flush, as perspiration popped out all over me. I'd need a bath as soon as I got home, and I would've left that second if I hadn't had to walk past them. And if I hadn't promised Ashley to direct her from afar.

As the first girl pranced down the runway, with Hazel Marie standing in for Etta Mae, who was just too busy to do her job, I tried valiantly to compose myself so nobody would know how shaken I was.

"I'm coming! I'm coming!" Miss Wiggins ran down the aisle toward the stage, laughing. Just so pleased with herself, after throwing herself at Sam, who was more than willing to catch her.

I could've strangled her. But just then, Ashley's name was announced and she walked out to center stage, slouching and hiding behind her hair.

I put my mind to the work at hand, determined not to let Sam and his new ladyfriend keep me from preserving my good name. That good name might always be *Springer*, but it didn't have to be spread all over creation, along with Sonny Sutton's, to be held up for ridicule.

Just as Ashley stepped onto the runway, she brushed one side of her hair aside, her eyes darting from one side of the auditorium to the other until they lit on me. I nodded at her, and put on a big smile that nearly killed me. She managed a small one in return. Then I stretched out my neck, lifting my head in an exaggerated manner, and saw her lift hers, too. As she began her walk, I sat up stiffly in my seat and threw my shoulders back, which served to put my top section in bold relief — all done to remind her to stand up straight and walk proudly.

Sitting there too straight to touch the back of the seat, with my chest poked out in military fashion, sending silent signals to Ashley, I felt Sam slide into the seat next to me.

"Julia," he whispered, his eyes on the uplifted part of my person. "I am so glad to be home."

Chapter 35

Gritting my teeth, I maintained my rigid posture until Ashley took her place with the other contestants at the side of the stage. As soon as I let down, she did too, so I had to keep bobbing my chin up and down to remind her that she was still on view. Just making it through her promenade without mishap wasn't nearly enough.

Sam tried to take my hand, whispering, "What's wrong, Julia? Having trouble with your neck?"

"No, I'm not having trouble with my neck. Don't distract me, Sam. I'm in the middle of directing Ashley in her comportment, and she needs my full attention."

I kept my eyes on the object of my instruction, lest one look into his blue ones did me in. It was all I could do not to get down on my knees, regardless of the dirty floor, and beg him to reconsider his decision to take his freedom and run. It tore me up to think that he was being taken in by that little twit in tight blue jeans.

"Well, by doggies, Julia," he said, trying

to jolly me up. "I thought you'd be happy to see me. Here, I've been gone for so long and you're acting like you didn't even miss me."

"Oh, I missed you all right. Missed you so much that I've been a nervous wreck these past few days when you couldn't find the time to call."

"I'm sorry about that, but Sonny had us on the move. He has investigators looking for Kincaid, and they were calling in with different reports every hour. I was hoping to have something definite to tell you, but, well, I don't."

"That's too bad." I could've told him what Sonny Sutton and all his investigators hadn't found out, but I didn't. As long as Sam thought we might be married, he'd stick around. He was too much of a gentleman not to. If I could keep him in the dark long enough to inveigle my way back into his heart, maybe he'd want to marry me again. And the next time, if we got to that point, I'd make sure it was done right.

But the whole mess so overcame me with grief that I had to widen my eyes to keep the tears from flooding out. I sniffed and began looking for a Kleenex in my pocketbook. "Allergy season," I mumbled.

"Why don't we get out of here?" he said.

"Let's go home where we can decide what we want to do."

Decide what we want to do? I knew what *he* wanted to do. His dalliance with Etta Mae Wiggins out in the foyer proved to me that he already considered himself all but free of any marital restraints.

I blew my nose. "I can't go home yet. Hazel Marie and Ashley need me here."

"I need you, too, Julia." He reached for my hand again, and I let him take it. He was so close, and smelling as fragrant as Mr. Pickens, that I was too weak to resist.

"Oh, Ashley, no," I whispered, suddenly brought back to the task at hand. The girl was standing alongside the other contestants with her shoulders drooping and her head down. I wanted to run up and tell her that she was drawing more attention to herself by being so different from the others. The idea was to blend in, even if that meant displaying herself in an unnatural manner. And they all looked unnatural to me, standing up there with locked knees, held-in stomachs, and plastered-on smiles. Except for Ashley, of course.

With a few delicate hand motions, I finally got her attention, and she made an effort to stand up straight. But by that time, she'd allowed her hair to fall down in her face, and she kept it that way.

"I'm going to get Hazel Marie onto that girl's hair, if it's the last thing I do," I said.

Sam leaned over to nuzzle my neck. "I hope it's not the last thing you do."

"Sam! Behave yourself," I said, jerking away from him. "People are watching."

I couldn't understand him. What was the purpose in getting all lovey when he'd already planned to throw me over? Just to let me down easy?

Well, I didn't intend to go down easy. And if I had anything to say about it, which I did, he just might have to make a few new plans.

When we all got home — in separate cars since we'd gone that way — Sam took my arm and said, "Let's go upstairs, Julia, where we can talk."

About that time, the Pruitts began a flurry of hammering upstairs, and Lillian began banging pots and pans in the kitchen. It was a din in stereo, and not at all conducive to an in-depth discussion of our sorry situation.

"Let me see what's wrong with Lillian," I said, unhanding myself, not at all eager to hear what he had to tell me. "When there's noise from the kitchen, I know she's upset about something."

Sam followed me as I pushed through the door from the dining room. I could tell, even without the noisy prologue, that Lillian was in a stew of major proportions. Instead of her usual cheerful countenance, her face was wrinkled with a deep frown and a downturned mouth. She crashed a lid on a pot, and turning to throw a pot holder into the sink, she stepped out of one of her slippers with the run-over heels. I thought she was going to break down and cry.

"Lillian," I said, hurrying over to her, "what's happened? What's the matter with you?"

She faced the sink and leaned against it, her head down in despair, unaware that Sam was in the room. "It's that James. He been over here, tellin' me Mr. Sam tired of my cookin' an' he movin' back home. That's not so, is it, Miss Julia?"

"Well . . ." I shot Sam a quick glance, not knowing what to tell her, because I didn't know, myself.

Lillian gave me a pleading look. "I don't want to be the cause of Mr. Sam leavin' you. If he don't like my cookin', I can change. You know I can."

Sam walked over and nearly gave her a

heart attack. She gasped when she realized that he'd heard it all. "Oh, Mr. Sam, don't leave us. I do better, I promise I will."

"Lillian, Lillian," Sam said, his easy smile and soft touch calming her down. "There's not a better cook anywhere than you. I wouldn't have you change a thing, and I'm going to have a word or two with James — you can count on that."

She wiped a tear from her cheek and tried to smile. "That man after me all the time, first one thing an' another, makin' me so mad I don't know what to do. You know what he say? He say he need to look after you so you pick Shandra Washington for the canine deputy queen. An' my cookin' do nothin' but give you a stomach-ache so you won't like her."

"Good Lord, Lillian," Sam said, laughing. "How could you believe such nonsense? What I eat won't have a thing to do with the way I judge a beauty contest. James is just trying to get to you, and I don't want you to pay any attention to anything he says. Look at me, now. I love your cooking, and I hope I'm here for a long, long time to eat it."

She gave him a weak smile, wiped her face again, and tried to believe him. I tried to, too. But if food wouldn't sway his vote for Miss Washington, what would incline him toward Miss Knowles?

Hazel Marie pushed through the kitchen door. "Miss Julia, we need you in the living room. You, too, Sam. Etta Mae's here, and we have to decide on the program."

I shot a quick look at Sam to see if his eyes lit up at the thought of Miss Wiggins's presence, but he was still reassuring Lillian. "I thought the program was already decided," I said. "What else is there to do?"

"We have to have more than just the beauty pageant. I mean, since there're only six contestants, we need some entertainment to make the evening worthwhile. If people're going to spend money on a ticket, they'll expect to get their money's worth."

"I hope you know we're going to be hard-pressed to find additional entertainment in this town." I started out with her, but then turned back. "Sam, I don't expect you're interested in this, so why don't you keep Lillian company."

"Oh, yes, he is," Hazel Marie said. "Come on, Sam. You may have some ideas we haven't thought of."

So, in he went — into the living room, where that man-hungry woman was just waiting to turn his head and sink her claws into him.

And there she was, sitting in one of the Victorian chairs by the fireplace, making herself as comfortable as you please. I pressed my lips together, nodded at her, and headed for the sofa. "Sit here, Sam," I said, patting a place next to me. I was determined to get the upper hand and not relinquish it. He wasn't free yet, and I meant to make sure they both knew it.

He spoke to her, calling her Etta Mae with a warmth that set my teeth on edge. I took his hand and held it, in spite of his raised eyebrows at the public display of affection, which usually did not meet with my approval. But there're a lot of things you do, which you might not ordinarily do, when the odds are against you.

"Okay," Hazel Marie said breezily, as she took the chair opposite Miss Wiggins and looked through her pages of notes. "Here's the thing. We need something before the girls are introduced, you know, just to get things started. I'm thinking that this would be a good place for Lieutenant Peavey to sing something."

"That'd be good," Miss Wiggins said before I could open my mouth. Actually, I was going to agree, but she didn't give me a chance. So I sat back and just listened.

"What could he sing?" Hazel Marie asked. "Any suggestions?"

Miss Wiggins was quick on the draw again. "Well, first, we'd better be sure he can sing whatever we pick out."

Sam laughed with her, and I edged a little closer to him. To remind him, you know.

"Well, I talked to him," Hazel Marie said, "and told him we'd want something that would fit in with a beauty queen theme."

"Lord, yes," Miss Wiggins said, giggling. "It'd be awful if he got up there and sang something like 'Maggie May.'"

Sam thought that was one of the funniest things he'd ever heard, but I didn't see the humor since I didn't know Maggie May from Sara Lee. I rubbed my thumb over his hand to regain a little attention.

Sam squeezed my hand, then said, "How about something like 'Shining Star'? That'd fit with your theme, wouldn't it?"

"Oh, yes," Miss Wiggins said, eagerly. "That's one of my favorite songs, Sam. I'm so glad you know it."

Sam? *Sam?* Where was the *Mr.* that would indicate the respect someone her age should show him? Lord, had they gotten so far as to be on a first-name basis? I watched with my heart in my throat as they smiled at each other, enjoying a common bond. I turned Sam's hand loose and looped my arm through his, pressing him close. She wasn't going to have him without a fight, I didn't care how many song preferences they shared.

Sam looked at me with a quizzical expression, the remnants of the smile he'd bestowed on Miss Wiggins lingering at the corners of his mouth. I leaned my head against his shoulder.

"Okay," Hazel Marie said. "That's decided, but we need something else. Oh, I almost forgot — Lieutenant Peavey'll sing the final song when the winner is crowned and she makes her triumphal walk down the runway. What do you think that should be?"

" 'Pretty Woman'!" Miss Wiggins said. "That's what the band'll be playing all through the contest, so we could end it with him singing the words. Oh, I wonder if he could do it like Roy Orbison. That would be so cool."

"Well, you know," Hazel Marie said, tapping a pencil against her mouth. "I wonder if we shouldn't switch it around. Have him sing 'Pretty Woman' first, because it's so

fast and exciting. You know, to get everybody eager for the show. Then do 'Shining
Star' for the winner's walk, since it's so uplifting."

"That's perfect," Miss Wiggins said. "Or
listen, how about 'Amazed By You'? That's
a great song, and was number one for
weeks and weeks. Let's suggest that to him,
too, and see which one he likes the best.
What about you, Sam? You like that one?"

"Either one would be fine," he said. "But
you'll need to check with the band, too. Be
sure what they can play."

I sat there, wondering why they'd wanted
me in on this planning session. I'd not contributed a single, solitary thing, nor had
Miss Wiggins given me a chance to.

"All right," Hazel Marie went on, "that's
settled. But I think we need something to
kill the time while the judges're making
their decision. Think of something else."

"You forgot something," Miss Wiggins
said. "Sheriff Frady wants to say a few
words."

I rolled my eyes at the thought, but
Hazel Marie said, "I'm putting him at the
very first. We'll let him welcome the crowd
and tell a little about what the winner will
do for the department. That'll be enough,
don't you think?"

"It will be," Sam said, "if you don't give him too much time. He'll give a campaign speech if you're not careful."

"I've told him ten minutes, and not a second over. Everybody's going to be so excited for the pageant to begin that they're not going to listen too long. Besides, the canine unit comes right after him, so he'll hurry along before that dog gets antsy. Okay, now think, everybody. What can we have while the judges are deciding?"

We all sat and thought, and Sam absent-mindedly stroked my arm. But his eyes were on Miss Wiggins as she twisted and squirmed in her chair. She was one of those people who couldn't sit still. Drawing attention to herself, don't you know. But by that time, I was so close to Sam that if I'd moved another inch, I'd have been in his lap.

"How 'bout this?" Sam said, leaning forward so that I almost fell into the space he'd vacated. "Have you heard Latisha do 'This Little Light of Mine'? She sang it for me one time, along with a lot of hand motions, and she was cute as she could be. With the voice she has, she'd knock the roof off."

"Who's Latisha?" Miss Wiggins asked.

Hazel Marie spoke up. "She's Lillian's great-granddaughter, and she's just darling. She's — what — five, six years old? Sam, I think that'd be great. Everybody would love her, and she'd add sort of a family atmosphere, don't you think?"

"Yeah," Miss Wiggins said, a frown of doubt wrinkling her forehead, which I could've told her was bad for the skin. I didn't, though. "But five years old? What if she gets scared and starts crying or something?"

"Oh, you don't know Latisha," Sam said, laughing. "She'd be in her element on that stage. You'll have to meet her, Etta Mae. I'll get you two together, and you'll see."

Oh, Lord, a flash of pain surged through my chest and I thought I was having a seizure. He was making plans to meet Miss Wiggins with only Latisha to chaperone, which was no chaperone at all. And doing it right in front of my eyes. If I'd had any doubt as to where his interest now lay, I didn't anymore.

Chapter 36

After Miss Wiggins left, and the Pruitts backed their truck out of the driveway at quitting time, and we'd finished supper, I knew I wouldn't be able to put Sam off much longer. All afternoon, he kept coming up to me, saying, "We need to talk, Julia," and I kept saying, "It's not a good time." So, now that things had settled down, there was nothing for it but to hear him out, at least until right before he got to the final words that would put the nails in my coffin.

I couldn't bring myself to tell him that he was a bachelor again, and that I'd heard it straight from that above-the-law preacher, himself. The only delaying tactic I could think of was to keep the conversation on the pageant, specifically Ashley's chances of winning the crown.

Hazel Marie helped by bringing up the pageant again, which was about all that was on her mind. As Lillian was getting ready to leave for home, Hazel Marie stopped her and said, "Lillian, we're thinking of asking Latisha to do a number in the pageant. Do you think she would?"

"Do what kinda number?" Lillian had just hung her apron in the pantry and was on her way out the door with an umbrella and a Winn-Dixie sack of leftovers.

"Oh, you know, a song or something. Mr. Sam says she can really sing."

"She think she can," Lillian said, smoothing the folds of her umbrella. "But I don't know, Miss Hazel Marie. Latisha, she got a mind of her own. No tellin' what she do, you put her out on a stage. That nice Miss Brickell what live next to our church, she been teachin' her some dancin' steps. An' all that chile been doin' is struttin' all over the house, sayin' she gonna be like Fantasia when she grow up."

"Who's Fantasia?" I asked.

Hazel Marie waved her hand. "Oh, you know, she won that show. Now, listen, Lillian. Would you ask her? See if she'd like to do it and not get too scared or anything."

Little Lloyd laughed. "You don't know Latisha, Mama, if you think she'd be scared. She'll do it. I know she will."

"Latisha never been scared of a thing in her life, but I ask her if that what you want." Lillian turned to face Hazel Marie. "I tell you somethin', though. You got to watch that chile like a hawk. No tellin' what she do, you give her a free hand."

"Well, why don't you bring her to-morrow? She can rehearse with us, and I'll see how she does."

"Uh-huh, I bring her, but you gonna have yo' hands full."

After Lillian left, Hazel Marie said, "I'm not sure Lillian was too thrilled about Latisha being on the program. I wouldn't want to do something she didn't like."

"She'd tell you if she didn't like it," I said, as sure of Lillian's responses as I was of my own. "It's just that the responsibility of that child weighs heavily on her, and she doesn't want her to disappoint you."

Sam put in his two cents then. "Latisha'll do fine, but I, for one, have had enough of the pageant for today. Hazel Marie, you'll have to excuse us, but Julia and I have some serious talking to do. Julia, upstairs, woman. I've got business with you, and I'm not going to be put off any longer."

"Uh-oh," Little Lloyd said, grinning at me. "You're in trouble now."

"Come on, Lloyd," Hazel Marie said, slapping her notes and lists down on the sideboard. "I've had enough pageant business today, too. Let's go in the living room and get comfortable. I haven't had a minute with you, and I want to hear all about your trip."

She put her arm around the boy as they started out of the kitchen. "I want you to start right from the minute you left town, and don't leave out a thing."

Sam looked at me and pointed to the back stairs. "Up there, where it's quiet."

I preceded him up the narrow stairs, dreading every step I made toward this momentous talk he was determined to have. I had never in my life understood women who tried to hold on to men who didn't want to be held. My attitude had always been: If he wants to go, then goodbye and good riddance. What kind of woman would want someone who didn't want her, anyway?

As I reached the top of the stairs, I realized to my dismay that I was that kind of woman. The thought of losing Sam made me weak in the knees, and it was all I could do to trudge down the hall to Deputy Bates's old room that was supposed to be Sam's new one.

The minute I walked in, I could tell that he'd not brought his suitcase from his house. The room was just as neat as the day he'd left on his trip. So there was another bleak sign that he was planning to leave my hearth and home.

"Come sit down, Julia," Sam said, taking his seat on the sofa under the windows that looked out over the back garden. "Let me tell you what I found out. Or, rather, what I didn't find out."

Suffering hot and cold flashes of panic, I made myself sit at one end of the sofa, trying not to break down in front of him. My hands were knotted in my lap, and I could hear my heart thudding in my breast.

Sam leaned over, an elbow on his knee with his chin in his hand, studying me intently. "First of all, Kincaid's gone and nobody knows where he is. We got at least one report that he's up in the hills of Kentucky, but it would be a fool's errand to look for him there." Sam stopped and rubbed his fingers across his mouth in a few seconds of silent contemplation. Maybe he was waiting for me to say something, but my throat was too dry to swallow, much less talk.

"But I'll tell you this, Julia, the Wedding Ring Chapel is even more upset than we are. They're having to track down all the couples that were married by him and break the news. Their business license is on the line, too."

"And well it should be," I mumbled, looking straight ahead, unable to bend for fear I would break in two.

"Yes, well, they're doing all they can to make amends. They've offered us a free deluxe wedding and another Dollywood honeymoon, including the special bridal suite, all on them." Sam glanced at me, but if he expected me to jump for joy at giving the chapel another chance to ruin my life, he was disappointed. "Somehow, I didn't think you'd be interested. Anyway, the town's Better Business Bureau is looking into the matter, as well." Sam sighed, then went on. "Of course, that doesn't help us, does it?"

"I guess not." I did a little sighing myself.

"And that church of Kincaid's — Sonny's investigators found out that it was only one unaffiliated congregation. It broke up several years ago, long before he showed up in Pigeon Forge." He put his hand on mine, but I still couldn't look at him. "The fact of the matter is, Julia, he was a self-proclaimed preacher, called, it seems, by the Holy Spirit, but who failed to notify the state of that calling." Sam took a deep breath of his own. "We might as well have been married by a stranger off the street, and I am just as sorry as I can be that it's turned out this way.

"Sonny's just as broken up over this as we are, and he's had to put up with it being spread all over the airwaves and in the newspapers. He's trying to make the best of it, but his lady friend's giving him a hard time — accusing him of tricking her into a sham marriage." Sam shook his head. "I feel sorry for him. He's just a country boy with more money and fame than he knows what to do with."

I couldn't muster up much sympathy for Sonny Sutton. If it hadn't been for his celebrity status, we wouldn't be facing a scandal of national proportions.

"Anyway," Sam went on, "I've hooked him up with Pickens, since there've been reports of Kincaid here in North Carolina, as well as in Tennessee and Kentucky. I swear," Sam said with some amusement, "the man's like Elvis — there've been sightings all over the place."

So I sat there, letting the silence lengthen as one thought after another ran through my head. What should I do? I could tell Sam what I knew, and watch him walk away, free as a bird to find another nest. Or I could let him go on thinking that we *might* be married, because as long as there was any question he'd *act* like we were married.

My mind cleared, as I deliberately put aside any qualms concerning proper conduct and moral rectitude. And honesty. I lifted my head and squared my shoulders. "Who knows about this?"

"Why, just you and me. And, of course, a lot of people in Tennessee and wherever there're people in the same boat we are. Why?"

"It's like you said at first, Sam. What people don't know won't hurt them."

He smiled. "I'm not sure I said that, but okay. What do you have in mind?"

"I have in mind keeping this to ourselves. As far as I'm concerned, we *are* married. And I *know* you've said that. Besides, after seven years, if we live that long, it won't matter one way or the other."

I thought he was going to laugh, but one hot stare from me sobered him considerably. "You're willing to be my common-law wife? I find that hard to believe, Julia."

"Well, believe it. That seems the simplest way to go about handling this mess. I know it goes against everything I've ever thought and said and believed, but . . ." I shrugged my shoulders and looked down at my lap, finding myself in the same hypocritical situation as all those who talk the talk, but who quickly change the rules when their own ox is being gored. I didn't like it, but what are you supposed to do when you want something so bad that the thought of losing it rips out your very soul? Besides, it wouldn't be like proclaiming to the world that we were flouting the proprieties. Unlike so many couples who live flagrantly in sin, we'd keep it to ourselves, and nobody'd ever know — if I could keep Aaron Kincaid quiet.

I said some of that to Sam, and watched as he slowly shook his head. "No, Julia, we're going to do this right, if we're going to do it."

If, he said if. I groaned inside, knowing that he was telling me he'd not only had second thoughts, but probably third and fourth ones, as well. And there was Etta Mae Wiggins, young and nubile, waiting in the wings to snatch him up.

Well, she wasn't going to get him. No, not as long as I had breath in my body to plead, beg, wheedle, and pile on the guilt. And I wasn't above doing it, either, although I never in my life thought I'd lower myself to cling to any man. But if it took courting him to keep him, I was going to learn to court with the best of them.

"Sam," I whispered, moving closer and molding myself to him. I wrapped my arms around him. "I want you to move down-stairs with me."

"Well, Julia, my goodness," he said, sur-prised by my unexpected forwardness. "You're about to take my breath away."

"That's what you do to me," I said. "It's about time I did it to you."

We didn't take the trouble to speak again for a good long while, but then he put his hands on my arms and pulled them away. "No, this is not the way," Sam said. "Not that I don't want to take you up on it, but, Julia, I know you. It wouldn't be long be-fore you'd be feeling guilty and ashamed. And then you'd start having regrets. No, no. Wait, now." He put his fingers on my mouth as I opened it to refute him. "It'd be only natural to be unhappy about living a lie. Of course, it wouldn't necessarily bother me, but I know it would you." Then his mouth curled up into a smile. "Besides, I'm afraid you wouldn't respect me in the morning."

"Oh, I would. I would."

Then, realizing that he was not only re-fusing my advances, but resorting to humor to do it, I unhanded myself from him and leaned back on the sofa, com-pletely undone.

"Well, then," I said, feeling the tears

spring up with the knowledge that he had rejected my most generously offered gift. "Well, then," I said again. "I guess that's it."

"Wait, now. Let's don't rush into anything. We need to think this through, because there's no real hurry. We may still find out that Kincaid is as qualified to marry people as Ledbetter himself. So, let's take a little time and give it some hard thought."

Oh, Lord, he wanted to think about it, and with that knife thrust to my heart, I knew I was on my own. If that wasn't a sign, I didn't know one when I saw it. Then I had a sudden, wrenching thought. Since we Presbyterians believe in predestination, what if all these signs meant that Sam and I had acted against what had been foreordained?

That sobered me considerably, but, I reminded myself, there was still the matter of free will. So, until I had irrefutable evidence to the contrary, I determined to exercise mine to the fullest extent.

"Well, then," I said again. "Will you do one little thing for me? Maybe two? While we're thinking it over, will you come back here? Just stay in the house until we decide?"

Pitiful, was what it was, and I never

thought I'd see the day I'd beg a man to stay. But I didn't want to put up with the tongues, like Thurlow's, that would wag if he up and left me flat. Appearances matter, even if they hide a multitude of deceptions.

Sam put his arm around me. "Of course, I will, Julia, if that's what you want. What's number two?"

"Ashley Knowles. I want her to win that contest, Sam. She deserves to win. Not on looks, I admit, but on talent. I would be so grateful if you'd help her out."

He looked at me quizzically. "You want me to throw my vote?"

"Well, not exactly. Just be, well, more inclined toward her than the others. I know you're fair and honest, but sometimes it doesn't hurt to be swayed a little. It's truly in a good cause."

"I don't doubt it," he said, laughing. "Any time you're involved in a good cause, I can be pretty sure there's something else going on underneath. But you know I'll give her every consideration."

"That's all I ask." It wasn't, of course, but it was a start.

Chapter 37

I slept, or tried to sleep, downstairs alone that night, comforting myself that at least Sam was under the same roof, if not under the same covers. How long that would last, I didn't know. Any day he could decide that he'd had enough of thinking it over, and say he was sorry for the inconvenience, but marriage to me was not all it was cracked up to be.

Then after that miserable night, I had to get up and face Hazel Marie's bubbling excitement about the beauty pageant that was practically upon us.

Lillian, I thought. *I'll lay it all out for Lillian, and she'll have pity on me.*

As I approached the kitchen that morning, I knew I'd have to continue to bear my sorrow alone. Latisha's piercing voice reached my hearing before I got through the dining room and pushed open the kitchen door.

"Great-Granny," she was saying, as I walked in, "I'm ready for that beauty contest anytime anybody else is. And I wish they'd hurry up. I ain't got all day to be waitin' around."

"Chile," Lillian said, "nobody worriet 'bout how long you waitin' around. Miss Hazel Marie be here soon as she get herself ready, so you jus' be patient an' mind yo' manners."

"Good morning, Latisha," I said, crossing the kitchen to get to the coffeepot. "My, you look nice this morning."

Latisha looked down at her white T-shirt, light blue shorts, and red tennie-pumps. Her head, with its braids and red beads, bobbed up after the survey. Then she said, "I know I do, but I'd look a whole lot nicer if Great-Granny'd let me wear my new Sunday school dress like I wanted to."

Lillian shook her head at the child. "You jus' gonna be practicin' today, an' I done tole you, you don't need to dress up for that. So, don't go on and on about it."

"Oh, yes," I said, pouring a lifesaving cup of coffee. "I hear you're going to be in the pageant."

"Yes, ma'am, I is. An' I'm plannin' on bein' the star of the show, 'cause that's what Miss Brickell tole me. She been teaching me how to dance, an' I'm real good at it."

Lillian turned bacon strips, and said,

"An' I tole you they don't want you to do no dancin'. You s'posed to sing, an' not do nothin' else. Now, set yo'self down, 'cause these eggs be ready in a minute. Miss Julia, you mind she eat with you, if you can stand all that talkin'?"

"Of course, we'll eat together. Have a seat, Latisha, and keep me company."

"Yes, ma'am, but I'm not much comp'ny when I'm eatin'. Great-Granny won't let me talk when I get my mouth full."

"And she's right, too. Here, have a biscuit. Your great-granny makes the best in the world."

"I know she do. I eat 'em most every day. But when's that Miss Hazel Marie comin'? I need to get started on my beauty contest song, see which one she wants me to sing. I know about two hundred of 'em, an' pickin' the right one's gonna be a hellava job for somebody."

"Latisha!" Lillian nearly dropped a bowl of scrambled eggs. "You better watch what you say, little girl. You not too big for a whippin', an' that kinda talk gonna get you one."

The threat didn't turn a hair on Latisha's head. She buttered her biscuit and bit into it, as unconcerned as she could be. I hid a smile, as I busied myself with helping my plate and hers. Maybe Latisha had the right idea. Nothing ever seemed to bother her, for she had the greatest confidence in herself and what she could do. Threats, reprimands, and scoldings just rolled off her back, as she pursued her own aims with a single-minded persistence that I could only envy.

Well, and perhaps emulate, I thought. Latisha was never discouraged, never side-tracked by anybody telling her she couldn't have what she wanted. She just kept on and on, until everybody threw up their hands and gave in to her.

That's what I could do. I would wear Sam down the same way, although I'd do it with a little more finesse and tact. No demands, no pleading, just sweetness and light and pleasant persistence until he couldn't help but capitulate.

"Lillian," I ventured in a quiet voice, as if my question were of no great import, "has Sam come down yet?"

"Yessum, him an' Little Lloyd, they get up early an' taken a walk. He say he need to clear his head, but they oughtta be back pretty soon."

Before I could begin to fret over what Sam was clearing his head of, I heard Hazel Marie clattering down the stairs in those shoes — *mules,* she called them — that flopped on her heels as bad as Lillian's. Except Lillian wore hers down over time, and Hazel Marie bought hers that way.

She bounded into the kitchen, looking fresh and bright in a sleeveless yellow-and-white top over a pair of yellow trousers. Her hair was pulled back in a fat ponytail, and her eyes were sparkling with excitement, ready for another round of rehearsals.

She stopped short when she saw Latisha. "Why, there's my little star attraction. Are you all set to rehearse, Latisha?"

"I been ready, an' . . . Oh, looka there." Latisha leaned over the table and pointed out the window. "There's that big ole white-headed man headed this way. An' he got that Lloyd boy comin' in with him. I better let 'em in."

She scrambled off her chair and opened the back door as Sam and Little Lloyd returned from their walk. There was a flurry of greetings among the three of them, with Lillian telling Latisha to finish her breakfast, and me leaving my own to fix a plate for Sam.

"Lillian," I said, edging up to the stove, "Sam needs some warm eggs. Where's a pan I can use?"

"What you mean, where's a pan you can use? I don't need nobody helpin' me cook, an' you can't cook no how."

"Well, but I want to fix Sam's breakfast. That's what a wife does, you know."

"Not in this house, she don't. You go sit down an' do yo' own eatin'. 'Sides, you in my way." She shooed me away from the stove, and, knowing she was right, I retreated to the table. I heard her mumbling as I conceded the kitchen to her. "First James, now somebody else, wantin' to take my place. I 'bout had enough of it."

I slunk back to the table, realizing that I'd come close to hurting her feelings. That had certainly not been my intention, so I busied myself with pouring orange juice for Little Lloyd and coffee for Sam.

I stood beside Sam, letting one hand rest on his shoulder, while I straightened his silverware. I opened his napkin and spread it over his lap. He smiled up at me, while I added cream to his coffee. "That's the way you like it, isn't it?" I asked, giving him a warm smile in return.

"Perfect. How are you this morning, Julia?"

"I'm fine. A little tired, but these are busy days. Did you two have a nice walk?" I let my hand slide across his shoulders as I passed behind him to get to my chair. Then I scooted the chair a little closer so that our knees could touch under the table.

Little Lloyd answered, saying, "We sure did, and I've worked up a big appetite. Thanks, Miss Lillian." He took the hot biscuits and eggs that Lillian had brought to the table. "That sure looks good."

"Here, Sam," I said, taking the bread basket from Little Lloyd and holding it out. "Have one while they're hot. And here's the butter. You want some jam with it?"

"Not quite yet," he said. "Thanks, though."

"I'll just put some on your bread plate," I said, spooning out grape jam for him. "Then you'll have it when you're ready. Here, you need some bacon." I put three strips on his plate.

All through my solicitous ministrations, Sam watched me with a bemused expression, while Hazel Marie and Little Lloyd exchanged glances. I didn't let any of it bother me. I was taking care of the man I was trying my best to keep.

Then Latisha, who'd been watching intently, piped up. "Great-Granny, that lady gonna be spoon-feedin' that ole man, next thing you know."

Everybody broke up, while I managed a sheepish smile to join in. So maybe, I thought, being too attentive wasn't the way to win friends and influence Sam, especially since he was laughing harder than any of them.

"Just trying to be helpful," I murmured in defense.

"And you are, Julia," Sam said, thrilling me with a soft touch on my hand. "I appreciate it, too."

"Well," Hazel Marie said, rising from the table, "we better get started if we're going to be on time. Etta Mae and the contestants will be there before long. Latisha, are you ready?"

"Yessum, I been waitin' all mornin' to get to that rehearsal."

"You jus' wait one minute," Lillian said, coming at her with a wet paper towel. "I need to wash yo' face an' hands 'fore you go anywhere. An' look here, you got jam on that clean T-shirt. What I gonna do with you, little girl?"

"It don't matter," Latisha said, as Lillian wiped her face. "I'm gonna be worse than this by the time I get back, 'cause when I sing I work up a big sweat."

Lillian took her hand and wiped each little greasy finger. "Law, chile," she said, "you too much. Now, you behave yo'self, an' do what Miss Hazel Marie tell you. Don't be runnin' 'round, an' gettin' in people's way."

"I won't. I'm jus' gonna do my singin'. Then I'm gonna set down an' watch them beauty queens so I'll know what to do when it come my time to do it."

Lillian rolled her eyes. "Miss Hazel Marie, if she give you trouble, you jus' call me an' I come get her."

"She'll be fine, Lillian. We'll be through around lunchtime, so I'll have her home by then. We'll go back for another rehearsal after supper, if she's not too tired."

Latisha said, "You don't need to worry about that. I ain't never been tired in my whole life."

"An' that's the gospel truth," Lillian said, looking about whipped herself.

"Lloyd," Hazel Marie asked, "are you going?"

"Yessum," he said. "Melanie's expecting me."

I glanced around, but nobody seemed concerned about that announcement. My word, but he was too young to be at the beck and call of Melanie Easley.

Little Lloyd said, "I'll look after Latisha when she finishes rehearsing."

"I don't need no . . ." Latisha began. But

Lillian said, "Hush, chile, you do so need some lookin' after, an' you better be thankin' Little Lloyd like I do."

Hazel Marie turned to me. "You want to go, Miss Julia?"

"Oh, I don't think so. Not unless you need me for anything. I'll go with you tonight, maybe, and see how Ashley does."

"Well, I've been wondering if you'd meet with the girls, and go over a few tips on poise and so forth. They're going to be so nervous when they're asked about their ambitions and plans for the future — you know, when they're up there in front of the audience and all. Could you do that this afternoon?"

I glanced at Sam, but he didn't say anything. "I'll be glad to, Hazel Marie. Maybe between one and three. Unless," I went on hopefully, "Sam has something he wants to do."

"Not at all, Julia," he said, as my spirits dropped. "I need to do some work on my notes before I get too far behind. I'll be working over at the house most of the day. But we'll go to the rehearsal tonight, if you want."

That's what I was afraid of, since Miss Wiggins would be there. I hid my feelings as well as I could, smiling at him in what I hoped was an agreeable fashion. I was bound and determined to show him I could be a good wife, even if it killed me. And from the way I felt inside at the thought of his imminent proximity to that flirtatious little twit, it was going to.

Chapter 38

When they'd all left, Hazel Marie with her entourage of children and Sam with his notes on the county's legal history, I continued to sit at the table with the dirty dishes.

"Lillian," I said, "come sit with me for a while. I'm not ready to face the day yet."

She poured a cup of coffee for herself and started toward the table. I began to feel better at the thought of pouring out my troubles to her. She stopped as truck doors slammed outside, and the rattle of tools announced the arrival of the Pruitts.

"Will they never be finished?" I said, sighing heavily and resigning myself to their arrival.

"Don't look like it," Lillian said, opening the door for them. "Mornin', Mr. Pruitt. Y'all come on in."

Mr. Pruitt and Willie entered with toolboxes and paint cans in both hands. They didn't stop, just nodded and greeted us as they passed through the kitchen on their way toward the back stairs.

As they tromped up the stairs, I beckoned to Lillian. "Come sit down. I need to talk to somebody, and you're the best one I know."

She pulled out a chair and began spooning sugar into her cup. "If you worriet 'bout James comin' 'round, they's not a thing I can do. I tole him I didn't want to see his sorry self over here again, but he don't listen."

"Oh," I said, waving my hand. "I'm not worried about James. Other than him bothering you. Sam'll take care of it. No, Lillian, I want to talk to you about . . ." I looked up to see Willie suddenly standing at the foot of the stairs, waiting, it seemed, for a break in our conversation. "You need something, Willie?"

" 'Scuse me," he said, with a shy smile. "Don't mean to interrupt, but I wonder, could I ask you something?"

"Yes, of course. But Hazel Marie's not here, and I'm not sure I can help you if it's something about her closets."

"No'm, it's not about closets. We're gonna start paintin' 'em today, and prob'bly be finishing up by the end of the week."

"Well, that is good news. Of course it's been a pleasure to have you and your uncle around, but it'll be good to get everything in its place again. What did you want to ask?"

"Well," he began, shuffling his feet and gazing off above my head. "Well, I don't want to butt in on anybody else's territory, but I was wonderin' if you know if Etta Mae is, uh, well, you know, seeing anybody?"

My spirits suddenly soared. "Why, no, Willie. I don't believe she is. Not that I know of, anyway. But even if she is, that would be no reason for you to hold back. Every woman likes all the attention she can get, and Miss Wiggins is certainly no exception."

He grinned widely, revealing that unfortunate gap where a tooth had once been. Although I must say, even though I worried about his oral hygiene, it did give him a rakish appearance.

"Well, okay then," he said, turning to leave. "Guess I better get back to work."

"Willie," I said quickly, not wanting to lose an opportunity to foist Miss Wiggins onto somebody — anybody — who would take her off the market. Sam was too much of a gentleman to intrude on an affair of the heart, if such should develop between Willie and Miss Wiggins. "Willie," I went on, "you might want to listen out this afternoon. She'll be here then and at the auditorium tonight. You might want to be there, too."

"I don't know," he said, as he prepared to climb the stairs. "I finished that runway, and that's all she wanted me to do. I don't know what she'd think, if I showed up again. She might get mad at me for hangin' around."

"Oh, I doubt that. But let me think a minute." I pondered the problem, absently stirring my cold coffee. "I know. You can say that I asked you to make sure the scrim works for Ashley. That way, you'll be up on the stage where Miss Wiggins is, and you can volunteer to work with the curtains and backdrops and so on. Whatever she needs, you'll be Johnny-on-the-spot."

His eyes lit up at the thought. "It's all right to say you want me there?"

"Yes, and you may be sure that I do."

"Then I'll be there." He started up the stairs again, then stepped back down. "Uh, Miz Murdoch, I don't know what a scrim is."

"Well, see, I hardly do, either. So that's something you can ask Miss Wiggins. Just tell her that I need to know if it's going to work right."

"Okay, thanks." He flashed a broad smile and bounded up the stairs, taking two or three at a time.

"Now, Lillian," I said, anxious to pick up where I'd left off. "Where was I? Oh, yes . . ."

The front doorbell rang, interrupting my train of thought again. "Who can that be this time of day?" I rose from the table, telling Lillian that I would see to it.

Lord, when I saw that it was LuAnne, I wondered how much more I could take. I unlatched and opened the door, but before I could barely get out a "welcome," she brushed past me and entered the living room.

"Julia," she announced, "we've been friends too long to let a few words come between us. I say, let's let bygones be bygones, and start over."

"I agree, LuAnne. I don't like having you unhappy with me, so have a seat and let's talk this out."

She plopped down on the sofa. "I didn't come to talk anything out. I just want you to know, even though you cut me to the quick at the book club, that I forgive you, and to tell you that I'm going to try one more time to have a reception for you and Sam. No, wait," she said, holding up her hand as I opened my mouth. "You may think you're above doing the accepted thing, but I am not. Everybody knows how close we've always been, and they'll wonder why I'm not doing anything to honor you. So I'm going to do something, whether you like it or not."

And she sat back on the sofa with her

arms crossed over her ample bosom, as if to say, *So there.*

I held my temper, although I was seething inside. "First off, LuAnne, it was *you* who offended me at the book club, not the other way around."

"I did not!" She almost sprang off the sofa. "All I did was speak the truth, and if that bothered you, then all I can say is, if the shoe fits . . . Besides, it wasn't me who got up and stomped out. And another thing, I was talking in general, but you — you made it personal."

"*I* made it personal? Why, LuAnne, everybody knew who you were talking about. You made that crystal clear. And I'll say this, you shouldn't start something unless you can take what you get in return. The trouble with you, LuAnne, is you think you can say anything you want to, and everybody'll just take it. Well, you need to know that I am a changed woman. I don't intend to sit back any longer and let people do and say whatever they please."

"Hah! When have you ever?"

"Plenty of times! Everybody thinks they can just run over me and I'll lie down and take it. No more, LuAnne. I'm not doing it anymore. And you can take that to the bank."

"Uh-huh, trust you to bring up money like you always do."

"I do not! And I'll have you know that I earned every cent I have. You try living with a man like Wesley Lloyd Springer, and see how you feel."

We glared at each other, each thinking up some other cutting thing to say. Then a smile pulled at her mouth until she couldn't help but start giggling. "No, thanks. Living with Leonard Conover's bad enough. I wouldn't take on another one for all the gold in Fort Knox."

Then we both began to laugh, sputtering and wiping eyes and expending all our ill temper. "Oh, LuAnne," I finally gasped. "I've missed you. Don't let's be mad anymore."

"I've missed you, too, Julia, and I'm glad we've got all that out of our systems. It was about to do me in." She pulled a Kleenex from her pocketbook and wiped her eyes. "Still and all, I'm going to have a do for you and Sam, I don't care what you say. It doesn't have to be a wedding reception, if you're so hell-bent against that. Although I still don't know what you have against having one. But call it what you will — a drop-in, a soiree, a dinner dance, whatever — but I'm going to do it. And I've already reserved the card room at the country club for next Saturday night. Now, don't say you can't make it. I know Sam's home, so you can't use that as an excuse."

"But, LuAnne, next Saturday's impossible. That's the night of the beauty pageant. Didn't you know that?"

"Oh, Lord," she said, doubling over on herself. "I forgot. And I bought tickets for it, too. Oh, for goodness sakes, Julia. What am I going to do? I just wrote out and stamped fifty invitations — that's a hundred people, and they'll all come. I was going to mail them on my way home."

"I am so sorry," I said in a doleful manner, although inside I was relieved not to have to pretend to celebrate a wedding I'd never had. The fact of the matter was, I was in no mood for a celebration of any kind. I had my hands full with trying to woo and win Sam before anybody realized that I'd lost him.

She sat still, her mouth screwing up and her forehead wrinkling in thought. "I know what I can do," she finally said. "I'll have something after the pageant. A supper dance, that's what it'll be. I'll just open the envelopes and change the time. It'll cost a fortune to buy all those stamps again. Now that I think about it, since everybody's going to the pageant anyway, they can just swing by the club afterward for a light supper and dancing. That thing's not going to last long, is it? I mean, with just six contestants?"

"I wouldn't think so. LuAnne, I've just had a wonderful thought. Why don't we make it a gala honoring Miss Abbot County Sheriff's Department and invite everybody associated with the contest?"

"Lord, Julia, I can't afford that! No telling how many would show up. And how am I going to address envelopes to people I don't know? I mean, nobody's asked me to help with the pageant, so how am I going to know who's associated with it?"

"Forget addressing envelopes!" I said, getting to my feet, so taken with the idea that I hoped would take the spotlight off Sam and me. "Well, except to the people you'd invite anyway. And for the rest, we can invite them in person. Just think of it! Your supper dance idea will make the pageant a huge success. It'll not only honor the winner of the title, but give the losing contestants a wonderful way to end the evening. And, LuAnne, think what it'll mean to all those brave sheriff's deputies to be able to have a night out with their wives and friends. And we'll have the sheriff and the mayor and the commissioners, and whoever else." And, I thought,

Etta Mae Wiggins and possibly her trailer park friends, as well as Mr. Pruitt and Willie, but I didn't mention any of them. "Why, everybody who is anybody'll be indebted to you. And Sam and I will be, too. But you know, LuAnne, we're private people and really don't like being the center of attention."

She had her head thrown back against the sofa, looking slack-jawed and overwhelmed with the all-out celebration I'd just described. "Julia," she gasped, "we live on Leonard's retirement, and we couldn't . . ."

"Oh, I didn't mean that you should do it all. My goodness, no. With that many invited, nobody could do it alone. I'll help, and so will Hazel Marie. But you should be the hostess and make all the arrangements and take all the credit. Because, after all, it was your idea."

"It was?"

"Of course. You just told me about it. And I'll tell you what, LuAnne. In all that crowd of people, we can gather a few of our close friends over in a corner and drink a glass of champagne to our future happiness. You'll be honoring Sam and me, as well as all those who've worked so hard, at the same time. It will be the perfect ending for the pageant, and I wouldn't be surprised if Sheriff Frady doesn't give you an award of some kind, and maybe put your name on a brass plaque to go on his office wall."

She gazed at me for the longest, her face becoming more and more skeptical. I might've overplayed it, but all I'd tried to do was get out of being the honoree at a wedding reception. And given her determination to celebrate *something,* I'd come up with the only substitute I could think of.

"Julia," she said, glowering at me, "now I know you're just stringing me along for some sneaky purpose of your own."

I felt my heart sink. "Why, LuAnne — why would you say such a thing?"

"Because you don't drink, so don't tell me you'd have a glass of champagne."

"Oh," I said, almost collapsing in relief, as I gave a little laugh. "Well, a lot of things change when a woman gets married."

"Tell me about it!" She hopped up and prepared to take her leave. "All right, I'll do it. And the first thing I'll do is switch to the ballroom, since we'll have a bigger guest list. So you might as well go ahead and give me a check. I'll keep track of all the expenses and we'll work it out when the party's over. But I'll tell you this, we're not going to have a big spread. That's too expensive. It'll just be hors d'oeuvres, dips, and so on." She stopped, bit her lip, then cut her eyes at me. "Unless, of course, you're willing to go a little fancier."

"Whatever you think, LuAnne. We want it to be the highlight of the pageant." I went to my desk and wrote out a generous check, rationalizing to myself that it would be money well spent. Handing it to her, I said, "Be sure to get a good band, so people will dance and enjoy themselves."

She looked at the check, then up at me. "You know, the more I think about it, the better I like it." She started toward the door. "But I'm telling you right now that I'm letting our friends know that it's a reception honoring your wedding. I'm not going to have people thinking that I don't know what's right. Now, I've got to get going. There're a million things to do. You know how it is when you're the hostess. Oh, and Julia," she said, her face lit up as she turned back to me. "I just thought of something. I won't have to pay back any social obligations for years to come. Everybody in town's going to owe me."

Chapter 39

I was certainly not in the habit of throwing money around, being of a naturally frugal nature, but I had no lingering regrets over the check I'd given LuAnne. What better reason to tap my bank account than to help preserve the semblance of my marriage for a while longer? I realized, though, that to keep up appearances even for that little while, I was going to need Sam's help.

I sat down in a chair by the fireplace, wishing it was winter so I'd have a fire to warm my icy hands. I was cold inside and out, shivering, as I thought of the pitiful state I found myself in. By this time, I had become convinced that Sam had one foot out the door and would soon be taking the other one out. So, as much as it would've ordinarily frosted me to do it, I knew I had to plead with him to continue in his usual uxorious manner, at least until after we'd suffered through that travesty of a wedding reception that LuAnne was so determined to have.

After that — well, I hated to think of afterward. Sooner or later, somebody was bound to catch up with Preacher Kincaid, so we needed to be truly married by then, unless, as seemed more and more likely, Sam wanted to be rid of me. But while everything was up in the air, he could help me out by putting up a good front for the sake of our long friendship, if for no other reason. It was the least he could do, if he was any kind of gentleman at all.

That way, in spite of our earlier sleeping arrangements on a number of nights, no one would know that we'd never been married. Well, no one except Hazel Marie, Lillian, Mr. Pickens, Aaron Kincaid, Sonny Sutton and his band of investigators, the people who ran the Wedding Ring Chapel, and whoever happened to see us coming out of a motel room in Pigeon Forge, Tennessee.

But I couldn't worry about that now. I had to concentrate on winning Sam back, and if that failed, I'd appeal to his better nature by begging him to pretend that it was I who'd kicked him out, and not the other way around. That would be poor compensation for the humiliation of such a short-lived matrimonial contract, but it was better than everybody knowing that he'd shown me the door. Of course, there'd be gossip, and Pastor Ledbetter would preach a few sermons on the present-day lack of commitment, the sacredness of the marriage vows, and the obligation to protect traditional family values — all aimed at me. But, I could tolerate that with my head held high, as long as no one knew that it'd been Sam who'd thrown me over.

Lord, it tore me up to think of losing him. Except, it looked as if I'd already lost him, what with his cavalier attitude toward our current marital mess and his flirtatious ways with Etta Mae Wiggins. I could've wrung that woman's neck. Yet, in the few moments I was able to think clearly, I realized that when a man begins looking around, almost any woman who presents herself will do. I just wished she hadn't presented herself so willingly.

"Miss Julia!" Hazel Marie's voice sang out from the kitchen, as I heard her and the children come clattering in from the rehearsal. "We're home."

I quickly pulled myself together, standing and smoothing my dress to appear my normal composed self. Walking through the dining room and pushing through the kitchen door, I was brought up short by the sight of Miss Wiggins sitting at the table.

I managed to speak to her in a civil manner, while hoping that Sam wouldn't show up for lunch, too. He probably would if he knew where she was. Lillian and Hazel Marie were putting plates of sandwiches and bowls of soup on the table, as Little Lloyd and Latisha kept up enough chatter to prevent my having to converse with the woman.

"Etta Mae's having lunch with us," Hazel Marie said as she took glasses down from a cabinet. "The contestants will be over in a little while, so this will save us some time."

"Delighted to have you," I said to Miss Wiggins, lying through my teeth as many social occasions require. "But excuse me for a minute. There's something I forgot to do."

I beat a hasty retreat out of the kitchen and into what was supposed to have been my and Sam's bedroom. I picked up the phone and dialed the number at his house.

"Sam?" I said when he answered. "I know you're busy, and I hate to interrupt your work. But I wanted to tell you that you might want to have your lunch over there. All the contestants will be coming over, so it's going to be a madhouse here."

"Well, sure, Julia, if that's what you want."

"I'm just thinking of you, Sam. And James. It would go a long way toward helping his feelings if you ask him to make lunch for you. You know, so he won't feel that you've thrown him over in favor of someone else."

"Not likely," he said, and I could picture his smile from the tone of his voice. "But a little reassurance never hurts. I'll see you later this afternoon, then. I'll miss you, Julia."

Uh-huh, I thought as I hung up the phone. And, if I could get rid of Miss Wiggins before he came home, he'd miss her, too.

Before returning to the kitchen, I quietly hurried up the stairs to Hazel Marie's new dressing room. I found Mr. Pruitt and Willie sitting on the floor, amidst open paint cans, sawhorses, wood shavings, and sawdust, eating from their lunch boxes.

Keeping my voice down so it couldn't be heard in the kitchen below, I invited them to the pageant gala. Mr. Pruitt grinned, but shook his head. "Too long in the tooth," he said, "to be kickin' up my heels that time of a night." But Willie, who was not too long in the tooth, but rather, short of one, lit up like a lightbulb. "You reckon . . . ?"

"She'll be there. She wouldn't miss it."

And having brightened his day, I went back downstairs with a feeling of satisfaction.

We sent the two children out in the backyard to play after lunch, while Miss Wiggins, Hazel Marie, and I gathered in the living room. Before long, the six contestants arrived in various stages of what appeared to me to be undress. I declare, if the fashions continued in this modern trend, there would be a lot of clothing stores going out of business. I'm not even talking about a lack of modesty, I'm talking about a lack of coverage.

But I kept my critical thoughts to myself and my eyes averted from the expanse of flesh available for viewing, if one were so inclined.

"Okay, girls," Miss Wiggins began, taking charge as she usually did. "We're going to work on your platforms today, and I hope you've all decided what yours are. The questions you'll be asked will be based on your platforms, and don't forget you'll be answering them in front of the audience. So be ready with real good answers. The judges will be scoring you on how well you answer, how poised you are in front of an audience, and how knowledgeable you are about your platform. Everybody ready?"

"Excuse me, Miss Wiggins," I broke in,

"but I have an announcement to make before we get too far along."

I'd not told her and Hazel Marie about LuAnne's gala before this, being too tightly wound at lunch to do much more than show up at the table. Besides, Miss Wiggins and Latisha had done enough talking for everybody.

When I had their attention, I said, "Mr. and Mrs. Conover are having a gala celebration immediately after the pageant. It'll be in the ballroom at the country club, and you're all invited. In fact, you may consider this your official invitation. Your parents're invited, too."

My announcement created an excited stir among the contestants. All of them, except for Ashley, who sat off to the side, turned to each other, talking and whispering to such an extent that I feared their platforms had flown out of their heads.

Melanie Easley turned to me. "Can we bring our boyfriends?"

"Yes, I think that would be acceptable. All of you will be guests of honor, especially, of course, the new Miss Sheriff's Department of Abbot County." Of course, there wasn't an *old* Miss Sheriff's Department, but that was neither here nor there. "We'll have a light supper and then dancing afterward, so I hope you'll all plan to come straight from the auditorium." I glanced to my side where Miss Wiggins was sitting. "You're invited, too, Miss Wiggins, along with everybody who's helped with the pageant. Willie Pruitt, too, I'm happy to say."

"Oh, Miss Julia," Hazel Marie exclaimed, "that's wonderful! I bet you had something to do with it, didn't you?"

"Well," I said, trying to hide a smile at being caught out, "maybe a little. But it was Mrs. Conover's idea, and I think it'll cap off the pageant quite nicely."

"Okay, girls," Miss Wiggins said, attempting to regain control of the meeting. "Girls! Listen, now. Here's what we're going to do. We're going to divide you into two groups of three and three. While one group stays in here with Miss Julia to work on the questions you'll get, the other will go with Hazel Marie to work on hair and makeup. Then we'll swap. I'll be going from one group to the other, helping out where I can. Hazel Marie, where do you want to take them?"

Before she could answer, I quickly intervened. "Take them upstairs to your room, Hazel Marie, where all your beauty aids are. That way, you'll have them close to hand."

She rose from her chair, saying, "That'd be easier than carting everything down here, especially since it's not so noisy up there today."

"The carpenters won't disturb you," I said. "They're painting now." And, though I didn't say it, with Miss Wiggins going in and out, Willie would have a chance to press his suit.

"Melanie," Hazel Marie said, "let's you, Tasha, and Heather go up and get started. Etta Mae, I'll need you to help me lay out all the stage makeup. Then you can come back down and see how Miss Julia's doing."

As I started to say there was no need for anybody to be checking on me, I bit my lip and held back. The three contestants, Hazel Marie, and Miss Wiggins took themselves upstairs, leaving me alone with Bethany LaVane, YoShandra Washington, and poor, nervous Ashley Knowles.

Hoping to give Ashley time to get herself together, I started with Miss Washington, who seemed to have a full measure of self-confidence. "Shandra, let's start with you. Tell us what your platform is."

Shandra leaned forward with a bright smile on her face. "Child Abuse Prevention!"

"Well," I said, taken aback by her enthusiasm. "That's certainly a worthwhile cause. Let's say you're asked what you would do to prevent child abuse. How would you answer?"

"I'd say that I'd go into the schools and tell children how to prevent it." She gave me another big smile, pleased with her response.

"But," I pressed, "just how would you tell a child to prevent it? Give some details, so the judges will see that you know your subject."

"Well," she said, more hesitant now that she was put on the spot. "Well, I'd say that, let me see now, I guess they could tell their teacher? Yes, they could tell their teacher. Oh, I know. They could tell a sheriff's deputy! That'd tie in with the pageant, wouldn't it?" She sat back, regaining her confident smile, satisfied with her quick thinking.

"Yes, I suppose it would, although I'm not sure that reporting abuse does much in the way of *preventing* it. That's more like stopping it, once it's started. I think you need to look into this a little more, Shandra. Maybe talk to some of the deputies who see so much of it."

That idea appealed to her. "I could do that. I know a couple of deputies already."

"Good. Now tell us, in case you're

asked, what your ambition is. What do you plan to do with your life?"

"Well, I still may run for president someday, but right now, I'm going to college and study to be a television anchorperson. They can do so much good, you know."

Well, no, I didn't know, since it seemed to me that all that position required was an ability to read what someone else had written and change expressions accordingly. And look good, of course.

"All right. Now, Bethany," I said, turning to Miss LaVane, "what is your platform?"

I steeled my nerves for Miss LaVane's halting country twang, but she surprised me with a ready response. "My platform's gonna be Skin Cancer Prevention and Awareness, and I'm gonna talk about the dangers of tanning beds and getting too much sun, like when you're fishin' or layin' out gettin' a tan. I'm gonna talk about SPF's, 'cause they ought to be at least fifteen and maybe even higher to prevent this terrible disease from ruining somebody's life. And then I'll tell about a woman I heard about who had a little skin cancer right here on her face. The doctor took it off, but five years later, she come down with liver cancer, which just goes to show, don't it?"

"I suppose so," I murmured, but it seemed to me that she had her medical facts mixed up. Then again, perhaps too much sun did play havoc with the liver. I mean, why else did liver spots pop up on your hands?

Miss LaVane had spoken with assurance and poise, though, and as I've always said, appearances do matter, although, I admit, often to the detriment of substance. Still and all, I said, "Since your time will be limited, I think, if I were you, I'd leave off the example. Now, you said earlier that you wanted to either go to medical school or learn how to do facials. I hope you've narrowed it down a little, so if you get a question about your life plans, how would you answer it?"

"My life plans? Well, I guess the first thing I want to do is graduate from high school. See, I have to go an extra year, 'cause of too many absences. So, it don't look like I'll make it to medical school."

"You don't need to go into that much detail," I said, trying to guide her into a halfway sensible answer. "Just tell us what you see yourself doing in, say, five years."

"Oh, well, that's easy. I'll probably have two or three kids by then. And, you know, I'll be helping others all I can, too. I think that's important, don't you?"

"Indeed. But, Bethany, you need to give a little more thought to your answer. You should give some specifics — like, just how you would help others. Think in terms of volunteer work and that sort of thing, if you're planning to have a family."

"Sure, I can do that. Whatever the judges want, I can do."

"Good," I said, trying not to roll my eyes at such supreme self-confidence.

Then I turned to Ashley.

Chapter 40

A burst of laughter from upstairs reminded me to hurry and finish before the others came down. At this point in my carefully planned campaign to help Ashley give a good showing, she didn't need a larger audience than the one she already had.

Fearing a stumbling, hesitant answer from her, I steeled myself and asked, "Ashley, have you decided on your platform?"

"Yes, ma'am, I think so." She fastened her eyes on me, trying mightily to ignore the interested and somewhat amused gazes of Miss Washington and Miss LaVane. "I don't know exactly how to say it, but maybe something about music appreciation."

I thought that was going to be it, but she surprised me by brushing the hair out of her face, and explaining further. "But I don't mean all music. I mean just old ballads and mountain songs and things like that."

"Why, Ashley," I said, "I think that's a marvelous idea, and you certainly know your subject. Why don't we call it Our

Mountain Musical Heritage? How does that sound?"

She smiled. "Real good."

"All right," I went on, pleased that she'd come through so well. "And what are your plans for the future?"

"Just to keep on playing music, I guess."

"Let's do better than that, Ashley. Why don't you say something like, I plan to continue learning as much as I can about our musical heritage, and —"

"Oh, wait," she said, reaching into her tote bag and pulling out a pad and pencil. "Okay, go ahead."

"Well," I said, somewhat taken aback at being transcribed as I spoke. "You could say that you are collecting old songs and melodies. If you are, that is. And that you plan to record them for posterity. And you might also mention that you hope to play professionally someday."

She scribbled it all down, then gave me a smile that beamed through the lanky tresses across her face. I was glad I hadn't mentioned that she wanted to play backup for some country music star. No need to give the others more ammunition for ridicule.

There was a sudden clatter on the stairs as the first group, all coiffed and beautified, rejoined us. Of course, my group had to ooh and aah over each one, while Hazel Marie stood by glowing in the compliments on her handiwork. And they did look good, although the farther away one stood from the heavily made-up faces, the better they looked. But that was the object of the exercise, I supposed.

I looked around and, not seeing my rival for Sam's affections, asked, "Where's Miss Wiggins?"

Hazel Marie smiled. "Talking with Willie. She'll be down in a minute."

"She doesn't need to hurry. Why don't you take the other group on up and join her? And Hazel Marie," I went on, drawing her aside, "Ashley Knowles is going to need your particular expertise. I wish you'd take her by yourself, and let Miss Wiggins work on Shandra and Bethany."

"I will. I can't wait to get my hands on her." Then turning to the others, she said, "Okay, girls. Let's go on up."

So I was left with Heather Peavey, Melanie Easley, and Tasha McKenzie, all with burnished, glowing, and glossy faces under coiled, curled, or upswept hairdos. I took a deep breath and plunged in.

"Settle down now, girls, and let's get started. Heather, if you get a question about your platform, how will you answer?"

Miss SWAT Team squirmed in her chair and twisted her mouth, as she gathered her thoughts. "Well, I guess I'm going for physical fitness, though maybe I ought to call it something else, since that's the name of the bathing suit competition. I think I'll call it Strong Minds in Strong Bodies. How does that sound? Because I'm interested in coaching young people, and it takes a strong mind to learn some of the rules. Especially soccer."

"That sounds fine," I said, not knowing one sport from another, much less the rules they were played by. "So what do you see yourself doing in a few years' time?"

"Being the women's volleyball coach at Chapel Hill," she declaimed without a moment's hesitation. "Y'all just better watch me, 'cause that's what I'm going to do." Then she gave us a big smile, leaving little doubt that she would.

"Excellent," I said, and meant it, too, since I was relieved that she'd not repeated her earlier ambition of replacing Sheriff Frady. "Now, Melanie, what about you? Tell us about your platform."

Miss Easley squeezed her eyes shut in concentration, then blurted out, "I can't decide! It's between Animal Protection, 'cause I kinda want to be a veterinarian, and Pain Prevention, 'cause I'm thinking about chiropractic, too. But I could say something about dancing, since I want to keep on doing that. What do y'all think?"

I opened my mouth to give her some guidance, but Tasha McKenzie beat me to it. "Oh," she said, with a careless wave of her hand, "do Animal Protection, and say something about the need for spaying and leashing and so on. Chiropractic pain prevention is too close to Heather's platform, since they both have to do with muscles and things."

"Okay, that sounds good," Miss Easley readily agreed. Then, to me, "What she said."

"So what do you see yourself doing in several years' time?"

"Well, I guess I ought to stick to my platform and say I'll be active in the SPCA, and maybe own a dog-grooming business. And, you know what?" She stopped as a new idea struck her. "There're some new programs out now that teach you how to do massages and stuff to sick animals. You know, like old dogs with arthritis? That'd tie in with my interest in chiropractic, wouldn't it?"

"Yes, it would," I said, striving with all my might not to say what I really thought.

"I'm sure that'll be fine, Melanie. Now, Tasha, let's hear your platform." Then I mentally girded myself for a replay of the girl's wide-ranging ambitions.

"My platform is Commitment to Christian Character," she said, surprising me with her brevity. "And I see myself in a few years' time as a witness to my faith in schools, churches, and on the mission field. With all I intend to accomplish with my various talents and abilities, I plan to serve as a role model of Christian character to young people everywhere."

"Very well said, Tasha," I said, and it was. What it wasn't, though, was anywhere near realistic.

Since my second group went faster than the first, maybe because I knew more about what I was doing, we finished before the others came down. Lillian, who always kept up with what was going on in the house, brought out a tray of lemonade and cookies, which made a nice break while we waited.

Before long, Bethany and YoShandra, fully made up and looking like models, if you could overlook their casual attire, joined us in the living room. The girls admired each other and themselves, preening in front of the mirror over the sideboard in the dining room. Miss Wiggins, having finished whatever she'd been doing, came down with them. She took a glass of lemonade and a seat beside me. She seemed to be smiling to herself and quite pleased about something. I hoped it had been Willie who'd put the smile on her face.

Turning to me, she said, "Hazel Marie'll be down in a minute. She's still working on Ashley."

"I assumed that was the case. How's Ashley looking?"

"Well, let's say it's a real change from the original." Miss Wiggins gave a little laugh, offending me since I had become so defensive of Miss Knowles. "But, you know, I always like to help someone who really needs it. The results can be so startling."

And, indeed, they were. Hazel Marie came down the stairs, with Ashley coming hesitantly behind her. Now, I'm not going to say that the girl took my breath away with a suddenly revealed beauty, because she didn't. Still, the transformation was remarkable. Hazel Marie had put Ashley's hair up in a thick coil on the back of her head. That alone went a long way toward making her a viable contestant for the pageant crown. The expertly applied makeup, especially around the eyes, made her seem a different girl altogether. I couldn't believe the contrast between her present appearance and what Lillian and I had accomplished with our amateur applications. I smiled to myself, thinking of telling Lillian that our school for beauty do-overs had to be put on hold until we'd mastered a few of Hazel Marie's magical techniques.

Miss Washington and Miss Peavey lavished compliments on Ashley, making her blush, but pleasing her, too. The other girls made an effort to say something nice, but I could tell they were none too happy about the added competition. Too bad, I thought.

"Hazel Marie," I said, drawing her aside. "My compliments. You have outdone yourself with that girl."

"She does look good, doesn't she? I told her that she should wear her hair up for the Physical Fitness and Beauty and Poise competitions, but it ought to be down, you know, flowing down her back, when she sings behind the scrim. Then if it falls in her face, nobody'll see it."

The doorbell rang just then, and Hazel Marie leaned over to look out the window. "Oh, look. It's the UPS man."

There was an immediate buzz of excitement among the girls, as they flocked around Hazel Marie when she opened the door. A young man, tanned and muscular in his brown summer uniform, said, "Got a delivery for you. Sign here, please."

Hazel Marie took his electronic clipboard, signed her name, and looked out the door at the package by his feet. "They're here! Oh, I can't wait to see them."

The UPS man said, "Better let me set it inside for you. It's heavy."

Hazel Marie stepped back to let him heave the large carton inside and set it on the floor. The girls watched in silence, but I didn't know if it was in anticipation of opening the box or from the sight of such shapely masculine extremities.

It didn't matter, for he was soon gone, hopping into his delivery van and heading off to his next stop. Attention then centered on the box, which Hazel Marie quickly tore into with the letter opener from my desk.

"Oh, my goodness!" She began pulling out one filmy and sequined garment after another. The contestants clustered around her, reaching out and calling, "That's mine!" and "I ordered the blue!" and "Dang! Look at that red one!"

Evening gowns. That's what they were,

and I couldn't help but roll my eyes. If Hazel Marie had bought them all, I needed to speak to her about fiscal responsibility.

She must've known what I was thinking, because she edged up to me and said, "They're rented, Miss Julia. Each and every one of them, because I knew some of the girls couldn't afford to buy an evening dress. So Etta Mae and I decided that they should all get a dress from the same place, so one wouldn't come up with something real expensive, and another with something homemade on a Singer."

That made me feel a whole lot better, and I was gratified at Hazel Marie's concern for those contestants who would've been outclassed in the Beauty and Poise competition.

Finally, the last of the girls were gone amid a great deal of chatter over their new faces and new gowns. Hazel Marie, Miss Wiggins, and I sat down for a few minutes of recuperation. And for another glass of lemonade. The respite was refreshing, for I was not accustomed to so much going and coming, and talking and giggling, on a slow summer afternoon.

The other two must have felt the same way, because we all sat in silence for some little while.

Just as I was beginning to wonder if Miss Wiggins was ever going to leave, she said, in a musing sort of way, "Have you ever wondered why they all have such great legs?"

"Who?" I asked.

Hazel Marie sputtered behind her napkin. "UPS men, Miss Julia. Didn't you notice?"

"Certainly not," I said, with a little sniff. "Besides, those were a little on the hairy side."

Hazel Marie and Miss Wiggins doubled over, laughing. I was finally able to join their amusement, surprised to find myself feeling somewhat companionable toward Miss Wiggins.

Miss Wiggins wiped her eyes, still smiling. Then with another laugh, she said, "Wonder if great legs is a job requirement. If it is, I'd like to be the personnel officer."

"I'd go for quality control," Hazel Marie said, and that set them off again.

Chapter 41

I smiled along with them, because I appreciated a pair of finely turned limbs as well as the next person. But, it was the pair of finely turned limbs on the man I'd tried to marry that was concerning me.

And I must say that as the pageant drew nearer, it was all I could do to keep up the appearance of excitement and interest in it. And even the little I managed to exhibit was only for Ashley's sake. Without my agreement with her uncle, I wouldn't have given two flips about who won the crown and who didn't. Keeping, or rather, getting a husband just about took up all my thinking.

And Sam? Well, he spent most of every day over at his house, working on that legal history of the county that nobody would ever read. Oh, I'm sure that the library would want a copy, and maybe a few students would eventually consult it. But let's face it, it wasn't going to be a national bestseller. But I didn't voice my opinion on the subject, not wanting to discourage him or nip his enthusiasm in the bud. It's always good for a retired man to have a hobby or some interest that takes him out of the house.

The problem was, it was taking him out of my house more than I wanted him out. And I was beginning to fear that that was exactly what he had in mind. He was as gentlemanly and as seemingly affectionate as he'd ever been, but I could read between the lines. He'd *said* he was giving me time to think about what we should do, and he'd *said* he didn't want to rush me. Well, I could've stood a little rushing.

Instead, he'd say things like, "Julia, I'm missing you." But if that was the case, where was he all day long? Not with me, I'm here to tell you. And when he sat by me on the sofa after supper, he'd take my hand and whisper, "You been thinking about me, Julia?" What did he think I'd been doing? What I wanted to know was who *he'd* been thinking of. Or, he'd sidle up to me when no one was around and say, "How about we slip off to the bedroom for a little while?" Which just tore me up, because he'd already turned me down when I'd suggested the same thing.

But the worst was when he'd say, "I don't mean to rush you, Julia, but I'm getting awfully lonesome." Now, wasn't that a warning that he was looking around, and it wasn't at me?

At any point, he could've said, "I'm tired of thinking. Let's get married, and do it for real this time." But he didn't.

So, why didn't I take the bull by the horns, fling my arms around his neck, and say I would never let him go? Why wasn't I willing to grab his hand and run over to Pastor Ledbetter's study, demanding a wedding ceremony right then and there? The average woman in my state of mind would've done just that, but I wasn't your average woman. For one thing, I could interpret the double meaning in everything Sam said, which meant that he didn't mean half of what he said. And for another, I was paralyzed at the thought of what the pastor would say, and do, if he learned we needed remarrying.

If I could just get through the pageant with my head held high, and if I could talk Sam into keeping up the pretense a while longer, then I'd either win him over or have to let him go.

I didn't know what to do. We couldn't pick up and go off somewhere to get married, not without missing the pageant. And if I missed the pageant, Ashley might miss her chance, and her uncle would send out a press release with our names on it. All I could think was that in a few days the thing would be over. Then I'd be able to give my full attention to reclaiming what I was about to lose. And, on top of wooing Sam, I had my hands full with all the little jobs Hazel Marie had for me to do.

"Miss Julia," Hazel Marie called before she appeared in the door of my bedroom. "Guess what? Binkie's going to emcee the pageant."

"She'll certainly do a good job," I said, trying to work up a little enthusiasm. "Binkie's never at a loss for words, and she has all that experience in a courtroom, too. But I thought Miss Wiggins would be the announcer."

"Oh, goodness no. I need her backstage, helping the girls get ready. They have to change several times, and their hair'll have to be fixed over and over. And somebody's going to have to see that they get out on the stage at the right time. It's going to be chaos. Just chaos." She flopped down in a chair across from me and closed her eyes. "I am wiped out. There're so many things to think about and plan for, and I keep thinking I've forgotten something."

"I don't see how, Hazel Marie. You've got the pageant organized down to the last contingency. I'd think by now you could relax and enjoy it."

"All I can think of is that something'll go wrong."

"It probably will," I said, "but you can't plan for everything. And, look at it this way. If anything goes wrong, the audience will likely never know. Or if they do, they'll get a big kick out of it. You know how people are."

"Yes, well, that's the trouble. I do know how they are, and if anybody messes up, that'll be all they remember." She frowned, twisting her mouth with the effort.

Thinking to distract her from worry, I asked, "Mr. Pickens will be there, won't he?"

That created a deeper frown. "He better be. I declare, his business is growing by leaps and bounds. Everybody wants him to work for them, because he's so good at finding people and investigating fraud and all those things. I'm proud of him, but looks like he could spare a little time for me."

I smiled. "You've been busy, yourself, here lately. But, Hazel Marie, take my advice. Don't get too busy for him. Men just naturally have a short attention span, and you have to keep reminding them all the time which side their bread's buttered on. I don't want you to get into the situation I'm in, neither one thing nor the other."

"Oh, Miss Julia," she said, leaning across and patting my arm. "I know you're having a hard time, and I appreciate all the help you've been to me. I just wish you'd get over worrying about what people will think and go ahead and tie Sam up good."

I sighed, grateful for her concern, but knowing she didn't understand. "What good would it do to tie him up, good or not, when I'm not sure he wants to be tied? There's nothing worse than holding on to a man who doesn't want to be held, as I've told myself a million times or more."

"But Sam does! You know he does!"

"Hazel Marie, you don't know all the ins and outs of what I've been going through. But, as soon as the pageant's over and I can get Sam's nose out of his book, I'm going to get things settled, once and for all."

"Oh, good. I'm so glad, but, listen. I wanted to ask if you'll help me and Etta Mae backstage. You know, getting the girls dressed and lined up? We'll have their outfits for the various competitions hanging in order, with the names pinned on them. All you'll have to do is be sure the right girl gets in the right outfit. And help with buttons and zippers and things. I don't want there to be a mad scramble with clothes flying everywhere."

Wardrobe mistress was not exactly how I saw myself, but I nodded.

"Oh, and, Miss Julia," she said, turning back to me. "Could you just be available if the judges need anything?"

"I suppose I could." And, with a lift of my spirits, I envisioned a multitude of opportunities that availability could produce. "You know, Hazel Marie, I'm quite anxious for Ashley to do well."

"Me, too. But I want all of them to do well, and let the judges' votes fall where they may."

"Yes, indeed."

Chapter 42

Mr. Pickens showed up just in time to have dinner with us the night before the pageant. He was in good form, laughing and teasing everybody and, in general, making a nuisance of himself. Of course, I was the only one who recognized the nuisance factor, although Hazel Marie was in such a tizzy here on Pageant Eve that she had little patience with him.

"Who wants to hear my good news?" he asked, flapping his napkin to the side, then draping it over his lap.

"I do!" Little Lloyd was always eager for anything Mr. Pickens wanted to dish out. "Tell us, tell us."

"Wel-l-l, let's see if everybody wants to hear it." He turned to Hazel Marie on his right. "You interested, sweetheart?"

"Don't mess with me, J.D. I have too much on my mind to put up with your foolery tonight." And she did, since the pageant was sold out, and everybody was expecting a great and wonderful event.

"How 'bout you, Miss Julia?" Mr.

Pickens asked, turning those black eyes on me. He was determined to drag it out and build the suspense.

"I'm sure you'll tell us sooner or later," I said. "But I wouldn't know good news if I heard it. I've had too much of the other kind here lately."

"Oh, just tell us, J.D." Hazel Marie rounded on him.

"Since you put it that way, then — guess who's coming to town?"

"Who? Who?" Little Lloyd was interested, even if no one else was.

"None other than your friend and mine, Sonny Sutton."

Forks clattered on plates, Little Lloyd beamed, Sam looked up with a surprised expression, and Hazel Marie threw her arms around Mr. Pickens, causing him to slosh water out of his glass.

"Oh, J.D.! How did you do it?" she cried. "That's wonderful. Oh, the pageant'll be a success now. Will he do a number for us? You think he would?"

"Hold on," Mr. Pickens said, laughing and trying to untangle himself. "He's coming because there's word that the fellow he's looking for might be in this area. Seems the man has family around here, and Sonny's hot on his trail."

"Who's he looking for, J.D.?" Little Lloyd asked, as I sat there blinking my eyes and cocking my head toward the child, trying to signal Mr. Pickens not to say too much.

"A Mr. Kincaid," Mr. Pickens answered. "He's got a few questions to put to him."

I closed my eyes in dismay. I could've answered every one of Sonny Sutton's questions, including the main one.

Sonny Sutton hit town the following afternoon, and you would've thought he was the president for all the excitement and carryings-on that his arrival engendered. He and his entourage took up almost all the Holiday Inn out by the interstate, and reporters from as far away as Asheville descended on us. Sonny was big news, and so was the state of his marriage.

I declare, I didn't see why the man couldn't just go ahead and get married again. I wondered if, deep inside or maybe not so deep, he was liking the publicity, especially after Hazel Marie told me that his most recent release had just hit number one on the country music chart. And even more especially after I heard the title of it: "I'm a Marryin' Man (But Somebody Stopped Me)."

"I just don't understand people who try to profit from personal tragedy," I said to Sam, as we waited for it to be time to go to the auditorium. "How in the world can he tolerate the publicity, much less help it along?"

He smiled. "Don't be too hard on him, Julia. People like Sonny express their experiences through their art. And their fans know it's heartfelt."

"Well, *I* wouldn't do it." Then I had to laugh. "Maybe that's why I'm not a country music star."

Although I would never announce to the world all my secrets, Sonny's openness made me wonder if I'd gone too far in the other direction. By this time, my head was so full of secret plans and what-ifs and help-me-Lords, that I didn't know if I was coming or going. You would think that Sam would know what was roiling around in my mind, and help me out a little. He could clear matters up in one fell swoop.

But he didn't. He kept waiting for me, and I wasn't the one to do it, especially since, for all I knew, he'd turn me down. You would think that a man would know what was in a woman's mind, and do something about it, wouldn't you?

Hazel Marie left early for the auditorium,

taking Latisha with her for one more practice of her song. Little Lloyd went with them, since he was charged with Latisha's good behavior. Lillian started to go, too, but decided that she'd get too nervous, worrying about Latisha's performance, and affect the child adversely. Before long, Mr. Pickens came by and picked up Sam.

"Hazel Marie's about to lose it," he said, in his joking way. "The judges' table won't fit where she wants it, and she expects you and me to figure it out."

About an hour before the event was to start, Lillian and I drove over to the high school. There were cars going up and down the streets, looking for parking places. Families crowded the sidewalk, waving to each other, on their way to the auditorium doors. Lines of people waited to get in, hoping, I thought, that Sonny would be there, since word had run through the town that he might be.

I finally found a place at a doctor's office to leave the car, figuring he wouldn't have office hours on a Saturday night. We went in at the back of the auditorium into absolute chaos, just as Hazel Marie had predicted. Half the contestants sat around in dressing gowns, their faces heavily made up, with eyes glazed over, scared stiff. Others, like

Tasha McKenzie, talked ninety miles an hour, giddy with excitement. Little Lloyd and Latisha were sitting on some boxes, out of the way but close enough to see everything. Little Lloyd smiled when he saw us, giving a little wave.

"Lemme look at that chile's dress," Lillian said, going over to Latisha. "Stand up, an' lemme see you got it dirty yet."

"I been watchin' out, Great-Granny," Latisha said, turning around in her bright red dress so that the petticoats underneath twirled with her. Her matching red patent shoes glistened on her feet. "I'm not gonna get it dirty. I'm gonna be the star."

Lillian snorted at that, then when Latisha pointed behind her, she turned and gasped. "Oh, my Jesus! Look at that thing!"

It was a combat-ready, black-outfitted deputy with a dog as big as a calf sitting beside him. "That's Max, Miss Lillian," Little Lloyd said. "That's why we're doing this — to get some more just like him."

"I hope he stay right where he is," she said, sitting down close to Latisha.

Sheriff Frady was over in a corner, looking over his introductory notes, and I veered away from him as I looked for Hazel Marie. Music emanated from the other side of the curtain, along with the buzz and shuffle of people finding seats.

I pushed past racks of the contestants' outfits, hoping to see Ashley. Lord, if she'd gotten cold feet at the last minute, what would I do?

Nothing, I told myself. Or rather, I'd do what I intended to do all along. Namely, get myself married if I could. Preacher Kincaid couldn't blame me if she failed to show, could he?

"Oh, Miss Julia!" Hazel Marie ran out of a dressing room, almost colliding with me. She was in a state. "Sonny's manager just called and Sonny's not going to sing. And he may not even come. And everybody's expecting him to. It's just awful."

"Now, Hazel Marie, they didn't buy tickets to hear him. All they were promised was a beauty pageant, and that's what they'll get."

She threw her hands up, wailing, "Oh, but . . ." Then she whirled away to help Miss Wiggins with another crisis.

I wandered around, dodging excited girls, and found a quiet spot in a hall that led to the classrooms. And that's where I also found Mr. Pickens. He was leaning against a wall, looking as if he'd rather be somewhere else.

I smiled at him. "You don't enjoy bedlam, Mr. Pickens?" He grinned at me, and I went on, "Hazel Marie can't understand why that Sonny person won't sing. Sam's been of help to him, and you're working for him. Looks like he could show some appreciation."

"He's got a broken heart, Miss Julia."

"No more broken than some people's, and we keep on keeping on."

Miss Wiggins stuck her head around the door. "The girls're getting dressed. Can you help?" Then, as Mr. Pickens made as if to respond, she laughed and said, "Not you. Miss Julia."

That was my call to duty, so I went to my post by the clothes rack. I pushed aside a few hands, eager to grab their own outfits with no concern for the others. Each girl snatched hers from me and ran for the dressing room. When only one garment was left for the first competition, I hung my head over it, overcome with disappointment.

"Miss Julia?" And there was Ashley standing behind me.

"Oh, Ashley, thank goodness. Hurry and get dressed, so Hazel Marie can fix your face."

She hung her head and whispered, "I really don't want to do this."

"Yes, you do. Just grit your teeth until time to sing, and you won't have to worry about anything else."

"My grandmother made me come. She said you're counting on me."

"Yes, and you don't know how much." I thrust the garment into her hands.

"I wanted to do it for you, but I'm so scared. Then when Uncle Aaron came, he —"

"Your uncle? He's here?" I looked around quickly, fearing he was about to run out and take control of the microphone to give a press conference.

"Yes, ma'am, and he wants me to do it."

I patted my chest, finding it hard to breathe. "You'll do fine. Just remember everything I told you, and it'll work out. Run on now, and get ready."

I rearranged the clothes on the rack, lining them up for the next category change. That would be Personal Expression, and the girls had chosen everything from jeans to jumpsuits, from shorts to sundresses. And all the time, my mind was in a worse jumble than the clothes rack. I had no idea in the world what Preacher Kincaid had in mind to do, nor did I have in mind what I could do to stop him.

I walked out to the side of the stage and

peeked around the curtain. The place was almost full, with more people coming in, searching for seats. The Piney Woods Boys — though they were hardly boys — were playing a rousing tune, adding to the hubbub. I saw Sam sitting right below me at the judges' table, along with Tonya and Thurlow. They had their heads together, discussing their scoring method, I assumed. Although Thurlow could've been telling them some long-winded and tasteless tale.

I searched the auditorium for Eunice Knowles, hoping to identify Preacher Kincaid by his proximity to her. I didn't see her, but I saw Helen and Mildred and the Reverend Abernathy and the Conovers and ever so many more. Sam looked up and waved to me, so I quickly pulled back out of sight.

There was only one thing to do. I dashed out to the back hall, where I saw Mr. Pickens just going through the outside door.

Chapter 43

"Mr. Pickens! Wait."

He turned around, half out the door. "Ma'am?"

"Are you leaving?"

"Just going around to the front."

"Well, listen. I just heard something you ought to know. Aaron Kincaid's here."

"Here? Where?"

"Somewhere in the auditorium. One of the contestants is his niece, and I don't know what to do."

He frowned. "Why do you need to do anything?"

"Because, Mr. Pickens." I took his arm and walked with him out on the stoop, letting the door close behind us. "Because Preacher Kincaid expects his niece to win — expects me to *make* her win, and the poor thing doesn't stand a chance. And when he finds that out, he's going public about the twenty-six weddings he performed under the auspices of the Holy Ghost, which as you well know is not anywhere near enough to satisfy the legal requirements. We've got to do something."

"Not we. You." He poked his finger at me. Then he grinned. "What do you have in mind?"

"I'm desperate, Mr. Pickens, so here's what I'm thinking. If you'll get the votes from the judges, you can slip behind the curtains on your way up to Binkie at the microphone. I'll be waiting, ready to switch votes with you."

He shook his head. "You don't want to do that. You'll have a riot on your hands."

"Well then, I'm at the end of my rope. I haven't had time to get to Tonya, but I've tried to persuade Sam and Thurlow to favor Ashley. And wouldn't you know, they've both taken the high road, which is easy enough to believe of Sam, but Thurlow is another matter. It makes me mad as thunder for him to suddenly get all upright and self-righteous when he's never been before."

Mr. Pickens looked so deep in thought that I wasn't sure he heard me. "Kincaid's in the auditorium?"

"That's what Ashley said."

"What does he look like?"

"I couldn't tell you. I only saw him the one time, and I wasn't paying attention to his looks. Big man, though, in a white suit." I frowned, trying to bring him to mind. "Black hair, but not much of it."

"I doubt he'll be in a white suit tonight, seeing he's out of the marrying business." Mr. Pickens turned to walk away. "I'll let Sonny know he's here. It's his best chance to catch him."

"No, Mr. Pickens! Don't do that. If that country star comes in with the crew that follows him around everywhere, and they start going up and down the aisles looking for Preacher Kincaid, it'll disrupt the whole pageant. And you know how Hazel Marie gets. She'll be beside herself."

"Right," he agreed. "What was I thinking?"

"Why don't you stand at the back of the audience and try to spot him. He'll be with his mother, Eunice Knowles, if that helps."

"It would if I knew Eunice Knowles."

"Don't be contrary, Mr. Pickens. Just keep an eye out, and find him. And get him out of there before Binkie announces the winner, because it's not going to be Ashley. And leave Sonny Sutton out of it, at least for tonight."

"Can't do that. He's paying me to tell him what I find out." He held up a hand as I started to argue. "Wait, now, let me finish. Sonny's coming, anyway, but nobody's supposed to know, especially the press. He says he's bored sitting around in a motel room."

"My word, he's only been in that motel room half a day. How could he be bored? But if he has to come, you tell him to leave those tagalongs of his somewhere else. It'll be a mob scene if they all come trooping in right in the middle of somebody's talent presentation."

"How about if we stand in the back till it's over, then wait outside for Kincaid? Sonny knows what he looks like, so he'll spot him when he comes out."

"Just be sure you wait till it's over, whatever you do. And, Mr. Pickens, please don't let that preacher say anything. He's going to be so upset about Ashley, and even more upset when Sonny catches him, he might start naming names and pointing fingers right there with half the town listening in."

He grinned and waved, which I took for agreement, as he went down the steps and on around the building. Hurrying back inside, I realized that the pageant had begun. Sheriff Frady's voice reverberated through the back of the stage, as he welcomed the audience and thanked Hazel Marie and "all those who pitched in to help her."

The contestants were lined up, waiting for their first entrance. All except Ashley, who was still being worked on in the dressing room. A burst of applause greeted the appearance of Deputy Ray Fields and Deputy Max von Rippen, as the canine unit walked out on the stage for a demonstration of their partnership.

I peeked into the dressing room, where Hazel Marie was doing something to Ashley's eyes, while Miss Wiggins pinned up her hair. "You look beautiful, Ashley," I said, hoping the girl could hold herself together for a while longer.

"There," Miss Wiggins said, with a last thrust of a bobby pin. "Stand up, so we can get your sash on. Now, go get in line. We've put you last, so you have plenty of time."

Ashley gave me a frightened glance, as she walked out with bent head to take her place. Then Lieutenant Peavey's astounding tenor took over in a rendition of something I didn't know.

Hazel Marie, Miss Wiggins, and I went out to stand by the girls as they waited their turn to be introduced. They were all jittery, excited, and nervous by turns. Ashley looked stiff and frozen, like she was going to her doom. I put my hand on her arm to reassure her. It was a shame that so many people were putting the girl through such a trial, and if I'd let myself dwell on it, I could've regretted having any part in it.

After the applause for Lieutenant Peavey

and his exit from the stage, Binkie took over. "And now, what we've all been waiting for — the contestants for the crown of Miss Abbot County Sheriff's Department! Let's have a big hand for each one."

She didn't have to urge them, for the audience was ready.

"Melanie Easley, Miss First Watch!" Binkie yelled, dragging out the syllables, and out went the first one to great acclaim. "YoShandra Washington, Miss Detective Squad! Ta-a-sha McKenzie, Miss Second Watch! Hea-a-ther Pea-a-vey, Miss SWAT Team!" Binkie had to wait for the whistles and yells to die down, for Heather was clearly the audience favorite. That might have been because her daddy was there. "Bethany LaVane, Miss Vice Squad! Oops, careful there!"

Hazel Marie whispered, "Oh, no! Bethany tripped. It's okay, she's all right."

I thought Ashley would faint dead away at Bethany's stumble, but Binkie carried right on, "And Ashley Knowles, Miss Third Watch! That's it, ladies and gentlemen. Just look at this lineup, and let them know how much we appreciate them."

Things went from fast to faster after that, with the girls running offstage, tearing off one outfit and pulling on another. I didn't have time to worry about anything, being so taken up with zippers and buttons and ties and the occasional safety pin. Before I knew it, they were going through the Expression of Personality competition, wearing their own choices of playwear. Each contestant went out alone to tell Binkie, for the edification of all, about her platform. Having heard all the grandiose ideas before, I was happy enough to help Miss Wiggins bring a semblance of order to the dressing room.

Hazel Marie came flying in. "I just feel so bad for Ashley. She was terrified, and even though Binkie practically put words in her mouth, it was pitiful to watch. And Heather got the giggles so bad that she never did tell about her platform. Tasha, though, sounded so professional. She didn't miss a beat."

My heart sank for Ashley. I hadn't expected her to excel, but I had hoped for better than she'd been able to do. I didn't have time to mourn the lost opportunity, though, for the girls were coming back in for another change.

Next up was the Physical Fitness competition, and out the girls went in nothing but smiles and the skimpiest of bathing suits, none of which would ever see water nor hold up in it if they did. This display of so many young women in so little clothing created havoc in the audience, accompanied by whistles, stamping of feet, and several uncalled-for catcalls.

In spite of all my signals to her, Ashley couldn't bring herself to smile even once as she walked out on the stage, down the runway and back again. She went through the motions with a grim expression, slumped shoulders, and nowhere near the smooth, scissoring walk that Miss Wiggins had shown them.

Finally, when the talent competition started, I had a chance to watch from the sidelines.

Binkie announced Miss LaVane, who played the piano with an excess of body movements, leaning over the keyboard, then throwing her head back as the music swelled. The audience appreciated her efforts, in spite of a few missed notes, and she came off, smiling. Then Miss Washington high-stepped her way onto the stage, looking trim and smart in her majorette uniform. She amazed me with her twirling batons, spinning them back and front, throwing them up and catching them on a spin, all to the rousing tune of a Sousa march. The only mishap was when she threw a baton way up into the rafters and it stayed there, hung up on some ropes. Miss Washington hardly missed a beat, just went right on with one baton. She did move to the side, though, just in case.

"It's still up there!" she whispered to Hazel Marie, as she came offstage.

Heather was next, and her selection, according to Binkie, was a Faith Hill song. Heather was every bit as good as her father, except for having to hum a couple of lines she forgot.

After her, Melanie Easley was announced, and Little Lloyd eased up beside me to watch her. It worried me that he was so taken with an older woman, and it worried me even more that the older woman was encouraging him. Miss Easley did what she called an original lyrical dance to the tune of Celine Dion's "Power of the Dream," and she did look dreamlike in a filmy lavender costume and ballet slippers. I didn't know much about dance moves, but it seemed to me that she worked her hands more than her feet. She did a lot of running on tiptoe, but hardly on the very tips of them. Still, the music set a mood, and the audience was absorbed in watching her — until Miss Washington's baton fell to the stage with a clang. Miss

Easley came off the stage in tears, raging at Shandra for spoiling her moment.

Tasha McKenzie took her place on a dark stage, lit by only one spotlight. She wore a long-sleeved, high-necked black dress that made her look spectral. That was the idea, I supposed, since her original poem, declaimed with great emotion and dramatic hand-wringing, was about the loss of life on Interstate 85, due to Jim Beam, Pall Malls, and a lack of commitment to Christian values.

Then it was time for Ashley. Miss Wiggins had done a good job on her, dressing her in a long, full calico skirt and a peasant blouse, with her hair brushed out, full and flowing. She gripped her guitar hard enough to untune it, which was something else for me to worry about. As the stagehands lowered the scrim and set up spotlights, I eased up beside her. "Don't pay a bit of mind to all those people out front, Ashley. Just pretend you're back in my pantry, singing for Lillian and me."

She nodded, or trembled, I wasn't sure which, then walked out on the dark stage. She took a seat on a make-believe rock with a mountainous backdrop behind her. By this time, the audience was beginning to murmur and rustle, impatient for the next performance. But all that ceased as the lights came up, and the hazy tableau opened before them. As Ashley strummed the first notes on her guitar, not another sound could be heard. And when she lifted her voice in a plaintive rendition of "O, Shenandoah," well, everybody knew they were hearing something rare and beautiful.

When the last notes died away, the applause nearly lifted the roof. Shouts of "More" and "Encore" rang out, as Ashley dashed to the sidelines. Binkie joked with the crowd, telling them they'd have to pay extra for a second helping. Hazel Marie hugged Ashley, and Miss Wiggins could hardly contain herself. Ashley had more than justified her place in the contest. I managed to get close enough to show my approval, while she cried with what I assumed was relief.

So then the judges went to work, while the girls came out of their costumes and donned their evening attire. Ashley was still trembling, but she was finally able to smile now that the worst was over.

As we waited for the judges to determine their choices, Binkie introduced Latisha.

That little girl skipped out to the middle of the stage, completely unafraid and ready to perform. Lillian stood by me, wringing her hands. "No tellin' what she do, Miss Julia."

"The audience loves her already," I said. "Just listen."

To great applause, Latisha spread her little red dress, curtsied, and nodded to the band. Then, as the music started, she commenced to sing "This Little Light of Mine," complete with hand motions, but minus a microphone. Her piercing voice had no trouble projecting to the farthest reaches of the auditorium, as she sang one verse after another. Then when I thought she couldn't think of another place for her light to shine, she broke into an all-out tap dance. Lillian gasped and hid her face, but the audience was clapping in time and Latisha was giving them a show.

At last, Binkie appeared on stage, holding a paper with the judges' decision. She gave the band a signal to wrap it up, which was probably the only way to bring Latisha to a close.

As the music stopped, Latisha announced, "You ready for another one?"

The audience clapped and yelled, but Lillian had had enough. She marched out on-stage and swept her up and off, with Latisha shouting, "But I'm jus' gettin' started!"

"Well, you finished now," Lillian said,

setting her down out of sight of the delighted audience.

"Ladies and gentlemen!" Binkie called out, "Here they are again!" At the prompt, the contestants, lovely every one in their rented evening gowns, went out onstage. "Now, for the big moment," Binkie went on. "And the judges' decision. The second runner-up is . . . Ashley Knowles, Miss Third Watch!"

I had to lean against the wall, so surprised that I could hardly catch my breath. She placed! But, Lord, would that be enough to keep Aaron Kincaid quiet? And as I realized how close Ashley had come to the crown, I could've shaken her. If she'd put more effort into her appearance and her poise in the spotlight, if she'd been able to show her personality more, why, she could've won it all.

But she hadn't, and that was that. All my efforts on her behalf and, I admit, on mine, too, had been for naught. So close, but not close enough. Was I looking at another sign, warning me away from Sam? Or did her third-place showing simply mean that she hadn't stood up straight?

I decided right then and there that the Lord would have to do better than send these signs that lent themselves to various interpretations. I needed something plain and clear, and until I got it, well, I wasn't going to stand around and wait for the clash between Sonny Sutton and Preacher Kincaid to make headlines and put us on *Entertainment Tonight.*

I didn't wait to hear the rest, but Binkie's voice followed me. She announced the first runner-up: YoShandra Washington, Miss Detective Squad, and finally, to great anticipation by the audience, the new Miss Abbott County Sheriff's Department: Tasha McKenzie, Miss Second Watch.

Sam was certainly going to hear from me about that. I'll admit that Miss McKenzie had made a competent showing. Well, to be honest, she'd done better than that. She had excellent bearing, thanks to her modeling classes, and had expressed herself with confidence and poise, but as she began her victory walk down the runway, crown awry on her head and arms full of roses, I knew Sheriff Frady had a loose cannon on his hands.

But that wasn't my problem. My problem was Aaron Kincaid and Sonny Sutton meeting up in a public forum, and, as the lights came up, I decided that the time had come to terminate this neither-nor state of affairs.

Chapter 44

Before I got down the few steps from the stage to the auditorium proper, a disturbance rose from the back where people were bunched up, waiting to get out. Looking over the heads of those sidling out of the rows and crowding into the aisles, I could see arms waving and hear cries of "It's Sonny Sutton!"; then, "Sonny! Sonny!"

I hesitated on the steps, not wanting to get caught in the crush of departing ticket holders, but needing to find Sam. I glanced back at the stage, hoping to find an easier way out. Latisha, freed from Lillian's grasp, was dashing from one contestant to another, admiring their gowns, with Lillian right behind her. Little Lloyd stood off to the side by himself, watching the turmoil. Some of the contestants crowded around Tasha, congratulating her and, I expect, envying her. Heather and Shandra were gracious enough to hug Ashley, and tell her they had no idea how talented she was. Parents and friends of the contestants pushed up onstage, along with the deputies whose units the contestants had represented.

I didn't know whether to go or come. Whichever way I looked, there was a crowd to be maneuvered through. I caught sight of Sam's white head edging around a group clustered at the judges' table. I waved to him, but he didn't see me.

"Julia! Yoo-hoo, Julia!" LuAnne yelled from the center aisle, as she waved her hand to get my attention. "See you at the club!"

I nodded, refraining from raising my voice above the din, which had increased as more people heard of Sonny's personal appearance among us. Still hesitating, I lingered, hoping to get Sam's attention before he was swallowed up by the crowd. Finally giving up the effort, I decided to go across the stage and out the back way. I wanted to waylay Sam before Sonny caught the preacher, and the preacher caught what was coming to him, at which time, he'd make good his threat to spew out a full confession. And if I couldn't keep the preacher away from Sam, my best hope was to keep Sam away from him. Maybe, I thought, since I was the only one who would know Preacher Kincaid by his proximity to Eunice Knowles, Sonny wouldn't recognize him, and the man would slip on through.

Maybe he'd be pleased enough with Ashley's showing, and go back to Tennessee and never be heard from again.

And maybe, if nothing worked out and Sam was willing, he and I could elope again, this very night, get married for real and true, and no one would ever have to know the actual date of our anniversary.

Then Preacher Kincaid could do all the announcing he wanted to, and we could smile and say we'd never trusted him in the first place, which was why we'd immediately remedied the situation. Then, regardless of the uproar over a celebrity's attempt to marry, we could simply be amused and above it all.

But I couldn't get it done by myself.

I hurried across the stage, edging around and through clumps of people ogling and hugging and congratulating the contestants, until I almost bumped into the Reverend Morris Abernathy. He was talking with Lillian, while a group of his deacons stood by, beaming at Shandra's success.

"I'm so sorry, Reverend," I said, backing right up against Lieutenant Peavey. "Oh, pardon me."

The Reverend Abernathy, that small, courtly gentleman who had once come to my rescue when Binkie and Coleman had badly needed some officiating, bowed gracefully. His dark, wrinkled face under curly white hair broke into a bright smile. "Mrs. Murdoch, a pleasure, madam, to see you again. This is Deacon Woodrow and Deacon Sims." He indicated the two smiling men beside him. "We are so proud of Miss Washington. The Lord has bountifully blessed her and us, too, as he always does."

I shook hands with his deacons, wanting to be polite but wanting even more to be on my way. "You should be proud of her. She is an exceptional young woman. If you'll excuse me, Reverend . . ."

And I sidled away, only to be engulfed by Hazel Marie as she threw her arms around me. "Oh, Miss Julia, it was a success, wasn't it?"

"It was, indeed," I said, disengaging myself. "You did a marvelous job, Hazel Marie. But I have to run. LuAnne wants me at the club as quickly as I can get there."

"I'll bring Lillian and Latisha with me, and we'll be there soon. Well, as soon as I find J.D. Have you seen him?"

"I think he's out front with Sonny Sutton."

"Sonny's here? Oh, my goodness, I hope I can get his autograph. I've got to find Etta Mae." And she hurried away, smiling at the praise heaped on her head as she went.

I finally got to the sidelines, thinking I had clear sailing to the back hall. I was brought up short by the sight of Little Lloyd standing alone in a dark corner.

Going over to him, I said, "Are you all right?"

He turned away from me, and my heart dropped as I saw the stricken look on his face. "Little Lloyd, what's the matter? Are you sick?"

He shook his head. "No'm."

"Well, come on with me. I'm looking for Sam, and we'll go to the party together."

"I don't want to go to the party." The child looked so miserable that for a minute my own troubles flew out of my mind.

"Has somebody said something to you?" I was immediately prepared to do battle. The idea that anybody would hurt him just tore me up.

He mumbled something, and I had to get him to repeat it. Finally I heard him say, "Miss Easley doesn't like me anymore."

I straightened up and looked around. There was Miss Easley by the dressing room, weeping on her mother's shoulder. "It's not fair," I heard her say amid convulsive sobs. "My talent was better than Shandra's, and her baton ruined my dance, and I'm prettier than Ashley, and it's just not fair."

So, I thought, that young lady was so taken up with her own misery that she'd spread it around, and to an innocent child, too.

"Come on," I said, taking Little Lloyd's hand. "You and I have no time for crybabies. Strike her off your dance card, Little Lloyd, and hold up your head. She's the loser in more ways than one. Now, I've got to find Sam, and I want you to help me." Still, I could've smacked Miss Easley good for hurting his tender little feelings.

We hadn't taken two steps when Miss Wiggins came running up and threw out her arms to hug me. I took a step back, and she thought better of it. "Wasn't it wonderful!" she cried. "And Ashley! I can't believe how good she was, and it was all because of you. I would've given up on her long ago, but you stuck with her and she was the highlight of the whole show."

"Thank you, Miss Wiggins, but I take little credit for her natural ability. I think she has a real future somewhere." I hoped it wouldn't be at McDonald's. "But you must excuse us, Miss Wiggins. I have to find Sam."

"I saw him just a minute ago," she said, glancing over her shoulder, as a flash of anxiety surged through me. How had she found him, when I couldn't? "But you can call me Etta Mae."

"Thank you," I said again, and moving away, I steeled myself to give credit where it was due. "You helped make the pageant a success, too, and I know Hazel Marie appreciates it."

Pulling Little Lloyd along, I wove my way through crowds of people that had spilled over behind the stage. Lord, where had they all come from? But still, I couldn't find Sam. I wouldn't have put it past Miss Wiggins to have steered me in the wrong direction, but I kept looking.

"This way, Little Lloyd," I said, pushing past a clump of people to return to the stage and through the back curtain, hoping to find Sam on the other side. I ducked just as a man threw out his arm in an expansive gesture; then I slipped through the opening in the back curtain. I raised up and found myself eye to eye with Deputy Max von Rippen.

"Oh, Lord!" I stepped back so quickly, I almost flattened Little Lloyd.

"He won't hurt you, Miss Julia. Deputy Fields has to give him a command before he'll attack."

"I'm taking no chances." I grabbed his hand again and veered away.

Finally closing in on the door that led to the classroom hall, I caught a glimpse of Sam in conversation with Tonya Allen. I saw him laugh and nod his head, as he gave her his full attention. You would think, being judges and having made at least one contestant so unhappy, that they would've put some distance between themselves and the stage. But Sam was always so pure and honorable in his dealings, that it rarely occurred to him that others might not be. My heart lurched in my chest as I watched him, so wanting him to want me, wanting to be within range of his goodness and have it slop over onto me, wanting to be his wife in holy matrimony. I didn't want to pretend anymore, nor act like a wife without being one.

"Sam," I said, hurrying up to him and feeling his warm eyes welcome me. "Forgive me, Tonya, but I have an emergency. Sam, we have to talk."

I took his hand, still holding Little Lloyd's with my other one, and led them both out into the hall. Hurrying into an empty classroom, I turned to Sam, the words rushing out of my mouth.

"Sam, I've thought and thought, until I'm tired of thinking. That's what you wanted me to do, and I've done it. I don't know what you've been doing, and —"

"I did my thinking a long time ago —"

"— and I know you might've come to a different conclusion. But I'm going to put aside my pride and ask you to marry me, once and for all, in spite of the fact that we might've already done it, so —"

"— I was just waiting for you."

"— so I want to do it now, this very night, and then whatever happens happens, and it won't affect us."

He was talking, but I wasn't listening. I needed to get said what I had to say. "Now, I know you may be attracted to someone else, but believe me, Sam, she is fickle and it wouldn't last. You'd regret it till your dying day. But I promise with all my heart that you will not regret choosing me. I will be your wife in every way possible, and I will be a good one."

I'll just tell you, I was at my wit's end by this time, dreading to hear him say that he needed to think more, or that he'd already thought enough and he'd made a different decision.

Little Lloyd said, "I thought y'all were already married."

"It didn't take," I said. "We have to do it again. Sam?" I put my hand on his chest to hold myself up. My limbs were shaking, as

I steeled myself, promising the Lord that if the ceiling fell in, I'd take that as a final and irreversible sign that Sam was not for me. I bit my lip, waiting for the crash of plaster and rafters and billows of dust to fall on my head.

"Julia," Sam said, as his arms went around me. "Anytime, anywhere." And there, at last, was a sign I understood.

I broke from his embrace and wheeled on Little Lloyd. "Run get the Reverend Abernathy. Hurry — don't stop for anything and don't tell anybody. Except your mother. Bring her, too."

Sam started laughing then. "Here? You want to do it here?"

"I certainly do. We need another witness. Who can we get that won't blab it all over the place?"

"I'll find somebody," he said, poking his head out the door, while I eased up behind him, afraid to let him out of my sight.

So that's how we came to be married in a classroom at the high school auditorium, with Hazel Marie and Deputy Fields as witnesses, along with Deputy Max von Rippen looking on with soulful eyes. Little Lloyd was there, of course, and if he'd been old enough he would've been an official witness, too. The Reverend Abernathy spoke about some legal aspects of when and what we had to sign the following morning, since he didn't happen to have his marriage book with him. In the meantime, he said with a complacent smile, he would trust us to hold ourselves pure and unsullied until all the T's and I's were crossed and dotted.

Other than that, the Reverend asked no questions, except the main ones, seemingly unperturbed by either the timing or the setting.

By the time our little wedding party got to the pageant gala, it was in full swing. Sonny Sutton was the center of attention, so nobody asked why we were late and nobody seemed to notice our postwedding glow.

Hazel Marie ran to find Mr. Pickens, and I saw him bend his head to her as she told him the news. He laughed and held a glass up to us, then made his way through the noisy celebrants to our side.

"Is it real this time?" he asked, and, as I put his mind to rest on that score, he leaned over and kissed my cheek. "To the bride. Congratulations, Sam."

Somewhat embarrassed by Mr. Pickens's greeting, I looked around the room, loud now with the beat of bad, bad Leroy Brown, and swirling contestants, still giddy with excitement. I smiled at the sight of Latisha dancing with Deacon Sims, and smiled even more when I saw Miss Wiggins doing some kind of gyrations with Sheriff Frady. Willie Pruitt might have been waiting his turn with her, but he was doing it with Miss Easley, whose tears seemed to have dried up. Heather Peavey pounced on Little Lloyd as soon as she saw him, and led him to the dance floor. Hearing a gust of laughter, I turned to see Lillian and James in deep conversation.

Over by the buffet table, LuAnne was holding forth, as Sonny's black hat towered above the crowd that milled around him. You would think he'd have the courtesy to bare his head when he came indoors, but that's the way some people are. For just a second I caught a glimpse of Ashley, smiling, but with a deer-in-the-headlights look about her.

Sam's arm stayed around me, enveloping me in the warmth and assurance of his love. He leaned close to Mr. Pickens so he could be heard. "What's the story with Sonny?"

Mr. Pickens gave us his devilish grin. "He spotted Kincaid coming out of the auditorium, and we had a little stir there for a minute. A few flashbulbs popped, because Sonny can never get away from them all." Not that he would want to, I thought.

"Anyway," Mr. Pickens went on, "since there were plenty of deputies around, he had Kincaid picked up for fraud. It won't stick, but Sonny thinks the effort will reassure his fiancée." Mr. Pickens looked at me. "Kincaid wouldn't tell Sonny anything, just said his lips are sealed until the seventh seal is broken."

Mr. Pickens looked puzzled, not understanding the reference, but I knew that Preacher Kincaid was promising his silence till the end of time.

But to be on the safe side, I drew Mr. Pickens slightly to the side. "Don't you agree that there's no need for anybody to know exactly when our wedding took place? If anybody asks, you could say we've been married for some time now."

He looked at his watch. "About thirty minutes?" Then he grinned at me, and whispered, "Your secret's safe with me."

Hazel Marie came running up. "Guess what just happened! Oh, I am so thrilled! Sonny's going to introduce Ashley to a record producer! She's going to Nashville to make a demo! And it's all because of our pageant!"

Well, not exactly, since it had taken Sam and me being only slightly married by her uncle, who then pressured me into keeping her in the contest, which lured Sonny Sutton to Abbottsville, where he just happened to hear her. That's how she got a record deal, and, somewhere in the middle of it all, that's how I learned to go after what I wanted, signs or no signs. I could only marvel at the mysterious ways our lives had intertwined.

"Here, Julia!" LuAnne pushed a champagne glass into my hand, and another one into Sam's. A waiter she had in tow supplied Mr. Pickens and Hazel Marie. "Even if we're weeks behind time, we're celebrating your wedding tonight." She raised her glass. "To the bride and groom, better late than never!"

Sam and I smiled at each other over our glasses, enjoying our precious secret, and after only the slightest hesitation, I decided that this was an event worthy of a taste of spirits. But I only took the teeniest, little sip.